Barefoot Bliss
Charleston Series
Book 6

Sue Langford

To the ones who craved the spice, had it and still crave more.
And to the ones who knew just when to
bring out the pom poms.

*"A soulmate is someone who has locks that fit our keys, and keys to fit our locks." —
Richard Bach*

Chapter 1

They'd had a vacation that turned into another level of hell, and almost an entire summer of watching their backs. Now, Faith was more worried that Ridge was gonna end up in jail instead of in her bed.

******

Faith, Ridge, Kellen, and Leo got back to the house, after a scenic drive through the middle of nowhere, and Faith was almost happy to see that big fireplace and her Dad's security waiting on them. "Welcome home," her Dad's security said. "Thank you," Faith said as Ridge shook his head. He went to help her bring everything upstairs and Kellen took over.

"You do realize that I can carry the bags right," Ridge asked. Kellen nodded with a smirk and took the bags upstairs for them.

Ridge opted to go talk to the security guys, telling them what they'd come up with when they were away. "We did wonder if that was the connection," her Dad's security said.

Ridge gave them all the information that they had. "We know it's not just Zack and his kid. Holden is doing IT on the side along with the dealerships. We know someone else is behind this. It's just a matter of going through the threats against…"

"We can take it from there. We heard there was a scuffle at the resort. Are you okay," her Dad's head of security asked.

"Bruised and sore, but beyond that yes. I'm gonna head upstairs and unpack," Ridge said. They nodded, got their things together and relinquished the office back to Kellen and Leo.

Ridge walked into the main bedroom to unpack and saw Faith sitting on the bed. "What's wrong," Ridge asked as he sat down beside her.

"Nothing is here right? Nothing in the walls or anything?"

"Worried," Ridge asked.

"I mean, yeah. After everything I heard when we were away in Jekyll, I'm more than worried."

Ridge kissed her, got up, closed the door, and walked over to her, pulling Faith to her feet. "What," she asked.

He kissed her, devouring her lips. "We're fine. We're home. It's all safe. The beach house is safe. I promise you."

She kissed him. "Tell me that we aren't making a mistake."

"With what," he teased.

"Ridge."

"We're good. I promise you we're good." She hugged him and with one hug, she was calm again. "Unpacked," he asked.

"And unpacked your stuff. Odd question, but those other

things you had in your bag to taunt your fiancée with. Did you want me to charge them or something?"

Ridge smirked. "Mad that we didn't try them or determined to try them out again tonight," Ridge teased.

"Both," Faith joked as he kissed her.

"Could be arranged, but your housekeeper and the guys may need earplugs." Faith shook her head and he kissed her.

He knew with one conversation that she was feeling better. She was getting back to the same old Faith. Even though she was mad as hell, she was back to the hot and bothered Faith that he loved. "What are we doing tonight," Faith asked.

Ridge laughed and shook his head. "What did you have in mind there woman? Round 965?"

"We never watched the movie."

He shook his head. "Dirty mind. Back to normal." She shook her head and kissed him. "Faith."

"What?"

"Is that what you really want to do tonight? You could end up in my room in the dark again."

"And that's why nobody is allowed to be in there except you and me," Faith teased.

He kissed her and wrapped his arms tight around her as

she sat him on the bed. "Faith."

"What?"

"It's 3pm."

"And?"

"I still kinda have work to get done," he teased.

"And you worked right through the entire vacation and vanished on me from what I remember. I say you…"

He kissed her, pulling her into his lap and wrapped her legs around him. "And what were you saying?"

"You owe me."

He shook his head. "Babe, you have no idea what you're saying."

"Yeah I do. We were gonna watch it when we were away. We never did."

"And?"

"And we're watching it tonight. Dinner, then movie."

"Where?"

She smirked. "If we can watch it downstairs fine. If not, up here."

"Then you're really gonna be in for it," he teased.

"Rules aren't really gonna work up here."

He looked at her. "And you think that doesn't mean you not coming near me?"

"Ridge."

"Movie. Nothing else if you make a move."

"Ridge come on."

"That's the deal Faith. Whether we watch it in here in bed, or we watch it downstairs." She shook her head, kissed him and he leaned her onto the bed. "Don't you have work to do sexy?" Faith shook her head, devouring his lips until his phone buzzed. "Faith."

"Nope."

"I have to."

She shook her head. "No, you don't." He kissed her, sliding his phone from his pocket.

"Yep," Ridge said answering the phone

"So, I think I figured out the connection," Kellen said.

"Be down in a couple minutes," Ridge said as he hung up. Faith looked at him.

"Couple minutes? Really?" He kissed her, devouring her lips, and pinned her arms to the bed. "What," Faith asked as they came up for air.

"Finish unpacking. I'll be back..."

She kissed him. "No, you won't," she said as she kissed him.

He got up, walked downstairs, trying his best to calm his body down, and walked into the security office. "What," Ridge asked.

"They put all of the threats and the people they thought were involved into a database. I was looking at all of this stuff and matching it up with that Holden guy. There are three options to who it can be. I think it's good."

"Send it over to her Dad's people. See what they say and we go from there." When Ridge's phone buzzed a minute or two later, he shook his head. One look at the picture message and he shook his head.

"Go take care of Faith. When I hear back I'll let you know," Kellen said with a laugh.

"I swear, she is totally asking for it," Ridge said.

"Asking for what," Faith asked as she came in behind Ridge and slid her arms around him.

"They may have determined who's behind all of it. We're letting your Dad's guys handle it."

"I need your assistance," Faith said as Ridge smirked.

He got up with Kellen and Leo almost laughing. "And what did you need my assistance with?"

Faith walked him into her office and closed the door.

"Faith."

"Come here."

"Faith, you do realize you have work to do right?"

She nodded. "I have the rest of the day off."

"Since when," Ridge teased.

"I checked emails while we were on the way back. It's fine. I have some queries to read and paperwork, but I'm off duty until tomorrow."

He shook his head, kissing her. "You do realize what's gonna happen if we watch that movie right," he teased as Faith got a grin ear to ear.

"Dessert," Faith teased.

"You have no idea," he replied as he kissed her.

Just as Faith was about to peel his shirt off, her phone went off. "Like I said, you have work to do. Try washing out that dirty mind of yours."

She kissed him and answered. "Yes," Faith said.

"Sorry to interrupt on your last day of vacation, but we have a slight issue. Someone hacked the computers at the office."

Faith shook her head. "Did you notify my Dad and the security staff?"

"Yes, but they asked me to call you. They're also doing a room by room search to make sure that nobody got in without us knowing."

"Meaning no emails," Faith asked.

"That's why I'm calling on my cell phone."

"There's nothing I can do except come down correct," Faith asked.

"If you can. I know that..."

"It's fine. Ridge and I will head over," Faith said.

"See you soon. I'll get your coffees for you," her assistant said as Faith hung up and looked at Ridge.

"No afternoon movies for you. Up and I'll get..." She kissed him again and he shook his head. "Faith."

"What?"

"Up." She shook her head and got up, going into her closet and pulling on something to wear into the office.

Ridge went and grabbed his dress pants and dress shirt, hopping into a quick shower before they headed in. When he stepped out, Faith had a smirk ear to ear. "Cut it out. We're going into the office."

"I know we are," Faith said as he could read her mind from across the room.

"Don't even think about it." He pulled on boxers, slid his

dress pants on and kissed her.

"Could've just gone in the jeans." He shook his head.

"And you could've shown up naked, but that's not happening either Faith." She kissed him and he slid his dress shirt on. When he looked at what she was wearing, he almost laughed. "Sundress?"

"Dress. I'm putting the blazer on if I'm cold," Faith teased.

"You better have something on under it." She kissed him and went and grabbed her heels. "I created a monster," he joked out loud.

"Just reminded me it was there," Faith replied.

They headed out a few minutes later, and Faith had her hand linked with Ridge's the entire way into the office. "Worried," he asked.

"Well, I can imagine that Holden does IT and whoever was after me or my Dad probably has him on their payroll. Holden could hack anything."

"You seriously think he'd be that stupid? Whoever is after your Dad and the company is coming after you first. I'm not letting you get hurt love. Not for anything in the dang world."

She kissed him at the light. "Holding you to it," Faith teased as she leaned her head on his shoulder.

When they pulled into the parking garage, her Dad's

security was there waiting. "Since when do my Dad's security guard the parking lot," Faith asked. Ridge hopped out of the SUV, went around to her side, and helped her out and they brought her inside while Ridge made sure the SUV was locked up and followed behind them.

They got up to the office and her Dad was waiting. "You alright," her Dad asked.

"We just got back from vacation. What happened," Faith asked as her Dad looked at Ridge.

"Remember that idea that you had about who could be behind all of this," her Dad asked. Ridge nodded. "I think that you might be right. My security found a connection." Ridge took a deep breath.

"That's why you wanted to double up security at the house and with Faith," Ridge asked.

Her Dad nodded. "The boys are beyond mad as it's supposedly ruining their social lives. At least you're listening to me," her Dad sad.

"Dad, I didn't have a choice. Besides. I kinda have a thing for my security," Faith teased.

"Faith." Ridge shook his head.

"All I meant was that I'm glad that he's here. There's stuff that happened that I wouldn't wish on anyone. Those photos made me lose it. Whoever is behind all of this is going down. They have to," Faith said.

"Did we ever do a search of the offices to make sure they weren't bugged," Ridge asked.

Her Dad looked at him. "Here?" Ridge nodded. "Really?" Ridge nodded. "We can get security to handle it," her Dad said.

"I can ask the guys to come if you want me to," Ridge asked.

"I may take you up on that. I was looking at other ideas," her Dad said. "Faith, for the amount of stuff they pulled out of your house and your beach house, I'm worried."

"We do know who was behind it though. It's a good step," Ridge replied.

"True. Honestly, I don't know what we would've done if you hadn't found them. You have one heck of a team," her Dad said as Ridge got a little more confidence.

By the time her Dad walked them upstairs, Ridge was giving ideas to his security detail. He got even more information on the guys that they had narrowed the issues down to. When Faith saw Ridge in his element, it was hot. Really hot. By the time they left, Faith got a grin ear to ear and walked to the elevator with Ridge. They headed to the parking garage and she kissed him in the elevator. 20 floors was just enough to get her hot and bothered to the point that she was ready to pounce.

They made it back to the house and Faith looked at him, sliding her heels off. "Faith."

"What?"

He shook his head. "Not in the SUV."

"I need a driver. That way we…"

"Faith, stop." She kissed him and he shook his head, hopped out, walked around her side and helped her out, locking up the SUV and walked into the house with her hand in hand.

"Ridge," Kellen said.

"What's wrong," he asked.

"They found the connection. The office was bugged," Kellen said. Faith looked at Ridge.

He took her hand and walked her upstairs to the main bedroom, closed and locked the door behind them and Faith lost it. "The office?"

He got her to calm down and kissed her. "Babe, it's fine. I promise you it is."

"My office."

"I did a sweep for them. I promise you."

"And nothing?"

Ridge shook his head. "No cameras, no bugs. You're alright."

She kissed him. "You sure?"

He nodded. With the number of things they'd done in that office, he'd never taken a chance that there might be a camera or microphone hidden. He'd checked the minute he was alone in the office when she'd headed off to a meeting. The fact that her Dad's security hadn't done those checks in the first place just irritated him. "Faith, we're fine in your office. Short of needing soundproofing, we're fine. I promise you." She shook her head and kissed him. "And who caused all that noise," he teased.

"You."

"Funny. Could've sworn I was the one..." She kissed him again and he smirked.

"What are you really worried about," Ridge asked.

"You know what. The same reason why I was worried about the beach house. How many did you really get rid of?"

"Cameras?"

"Both Ridge. How many?"

"Over 20. Leave it at that."

Faith shook her head. "You do realize what that means right?"

He kissed her. "You're starting to lose it baby. It's fine. Your house is safe. The beach house is safe. Your office is more than safe. The rest of the offices are a different matter. That's up to your Dad's security to handle."

"I have a feeling he's gonna be really stunned when he finds out what they find. Maybe that's…"

Ridge kissed her. "Babe, I love you, but I don't want to talk about the office, and I definitely don't want…"

She kissed him back and wrapped her arms around him. "Better," he teased.

"What," Faith asked.

"Babe, no more worrying. You have me here for a reason, and it's not just to keep the bed warm. I promise you. I have it handled."

"I like the bed warm," Faith teased.

He kissed her again and she got a grin ear to ear. "I bet you do," he teased.

Faith shook her head and he slid his arms around her, picking her up and wrapping her legs around his hips. "Ridge."

"Yes sexy."

"Are we gonna have the movie night?"

"Depends on whether you can make it through. That was always the deal beautiful."

"Taunting." He leaned her onto the bed and undid the dress.

"Really," she said.

Ridge smirked. When the dress slid off her shoulders, when the bra slid to the floor along with every inch of clothing from her body, he kissed her until she was ready to pounce. "What," he asked as she went for the button of his jeans.

"Ridge."

He shook his head. "Faith, I told you."

She pulled at his shirt, pulling him into her arms as she slid his dress shirt off. "I love you, but you're way too overdressed," Faith said.

"Babe, behave."

"Never," she teased as he leaned into her arms and kissed her.

"This is what you want? Now?"

She kissed him and wrapped her arms tight around him. "I wanted to finish our vacation the way we had it before we left," Faith teased.

"I know what you're saying Faith. I told you no."

"Ridge."

"The answer is no. I told you."

He went to get up and Faith refused to let go. "Ridge, just stay here."

He pulled her off of him and got up, walking into his closet, and sliding into jeans and a tee. Just as he turned to leave the closet, Faith walked in wearing her silk robe. "What," Ridge asked.

"We were alright. We were in Jekyll and we were good. What happened," Faith asked.

"I'm not having this discussion." Faith put her arm across the door, determined to get him to say something.

"Ridge."

"If that's what you're so damn determined to do, I'm not gonna be there. I'm not playing this game Faith. I say no, I don't mean go ahead and do it regardless. Leave it."

"Ridge."

He shook his head, kissed her cheek, and walked down the steps. The mood was gone. Long gone. Ancient history gone. He went into the security office and Kellen looked at him.

"What's wrong?"

"Nothing. I need to get some air. I'm gonna do a check outside," Ridge said.

"Dude," Kellen said.

Ridge walked out of the office and went outside, opting to get as far as he could without leaving the property. He checked the cameras, checked the gardens, the grass, the property line. Anything he could possibly to do to be away from everything.

When he went to walk back up to the house, Faith was sitting on the front steps. "What," he asked as he walked over to the front steps.

"Can we talk," Faith asked.

"No."

He went to walk back inside and Faith followed him. "Ridge."

"Leave it." She took his hand and walked him into her office. She closed the door and he sat down on the sofa. "Faith."

"Tell me what I have to do. Tell me. I just want to be with you Ridge."

"Then stop pushing. You want something I'm not gonna let you do. Not again. I told you Faith."

"Ridge, I love you. All I'm saying is that…"

"Faith."

"There's nothing wrong with it. You know there isn't. I love you."

"Faith, stop." He went to get up and Faith stopped him.

"So, you're just gonna avoid being around me?" He shook his head and Faith got up and slid into his lap. "I love you."

"I get it Faith. I do. Just get…"

She kissed him, leaning into his arms and hugging him. "I get that you don't want…"

"Faith, please just leave it."

She kissed him. "Fine. I won't do it."

"Faith." She held on a little tighter. "I don't want us fighting about this. Tell me what you want," he asked.

"I want the Ridge back that was there in Jekyll."

He took a deep breath. "I get that you want to. I get that you want the world. I'm not a toy Faith. You can't just do whatever."

"Ridge."

He kissed her. "I need to get up."

"Not until you tell me that we're okay."

He shook his head. "Babe, we're good. Just leave it be." She kissed him, wrapping her arms around him again as his hands slid instinctively to her backside as he got up and set her on her feet.

"Are you gonna watch a movie with me tonight," Faith asked.

"We'll see. I'm gonna get work in and sit outside."

Faith looked at him. "Am I allowed to sit with you?"

He kissed her. "Fine," he said as he went and grabbed his phone and laptop.

He walked outside, putting his feet up, and went through emails. He checked over his financials, realizing that a giant check had been deposited. He shook his head and went through everything, realizing that the money was from her Dad. He went through everything else and saw 3 emails from random women he'd known:

> *So, I heard you and queen bee are engaged. Not exactly surprised, but you could've done so much better. I know you miss me. Don't worry. We can keep it a secret – Emily*

> *I heard about the engagement. You're making a mistake Ridge. A big one. She's psycho. - Cara*

> *Tell me it isn't true. I know you still miss me. Come over. Please? – Sammy*

He shook his head. "What are you reading that has you all irritated," Faith asked as she sat down beside him.

"Old girlfriends that never worked. None of them are happy that we got engaged. I'm not sure how they would've found out," Ridge said.

She kissed him. "You know how."

"Lacey," Faith replied.

Ridge shook his head. "Babe."

"I love you," she said.

"That's how you scream things from the rooftop?"

Faith nodded. "Sorta. You wanted me to tell people because you thought I was keeping it a secret. I told her. She told everyone we knew in high school and probably 90% of Charleston. Hell. I'm surprised she didn't take out an ad in the paper and declare it to the world."

He took a deep breath. "Faith, I get it."

"You wanted me to tell people."

"Faith, I love you. I get what you're trying to do."

She looked at him. "What if I gave everyone a night off so we could be home alone."

"Since security is staying you mean."

Faith looked at him. "I can give the housekeeper the night off. We can be alone."

He shook his head. "If you want to watch the movie, fine." Faith kissed him and got up. "What are you doing?" She smirked, walked inside, and poured them each a drink, walking outside and handing him a Jack and Coke. "Faith."

"And according to the housekeeper, we're having seafood pasta for dinner."

He smirked. "Nothing to do with you asking," he teased. Faith kissed him and she slid into his lap. "Determined to distract me?" She nodded with a grin.

"I love you," she said.

"I love you too. I just don't know what to think," Ridge said.

"About what?"

"Babe, I never stopped loving you all that time. You may have gone on and dated and been with a million other people, but I didn't. I was trying to let people in. I was determined to never have a broken heart. I dated, but I never let anyone in but you."

She looked at him. "Really?" He nodded and Faith instinctually hugged him.

"I was waiting for you."

She looked at him. "Come with me?"

"Faith."

"Come inside."

He shook his head. "I'm just gonna relax for a while."

Faith looked at him. "Okay," she said. The mood was, at that moment, on another planet.

They curled up on the sofa outside and he finished going through emails while Faith did her best to work. When he finished his emails, her legs slid across his lap. She read through the queries and the rest of her work and then slid in closer to Ridge. "I love you, but quit teasing," Ridge said.

"Why," she asked.

He shook his head, got up, brought his laptop inside to charge and Faith fully believed that he was avoiding her. When he walked back outside in his swim shorts and dove into the pool, Faith smirked. She walked upstairs, slid into her bikini, and came back outside with the beach towels. She slid into the pool, and he shook his head. "Faith."

"Fiancée," she replied as she slid under the water and surfaced right in front of him. He shook his head.

"You are so bad," he said as he noticed the naked bikini.

"Your favorite one," she joked as he leaned in and kissed her.

"Trying to make up for…"

She kissed him. "Yes," Faith replied.

"It works," he teased as his hands slid to her backside and wrapped her legs around him.

"I love you handsome."

"Faith."

"What?"

"What if we just went on a real date."

"Where," Faith asked.

"Has she started cooking?"

Faith shook her head. "Let her know we're going out for dinner."

Faith kissed him and he sat her on the edge of the pool. She went inside and let her housekeeper know they were going out and came back outside to see Ridge swimming laps. She smirked and slid into the pool, leaning against the edge as he swam over to her and kissed her.

"And," he asked as she slid her legs around him.

"What?"

"She good with us going to dinner?"

Faith nodded. "She was doing laundry," Faith joked.

He shook his head, kissed her and they slid underwater. That kiss just got hotter. When they surfaced, he kissed her again and sat her on the edge of the pool. "What," Faith asked with a smirk.

He kissed up her torso and Faith shook her head. "You wear the bikini, you end up going inside naked," he teased.

When she slid back in, she smirked. "Promises, promises Ridge."

He slid her legs around him and untied her bottoms. "Really?" He nodded and kissed up her torso. Whatever the saltwater pool had caused was at least putting him in a better mood.

"And where are yours," she asked.

"Staying on."

Faith shook her head, and he leaned her against the side of the pool. "Ridge."

"Yes."

"Can we go upstairs?" He shook his head and her arms slid around him. He walked her over to the jets of the pool and leaned her against it.

"Crap."

"Hot tub," he joked.

Faith nodded. He walked to the steps of the pool, stepped out and walked the 5 steps to the hot tub outside. When they slid into the steamy, hot water of the hot tub, Faith couldn't help but laugh.

"What," Ridge asked as he kissed up her neck.

"I guess you're feeling better."

"I needed the fresh air and the water. That's all."

She kissed him and was about to attempt to rid him of his swim shorts when his phone went off. "Don't answer it," Faith said as he kissed back up her neck. He grabbed his cell and saw the one name he didn't ever want to see again. He ignored the call, throwing his phone on top of the beach towels and kissed Faith again. "I guess it wasn't work stuff."

"Nope," he joked as Faith slid her legs around him again

and he devoured her lips, deepening the kiss until she was even more turned on.

"Ridge," she said as he kissed down her neck and went for the tie of the bikini top.

"Faith."

"Inside."

"Why," he asked. She only had to give him one look to tell him what she was thinking. He shook his head with a smirk, got up, and grabbed the towel, wrapping her up in it, and carried her inside and up the steps to the bedroom, leaning her back onto it. He slid his phone on the charger and closed the bedroom door. He walked back over to her and the bikini top was gone. When she went for the tie of his swim shorts, he knew.

"Faith."

"What," she asked as he leaned into her arms and linked their fingers, pinning her to the bed.

"You move your hands and I am seriously not letting you win tonight."

"Meaning what?"

"Meaning second entrée, dessert and appetizer times 10."

Faith looked at him and shook her head. "You wouldn't."

"It's a bonus with that super dark blackout room."

"Ridge." He kissed her and his phone went off again. He looked at the call display and saw Calvin's name. He grabbed it and Faith looked at him.

"What's up," Ridge asked.

"Package showed for Faith. What do you want me to do with it?"

"Did you scan it?"

"Yep. Not what she's expecting. That I do know," Calvin said.

"I'll grab it in the morning."

"Alright," Calvin said as they hung up and Faith was undoing the drawstring of his shorts. He put the phone on the charger and grabbed Faith's hands.

"You're taking too long," she teased.

"Faith." He kissed her again and leaned her back on the bed, leaning into her arms.

"Now where was I?"

She smirked. "What did..."

He kissed her, devouring her lips and making her forget what she was about to ask him. "Now what were you saying," he asked as he let her up for air.

"Hmm," she teased.

He smirked again and her phone went off. "Like I said, you had work to do," Ridge joked as he slid her phone into her hands.

She answered and heard her Dad's voice. "What's up," Faith asked as he kissed down her torso.

"He was right. About the cameras and the microphones. There were some in my office and in the boardroom. Luckily, they got rid of them. Thank Ridge for me."

"I will. Did they do a search anywhere else?"

"There was one or two. The boardroom on your floor and the extra office. None in your office at all. Where are you two now?"

"Home. Just about to watch a movie," Faith said as he got to her hip and her toes curled as her legs slid over his shoulders.

"Tell Ridge I said hi. I need you to come in tomorrow. You okay with that?"

Faith was about to scream yes, but knowing who was on the other end of the phone, she nodded. "Okay," Faith said.

"And by the way, your Mom is going to do that book tour that we discussed. It means us being away for a while," her Dad said.

"I'll get the dates together for her," Faith said as her head slid back and her body started throbbing for him.

She finally got off the phone with her Dad and Ridge took over taunting her with his fingers as he kissed back up her torso.

"And how was your call," he teased.

"You are so not playing fair," she teased.

"Really? You think that was taunting?"

"Don't."

He kissed her, devouring her lips when the goosebumps re-appeared. "Now, what did your Dad want," he asked as he kissed down her neck.

"Doesn't matter," Faith said as he wrapped her legs around his hips.

"And," he teased.

"Having more fun with this," she teased. He slid her tight to him and kissed her again.

"Finish telling me what's going on."

"They found them on the floor with my office. In the boardroom or something."

"And," he teased.

"My office is good."

He snuggled her to him. "Like there was any doubt." When he devoured her lips, they had sex. There was nobody trying to make a move that they didn't want. There was no doubt. There was nothing but passion between them.

Just as her nails were digging into his back and her body was on the verge of climaxing, her phone went off again. He smirked.

"Not happening," Faith said as Ridge kept going. When it went off a second time as he collapsed to the bed, she shook her head. "Crap," Faith said as she grabbed her phone.

"Yes," Faith said as Ridge got up and cleaned up.

He got re-dressed and went to head downstairs when she grabbed the belt loop of his jeans and pulled her to him.

"I will," Faith said as she hung up.

"What," he asked.

"Come back to bed."

"Babe, you are gonna get back to back calls. I have work…"

She kissed him. "Come back to bed," Faith said as she went to undo his jeans.

"I love you Faith. I do. You have work to get finished, and I have a reservation to make for dinner and a movie night to plan," he teased as he kissed her again.

"Ridge."

"You finish up work, I'll get my work stuff done then we go

out for dinner alone.

"Really," Faith asked. He kissed her and pulled a shirt on, heading downstairs.

Kellen came in to grab a drink and saw Ridge. "What," Kellen asked.

"Nothin. I need a favor."

"What?"

"You know that limo service that we were talking about?"

Kellen nodded. "The grand gesture night," Kellen asked quietly. Ridge nodded. "What restaurant?"

"Circa 1886."

Kellen nodded. "Done," he replied.

Ridge made a quick call and managed a private dining room in the back, away from everyone and everything. He took a deep breath and got the flowers ordered, her favorite wine brought in and when Kellen looked at him, he was almost laughing. "What," Ridge asked.

"Never in my life did I think that I'd see you doing that," Kellen teased.

"I told you that when I found the right one, I'd do anything," Ridge said.

"And you are," Kellen joked. Ridge nodded.

"And you are what," Faith asked as she walked over and kissed Ridge.

"Nothin. Just surprising you with a night out. How's work," Ridge asked giving Kellen a look.

"Thanks to someone mentioning the camera stuff, Dad's now freaked and getting his security to do a check of their house too."

"They should've done that long ago," Kellen said as he walked back into the security office.

"And since he's all worried, he decided to stay at the beach house. My beach house."

Ridge kissed her. "And there's a problem why," Ridge asked.

"Well, I was gonna just take you there on the way home from wherever we're going. I told them that we're going tonight. He got a suite for them at Belmond Charleston Place instead. He said it was like a honeymoon 2.0 for a night."

"Fun," Ridge teased. Faith shook her head. "You good with that beach plan idea?"

She nodded. "Wherever we're going, I kinda want to go down to the beach for a while."

Ridge nodded. "Works."

"And where are you taking me," Faith asked.

Sue Langford

"You'll need a dress, and a pair of heels."

Chapter 2

"And where are we going that I need a fancy dress and heels?"

"You'll see when we get there. We're going to dinner."

Faith shook her head and kissed him. "And what are you wearing," she asked.

"You'll find out." She kissed him again and headed upstairs, figuring out what dress to taunt him with all night.

"You actually got a reservation," Kellen asked.

Ridge nodded. "She needs this tonight. If you can make sure that things are okay at the beach house so she isn't worried."

Kellen nodded. "Flowers," Kellen asked. Ridge nodded. "I'll get them brought to the beach house. Go get ready." Ridge smirked, double checked emails and Kellen grabbed his laptop. "I'll take them over to the beach house. Breathe dude. Go have a date night with your woman."

Ridge patted him on the back and went upstairs. Faith was coming out of her closet in nothing but lace lingerie. "You know that isn't gonna be enough clothes for dinner right," Ridge joked.

"I was considering this and a trench coat," Faith teased.

"I'm thinking more like a dress." She showed him two

options, and both were way too tempting for her to wear anywhere.

"Faith."

"What?"

"You sure you want to go there?"

Faith nodded with a smirk ear to ear. He shook his head and went into his closet, grabbing his black dress pants. When she came in behind him, he shook his head. "Ridge."

"What?"

He turned to face her, and Faith smirked. "Which do you want me to wear?"

"Both are illegal. You're seriously tempting fate with those dresses."

"So, you want me to wear something else?"

"I want you to put on what makes you feel good. Those dresses are sexy as all get out and you dang well know it."

"Oh, I know." She kissed him and he smirked.

"I know what you're doing."

"And what do you think that I'm doing," Faith asked.

"Taunting me until I call off dinner and just curl up in bed with you. You have a movie to finish tonight. Until..."

She kissed him and slid in closer to him. "Until what?"

"You don't make it through the movie, that bed is gonna be mighty cold," he teased. Faith kissed him. "Until then, you have to behave for a while. Go put something on that you can't see through so I can take you to dinner, fiancée."

She kissed him. "Fine, but you can't get mad."

He shook his head. "Get goin," he teased.

Faith kissed him again and went and got dressed. Ridge slid into his dress pants and dress shirt, slid his black and silver tie on and saw her in the dress. "Can you zip it up for me," Faith asked as he zipped up the barely there zipper. He tied the top for her and she turned to face him with a smirk. The ultra-low front, the draped back, and the sparkle. With one move, she would show him everything. She'd practically be naked in the middle of the restaurant.

"Literally the closest you could get to walking around naked," he teased.

"You told me to choose."

He shook his head. "You're wearing a sweater."

She smirked. "Nope." Faith changed purses and went to grab her laptop when Kellen smirked.

"What," Faith asked.

"Already at the beach house."

"What?"

"The laptops and an overnight bag are already over there."

Ridge came downstairs and saw Faith on her phone.

"Are you putting it down tonight," he teased. She slid her phone in her bag and saw him in a suit. She slid her heels on and he kissed her.

"Which car are we taking," Faith asked. Kellen nodded that the truck was at the beach house and they went to head outside when she saw the fancy car waiting outside for them.

"What's this?"

"I'm not driving. We got a driver," he said with a smirk.

"What?"

"Easy. That way we can both have a couple drinks. Start that night that you wanted off with a nice dinner."

She shook her head and the driver opened the door for them. "What's all of this for," Faith asked.

"Woman, get in." She smirked and slid into the car, and he slid in beside her. The driver put the window up between the front and back seat and Faith shook her head.

"Are you gonna tell me what all of this is about," Faith asked.

"I wanted to do something nice for you. Is that not allowed?"

"You're going all out aren't you," Faith asked.

Ridge slid his arm around her. "I'm allowed. I have a pretty amazing fiancée. Thought she needed an all-out fancy night out complete with doing whatever we want." Faith kissed him and slid her head on his shoulder. "What," he asked.

"I love you too." He kissed her and they made their way to the restaurant.

When they walked in, Faith fully expected to be seated among the other patrons, but when they got their own private dining area, she smirked. "You overdid this too didn't you," Faith asked.

He kissed her, held her chair for her and they sat down to a fancy amazing dinner. The wine, the food and everything else was perfect. When they headed out and made their way to the beach house, she still had a grin ear to ear.

"What," he asked.

"Thank you."

"For what? Dinner?"

"All of it. For distracting me. For loving me and my insanity. For knowing what I need when I don't. I needed tonight. You may have gone overboard just a little, but it's perfect." Faith kissed him and he snuggled her to him as they pulled into the beach house. The lights were all out.

"Don't move," Ridge said.

"What," Faith asked.

"Stay in the car." He grabbed his bag out of his truck and she saw the handgun. He walked into the house and Faith said a prayer. She just needed to see him. No gunshots, no fire, no nothing.

Ridge walked into the house, walked into the security office and there was nobody there. He checked upstairs and the guys were gone. He called Calvin and heard a phone. He followed the noise and saw them having dinner back in the other sitting area. "Gees. I thought you two vanished," Ridge said as he put his handgun away.

"Candles are out. I thought you'd want us away from y'all," Calvin said. Ridge shook his head, lit the candles, and came outside, got Faith's door, and walked her inside.

"What happened," Faith asked.

"I thought the guys had vanished. Unfortunately, they're still here," Ridge joked.

"You scared me."

He kissed her and walked her into the TV room and she saw the candles, the Jack, two glasses and a blanket on the sofa. "I kinda knew you'd be pissed, so I set this up," Ridge joked.

She shook her head. "You do know that I'm changing before we watch it right," Faith teased.

He kissed her, devouring her lips. "Kinda liking the dress."

"And you said it was too much."

"It is fiancée. I mean, if it were a shirt you might not be able to wear it at all. It would keep falling open," he teased.

"Funny." She kissed him and went upstairs, sliding into his t-shirt and washed the makeup off. She headed back downstairs and Ridge was pouring two glasses. "You aren't changing," Faith asked as he looked over and saw her in his t-shirt.

"Faith."

She kissed him with a smirk and sat down on the sofa. "I'll be down in a few minutes," Ridge said as he shook his head and went upstairs to change. He slid into his comfy beat-up jeans and a t-shirt and came downstairs. "You ready," Ridge asked as she turned and almost drooled.

Ridge in comfy beat-up jeans, the comfy t-shirt and barefoot was hot. The ideas running through her head would've made the devil blush. "Faith, stop staring at me like I'm dessert," Ridge said.

"You are," she teased as he handed her a glass.

"Good thing you're marrying me then." She nodded with a smirk.

"Ridge."

"Don't even say what I think you're going to."

"All I'm saying is that we could just hold off and watch it…"

He kissed her neck and down to her shoulder. "We're watching it."

"We're going to do a search," Calvin said with a smirk as he did a perimeter search of the property.

"You sure you want..."

He kissed her again. "Woman, we're watching it like it or not," he said.

He flipped the TV on and started the movie. She slid in close to him, wrapping his arm around her and got as close as she could short of jumping into his jeans. "Faith."

"What," she asked as he paused the movie.

"What are you up to?"

"Nothin."

He shook his head. "You couldn't get closer unless you were on top of me."

"And?"

He leaned his head forward as he whispered in her ear. "You keep trying to taunt me. You're the one that has to behave," he teased as Faith kissed him.

They curled up together, watching the movie and when the first of a million steamy Moments appeared on the screen, he kissed the nape of her neck. He knew the reaction she'd have to it. The reaction she always had. "Ridge, you're taunting."

"I know." He smirked and Faith shook her head, determined to watch the movie. When he pulled the blanket up a little, Faith shook her head and his hand slid down her torso.

"Ridge."

"What?"

"I know what you're doing."

"Good." When his hand slid to her inner thigh, Faith shook her head and he kissed her neck. She could feel the warmth of his hand near her and she shook her head. "Mine," he whispered.

Faith nodded and he smirked. "You don't cut it out, I'm pausing it."

"And you'll lose the bet." Faith felt his fingers start teasing and her toes started curling. "Fiancée."

"Then stop."

"Nope," he teased.

"You are seriously determined. You need to quit."

"And why's that sexy?"

She shook her head and smirked. He kissed the edge of her ear and she smirked. "You are so not being fair right now."

"You seriously thought that I'd play fair with you? The one who wears the lowest cut dress that she could wear to try

41

and taunt me? The one who tries things when I'm sleeping that you think I don't notice? Really fiancée of mine. I'm not playing fair," he whispered as he could feel her getting even more turned on.

"Ridge."

"Yes beautiful," he said as he snuggled her close to him. When he saw her eyes close, he knew. He intensified the teasing and felt her body clench around his fingers. "How's the movie," he joked.

"You have to stop."

"Never."

He smirked and Faith shook her head. "You're so not behaving," she said.

"I know," he whispered.

Faith took a breath and he nibbled her neck. "Ridge, I swear."

"Pause it."

"Cut it out," Faith said almost laughing.

"I dare you to pause it."

Faith shook her head. "Then..."

"What?"

"I'd lose."

"You like losing the bet," he teased. Faith smirked and he grabbed the remote, pausing the movie. She turned to face him as he pulled the blanket up to cover her bare backside. She straddled him on the sofa and kissed him.

"You sure you want to watch the rest?"

She nodded. "You have to quit teasing," she said.

"Like this," he said as his fingers started taunting her all over again.

"Ridge."

He kissed her, devouring her lips and she went for the button of his jeans. "Nope," he said as he broke the kiss.

"You don't get to taunt me without repercussions." He moved her hand away from him.

"Ridge."

He kissed her. "No touching."

She kissed him. "Then you can't taunt me either."

He smirked. "Fine," he joked.

She kissed him and he smirked as she turned and got comfortable again, sliding in tight to him. "Okay. Watch the movie," he teased.

"I swear, if you start again, you're not gonna be sleeping tonight either." He smirked and kissed her neck. He pressed play and it got to an even hotter scene. He smirked and kissed her shoulder. "Ridge."

"What?"

"I mean it." He smirked and took a gulp of the drink and she put her glass down. Ridge refilled her glass and handed it back to her. She shook her head.

"All yours beautiful," he teased. They kept watching and he could tell she was squirming. When she linked their fingers, he got a grin ear to ear. "I love you too," he whispered.

When it got towards the end, Faith shook her head and he kissed her neck. She turned it off, turned to face him, put her drink down and kissed him.

"And?"

"Fine. You win."

He smirked. "You sure?" She kissed him again and went for the button of his jeans. "Not down here."

He picked her up, wrapped her legs around him, bringing the blanket with them and walked up the steps to their bedroom. He closed and locked the door, leaning her against it and dropped the blanket. He walked over to the bed and leaned her onto it, peeling his shirt off of her. "Ridge."

"What?"

"What's for dessert," Faith teased.

He shook his head and peeled his shirt off.

"You keep your hands there," he said as he kissed her and put her hands at her side.

"Ridge."

He covered her eyes with the shirt and she shook her head. "Faith."

"Why," she asked.

"You'll find out," he said as he grabbed a few things from his bag.

"Ridge."

He kissed her and she heard a quiet buzz. He messaged the guys that they'd gone to bed and walked over to her as he saw her toes starting to curl already. One slight touch and her toes were in knots. "Now, what were you saying about not fair," he teased.

"Ridge."

"What?"

"Come here." He intensified the buzz and kissed her as she nibbled at his lips.

"More," he asked.

"You sure you want..." He kissed her again and the buzzing intensified even more.

She was almost climaxing just from the buzzing. "Didn't think I'd make it that easy did you," he teased.

The buzzing disappeared and she smirked. "Ridge."

"Mm," he said as he kissed up her inner thigh.

"I know what you're doing," Faith said.

"Nope." He taunted and her toes curled even tighter. He taunted, nibbling and kissing and nibbling some more until she was almost shaking. One kiss and she shook her head.

"Ridge."

"What?"

"What are you up to?"

"Dessert." He kept taunting and grabbed something else from his bag.

"Ridge."

"What baby," he asked.

"I need you."

"For what," he teased.

"Now."

He shook his head with a smirk. "Not yet."

"Now." She reached for him. When the buzzing started again, she tried grabbing his hand. It got even more intense. "Ridge, now." He kept going and kissed her. "Jeans off."

"Nope."

"Ridge, seriously." He kissed her again and kept going, making it more intense.

"Seriously." He kissed down her neck and she pulled him to her.

"No more taunting." He kissed her again and turned the buzz up. "Crap," Faith said as he could see her legs shaking and her toes in knots. "Ridge." He slid the buzzing away from her and she reached for his jeans.

"What are you up to wife to be?"

"I want you. Now."

He kissed up her neck. "I have so much more taunting to do."

"Ridge."

He kissed her. "Flip over."

"Not on your life," Faith replied as he kissed her and turned her so she was face down on the bed. "I mean it," Faith said.

When she heard the zipper of his jeans, she slid closer to him. He was past turned on. Way past. It was almost painful. They had sex. It was hotter when she was almost craving him. It always had been. He went deeper, harder when she demanded it and her body was almost exploding around him. "Ridge," Faith said.

He smirked. "Yes sexy," he said as it got faster.

"Kiss me." She turned to face him and he devoured her lips and it got harder. "More," Faith said as he continued taunting her. They kept going until she was on top. It got more and more intense until he was overheating and her body had exploded more than once. When his body exploded into her, he pinned her to the bed. "Don't move," Ridge said.

"I can't," she said as his body finally came down from the intensity. He devoured her lips and grabbed the buzzing item from the floor. "What," Faith asked.

"Eyes closed."

"Ridge."

"I gave you a break," he teased.

"That wasn't a break," she joked.

"Yeah it was," he said as he kissed her again. The buzzing slid up her inner thigh and her toes curled back up again.

"Ridge."

"What sexy," he said as it hit the apex of her thighs.

"Crap."

"Too much," he asked with a smirk ear to ear.

He had to admit it. All of the taunting and watching her body curl was hot. It was really hot. It was becoming an addiction. "Ridge."

"Too much?"

"Yeah," she said as he turned it down.

"Don't." He smirked and turned it back up. He nibbled at her breasts and worked his way up, kissing her as she was almost gasping for air. The kiss was even hot.

"I love you," Ridge said.

"I love you more...ahh."

"Really," he teased.

"You're so not playing fair."

"Never do around you," he joked as he kissed down her torso and intensified the buzz.

"Crap," Faith said.

"Like I said sexy. Dessert," he teased.

When her body climaxed again, she was almost shaking. He turned the buzzing off and taunted her in complete silence. "Ridge."

"Baby."

"Come here." He kissed back up her torso and she reached for him.

"What," he asked.

"Come."

He kissed her and she devoured his lips as his fingers taunted her even more. "Ridge."

"You told me that I'd be the one that wasn't getting any sleep," he teased.

"Fine. You win."

When the taunting got worse, she grabbed his hand. "Stop."

"Too much," he asked.

"I can't stop shaking." He kissed her and they had sex again.

It was making love. Her body was spent, and by the time he collapsed into her arms, neither of them had an ounce of energy left. He kissed her again and devoured her lips.

"All mine," he teased.

"Forever," Faith replied. He smirked and snuggled her tight to him. Her head rested on his shoulder and before he even managed to catch his breath, she was nodding off.

"You okay," he asked.

Faith nodded and kissed him, snuggling in tight to him. "Now, no doing what I know you're going to. Not tonight."

"Tomorrow," Faith teased.

"We're going for a swim. You good with that," he asked. Faith nodded and yawned. He slid her to the pillows and pulled the blankets up. "Where are you going," Faith asked.

"Clean up a little. I'm getting us water." She kissed him and he got up.

He cleaned up, put his joggers on, hid the toys in his bag, and walked downstairs. Both glasses were in the washer and the Jack was away. "Thank you," Ridge said as Calvin came out of the security room.

"Everything good," Calvin asked.

"Just getting water. Everything secure?"

He nodded. "I still think you need…"

"Cal."

"I get it, but you need to."

Ridge nodded. "Not happening."

"Dude, it's not bad."

"Yeah it is. Leave it." Ridge got the water for them and went back upstairs. Faith had his t-shirt back on and was curled up in the blankets. He put the water down, kicked his joggers off, slid into bed behind her and kissed her shoulder, sliding his arm around her.

"What were you two fighting about?"

"Nothing. Old crap," he said. He kissed her shoulder again and she slid in tight to him.

"Faith."

"What?"

"I thought you were tired."

She kissed him and turned to face him. "I am. I was missing my man," she said as she snuggled up to him.

"Faith."

"What?"

"Off limits."

She kissed him. "I know. I promise."

He shook his head. "I also know when you have your fingers crossed. I mean it." She nodded and he turned her so that they were curled in tight together with his arms around her from behind. "Now sleep before I have to start round two," he whispered.

They finally managed to fall asleep. The next morning, he woke up still curled up with Faith. He kissed her shoulder and she rolled over, snuggling back up to him. "Sleep."

"Going for a run."

"No."

"Sleep. The guys are here. I'll be back in an hour."

"No Ridge." He kissed her and got up. "Not allowed," Faith said half-asleep. He kissed her again and pulled on his boxers, joggers, and a hoodie. He slid his socks and sneakers on, grabbed his AirPods Pro and phone and came downstairs.

"Morning," Carson said.

"Hey. Can you keep an ear out for Faith? She's sleeping in. I told her I was going for a run."

He nodded. "Cal said you two had words."

"Don't bring it up. What happened there stays there," Ridge said.

"It's not a bad thing."

"I don't care. No." Ridge shook his head, grabbed his water, and freshened up then headed off for his run. He was gone for an hour and a half and when he made it back, Calvin was sitting on the back steps. "Hey," Ridge said catching his breath.

"You need to."

Ridge shook his head. "You bring it up again I swear I'll rip your tongue out." Ridge walked back inside and washed out his reusable water bottle, refilled it and made himself a protein shake. He guzzled it down and walked back upstairs. He went to head into the washroom and shower and Faith smirked.

"You could just come back to bed," she teased.

He kissed her, peeled his shirt off and walked into the bathroom. He kicked his clothes off, throwing them into the hamper and walked into the shower. He leaned under the hot water and it almost felt too good. Taking off and diving into the ocean without her would've been unfair, but he needed it. He washed his hair and was about to wash up when her arms slid around his waist.

"Morning beautiful," he said.

"You are such a party pooper."

He smirked and turned to face her. "And why is that," he asked as he leaned down and kissed her. She deepened the kiss and he picked her up, wrapping her legs around him and leaned her against the wall.

"You vanished on me."

He kissed her. "You knew where I was. Your Dad said hi by the way."

She kissed him. "I don't wanna talk about my Dad right now sexy fiancée," Faith teased.

He kissed her and Faith slid her arms around his neck. "And what do you want," he teased.

"Want a hint?"

He kissed her. When his hand slid down her legs and to the one tender spot that had driven her crazy the night prior, she smirked. "Really? Interesting," he teased as they started making out and then started having sex in the shower. When he kept going, she wouldn't break the kiss. He sat down on the shower bench and she kept going.

"Mine," she joked.

"Think so do you," he joked. Faith nodded and his hand kept going, taunting her even more until her body exploded around his. He pulled her tight to him.

"Ridge."

"Sexy," he said as his body found its release.

"Promise me," she said as he kissed her.

"What?"

"That we never ever change." He smirked.

"We'll have to find another movie for movie torture night," he said with a smirk ear to ear. She kissed him. "I love you."

"I love you back," Faith replied as he picked her up and walked her into the stream of hot water. He grabbed her shampoo, washing her hair for her, rinsed it out and then slid her conditioner in. "I meant what I said," Faith said.

"Nothing is gonna change. Maybe not as much time, but we're not gonna change baby. I promise you we aren't."

She kissed him. "Good, because I don't know that you're gonna be able to handle it if I manage to win one round."

"Babe, I can taunt you for hours if you didn't keep tapping out," he joked. She kissed him with a smirk, rinsed her conditioner out and stepped out of the shower while he finished cleaning up.

He stepped out of the shower, wrapped a towel around him and went and shaved, freshened up and came into the bedroom to see Faith in a bikini. "You shaved."

"Just a little. Babe, if I don't I'm gonna end up with a full beard."

He kissed her and went and pulled on swim shorts. "Ridge," Faith said as she walked into his closet.

"Yes beautiful fiancée."

"Are we staying," she asked.

"We can head back whenever. My truck is here."

"Can we?"

He smirked and kissed her. "Whatever you want."

"Did you really see my Dad," she asked.

"He was going for a run."

"I thought they were going away?"

"He said they were leaving today. I just wanted to make sure he was alright. I know how shaky you were when we were dealing with the camera stuff."

She kissed him. "Thank you for checking."

"Babe, I love them too. Always have even though your Dad kinda freaks me out now."

She smirked and wrapped her arms around him. "He isn't that scary."

"Yeah he is when we're dating," Ridge replied as he grabbed beach towels and walked her downstairs.

They made their way outside and went straight into the water. He knew that it was almost calming being in the waves. When she swam to him and right into his arms, he smirked and kissed her. "What," he asked. Faith dunked him and swam over the waves.

"Oh, you really think that you're gonna get away with that," Ridge asked as he splashed her. The two of them played in the waves for what felt like hours until he pulled her to him and her legs slid around his hips.

"What," Faith asked.

"Hungry," he asked.

"Actually yeah." She got a smirk and he shook his head.

"That's not what I meant," he said.

"Still," she teased.

"Faith." She kissed him and he walked her up to the shore, walked up through the sand and sat her on the steps. He rubbed the sand from their feet and she smirked. "Faith, cut it out."

"I didn't say anything," she said with that smirk that said she was totally and completely up to something.

"I know the look."

He kissed her and walked inside to make breakfast. She followed and he made omelets for everyone. She made coffee and handed Ridge a mug. "Faith."

"Ridge," she teased. He kissed her and she went and sat down. He gave the guys their breakfast and came and sat down with Faith on the high-top chairs. He plated their omelets and bacon, put some melon on the side and handed her the breakfast plates. "Thank you," Faith said.

"Maybe now you'll quit staring at me like I'm dessert," he teased.

Faith kissed him and they ate. Somehow, after a long run and swim, the food tasted even better. They finished breakfast and he cleaned up. "Ridge."

"What?"

"We're staying today."

"Alright beautiful." He messaged Kellen and Leo to let them know they were staying another night at the beach and Ridge's phone rang.

"Good morning," Ridge said as Faith smirked.

"Mornin. We had a little situation. One of the windows

was shattered," Kellen said.

"Where?"

"TV room and we found a bullet casing. The cops are taking care of it, but I wanted to let you know."

"Thank goodness we weren't there," Ridge said.

"The glass is being replaced this afternoon. It won't look any different."

"Okay," Ridge said as he looked at Faith.

"It's a really good thing you weren't. The bullet casing was on the sofa," Kellen said.

"Shit. Okay. You sure you're good?"

"Don't bring her until the window is fixed. Tomorrow."

"Done," Ridge said. They hung up a minute or two later and Faith looked at him.

"What," Faith asked.

"I love you. I always will."

"Say it," Faith said.

"One of the windows was broken. Someone shot through the window."

"What?"

"The bullet casing was on the sofa."

"But they didn't get in?"

He shook his head. "The cops that were on security detail heard it and got what they needed. He's replacing the window today."

Faith shook her head. "So much for relaxing," Faith said.

He came around the counter and wrapped his arms around her. "We're safe. Whoever it is knows that they can't hurt you with me around. We're good baby." Faith shook her head and walked upstairs, grabbing her laptop.

Ridge came into the bedroom behind her and Faith sat down on the edge of the bed. "Babe."

"I don't want Dad worrying." He kissed her head and took her hand, walking her downstairs to the TV room.

"Do you want to go see him," Ridge asked.

"Is it gonna ruin the day?"

He kissed her and shook his head. "We'll go together."

They got dressed and Faith smirked. "What?"

"You sure," she asked.

He kissed her. "Babe, get dressed and we'll go." She kissed him again and they hopped into the truck and went over to her Mom and Dad's beach house.

"What on earth are you doing over here," her Mom asked when she answered.

"We were down at my place. I wanted to make sure that you two were alright," Faith said.

Her Mom gave Faith and Ridge a hug and they all sat down. "I must say Ridge, those guys that you have working with you are amazing. One of the guys came down and went through the house with our security and found the cameras. The house doesn't look like anything was ever there," her Mom said.

"That's kinda the bonus. They did construction before we all met. They fixed up Faith's place like it was nothing," Ridge said.

"I thought I heard voices. Ridge. Nice seeing you again," her Dad said as he gave Faith a hug.

"She wanted to check on you both before you headed out," Ridge said.

"What's wrong," her Dad asked.

"Well, there was a small issue last night. We weren't at the house anyway, and the police were guarding the house. They have everything that they need," Faith said.

"What happened," her Dad asked.

"Someone shot at the house. It hit the main floor living room window and shattered. They found the bullet on the sofa," Ridge said as her Mom grabbed Faith's hand.

"Thank goodness you two weren't there. Oh, my goodness," her Mom said.

"They're fixing the glass today, but Faith wanted to make sure you knew," Ridge said as her Dad a silent thank you.

"Nobody was hurt," her Dad asked.

"No. Just on edge. The police are going through security tape and they're taking care of it. We're staying out here for a few days then heading back once things are settled," Ridge said.

They stayed and visited for a while then headed back down to Faith's. "What if we went for a walk," Faith asked.

"Where?"

"Waterfront?"

He kissed her at the light. "Done." He linked their fingers, kissing her hand and made their way into parking for the waterfront park. "Do you want a soda or anything," he asked. Faith kissed him the minute the truck was in park. Her arms slid to him and he knew what was coming.

"What," he asked. She hopped over the console and slid into his lap, straddling him on the seat. "What," he teased.

Faith shook her head. "I love you," she said.

"And I love you. What's wrong," he teased.

She undid his jeans. "Faith."

"What," she asked as he felt her hand slide his zipper down.

"I know what you're doing."

"Good." She kissed him and he felt her hand on him, gripping him and getting him turned on.

"Here? Now?" She nodded and kissed him as her hand started moving faster. "Faith."

"What," she asked as he grabbed her hand, slid it behind her back and pulled her panties off from under the hem of her dress.

"You're doing this now."

"Tinted windows."

He slid her on top of him. "All yours," he teased as he held her hands behind her back.

"Really," she teased.

"You wanted it." She shook her head and he kissed her, pulling her body to his so he was deep inside her.

"Crap," Faith said.

"What? Too much," he teased as Faith kissed him. He pulled her to him and they started having sex in the truck. Hot wasn't enough to describe it. She kept going. Harder. Faster. Deeper until her body was throbbing around him. "Faith."

"Mine," she replied.

"Always," he replied as it got harder. Her body was

addicted and so was she. He was the one man she'd always wanted even if she didn't know it. When his body started to stiffen, she'd already crumbled into his arms. They kept going until he found his release and let go of her hands.

"Damn," Faith said catching her breath.

"Woman, I swear, you are so bad."

"And you love me," she replied as he held her tight to him and refused to let her move.

"That, my love, is one very immense understatement."

She kissed him and went to move when he stopped her. "What?"

He kissed her again. She sat up just long enough for him to slide his boxers back up. "And what are you gonna do when we're out there on the dock?"

"Kiss my man."

He kissed her again and she slid back over to her side of the truck, hopping out. He grabbed the lace panties from the seat, sliding them into his pocket, zipped up his jeans and buttoned them, then slid out of the truck, locking it behind him. "You just keep taunting their fiancée of mine. Someday, you'll go too far."

She kissed him and took his hand. "You left something in the truck."

"I know."

He shook his head. "Faith."

"What?"

He shook his head. "Front pocket."

"Yours."

He shook his head. Thankfully, the sundress was long enough to cover. "You are seriously asking for it."

"I know," she teased as he slid his arm around her and walked her to the end of the dock.

"Now what beautiful," he asked.

Faith kissed him. "Now I get time alone. Nobody bugging us or interrupting," Faith said.

He kissed her, keeping a close eye on everything around them. "Hungry," he asked.

Faith kissed him. "For lots of things," she teased.

"Insatiable." She kissed him and he picked her up, walking over and sat down on the iron porch swings. He slid her legs across his lap and she kissed him again.

"I love you."

"I love you back." When he could hear her stomach grumbling, he smirked. "Come on."

"What?"

"Food." He got up and took her hands, walking her to the truck.

He got her door for her, helped her in and they headed over to get Cane's chicken. "This is what you want?"

Faith nodded and linked their fingers. He shook his head, got the takeout and they headed back to the beach house. When they walked in, the guys were having lunch. "Hold up. Do I smell Cane's," Calvin asked.

"Mine," Faith replied.

"Come on. One," Connor said.

"Nope," Faith teased as they walked outside. Ridge got them each a Jack and Coke, handing one to Faith and sat down on the porch with her.

"And," he asked.

"This is exactly what I needed," Faith teased. He shook his head with a smirk. "What?"

"You are so bad. First this morning, then the park," he said.

Faith kissed him, devouring his lips. "And," she teased as she came up for air and fed him the last chicken finger.

"Thank you," he said.

Faith kissed him. "Now, what did you want to do," Faith asked.

"You're getting work done, or at least check over emails. I have to check over..." She kissed him and took his hand. "What," he asked.

"Roll up the jeans. We're walking." He slid his phone in his pocket, put hers in his other pocket and walked down to the water. She rolled her jeans up and they walked along the water.

"You good," he asked.

Faith smirked. "Yep."

"I know that look. What's going on," he asked.

Faith turned to face him. "When this stupid threat stuff is over, why don't we just get married on the beach?"

He looked at her. "And we're back to wedding talk," he teased.

"What would be wrong with that?"

"Because you wanted the wedding at the church where your Mom and Dad got married."

"We can do both. This one is you and me. The other one is for everyone else."

He shook his head. "And have your parents murder me in the middle of the beach? I'd say no."

Chapter 3

"I doubt he'd do that. I just want a little piece of it to be just ours," Faith said.

"Then we come up with a date. We plan something that's just for us."

"Such as?"

Ridge kissed her. "Remember that show you watched about people in Scotland? They did handfasting or something like that."

Faith looked at him. "You remembered a show I watched when I was a teenager?"

"The first time that I kissed you."

Faith looked at him. "No, you didn't."

"You fell asleep on my dang shoulder. I did."

She looked at him. "Seriously?"

He nodded. "When I got my first truck."

Faith looked at him and shook her head. "If I'd known..." He kissed her again and picked her up, wrapping her legs around him. "No, you didn't," she said. He nodded.

He leaned down, leaning her onto the sand and sliding into her arms. "Yeah I did. I didn't say anything before. I didn't even tell my Mom then. I liked you then. I always did."

Faith kissed him and he nibbled at her lips. "What do you want," he asked.

She kissed him and went for the button of his jeans. "No," he said.

"Why?"

"Not happening Faith. Not out here."

She kissed him and undid the button. He shook his head, did the button back up, and picked her up, walking her back down the beach. "Never ever behave."

She smirked. "We could just jump in the water."

"And you could just go home and change into a dang swimsuit."

She kissed him. "No adventure at all," she teased.

"I swear, you are taunting the wrong dang man."

"Really? Says who," Faith asked.

He shook his head and walked her back to the beach house. "Get emails in and I'll go change."

"Ridge."

"What?"

"I'll meet you in the water." Faith kissed him.

"I swear, you are never ever gonna behave."

"Nope." She kissed him and he picked her up, carried her inside and sat her on the bed.

"Swimsuit." She shook her head. "I mean it Faith." He walked into the closet, grabbed his swimsuit, and pulled it on and Faith intentionally grabbed her skimpiest bikini. "Don't you dare."

"Why," Faith asked.

"Might as well walk out there naked. Put on an actual swimsuit not just string. Please?" She kissed him, grabbed the other bikini that was almost as bad and pulled it on.

"Faith, you do know that walking around half-naked isn't exactly necessary right?"

"And I know that I only do it to taunt you."

"You do know that a naked bikini isn't about to taunt me."

"So, if I decided to swim naked?"

"I'd suggest that you didn't with security watching."

"Ridge."

"What?" He kissed her, devouring her lips. "Stop taunting me and I stop taunting you," she said.

"That wouldn't be any fun, but I don't know that your Dad would..."

She kissed him. "And that's gonna stop me?"

He shook his head and nuzzled her neck, picking her up and leaning her onto the bed. "Here's the deal. You put on an actual bikini or something other than the dental floss see-through stuff, and you won't get taken back to the house in that room that you love. You won't have your hands tied. You won't be taunted until your body is exploding and then do it over and over again until you have no energy left." Faith kissed him and he slid his arms around her. She smirked and grabbed his hoodie, walking downstairs. He shook his head. He slid his other hoodie on and followed her downstairs, grabbing the beach blanket and two towels.

"What's up," Connor asked as they came downstairs.

"When we come back in, we're heading back to the house. Just let the guys know."

Connor nodded. Ridge walked outside and saw Faith on the steps waiting for him. "What," Faith asked as he came down the steps.

"We're going home tonight."

"Ridge." One look and she smirked. "If you have to go all..."

He kissed her. "Now miss showoff. Go get in the water."

She took his hand, pulling him to his feet and walked into the water with him, throwing the hoodies on the sand. She swam under the waves until she felt hands pulling her to the surface. She came up face to face with Ridge as he kissed her. "You need to quit taunting."

"Ditto," Faith teased.

He picked her up and wrapped her legs around his hips and walked further into the water. "What?"

He kissed her. "Be prepared."

"For what?"

He untied the sides of the barely there bikini. "Ridge."

"This is the least of it," he teased. Faith looked at him and he kissed her, nibbling her lips and deepening the kiss until her toes were curling. She felt his hand slide from her backside down her legs and grazed the one sensitive spot that he knew would get her going.

"Ridge," she said as he broke the kiss for a half second.

"What," he teased.

"We doing this out here? What happened?"

"Dental floss," he replied as he kissed her again and they slid under the water. She could barely think straight let alone break that kiss again. When they surfaced, he had a smirk. "I know that look."

"This what you wanted," he asked.

Faith shook her head. "What?" Her hand slid down the front of his swimsuit and he shook his head.

"I love you, but cut it out." She shook her head and kept going. "Faith."

She kissed him and pulled her legs tight around him, pulling her hands behind her back. They had sex in the water, the waves crashing around them as her body trembled in his arms. "Ridge," she said. She was far enough out in the water so nobody would hear them other than the dolphins. When his body tensed, her nails were digging into his back.

"Faith."

"Don't move."

"What?" He felt her body tense around him and he shook his head.

"Mine," he whispered as a wave crashed beside them. "Still determined to taunt me back," he asked.

Faith nodded. He slid her bikini bottoms back together, slid his swimsuit back up and walked her back into the house. She slid to her feet in the water and walked in with him hand in hand.

"Now, before you do something else that they're gonna tease us about, go get clothes on and we can go." Faith smirked, kissed him, and headed upstairs as he shook his head. When he heard the swish of the sliding door behind him, he half-expected it to be Faith taunting him even more.

Callon handed Ridge his cell phone and headed back in.

He looked at the call display and shook his head. "What's up," Ridge asked.

"The cops were just back in here. There was another freaking package."

"And?"

"It had her Dad's name on it. The cops have it."

"We're coming back to the house." Ridge hung up with him, walked upstairs, grabbed his bag and pulled his jeans back on with his t-shirt. He put his laptop, his charger, and his toiletry bag back in his bag and slid in all the toys from the night prior.

"What's the rush," Faith asked.

"We're leaving in 15."

"Ridge."

"What?"

"What happened?"

"I'll meet you downstairs." He walked downstairs, slid his socks and sneakers on and put his things in the truck. Faith walked downstairs with her bag, slid her laptop into it and he grabbed it, putting it in the back seat. "Purse," he said.

"Are you gonna tell me what's going on?"

"Just hop in," he said getting her door for her and helping her into the truck.

"Are you gonna tell me what happened?"

"Another package, but it had your Dad's name on it," Ridge said as he stopped and got them coffees then drove to the house.

"What?"

"I think we need to upgrade the windows. They have to be bulletproof."

"Wait a second. What do you mean it had my Dad's name on it?"

He shook his head. "The police have it."

Faith looked at him. "What was it?"

"I don't know. As soon as I found out, I packed up our stuff." Faith shook her head and held his hand the entire ride home.

They pulled through the gates and went up to the door to see Kellen waiting. "What was it," Ridge asked.

He looked at Faith and Ridge shook his head. "Either you two tell me, or I swear."

"It was photos and a baby blanket," Kellen said.

Faith looked at them. "Of what," Faith asked.

Ridge shook his head. "Babe, the cops will handle it."

"Kellen," Faith said.

"Miss Faith..."

"Don't Miss Faith me. Say it." Ridge shook his head and walked upstairs, putting his things in his closet. When he came back downstairs, Faith was ripping Kellen a new one.

"There is no way in this damn world that my Dad would ever even think about it. Never. Don't you dare tell me that you believe some photoshopped photos," Faith said.

Ridge took her hand and walked her into her office.

"Ridge."

He kissed her. "Breathe. I'm gonna talk to your Dad's security and get more information. At least we'll have confirmation that it's crap. Just calm down."

Faith glared at him. "Go shower and..."

"No. You find out the answer then I get the real answer."

He shook his head and called her Dad's security. "Ridge."

"Were you notified about the package," Ridge asked.

"Yes."

"I was a little concerned. I don't believe that he would ever do that to Miss Lily. Has he," Ridge asked.

"Ridge."

"Faith is just as worried." There was an awkward silence. One that he wasn't happy with. "Is that a yes or no," Ridge asked.

"There was an incident years back. She thought he had, and he said he didn't. Truthfully, there's a chance that he did."

"And?"

"We'll get the information about the sender. Just please don't say anything," her Dad's security said.

"Thank you. Just keep me posted," Ridge said.

"And," Faith asked.

"They don't know."

Faith looked at him. "You're full of it," she said closing the door.

"Faith."

"What did he say?"

"That there was an incident but he doesn't think it's true."

She looked at him. "My Dad? Mine? My Dad cheated on my Mom," Faith asked.

"I don't know and either do they. It's probably a load of crap. Threats like that usually are."

Faith grabbed her phone and he took it from her hand. "Don't."

"Ridge, if he cheated on my Mom..."

"Don't go there." She took her phone back and called her Dad.

"Baby. What's wrong," he asked.

"I need to ask you something and I need the truth. All of it."

"Meaning what," her Dad asked.

"A package showed…"

"I know."

"A baby blanket and pictures of you with another woman."

"Faith."

"Did you cheat on Mom?"

"Baby, I love you, but this is between…"

"Not when it's on my doorstep. Did you?"

"Something happened at one point, but nothing that would result in a baby. I promise you that."

"Dad."

"I'm coming to the house." Faith hung up and shook her head.

"Babe, breathe," Ridge said as she shook her head.

"If he could do that to her…"

He kissed her. "Not happening with us. Not now, not ever. I promise you that," he said. Faith hugged him and he picked her up and carried her to the sofa. "Sit. Breathe. We'll figure it out. Just remember that I am never in my life ever doing that. I promise you Faith." She nodded and kissed him.

He went and got her a Jack and Coke, handed it to her and poured himself a Jack. They sat down and Kellen came in. "What's up," Ridge asked.

"It wasn't from a woman. They found out who sent it. The idiot actually thought we wouldn't look."

Ridge looked at him. "Meaning what," Ridge asked.

"Zack sent it."

"And?"

"I don't know what his deal is, but the cops said that they're handling the rest of it. At least we know what part of it was about," Kellen said as he headed back into the office.

"If he cheated on my Mom, I don't know that I could forgive him Ridge." He kissed her.

"Just remember. If it happened a long time ago, it's not up to you to forgive him. If it did happen, your Mom is the one that needed to forgive him." Faith nodded and he saw her hands were shaking. "Babe, maybe go try and relax. Have a shower. When he…"

"No."

She finished her drink and her Dad showed. Alone.

"Sir," Ridge said.

"Where's Faith?"

"Sofa." Her Dad came in and sat down with her.

"And," Faith asked.

"Baby, things happen in life. I can tell you that nothing happened. I was never with anyone else like that. Your Mom and I have lots of people around us, but I didn't cheat on your Mom. I wouldn't. I couldn't."

"Then why would someone say that you did," Faith asked.

"There was a time when something almost did happen, but nothing happened baby. I promise you," her Dad said as he gave her a hug.

"If you're lying to me, I swear…"

"Baby, Mom and I have both had our moments, but nobody ever cheated on anyone. Zack tried to talk her into it, but she never did and either did I." Faith looked at him and he shook his head.

"Drink," Ridge asked.

"Sweet tea if. You have it," her Dad said as Ridge went and got him a glass of sweet tea. He handed it to him and saw them talking through things. When his phone buzzed, he went back into Faith's office and answered. "Yep."

"Ridge, baby, where are you two?"

"At the house Mom. Why," he asked.

"Her Dad just took off like a bat out of hell. What's going on," she asked.

"It's fine. Something showed here and it freaked Faith and I out a little. She needed to talk to him alone."

"Are you two alright," his Mom asked.

"Yes. She's fine and no she's not pregnant," he joked.

"Did you two decide on anything?"

"Mom, I appreciate that you want to help, but we aren't even close." He took a deep breath.

"Do you remember when I told you about your Dad and I getting married," she asked.

"Yeah. What about it?"

"We sorta did something for just us before the wedding. We did a handfasting. It was a day or two before the wedding. We went off to the beach where we'd had our first date and did it just us and a priest from the church. We still had the ceremony, but the handfasting was just for us."

Ridge smirked. His Mom knew him. She also knew that a long, drawn-out thing wasn't his style. He also knew that

Faith wanted a ceremony like her Mom and Dad had. "I have no idea what she wants to do, but I wanted to do something for us alone. When we figure it all out, I'll tell you."

"She's okay though right," he heard.

"Her Mom's with you?"

"Yeah," his Mom said as she put Faith's Mom on the phone.

"How is she doing," Faith's Mom asked.

"She got freaked out with a package that showed while we were at the beach."

"I heard. All of that stuff was a long time ago. Nothing ever came of it. Just make sure she knows that things are fine. That she has nothing to worry about."

"I'm trying. She's really concerned and I knew the only way to fix things was for her to talk to her Dad. She seems okay now," Ridge said.

"Alright. If either of you need us let us know," his Mom said.

"I will. Love you guys." He hung up with them and went into the living room to see Faith on her laptop and her Dad gone.

"You alright," Ridge asked as he came in and sat down beside her.

"I'm not impressed with all of this," Faith said.

"Either am I. Babe, it's fine. They're determined to screw with you. What's done is done." He slid his arm around her and she leaned into his arms.

"Ridge."

"What?"

"I love you."

He kissed her forehead. "Babe, people in this life are gonna mess with anything and everything. They always have and they always will. Even in high school people tried to mess with us. We're good love. We always will be."

"Promise me that I never ever have to go through that," Faith said.

"I promise that for as long as I live and breathe, the only woman I'll ever want is you. If we have babies, that is the only other woman that I'll love as much as I love you."

Faith kissed him. "And what's with the if?"

"We could have boys."

Faith smirked and shook her head. "Ridge, you are ridiculous."

"And I made you laugh. Babe, you need a night off of all the stress. We watch one of those sappy movies you love," he teased.

"Funny," she joked.

"Go pick one, we'll have dinner and have a night to just relax."

Faith looked at him. "Don't."

She got up, took his hand, and walked him upstairs. "Faith."

"Come here," she teased.

They walked into the bedroom and she closed the door. "And what do you want beautiful?"

"Remember what you…"

"Faith."

"Remember what you said last night?" He nodded. "Then we're watching it tonight."

He took a deep breath, looking at her. "You just had the day from hell with that package…"

"I don't care. I want us to watch it. Since we both know that I'm not making it through that movie, I'll put my charger in your old room."

He shook his head with a smirk. "If you really want that tonight, then you're gonna have to at least attempt to behave."

"Never," Faith said as she went and slid out of her jeans and slid into a sundress that was damn near wrong. The totally open back, the slit that went right up to her hip, the fact that she intentionally took off anything and everything underneath it. Ridge shook his head, slid into his looser jeans and tee, and headed downstairs.

"I'm putting dinner together. Grilled lobster and sliced steak," her housekeeper said.

"Let me at least do something," Ridge asked.

"Steak is grilling with the lobster and the salad and baked potatoes are ready whenever y'all are. Dinner should be done in 15," the housekeeper said.

"I'll get the drinks then," Ridge said as he went and poured two Jack and Coke's. He put them at the table, put the salad out and saw Faith coming downstairs, wearing the perfume she wore the first time they were together.

"Faith," Ridge said as she came down the stairs.

"Hey handsome," Faith teased. She smirked and he instantly got a grin ear to ear.

"Much better mood?"

She nodded and kissed him. "Everything is ready. Enjoy your dinner. Are you alright with me going to that movie," her housekeeper asked as Faith nodded.

"Just be safe."

"I will. Thank you and enjoy dinner." Her housekeeper headed off and left Faith and Ridge semi-alone. Kellen and

Leo were hanging in their sitting area, away from the kitchen so Ridge and Faith had privacy.

"Come sit," Ridge said as he grabbed the plates and put them on the table, pulling her chair out for her.

"Thank you," Faith said.

"I literally did nothing. I promise," Ridge joked.

"I needed that today after everything that happened," she said.

"Your Mom called while you two were talking."

"And?"

"She says hi. She also mentioned that thing we were talking about."

Faith looked at him with a grin ear to ear. "Faith, we can do something that's just us, but I still think..."

"I had a better idea. What if we went and did something alone first. Completely alone."

"Like a honeymoon before the honeymoon?"

She nodded. "We make promises to each other alone. Just you and me and a beach."

"We can do that here."

"Somewhere away from everyone else." He smirked. An idea popped into his head that would not only be romantic, but sentimental as well. "What," Faith asked seeing the look on his face.

"I know the perfect spot." She kissed him and they ate dinner in the peace and quiet.

Once they finished, Ridge cleaned up, refilled their drinks, and lit a few candles. "And what's all of this for," Faith asked.

"Before we start, you take a dang breather. You've been running around continually for days. Breathe baby."

She kissed him, sat down with him on the sofa and slid into his lap. "Faith." She kissed him, devouring his lips as he pulled her tight to him. "What do you want," he asked as he slid his hands to her face and kissed her with a kiss that would make most women melt.

"I love you."

"And I love you," Ridge said. She hugged him and somehow, it was the glue that put her back together again. "You have me for life Faith. You always have and you always will."

"How in the world did I ever find you," Faith asked.

"The right time. If this had been when we were still teenagers, who knows," he replied.

They curled up together and watched one of her sappy movies then she turned on the last part of 365 days as he refilled their glasses. "So, what are we doing after this,"

Faith teased.

"You mean when you don't make it through the movie again?"

She nodded. "Full meal," he whispered as she got goosebumps head to toe.

"Ridge." He kissed her, devouring her lips until her toes were curling. "Don't want to just bypass the movie?"

He smirked. "Nope. I can do whatever I want to taunt you until you flip it off."

"That's the rule is it," Faith joked.

He nodded. "You ready," he asked.

Faith kissed him. "I love you handsome."

"Remember that when you're clawing up my back again," he whispered.

"And if I can't walk?"

"Then you stay in bed."

He kissed her and she smirked and turned to watch the movie as he pulled the blanket from the back of the sofa over her. "Really," Faith asked as he pulled it right up. "Ridge."

He kissed her neck and flipped the movie on. "Just remember the deal," he whispered as he kissed and nibbled down the edge of her ear.

"At some point you have to play fair," Faith said.

"Oh I am. It's up to you to make it through the taunting." The movie started and Faith took a gulp of her drink. When she refilled it in the second scene, he smirked. "Fiancée of mine," he whispered.

"Handsome." She slid his arms around her and his hand slid to the slit of her dress. When it was gently slid out of his way, she slid in a little closer.

"Faith."

"You started it."

He smirked and kissed the nape of her neck. "All mine," he whispered as she got goosebumps on top of the goosebumps. They kept watching and his hand slid up her inner thigh.

"Ridge."

"Mm."

"You sure," she teased. His hand slid to the apex of her thighs and the taunting started. When her hand slid on top of his, he kept going and it got worse. He knew just how long it took to get her turned on. He also knew that taunting her even more would have the guys wondering what they were up to.

He nibbled the nape of her neck and intensified the taunting. "You sure you can do it," he whispered as she leaned back harder against him.

"I swear. You are doing this intentionally."

"Yep."

Faith smirked. "Ridge."

"What?"

"If you don't stop, we're gonna..."

"Watch the movie," he said as he kissed her neck. He knew she wasn't going to be able to take much more when the taunting deepened. Her nails gripped his thighs.

"Ridge."

Her body was throbbing and he could feel it. "And," he whispered.

"Maybe I should stop the shots."

He paused the movie. "What?"

"Maybe I should."

"And maybe we should talk about it before you do that."

"Turn..."

"Faith."

"I was thinking about it. That's all."

He shook his head. "We'll discuss it tomorrow," he said as he turned it back on. The taunting went into overdrive by the time they were 60% of the way through.

"Fine. Off," Faith said as he had her legs almost trembling.

"I was wondering when you'd say that," he teased. He kept going and Faith's nails dug into his leg.

"Upstairs."

He kissed her shoulder and went to get up when she turned to face him and tried to undid his jeans. "Faith."

"What?"

"Don't."

She kissed him and unzipped his jeans. "Faith." He stopped her and got up, zipping and buttoning his jeans. She grabbed the glasses, refilling their drinks and followed him up the steps to his old bedroom.

When she walked in behind him, she put the drinks down and slid her arms around him. "Come sit," he said. She sat down on the edge of the bed, he slid the phones on the charger and he smirked.

"I know that look," Faith teased.

He kissed her. "Good," he teased as he closed and locked the door behind him.

"Ridge."

"Yes sexy," he asked. She motioned for him to come closer. He leaned over her and kissed her. When she went for the button of his jeans, he stopped her. "Don't even go there."

"Ridge." He shook his head. "Someday," she teased.

"Then I'm going to have to make sure you can't touch."

"Don't you dare." He smirked and flipped the light off.

They were in complete darkness and he loved it. She couldn't grab at him, and she definitely couldn't see him. When she felt him undo her dress, she slid out of it and he slid her into pillows. "Ridge."

"Faith."

"Please."

"Please what?"

She reached for him and he was out of reach. When she felt him kissing up her leg, her toes curled. "Mine," he teased. Faith shook her head and when he reached her inner thigh, Faith's toes were like pretzels.

"Taunting," Faith teased. When she heard a quiet buzz, she shook her head. Instead of what had happened last time, it was more intense. Way more. Her body clenched and she felt warm against her. "Ridge." Then a nibble. "I need you," she said.

"I know you do," he teased as he kept going until his fingers kept going. He kept going until her body was exploding around him then intensified it even more.

"What…" He kissed her and she felt pressure and throbbing in places that she never had before.

"Good," he asked.

"Damn it."

"Much better," he teased.
"I want you."

"I know." She reached for him, catching a belt loop and pulled him closer. When her body crashed into another orgasm, he got a smirk ear to ear. He released what was causing pressure and her legs were trembling. She felt him kissing up her torso and she reached for the belt loop. "Nope," he teased.

"Ridge."

"Faith."

"I need…" He kissed her and she got her hand on the button of his jeans.

"Don't."

He pried her finger out of the belt loop and pinned her hands to the bed with what she could only imagine was a tie or a belt. "What are you doing?"

"You can't keep your hands…"

She kissed him. "That's the deal Faith."

"Then let me."

He knew exactly what she wanted, and he wasn't giving in. If she'd made it through, she could've had her way. She kissed him and her hands were slid away from him. Her dress slid off and he kissed back down her neck. "That all you have planned," Faith teased.

"Baby, you have no idea what I can do."

"I have a few ideas," she teased.

"That was child's play Faith." He kissed her hip and her toes started curling. She heard a zipper and smirked. She fully expected that they'd be having sex, but that wasn't the zipper she heard. She felt something against her leg then felt something pulsating.

"Ridge."

"This what you wanted," he teased as the throbbing started again.

"I ..." He smirked and then slid the pulsating item closer and her legs started trembling. The feeling got deeper, harder, hotter and then she felt him against her. "All hot and bothered and nothing there to fix it," he teased as they started having sex. It was so much more intense. Way more than she thought possible. She exploded over and over again like it was in waves and intensified with each wave. When his body exploded into her, he reached up and untied her hands. They instantly slid forwards and he barely moved. When her body exploded again, the pulsating went away.

"And," he teased.

"I can't move even if I wanted to," she said as he kissed

her neck, then her shoulder.

"More," he asked.

"I can't even move enough to get up and get our drinks."

"Good." He got up from the bed and grabbed the drinks, handing Faith her glass. "Better," he teased.

"I don't think I can walk."

"Good thing we have everything we need in here then," he teased as he noticed it was close to midnight.

"Taunting your fiancée until she can't move. That's one for your resume," Faith joked.

He kissed her, leaning back into her arms. She still couldn't see him, but he could see her. Sated. Still turned on and craving him even more. "Fiancée."

"Yes handsome," she said as her legs slid around his hips.

"More," he asked.

"I don't know that I even can," Faith said as he leaned back into her arms. He devoured her lips. When she heard his phone buzz, Faith shook her head.

"Don't you flipping dare," Faith said.

He kissed her neck. "I wasn't planning on it," he whispered.

His hand moved and her legs started trembling again.

"Faith."

"What," she asked as her body started clenching all over again. "Ahh," she said.

"Still think you need to walk," he teased.

"Not tomorrow." He smirked and nibbled at each breast, taunting even more until her body was exploding for the millionth time. "Ridge."

"Baby," he said from behind her as she felt pressure in places she had never felt it before. "All mine," he whispered as her body trembled in his arms.

"I don't think I can move," Faith said.

"Good," he teased as they both laughed. When she felt something cool against her, he nibbled her shoulder. "What was that," Faith asked.

"Taking care of my woman," he teased as he kissed her neck.

By the time that he pulled the blankets up, she was asleep in his arms. He kissed her shoulder, finished his drink, and cleaned up a little, slid into boxers and curled up in bed with her. He kissed her shoulder and wrapped his arm around her, sliding her tight to him. He laid his head down and she linked their fingers. "Sleep baby." She went right back to sleep and he smirked. "I love you," he said as he went to sleep. That was the best night of sleep he'd had in days. He'd been on the defensive for weeks, but now, with her in his arms, she'd managed to calm him.

The next morning, Ridge woke up and Faith's head was on his shoulder. Her arm was wrapped tight around his torso. He smirked and kissed her forehead and her leg wrapped around his. "Baby, I love you, but you have to move the leg."

"No."

"Babe." Her eyes were closed, but he knew better.

"I have to get up."

"No," Faith said as he felt her hand move. He grabbed her hand and she woke up.

"We're not doing that." She kissed him. He slid out of bed and went and slid his joggers on. He pulled on his shoes and a t-shirt and went to get a full workout in before she really woke up.

He was finishing his run when he felt like someone was watching him. He stepped off the treadmill and looked over to see Faith on the steps with her coffee. "You woke up," Ridge teased.

"And you're staying in bed tomorrow with me. No more vanishing."

"I do a workout every morning love. I have for years."

"One morning just stay in bed with me."

"Faith, I know what you want." He sat down and started doing his weights. She just watched. "Faith." She watched him put the weights down and walked over to him. "What," he asked. She kissed him and he pulled her into his lap. "I mean it."

"I know you do. You also know that…"

She kissed him again, devouring his lips. "Faith."

"Come to bed."

He kissed her. "Give me a half hour."

She kissed him and he shook his head. "Fine, but if you aren't back in bed then I get payback from last night."

"I'm surprised that you're even walking."

"It was not as easy as it normally would be."

He smirked and kissed her then got up. "Fine. Come on," he said as he flipped her over his shoulder and walked back upstairs to his bedroom, closing the door behind him, and flipping the light back off. "Ridge."

"What?"

"Come here." He smirked and curled up on the bed, pulling her to him. "What did you want," Ridge asked as he kissed her neck. She tried to turn to face him and he wouldn't let her. He knew what she was trying to do, and he also knew that she wasn't getting what she wanted. "Ridge."

"Faith." She leaned back and kissed him.

"Tell me what you want," Ridge asked.

"I'm turning around."

"Nope." Faith was about to try to do it another way and he slid her to her stomach and pinned her hands. "What do you want," he asked.

"You know," she said.

"Answer is no."

"Ridge."

"No." He got up and shook his head.

"Where are you going?"

"Faith, I told you. No. Not happening," he said. When he felt her arms slide around his torso, he shook his head.

"Come back to bed."

"Let go Faith."

"Seriously? You're walking out the door. Now."

"What do you want me to do Faith?"

"Sit down," she said as she flipped the light on. He did and she slid into his lap. "Why are you so damn determined to not let anyone..."

"Faith."

"Why?"

"Because I said no." He shook his head and got up.

"Ridge." He walked out of the bedroom and went and hopped into the shower. Now he was pissed. Beyond.

He showered, finished washing up and was rinsing his shampoo out when Faith stepped in with him. "Ridge, talk to me."

"I said no, and I meant it."

"But when we were in Jekyll…"

"Faith." He rinsed the shampoo out and went to step out of the shower when she got him to sit on the bench.

"Tell me what you want me to do Ridge. You shut yourself off."

He shook his head and Faith looked at him. "I told you that I didn't want you to and you keep pushing."

"You aren't making this easy Ridge." He shook his head and got up, stepping out of the shower. He wrapped a towel around him, freshened up and before she could step out of the shower, he was in his closet and getting dressed. He pulled jeans and boxers on and slid a t-shirt on and went to try and leave when she caught his hand.

"Seriously? You're just gonna walk off."

"I love you, but yeah." She pulled him to her and walked him into the bathroom. "What," Ridge asked.

"Tell me why you don't want…"

"Faith."

"Tell me." He shook his head.

"Because you aren't going to even if I have to tie your hands up." He walked out of the bathroom, walked downstairs, and saw Eggs Benedict waiting. He grabbed a coffee, grabbed his laptop, and sat down to eat while he went through email.

Chapter 4

Faith walked downstairs and saw him on his laptop and shook her head. Whatever had irritated him that much had done a number on him. She walked over to him and grabbed her breakfast. "Ridge."

"Babe."

"How long have we known each other?"

He knew exactly where that conversation was going. "We turn 32 this year. Why," he asked.

"Then why can't you just tell me all of it. Why you won't."

"Faith." He ate the last bite of his breakfast and put the dishes in the washer.

"Come here," she said.

"I'm not having this conversation in the middle of breakfast."

"Sit down Ridge."

He shook his head and sat down. "Was last..."

"Ridge, I mean it."

"Because I don't want you to. That's not a good enough reason?"

"No."

He shook his head and got a refill of his coffee. He went

and sat down on the sofa. When she finished her breakfast, she put the dishes in the washer and grabbed his hand, walking him into her office and locked the door. "Faith, we're not talking about this."

"Yeah we are Ridge. We're getting married. You don't think that maybe I should know the entire story?"

"I don't want you..."

"I don't care what you want right now. I want the entire story."

He shook his head. "We're not..."

Faith stood in front of the door. "Talk."

He looked at her. "Faith, I told you."

"And there's something else to it. There has to be. You literally coiled away from me like a damn snake. Say it."

"It's a respect thing Faith. I don't..."

"Liar. When we were away, you went along with it and everything was fine. Now, you walk away before I even get close."

He shook his head. "Faith."

"What Ridge? Just tell me. You don't like the way I..."

"Has nothing to do with you. I'd rather us be having sex instead of that."

"And?"

"What Faith?"

"If I did before we were…"

"Faith, are you seriously gonna start a fight about this?"

"You're the one fighting."

Ridge shook his head. "I'm done having this conversation Faith. I don't want you to."

"Because?"

He looked at her. "Faith."

"Answer me and you can leave."

"Because I'm not in control. Happy now?" He walked out of the room, walked into the hall and into the security office.

"Everything good," Kellen asked.

"No."

Faith went and sat down outside, getting her emails cleared up and sent one to Ridge:

> *Come for a drive with me. Alone. Just us.*

Ridge ignored it and kept going through whatever he could to distract himself altogether. He didn't want to think about it. He wasn't about to give in and let her do what she wanted. He couldn't stop her, but he could dang well try. Fine. It felt good, but there was something about it that made him feel like he was a disgusting person. She needed to stop pushing, but he also knew that she never gave up on anything she ever wanted. Hell. She never gave up on getting him to kiss her. He took a deep breath and walked into the living room to see her on the sofa.

"Are you coming with me," Faith asked.

"Depends."

"Ridge."

"Fine but leave everything else alone." She nodded and got up. He shook his head, grabbed his truck keys, and walked her outside, sliding his phone in his pocket. He got her door and Faith stopped him. "What," he asked. She motioned for him to come closer. He leaned down and Faith kissed him as he picked her up and sat her in the truck.

"No more fighting." He nodded.

They headed off and went for a drive. She really didn't care where they went. Ridge was determined to just get away. "Where are we heading," Ridge asked.

"Wherever."

He shook his head and started driving. "Ridge."

"What?"

"One word."

"What?"

"Why?"

"Because it makes me feel like a piece of crap for letting it happen. Happy now?"

She looked at him. "Pull over."

"What?"

"Pull over Ridge."

He took a deep breath and pulled over. "What?"

"If I wanted to, because I wanted to, would it be that bad?"

"What happened to not having this discussion?"

"Ridge."

"Faith, why can't you leave it alone?"

"Because I want to do something for you. All of those nights that you were taunting me...you won't let me near you."

"Then win."

He pulled back onto the road. "Where are we going?"

"You'll see when we get there," Ridge said. It was the one place that he'd always felt good. Where he'd always had calm and serenity. When he pulled into the parking area, Faith looked at him.

"Where are we?"

"Old Sheldon Church." He went to hop out and she locked the doors. "What babe," Ridge asked.

She slid into his lap. "Faith."

She kissed him. "I love you. I always will. Just stop worrying about me okay? If I do, it's because…"

He kissed her, opened the door and set her on her feet. "I don't want to talk about it Faith. Leave it alone."

He walked her over to the ruins and she saw what he meant. Something was so calm. The summer breeze was blowing through the live oaks. The grass was perfectly manicured. All of it was beautiful. They sat down on the bench and he kissed her. "Just enjoy the surroundings. I don't want the conversation about it Faith. I really don't."

"I get it. I trust you Ridge. More than anyone in this entire world, I trust you. You have to trust me. That I'm not gonna do something you don't want. That I'm not gonna intentionally hurt you. I love you. I have for my entire life. Breathe."

He kissed her and devoured her lips. "Tell me that you'll hear me. That if I ask, you do what I ask."

She kissed him. "I also promise that I'm gonna win someday."

He smirked. "You keep tryin. Go for it." She kissed him. They got up and walked around a bit, looked at the ruins and Faith smirked.

"I know that look. What's going on in that head of yours," he asked.

"It's still here. It's been burned to the ground twice and it's still standing. Honestly, it's the perfect..."

He looked at her. "What?"

"The perfect place for wedding photos."

He looked at her. "Better plan. Engagement photos."

"Here and our beach."

Ridge nodded. "This mean that you're gonna let me marry you," Faith asked.

"So long as you don't plan it for tomorrow morning." She kissed him.

"Promise me something," she asked.

"What?"

"That when we go away next time you let me win." Ridge shook his head.

"Woman, you are stubborn as a damn ox."

She smirked. "And that's why you love me."

He smirked. "I wish."

Faith shook her head. "Why do you then," she asked.

He looked at her. "Because you are the woman I dreamt of marrying even when I was a kid. We fight continuously and we butt heads like no tomorrow, but I would never fight anyone like that unless I loved them. Baby, you are a pain in my backside and you always will be, but I still love you."

She smirked and he kissed her. "Do you want to stay for a while?" He nodded and they relaxed on the bench under the tree.

"Ridge."

He took a deep breath. "Wife to be."

"What do you want to do tonight?"

"No, we aren't having a rematch, and we definitely are not watching that movie. Dinner. Maybe a swim. Whatever you want to do."

"I want us to have a swim and whatever we do after..."

"Faith." She smirked and he shook his head. "We're leaving. Period."

"Ridge." He shook his head.

"You are so damn stuck on that. You're ruining the damn..." She kissed him. "You're ruining the day Faith."

He walked off and walked back to the opposite side of the church. He was past mad. He needed to calm himself before he blew a gasket. Before he ruined everything. Before he walked off and made her walk back. He took a deep breath and saw her walking over to him. "Don't."

"Ridge." He shook his head, took her hand, and walked her back to the truck. He unlocked the doors, sat her in the truck and sat down on the tailgate to calm himself before he drove.

When he calmed down, he walked back over to his side and hopped in. "Are you okay," she asked.

"No." He pulled out and headed back towards the house, stopping off to get a drink. He handed Faith an ice water and hopped into the truck with an oversized soda.

"Ridge."

"Not having this conversation Faith." They got back to the house a while later, he got her door for her and brought the drinks inside. He locked the truck up and walked outside to the pool, kicking his socks and sneakers off. He was past being mad. If he could've walked out and gone anywhere else, he would've.

He got more emails finished and Kellen came outside. "What's up," Kellen asked.

"Nothing."

"Dude, you're pissed. What the hell happened?"

"Leave it Kellen. It has nothing to do with you."

He looked at Ridge. "What has you all mad then?"

"Kellen."

"Dude, fine. I haven't seen you this damn mad since…"

"Kellen."

He shook his head. "Fine. I have a question then."

"What?"

"Do you remember Kim?" Ridge glared at him. "Okay then," Kellen replied.

"She messaged me and asked if I wanted to go for a drink."

"Then go."

Kellen looked at him. "If you're all mad about what I think you are, I'm going to say one thing and only one. The solution isn't in the bottom of a bottle, and it's not gonna change anything if she wins. She loves you. Let her have her chance once in a damn while. She's not gonna do anything Ridge. She even told me that she thinks something more is wrong."

Ridge shook his head. "Keep an eye on Faith."

"Where are you going?"

"Out." Ridge grabbed his keys and his phone, slid his sneakers and socks on and took off. Faith came out of her office and saw Kellen.

"Where did Ridge go," Faith asked.

"He said he needed to clear his head alone."

Ridge drove out to the beach, parked at the house, and walked along the white sand. He needed to be away from it. From the constant questions about why he wouldn't let her put her lips on him. Why she couldn't do it when she wanted to. It was stupid. All of it was. If she'd said no she didn't like something, he wouldn't have touched it and would've never questioned her. Never. He walked through the sand and when his phone buzzed, he shook his head and kicked his socks and shoes off. "What," Ridge asked.

"Where the hell did you go?"

"For a walk alone."

"Seriously?"

"Faith, leave it."

"You can't just take off on me Ridge. I'm your fiancée."

"I'll be home in a while," he said as he went to hang up.

"Where are you?"

"The beach."

"Fine. I'm coming..."

"No. I needed to go for a walk alone Faith. I'll be back in an hour or so." He knew it'd probably take longer than that to get back with all the traffic from the summer tourists. He hung up with her and wanted more than anything to have someone or something to pulverize. When he saw Conner come outside, he shook his head.

"You good," Conner asked.

"I just needed a walk. Everything good," Ridge asked as Conner nodded.

"Calvin is doing an inside search. He saw you and I came out to make sure things were alright." If he could've, Ridge would've stayed out there alone that night. He knew it was damn near impossible to pull off, but he needed a break.

"I'm fine. Just decompressing," Ridge said.

"I'll grab you a beer if you want one."

Ridge shook his head. Alcohol wasn't going to help his foul mood. When he felt his phone buzz, he knew:

> *Are you intentionally avoiding me? Come home.*
> *Either that, or I come to the beach.*

He shook his head. Five minutes. Five. No interruptions, no calls, nobody keeping an eye on him. He needed 5 damn minutes to be mad and kick his own backside into not behaving like a child. The last woman who'd intentionally forced him to let her suck him off had used it as a power tactic. She'd done it to try and get his credit cards, truck keys, money, gifts. It wasn't a barter system. It never should have been. She made him feel weak, and he wasn't about to let Faith do that to him. Not when he needed to be strong and protect her:

> *It's not a power tactic. You want to do it. Fine. I*
> *can't control a damn thing with you. You want it,*
> *fine. Do whatever the hell you want to Faith.*

Happy now?

He stared at the text and knew that the words wouldn't hit the way he wanted. He deleted the message and tried again:

> *To me, it's like trying to make me weak. I don't want that feeling around you. If you're determined to get your way, fine. Just know that it's not ever gonna be my thing.*

Before he even thought about it, he'd pressed send. He'd done it. He'd screwed up the entire relationship with one stupid idiotic text. He walked through the water, went inside, and pulled on a swimsuit and came back outside. He put his phone on the towel and dove into the water.

He felt like he'd been out there for hours, and when he finally headed back in, Faith was sitting on the steps. He shook his head and walked up to grab his towel.

"Ridge."

"No."

"What do you mean no?"

He put the towel on the sand and sat down, determined to let the sun dry him off.

"What in the...what do you mean no Ridge?"

"No, I don't want to talk about it ever again. No, I don't want to talk about the stupid text." She walked over and sat down in his lap.

"You're gonna listen to me if I have to sit on you to make you listen."

"Faith."

"Now. It's called me doing what you did to me last night. Me turning myself into knots with how hot we were together. There's nothing wrong with you doing..."

"Up."

"No. There's nothing wrong with making each other happy. Nothing."

"That doesn't make me happy."

"Then tonight, I get to taunt you." Before he could object, she kissed him and slid her legs around him so she was straddling him on the beach towel. "Husband to be, we're staying here."

"Faith." She kissed him before he could object. "Laptops."

"On the kitchen table." He shook his head and her arms slid around him. "I'm gonna be your wife Ridge. You can't..."

He kissed her, got up and carried her inside. "Go put your swimsuit on."

She walked upstairs to the main bedroom and Ridge let Kellen and Leo know they were staying at the beach house. "Who brought her over," Ridge asked.

"Leo," Conner said.

He shook his head with a smirk. He grabbed another beach towel and walked back out into the water, diving under the waves until he was past being able to walk on the bottom. When he felt arms around his waist, he smirked and she surfaced.

"Now. Are you cooled off enough to…"

"Faith."

She kissed him. "Fine." He swam back just enough to touch the bottom and felt Faith's hands.

"Seriously," he teased.

"For once Ridge, just once, I'm taunting you."

He shook his head. "Not in the water you aren't."

"Really?" When she felt her swimsuit get loose, he kissed her and she shook her head.

"That what you want?"

"Nope." He slid the top of his swim shorts down just enough and pulled her legs around him. When she sharply inhaled, he nibbled at her neck. "Faith."

"More," she whispered as they started having sex in the water. When she said his name, nibbling his ear, he knew she was spent.

"Really," he teased.

"That is so not fair," she said a matter of 5 minutes later as her body throbbed and tightened around him. He slid his shorts up and retied the bottoms of her bikini.

"You were saying?"

"Ridge."

"What," he asked.

"I love you. I don't want us fighting about it anymore," Faith said.

"Then don't bring it up. If you're all determined to get away with it, fine. You manage to pull it off, fine. You know how I feel about it."

Faith kissed him again, devouring his lips until they were back past neck deep in the water. "Babe."

"What?"

"Are we still okay?"

"You do know that you're just as stubborn as I am right," Faith teased.

He smirked and kissed her. "We're going in. No more stress. Deal?"

Faith nodded and kissed him. They made their way back in and sat down on the beach towel. "Ridge."

"What?"

"What if we just relaxed tonight and hung out. We can watch gone with the wind or something."

He kissed her shoulder. "I know that you're up to wife to be. I know exactly what you actually want."

"Oh really," Faith teased as he shook his head.

"Faith, I needed time to clear my head. Alone. You have to give me space."

"I did. You losing your mind all day over something that isn't that..."

"Faith."

"That you don't want wasn't a good idea," she said continuing where she left off.

He shook his head. "If I need to cool off, I need to. Alone. You need to know that. You're upset and you need space, I give you space."

"Ridge."

"What?"

"Don't vanish on me again."

"The guys were with you. They knew where I was. I was gonna head home."

"Don't vanish on me. You want to be mad then be mad, but don't take off."

He looked at her. "You do realize that sometimes, it's not world pushing to get your way right?"

Faith looked at him. "We can fight about this until we're 102 Ridge. Unless we talk, nothing gets resolved. You don't feel comfortable with that idea, fine. You don't want me doing anything like it, fine. I love you. You need to see that somewhere in this. I just wanted to do something to get you the way that you get me after those movie nights. That's it."

He shook his head. "For now, leave it." She nodded and he slid an arm around her, snuggling her to him.

Once they dried off, they headed inside and she walked him up to their bedroom. "Faith."

"Go." He shook his head, walked into the bedroom, and went to get changed.

"Are we staying tonight," Faith asked.

"No." She looked at him. "Faith, we're going back to the house. I just needed to get air. I needed space. That's it." She kissed him and pushed him onto the bed. "What are you doing," he asked.

"We're sitting."

"Faith."

"What do you want to do tonight," she asked as she grabbed her jeans and hoodie from the closet.

"Sleep."

"Ridge, talk."

"You're sleeping."

She looked at him. "Meaning what?"

"Meaning I'm sleeping in my room. Just for…"

"No."

"Faith." She gave him a look that he knew he never wanted to see again.

"One night."

"No."

"Faith."

"Don't you dare even think about it." He shook his head, got up and pulled his jeans and hoodie on and walked downstairs. He grabbed his laptop and sat down outside on the porch chair. Faith walked downstairs, grabbed two glasses of sweet tea, and walked outside, handing one to him.

"Faith."

"I love you. You know I do. Why are you doing this now?"

He took a deep breath and shook his head. "Because you keep pushing that button. You keep trying to push."

"We just talked through things Ridge. At least give it a

chance." He shook his head and walked back down to the beach, rolling his jeans up and walked along the water's edge. He needed one night of no stress, no drama, nobody pawing at him and nobody attempting to get him turned on in 2.3 seconds. He walked until his body and mind turned him back towards the house. He shook his head and when he came back, Faith wasn't outside. His shoes sat on the step with his socks. His sweet tea had a napkin over it and was there alone.

He shook his head, grabbed his shoes and drink, and walked inside. "Where is she," Ridge asked.

"Her office. She was kinda upset when you took off again." Ridge shook his head. He walked upstairs, walked into the bedroom, and peeled his clothes off, hopping into the shower. He took a deep breath, let the water wash the feeling off and sat down on the bench as the water washed the bad feeling away. The feeling that he'd screwed up yet again. That he'd pushed someone away. He washed off and stepped out to see Faith leaning against the door frame. He wrapped a towel around his hips and she looked at him.

"What," he asked.

"You don't want me near you now? Since when?" He took a deep breath and walked out of the bathroom, pulled boxers on, and pulled his jeans and shirt on. "Ridge."

"I said I needed one night to relax. I needed to get a decent night of sleep. I needed to clear my head and just chill out. That's it. Not hating you, or wanting you gone. I

121

just wanted a night to just breathe Faith. It doesn't mean that I don't love you, and love waking up with you. It means I need a night to go to bed without worry." She looked at him. "What?"

"You really think that I'm just gonna pounce like a cat with a mouse? Seriously Ridge."

He took a deep breath. He wasn't about to have world war three part 202 with her. "I am not having this conversation Faith. If you can't deal with one night then I'll stay here and you can go to the house."

"You're gonna avoid me?"

"I'm giving you a night off. One without me in your way when you go to sleep. I love you Faith. I do. Just breathe."

"Tell me what you want Ridge. Right now, it's like you're intentionally shutting me out. I don't like it."

He took a deep breath. "I love you alright? It has nothing to do with anything else other than me. If I take off for a run, you worry. If I go for a drive, you snap that I didn't let you come with me. I need to wrap my head around all of this. I want more than anything to just run off and plan a wedding with you, but I can't do that. Something is pushing me back from doing it. Until I can..." He saw her eyes welling up. "I need to straighten it out in my head Faith. 24 hours. Then we can pick a date, plan whatever we decide to do. I just need to breathe." He looked at her. "What," he asked.

"You're pushing me away. What did I do wrong Ridge? What did I do that upset you that damn much that you push me a million miles away?"

"I need to straighten out my mind Faith. I need to make my head stop spinning. That's it."

When he saw the first tear fall, it killed him. "Faith."

"It's because of me." He walked over to her and she shook her head and backed away, walking downstairs. He shook his head. He was spilling his guts to her and she was in tears. He'd screwed up all over again. He'd thrown her away like garbage from the night before. He shook his head and walked downstairs, walked past her, and walked outside, sitting down on the sand. All he was doing was telling her how he felt. He wasn't raising his voice. He wasn't insulting her, and he wasn't doing anything other than being honest. He sat out there for what seemed like hours.

Around dinner, he was kicking himself. He'd lost her. He knew that he'd walk back into that house and the ring would be sitting there. His things would be in a box like they always were when he screwed up a relationship. Running off and getting the biggest bottle of Jack he could find and drowning in it was his next task. He got up and saw Faith sitting on the steps. Two glasses of amber liquid sat beside her. One was a lot fuller than the other. She brushed tears away and looked up, seeing him not 10 feet in front of her.

He couldn't move. It's like his feet had turned into

concrete in the sand. She couldn't move either. "Ridge."

"What?"

"Are you gonna have the drink or what," Faith asked.

"Come here for a minute." She looked at him like he was growing fangs or horns somewhere. She got up and walked over to him, handing him the drink. "Faith." She shook her head and walked back over to the steps, sitting down. "Please." She shook her head. He took a deep breath and walked towards her. "Come inside at least." She shook her head.

Ridge took a deep breath, grabbed her hand, and walked her in. "Ridge, let go."

"We're going to get dinner." He didn't ask her. He didn't say please. He put the drinks into the fridge and walked her out to the truck. He sat her in the passenger seat, hopped in his side and headed off.

"Where are we going?"

"Getting something to eat before the Jack burns a hole in your stomach."

When they pulled into the line for the chicken that she loved, Faith looked at him. "This?"

"Either this or we go to dinner." She looked at him. He pulled out of the lineup and took her to the one place that she had no choice but to talk. They pulled in, parked and made their way into the Charleston Crab house. It was risky considering what had happened the last time they'd been in Shem Creek. When she looked at him, he shook his head. "What?"

"The last time we were here, we bumped into Holden."

"And I got you out of it. We're eating and leaving."

"Walk," Faith asked.

He looked at her and nodded. "And a walk."

By the time they finished dinner, they'd managed to make small talk for almost an hour. When they were out of the crowd, they made their way down the boardwalk and things went quiet again. All they could hear were the flapping of bird wings, the sounds of the water, boats coming into dock, and the distant sound of cars going over the bridge. Quiet enough that their conversation was quiet and private.

"Still don't want me near you," Faith asked.

"I never said I didn't. I needed a night to figure myself and my idiot ways out. That's it."

She looked at him. "Ridge."

Before she could say another word, he slid his arms around her and hugged her. They sat down on the covered benches along the pathway, and he kissed her. "I half expected you to have walked out. I thought I'd go inside to see the ring on the counter and my stuff in the back of the truck," he said.

"You're an idiot sometimes Ridge. It doesn't mean that I'm leaving. I was waiting for you to get out of your own way."

He took a deep breath. "I've had a screwed-up life Faith. I have money, but it never did me any good. Women I tried to date would do what you wanted to do, and figured they'd get my credit card or my wallet. It just sits bad with me. That's it."

"Ridge."

"What?"

"I'd never do that. You know that right?"

He nodded. "It just makes me feel like I'm being used. I get that you want to make me happy. I want to make you happy too. I just don't think that…"

She kissed him. "I get it. No more talking about it." He kissed her again and she slid into his lap, straddling him. "What," he asked.

"No more fights." He kissed her and with one nod, the silence, the pain, the anger, and the tension just melted away into the water. It's like one tiny wave had washed it all away. One wave of her accepting him the way he was. One wave of him respecting her more than anything in the world. One wave of them loving each other through it all. He kissed her again and she slid out of his lap. "Take me home?"

"Which one?"

"Doesn't matter. You are my home."

They made their way back to the beach house in silence. Not the awkward kind they'd driven in as they made their way to Shem Creek, but a comfortable one where they listened to the sound of the water with all the windows open. He kissed her hand as they made their way and when they pulled in, she slid over the console and into his lap as he slid the seat back. "What," he asked.

Faith kissed him. "I love you."

He smirked and slid his hands to her face. "I love you back fiancée of mine. Forever." He kissed her and she hugged him. He smirked, slid his door open and wrapped her legs around him as they headed back inside. He locked the truck, and walked upstairs, leaning her onto the bed. He kissed her again and locked the door.

"Ridge."

"What," he asked as he slid her up the bed to the pillows and slid into her arms.

"Promise me that we're okay." He kissed her, devouring her lips, slid her sandals off and wrapped her legs around his hips as he kicked his shoes to the floor. He didn't want to talk about it. He didn't want her upset, and damn well didn't want to bring the entire fight back to light.

"Faith, I don't want..."

She kissed him. "Are we okay?"

He nodded and kissed her. He didn't want to talk about it. Not even for a half second. He slid her jeans off and she slid him to his back. "What," Ridge asked.

"Do you trust me?"

He knew that the only thing he could do at that moment, short of kicking her to the floor was to close his eyes and separate himself from it. "Faith."

"Do you?"

"Yeah. Why?"

"Ridge."

"What?" She slid into his lap and kissed him, leaning into his arms. She could feel the tension when he thought she might make a move.

"What's wrong?"

"Nothin," Ridge said as he sat up and pulled her to him.

"Ridge."

He kissed her, determined to get that feeling gone from his system. "What," he asked.

"Am I allowed to ask you something?"

He looked at her. "What?"

"Are you really that uncomfortable?"

"Faith, we agreed we weren't talking about it."

She nodded and he slid her shirt off. "I love you."

"I love you too," he said, knowing full well that at some point, and probably that night, something was gonna happen.

She kissed him and he knew he had two choices. One, he slid her to her back and went on as normal. Two, he gave in. He let her do what she wanted. When she slid the light off, they were alone. The darkness in the room was soothing somehow. "I have an idea," Faith said.

"What?" She smirked, slid out of his lap, and walked into the bathroom. Within a matter of minutes, he heard the hot water running and the tub filling with water. Fine. She came up with a much better plan. One that would make them both feel a lot less awkward. He got up, sliding his shirt and jeans off and walked into the bathroom, seeing her in bubbles and in the massive tub. "Really," he asked.

"You grab drinks and get your butt in here." He kissed her and grabbed two glasses of Jack, walked upstairs, and handed them to her as he kicked his boxers off and slid into the hot water with her.

"Better," Faith asked.

"What?"

"Your shoulders are back to normal. You tensed up like a dang turtle." She put her drink on the edge and slid into his arms.

"Faith."

She kissed him. "What?"

"I love you. You know I do." She kissed him again and he slid her onto his lap.

"Good," she replied as he smirked.

"I'm never gonna stop either. I promise you." She kissed him and he devoured her lips until she got a smirk ear to ear. "Woman."

She kissed him. "What handsome," she asked.

"What you up to?"

"Nothin," Faith teased. He shook his head and kissed her again as she slid out of his lap.

"Faith."

"What?"

"Where you goin?"

"Getting my drink." He kissed her hand and pulled her back to him. She took a gulp of her drink and he tried to pull her into his lap. He took her glass and Faith smirked.

"What are you up to?"

"Nothin," she said as she slid closer to him. He shook his head.

"I know you're up to something." She kissed him and he felt her hand against him. Faith could tell that he was hot and bothered.

"What," she asked.

"Faith."

"What?" He managed to brush her hand away and pulled her into his lap. He devoured her lips and she slid on top of him.

"Faith."

She leaned into his arms. "Mine," she whispered. The sex went from the tub, to over the edge of the tub to the counter of their bathroom. When they both slid to the floor of the bathroom, she smirked.

"Was that so bad," Faith teased.

"I swear, you're seriously..."

She kissed him. "And you love me."

"Faith."

"What?"

"Enough taunting tonight."

Faith kissed him. "Are you gonna stay and sleep in my bed with me?"

"Maybe."

"Maybe what," she asked.

"You gonna sleep?"

"Maybe. Stay in bed with me. No vanishing for a workout. Deal?"

"Nope. I have to look good for my fiancée woman."

He kissed her. "Your fiancée likes you the way you are sexy man of mine." He kissed her, devouring her lips. "You're stuck with me."

Faith got up, grabbed his hand, and helped him up. He grabbed the drinks, put them on her side table, put the phones on the charger and slid into bed with her, snuggling her into his arms.

"Happy," he asked.

"Better than earlier."

"And?" She turned towards him and kissed him.

"I love you. I will for the rest of my life handsome."

Chapter 5

Ridge woke up the next morning, feeling refreshed for the first time in days. When he opened his eyes, he shook his head. "Faith."

"Mm."

"Come here."

"No." When he saw where she was and what she was doing, he shook his head.

"Faith," he said as his body was starting to overheat. She slid into his arms and they had sex. Hot, out of control and could care less, sex that had his body tensing at her touch. "Had to," he teased. Faith nodded feeling proud. "Happy," he asked.

Faith nodded and her body crumbled around him. She fell into his arms and he pinned her onto the bed. "Had to," he asked. Faith nodded and kissed him. He shook his head. "Wife to be, you are seriously asking for it."

"In other words, movie night."

"In other words, you're lucky I don't go find more things to completely taunt you with."

"Such as," Faith asked.

He smirked. "I could find more online." She shook her head and he kissed her. "Daring me," he teased.

"Ridge."

"I'll take that as a yes," he teased as he kissed her.

"Where are you going," Faith asked as he managed to get up.

"Shower then home. Are you comin or are you staying out here," he teased.

"And if I said that I wanted to go for a swim first?"

"Since it's raining you mean."

"Fine. Breakfast then we go home."

He kissed her. "You getting up?"

She smirked. "Nope. Staying over here," she teased as he went and freshened up and showered.

He got cleaned up and when he went to step out of the shower, Faith was freshening up. "Wife to be," Ridge joked as he came up behind her and kissed her neck.

"I love you," she said.

"Love you back," she said as she splashed water on her face.

"You okay?"

Faith nodded. "Babe."

"Nauseous."

He looked at her. "So, I was right about that so-called shot," he teased.

"You aren't funny."

"You started it," he teased as he kissed her shoulder. She looked at him. He went and grabbed his hoodie, her jeans, and her sneakers. He grabbed her lingerie that she loved and handed them to her.

"Ridge."

"What?"

"Can we..."

"Two steps ahead of you. I'm driving us back." She got dressed and he grabbed the phones and his bag and walked her downstairs.

"What's wrong," Conner asked as he poured himself another coffee.

"Nothin. We're good. Just tired. Breakfast," Ridge asked.

"Whatever you're makin," Conner replied as he went into the office.

Faith sat down at the counter and watched him cook. He brought the guys breakfast and handed Faith a plate. When she looked like she was about to be sick, he shook his head. She ran for the bathroom and he went and made her granola and yogurt instead. He ate her breakfast and when she came back in, she gave Ridge a look. "I did try to warn you wife to be."

He kissed her forehead and they finished breakfast. He

cleaned up, handed her a ginger ale, and walked upstairs, changed the bed sheets, threw them in the washer and let the guys know, and then they headed off.

Ridge stopped off at the store, and when he emerged 10 minutes later, he had a 5 pack of pregnancy tests, a 6 pack of ginger ale and a box of saltines for her. He handed everything to Faith and she looked at him. "What?"

"What's the other box?"

"If you aren't, making sure that you stay that way until we're ready."

She looked at him. "Can you handle your latte?" She shook her head.

"Frozen juice thing it is," he teased. He kissed her, went into Starbucks, and got her a frozen juice drink, handed it to her and gulped down his iced latte.

"Ridge," she said as he linked their fingers and kissed her hand.

"Yes love."

"Can we get on with the wedding planning?"

"Once we know if you are or not."

They got back to the house and she took the bag upstairs. Ridge went and talked to the guys alone.

"What's up," Kellen asked.

"Anything go to crap when we were gone?"

"Depends. You two talking?"

Ridge shook his head with a smirk. "Yes. We talked. And?"

"Package. Cops have it."

Ridge shook his head. "There's gonna be an order that comes in. Not a word to her."

Kellen looked at him. "What are you up to," Kellen asked.

"Taunting my fiancée. It's almost like a game now," Ridge teased.

"Fine. I don't want to know. Just let me know when it's supposed to be here. Beyond that, I'm still convinced that the bulletproof glass is a good idea," Kellen said.

"I agree," Leo said.

"Would you two stop," Ridge asked.

"Depends. Are we refereeing today," Kellen joked.

Ridge shook his head, grabbed his laptop, and went and sat down on the sofa.

Faith came downstairs and saw him. He was calm for once. Settled. He wasn't on edge. He wasn't watching over his shoulder. She went into her office and grabbed her laptop, making sure it was charged, then came and sat down on the sofa with him. "What," Ridge asked.

"Nothin. You'd be stunned at how many emails that I have," Faith said.

"You mean since you played hookie for a few days?"

"Ridge."

"You did. How many did you get," he teased.

"872," Faith said as he shook his head.

"Then you don't get to play hookie anymore. Too much work to do wife to be," he said.

"If my fiancée would stop vanishing, there wouldn't be an issue."

"And if you would answer some of those emails, we could go enjoy our day beautiful," he replied with a smirk. Just as he said it, an email popped up on her screen:

> *Fiancée of mine. Please stop staring at me like I'm your dessert. You had dessert already. Tonight is my dessert and entrée, and appetizer. Dinner backwards.*

Faith gulped and he smirked:

> *Then the appetizer, entrée, dessert, second dessert and champagne. Yes, all in one night.*

When she looked at him, he got a grin ear to ear. "What?"

"Taunting your wife during business hours?"

"You're the one checking personal emails on your work computer," he teased.

"Ridge."

"What?"

"You do realize that we still have to check that thing." He kissed her and slid her laptop off her lap, put his aside and walked her upstairs.

"Where is it?" She walked into the bedroom and opened the bedside table. She took it out and it said error.

"What in the freaking world," Faith asked. He kissed her and Faith ran into the bathroom to be sick yet again.

"Try another one," he said.

When she came into the bedroom 15 minutes later, she had the test in her hand and looked like she'd seen a ghost. "What," he asked.

"We need to go into town." He took it from her hand and it said pregnant.

He shook his head, handed Faith her phone and walked her downstairs. "We're heading downtown. We'll be back in an hour or two," Ridge said.

"What's wrong," Kellen asked.

"Doc appointment," Ridge said.

"I'll take you," Kellen said as they headed out and Kellen

pulled the SUV out, taking them to the appointment. "Everything alright," Kellen asked.

"Yep. Just need to make sure," Ridge said.

They got to the doctor's office and went straight in within minutes. "Is it possible that it was a faulty batch or something," Ridge asked.

"Highly unlikely, but we need to redo the pregnancy test. Faith, if you can please." Faith nodded and left the room.

"Is it possible," Ridge asked.

"It takes a week for full efficacy. It's possible that we did it too late, but I don't think so," the doctor said. Faith made her way back in a few minutes later and handed the sample to the doctor. She went off and did the test while Faith took a deep breath.

"We figure it out either way. Promise," Ridge said.

"I can't get married when I'm as big as a dang house," Faith said.

"Babe, you're beautiful no matter what. It doesn't matter."

"Yeah it does."

He shook his head. "Not to me." He gave her a hug and was about to kiss her forehead when the doctor came in.

"And," Ridge asked.

"Well, we have to do a blood test to confirm, and probably an ultrasound or two, but it seems that you are. That means no alcohol, eating healthy..."

The doctor's words just melted into the deaf ears. All Faith could hear was that she was pregnant. They'd had Jack the night prior. Too much Jack. They'd had Jack almost nightly for...

"Faith," the doctor said.

"Yep."

"Next week. Monday. 8am. We'll do an ultrasound and get the bloodwork back. Go from there. I may have to notify that drug company." Faith nodded. "Vitamins, healthy. If you need anything, call me, and tell me and I'll come to the house. Just don't do anything ridiculous like tell the world alright?" Faith nodded and the doctor headed out leaving them alone, surrounded by pamphlets about pregnancy do's and don'ts, what to expect when you're expecting, photos of how big a baby is. All of it was overwhelming.

"You okay," Ridge asked.

"No." He kissed her and helped her off the exam table, walking her out and down to the SUV with the vitamins in her purse.

"Everything alright," Kellen asked.

"Thank you. I was a little distracted," Ridge said as they hopped in.

"I needed the fresh air. Miss Faith, are you okay?"

Faith nodded and leaned her head on Ridge's shoulder. She looked at him and he snuggled her close. Ridge opened the windows for some fresh air as they made their way back.

"Starbucks run," Kellen asked.

"Please," Ridge replied as he mobile ordered them their drinks. Hers was intentionally decaf. They got them and when they got home, they hopped out and Ridge walked Faith right up to the bedroom, closing the door behind them.

"Not exactly the way we hoped," Faith said.

He smirked. "What?"

"Well, at least we won't have to worry tonight," he joked as Faith threw a pillow at him. "I'm just saying love."

"Not funny Ridge."

She sat down on the edge of the bed. "If this sticks, you do know that the whole wait until Christmas thing isn't gonna fly right?"

"Babe, we can wait until after."

She shook her head. "No. We need to plan this out Ridge. Now. Before I end up being a damn whale."

Ridge shook his head. "You do know that your folks are gonna figure it out if you start rushing into planning it. If we wait until May or June..."

"Ridge."

"Fine. We give ourselves a week or two then we see if it'll stick. You need a different dress more than anything. You also need a maid of honor."

"Your sister."

He shook his head. "Seriously?"

Faith nodded. "You do know that she doesn't even know we're dating right?"

"Like your Mom hasn't told her. What if we get everyone together for dinner? We haven't done a low country boil in forever. Mom's birthday is coming up anyway," Faith said.

He looked at her. "Faith."

"What?"

"You sure that you want to do that and have everyone assume you're gonna tell them that we're pregnant?"

"Ridge, I love you, but I want everyone together. We did it all the time when we were younger. Why not," Faith asked.

"Fine. Pick a day, we can do a tent thing outside or something."

Faith kissed him. "Or we do it at Mom and Dad's." He shook his head.

"Here or the beach."

"14 people?"

"Or at Mom and Dad's." Ridge wasn't happy with the idea, but it made Faith happy.

"You sure that you want to do that?"

"Ridge, I love you, but I think they all sorta have a feeling. My brothers probably know via my Mom. I just…"

He kissed her. "You, my love, are insane, but I get it. I'm not exactly sure about my sister at all, but I think that maybe we should…"

"For our birthdays. Gives us time, plus we can hang out and if it does stick…"

He kissed her. "I love you, but no."

"Ridge."

He kissed her. "Not happening."

"Why?"

"Because I don't want anyone causing crap in the middle of it. We still…"

Faith kissed him. "I love you. I get that you're still worried, but I know deep down you wanted me to scream it from the rooftops. This is sorta my way of doing that. We tell all of our family at once. If it does stick, we decide when we want to tell them."

"You sure?" She nodded and slid into his lap.

"What are you doing fiancée," Ridge asked.

"Nothin," she replied.

"You do realize that you in my lap isn't gonna change my mind right," he teased.

Faith kissed him. "You sure," Faith asked.

"I'm sure. Getting everyone together is probably not a good plan. My sister..."

"Ridge."

"And your oldest brother."

She shook her head. "Go figure. Still. He's kinda dating someone anyway. She's not his level, but she's a decent enough person. Honestly, the two times I met her, she was wearing the lowest..."

He kissed her. "Faith."

"I never would've worn a dress like that."

"You did. When we went out for dinner and you were determined to get me in bed."

"If I remember correctly, I succeeded," she teased. Faith smirked and he shook his head. "Faith, if you're that determined to have everyone together then fine but don't start getting..."

She kissed him. "I know who you really are wife to be."

She shook her head. "You started it," she teased.

He kissed her and just as he did, her phone buzzed. "Work is calling," he said.

"Oh, I know husband to be." She kissed him and answered.

"Yes," Faith said.

"Miss Faith, there's a slight issue," her assistant said. Faith shook her head, got up and kissed him and took her laptop into her office, finishing the call. Ridge smirked and called his sister.

"What's up," Sammy said.

"You still civil with Faith's little brother?"

"You mean Kevin?"

"Don't play dumb little sis. Yes or no?"

"Civil. Beyond that, no. Why?"

"What would you think about coming home to visit," Ridge asked.

"Why? Did you finally find a woman who was enough for you?"

"I met her when I was 2 days old," Ridge replied.

"You aren't seriously trying to tell me that you and Faith..."

"We're engaged," Ridge said.

"No, you flipping didn't. Ridge, what on earth are you thinking?"

"That she's the one I've been in love with most of my damn life. Don't start little sis. I can take care of myself."

"And?"

"What?"

"When's the big day?"

"We haven't decided. Probably fall. Are you gonna object?"

"Funny. Depends," his sister said.

"Do me one big favor. Get the stick out of your butt and be civil."

"I'll get a flight. Just don't go getting her knocked up before I get back," she teased.

Ridge shook his head. "Maybe you might actually get your personality back and learn manners," Ridge joked as they hung up.

Faith came back into the living room and saw him hanging up. "What," Faith teased.

"My sister says hi," Ridge said lying through his teeth.

"Your sister and I never did get along. I know that you are

totally full of it. Why are you calling her," Faith asked.

"If you want to do the dinner thing, I kinda have to get her back in North America. She said she's gonna book a ticket. Whenever you want to do this thing, we can. I still don't think that we need the giant family dinner."

"Meaning she still hates my brother."

He kissed her. "Meaning I don't think that she's capable of being polite for more than 30 seconds when it comes to him."

Faith shook her head. "And what's going on with work," he asked.

"Remember that author I told you that I hated working with?"

He nodded. "Still hate him."

"Meaning what?"

"Meaning he's holding back the chapters. He claims that he can't finish it. That he's stuck."

"Would a cattle prod help," Ridge joked.

"Funny, but yes," Faith said.

He kissed her and she slid into his lap again. "This mean you're going into the office?"

Faith shook her head. "Not today handsome. I got legal to forward him a letter about his contract and returning his advance."

Ridge shook his head. "And what did you want to do the rest of the afternoon then," he asked.

"I had a few ideas. None of which involve me going back into the office."

He shook his head. "My, my, my, fiancée of mine. You have a dirty mind and a..."

She kissed him and slid into his lap. "And all yours."

"I have created a monster," he teased.

"Yep. Not ashamed to show it either. Now, what are we doing today really?"

"You're planning the dinner you wanted to have at your Mom and Dad's. My sister already knows which means calling your brothers."

"Great. Super fun," Faith teased.

Ridge kissed her and he heard bustling in the kitchen. "We're doing grilled chicken and asparagus with brown wild rice. Any objections," the housekeeper said.

"As long as you let me do something to help," Ridge said.

"You can set the table," the housekeeper joked.

Faith kissed him and he shook his head. "You go call butthead 1 and 2 and I'll set the table," Ridge said.

Faith shook her head, kissed him again and got up, walking into her office. "So, what is Miss Faith planning," her housekeeper joked.

"Telling everyone about the engagement. She wants to do a big party. I'm not exactly the big party type," Ridge said realizing how much those words meant.

They were complete and utter polar opposites. Their personalities didn't even match up. She loved the high life and the oversized parties. He was more a homebody and a quiet small get together type. Who knew how they managed to make things work. The control freak learning how to lose control and the military man who was disciplined, becoming the undisciplined. Literally, they were and always had been opposites. Somehow they ended up being the perfect puzzle pieces. They fit no matter which way they were put together. He got up and set the table, got them each a glass of sweet tea and saw the housekeeper looking at him.

"What," Ridge asked.

"Since when does she have sweet tea and not wine?"

"We're attempting to cut back," Faith said as she emerged from her office.

"And did you hear from your brothers?"

"They aren't happy that I won't tell them why, and I managed to get them to leave their idiot girlfriends at home. We're all good, plus I let your sister know when and where. Mom and Dad are on board, and I let your Mom and Dad know. We're good," Faith said.

"And," Ridge asked. She kissed him.

"And what?"

"And when did you decide that we have to do this whole big family meal thing," Ridge asked.

"Weekend of our birthdays."

Ridge shook his head. "Had to didn't you," Ridge asked.

She nodded and kissed him. "Mom suggested it. Wasn't all me handsome."

He kissed her and shook his head. "You two get. I'm going to start on dinner. I'll let you know when it's ready."

"Thank you," Faith said as Ridge walked her outside.

"Are you sure that you really want to have a big party," Ridge asked as he closed the sliding door to the porch.

"Ridge, I'm good. I was nauseous for a while, but we're fine. I promise. Honestly, I'm surprised we even ended up in this situation." Ridge smirked and almost laughed. "What?"

"I did warn you if you didn't quit taunting that we'd put that shot to the ultimate test. You started it. We could've..."

"Ridge."

"What?"

She shook her head. "If it weren't for you," she joked.

"Excuse me fiancée of mine, but if it weren't for you and your movie nights, this would not have ever happened." She smirked.

"50/50," she teased.

He kissed her. "Faith."

"What," she asked as she curled up to him.

"You sure that you're ready for all of this?"

"No. I doubt that I can be. I love you Ridge, don't get me wrong, but a baby is a big thing." He kissed her forehead.

"And I know more than anything that I love you. We'll figure it out whether it sticks or not."

"And if it doesn't," Faith asked.

He kissed her. "Then we go back to using something to make sure it doesn't happen until we're ready. We have time love. We always will."

He kissed her forehead and she smirked. "What?"

"I had an idea." He shook his head, knowing just how insane some of her ideas were. She's the one that had come up with the movie idea. The one who'd started the teasing. True, he was the one that had taken it that much further with all of the taunting until her toes were pretzels. But if she hadn't been there almost naked in his arms on the sofa and sliding as tight to him as she could, he never would've made the move.

"So, if it's a girl?"

"Let's pray she doesn't have your sass or attitude," Ridge joked.

"Names silly."

"Cami."

Faith looked at him. "As in your first girlfriend," Faith joked.

"As in Camelia the flower."

"Aria."

Ridge smirked. "Okay. That one I like. And if it's a boy?"

"Matthew," Faith said.

"So, we're basically sticking with bible type names." Faith smirked.

"I do kind of like it."

"Matthew Sams."

Faith smirked. "Matthew Carter Sams."

Ridge smirked. "Aria Lily Sams," he teased.

"Too much," Faith teased.

"Aria Melissa?"

"Who's Melissa?"

"Great gran," Ridge said.

"That's not the one who always sent you those Christmas checks is it?"

He nodded. "I like it. Still though, what if it doesn't stick?"

He kissed her. "Like I said, we have time. Babe, I don't want you getting all stressed about it. That's the last thing that you need. We figure it out. If it doesn't, life still goes on. We take time to deal with it, we figure things out and hold on tighter to each other. That's all we can do." Faith hugged him and he carried her over to the pool.

"Don't you dare throw me in," she teased.

"I mean, I wasn't considering it, but if you..."

He smirked, kissed her and sat down, rolling his jeans up and pulling off his socks and shoes. She sat down beside him, slid her shoes off and they talked.

When Faith got a text that the dinner was ready, they both came back in, hand in hand, and sat down to dinner. The guys came and sat with them and Faith invited the housekeeper as well. "We wanted to tell you guys what was going on," Faith said as they all sat down to eat.

"What's up," Kellen asked.

"Y'all already know that we're engaged. We sorta had a

little bit on a surprise," Ridge said.

"Yeah…what else is going on," Leo asked.

"This stays between us. Not even the wife Leo," Ridge said.

"What's so big that you can't tell anyone," Leo asked.

"That appointment this morning," Faith said.

"Until you're three months, you shouldn't be…"

"What," Faith asked.

"I know the signs. I have two of my own," Leo said.

"Oh," Faith replied.

"So, you can all understand why we didn't want to tell anyone," Ridge said.

"Not a problem. If you need anything, please let me know," her housekeeper said. Faith nodded and Ridge slid his hand in Faith's.

They all finished dinner and Ridge helped with what he was allowed to. When Faith curled up on the sofa, he smirked. He walked over to her and sat down on the sofa beside her. "And what did you want to do tonight," she asked.

"That's kind of up to you fiancée," Ridge teased. She slid into his arms and kissed him.

"Old movie."

He smirked and kissed her neck. "Faith."

"Gone with the wind."

He smirked. "I figured you'd say something a little more than that. Nothing like that movie plan from earlier," he teased.

"I mean, we could watch it, but I'd suggest watching it upstairs," Faith whispered.

"Faith, please just try to behave for once," he whispered.

She shook her head and kissed him. "Never."

She went to grab her wine and he shook his head. He got two glasses of sweet tea, and she grabbed his Jack. She walked upstairs and put the bottle on the bedside table.

"Faith."

"What," she joked.

"The Jack isn't needed baby." She kissed him and went and closed the bedroom door.

"Even if you can't get me tipsy enough..."

He kissed her, devouring her lips. "Never needed a single drop and either did you. You know that right?"

"Helped."

"With what," Ridge asked as she curled up on the bed with him.

"Me being nervous."

"About? I've had a crush on you since we were 10 Faith. My first kiss, my first crush. How could you have been nervous?"

Faith kissed him. "I was. Nervous that you wouldn't want me. That you wouldn't want to be with me. That things wouldn't click. I didn't know what to think. That movie was sort of the olive branch that burned up in a ball of flames."

"Flames?"

She kissed him. "Actually, you were kindling and I dumped gasoline on you and we fell into the fire."
"I kinda like that. I need to write that down and put it in vows or something."

She shook her head. "Ridge."

"Babe, I didn't need the alcohol to talk me into anything."

She kissed him. "You sure," she asked.

"Never have and never will. I love you Faith."

"But, the movie thing..."

"All it did was push me into doing what I knew you wanted to. That's it. Nobody else in the entire world would ever get me to do that if I didn't want to. No amount of Jack could get me to."

She looked at him. "Meaning what?"

"I knew you were nervous the first time we were up here. That's why I went along with it beautiful."

Faith looked at him. "So, all this time that I thought you needed liquid courage, you were playing along?"

He kissed her and pulled her into his arms. "Trust me. I didn't need one single drop. I wanted you comfortable," he said.

Faith kissed him and he leaned her onto her back, pulling her legs around his hips. "What," he asked seeing the smirk.

"What would you think about us re-watching that movie," he teased.

"The one that started all of this?"

"The one you thought would get you some the fastest," he teased.

Faith kissed him. "We don't need a movie, just like you supposedly don't need Jack," she teased.

He kissed her, peeled her clothes off little by little and got up, closing the shutters, the blackout curtains and peeled his shirt off.

"Ridge," Faith said as she went to flip on a light.

"What," he asked as she felt his lips kissing her leg. She slid her skirt off and he slid it to the floor.

"What are you doing," she asked.

"Starting over."

"Ridge."

"Yes sexy," he said as the kisses made their way to her inner thigh.

"You sure you don't want a drink?"

He smirked. "There's a sweet tea right there," he teased as he kissed her hip.

He grabbed a glass and handed it to her. "Ridge."

"Faith." He slid into her arms and her legs instinctively wrapped around him. "You're the one that needed the wine." She shook her head and he devoured her lips. "You okay," he asked. Faith nodded and kissed him.

"Babe."

"What?"

"You do realize that we could just watch..."

She kissed him and he smirked. "You sure?"

"Ridge."

"Yes or no?"

"I'm sure that if you don't, I'm gonna..." He kissed her and slid her bra off. "Ridge."

"Sexy woman of mine."

"You sure that you don't want to..."

He kissed her again. "Movie?"

"What do you think," she asked.

He knew she needed the liquid courage. "Up to you."

He kissed from her neck to her breasts then back down her torso. When he got back to her inner thigh, her toes were curling. "Faith," he said as he could see her stomach trembling.

"What?"

"You sure?"

It took two minutes. Two. Her body was already trembling. Two minutes of his lips against her. Two minutes of him taunting her. He kept going and let his fingers take over as the kisses worked their way up her torso. "Wife to be."

"What," Faith said breathless and getting even more turned on.

"You sure?"

"More," she replied as he kissed her.

"Faith."

"What?"

"Are you sure?"

She nodded and kissed him as he kept going. When the

taunting got more intense, he smirked. "What," Faith asked.

"Don't move."

"Ridge."

"Don't move."

He grabbed his bag and she heard buzzing. "I swear," she teased.

"Don't move fiancée of mine."

"Ridge." She felt the buzzing slide closer to her. When it touched her skin, it's like it sent lightning strikes through her body. It was more intense than last time. It was hotter.

"Ridge," she said.

"Yes beautiful," he said as he nibbled at her inner thigh and her legs tightened.

"You're taunting."

"I know. I'm very good at it. Adding it to the resume," he teased. He kept going until he knew that she was at that point. He had two choices. Take full advantage and keep going until she was begging him to sleep with her or having mind-blowing sex with her immediately. Hell. He was already turned on so badly that his loose and baggy jeans were already too tight.

"Ridge, come here." The decision had been made.

He slid up her torso, sliding into her arms and he felt her legs tighten around his hips. "What," he teased.

He kissed her and devoured her lips until she was pulling at his jeans. "Faith."

"What?"

"What you doin," he teased as he kissed her neck.

"Getting what I want."

He shook his head. "Faith."

"What?"

"Hands off." He kissed her, sliding his hands in hers and pinned her hands to the bed.

"Ridge."

"What beautiful?"

"Take them off. Now."

He smirked and kissed her. "Nope."

She managed to get one hand free and he felt her hand against him. She'd bypassed the button and the zipper altogether. "Faith."

"You taunt me, I taunt you. Mine," she said.

He shook his head and kissed her. "Faith, let go."

"No."

Her hand wasn't just holding him. She was turning him on even more. "Faith."

"Then come here." He shook his head and undid the zipper and the button and she slid his jeans down. They had sex and he was way past just turned on. She felt too good and she always had. He kept going, deeper and deeper until she was digging her nails in his back. Hell. That was even hotter. When he neared his climax, she was holding on even tighter and he kissed her with a kiss so deep that he could feel her toes contorting into knots.

"Faith." She held on even tighter and he couldn't move. When her body throbbed around him, he couldn't hold back. His body exploded into her and she wouldn't let go. "Baby, let go."

"No."

He needed to move and she wouldn't let him. He nibbled his way up her neck. "I need to move baby." She shook her head and kissed him. He felt something wet on his shoulder and he managed to pull away just enough to see the tears.

He brushed them away with his thumbs. "What's wrong," he asked.

"What happens if we can't make this stick?"

He kissed her, devouring her lips. "Babe, we have time. We can keep trying if that's what you want. I promise you."

He hugged her and slid her to her side. He managed to get

just far enough apart that his body had time to cool off. He pulled a blanket up over them.

"Is that what you're really freaked out about?"

Faith nodded. "I mean, yeah, we weren't expecting this, but now I kinda want to," Faith said.

He kissed her forehead and she slid into his arms. "Babe, there's time. We can do whatever you want to. Are you worried that something's wrong?"

Faith nodded. "That I screwed up. That the wine and the Jack screwed things up. That all the stress..."

He kissed her. "We have time. When we go to the doc for the ultrasound, we make sure things are okay. If you're not feeling well and something's wrong, then we go to the hospital. Whatever we have to do."

"And if I lose it?"

"Then we figure it out. We try again if that's what you want."

She kissed him. "Ridge." "What?" "I love you." He curled her to him. He knew deep down that she was scared. She was worried and scared.

"I need to get up for a second," Ridge said.

"Why?"

He kissed her. "Back in 2 seconds."

He went and cleaned up, put in an order with the florist for her favorite peonies and roses and came back into the bedroom to see her looking at the movies online.

"Which one are we watching," he asked as he took a gulp of his sweet tea and curled up in bed with Faith.

"Up to you. Casablanca, gone with the wind."

He shook his head and kissed her, flipping on a movie on Netflix. "What are we watching?"

"Something that it doesn't matter if we don't watch it or talk through it," he said as she saw a nature movie come on.

He put the remote aside, handed Faith her sweet tea and they talked. They talked until the tears dried, until the worries passed, until she was calm and content again. "I need to ask you something," Faith asked.

"G-rated," he teased.

One look and she smirked. The old Faith was back. "How long have those little buzzing things been around?"

"I got them a while ago. Never had a reason to use them. Never bothered to. Why?"

"What do you mean never bothered to?" He took a deep breath.

"I had one girlfriend before we got together and it was a good 6 months before I showed up on your doorstep."

"And you dated her how long?"

"A month. I had got them then, but never had the chance to use them. I caught her with one of my friends, in my bed, in my condo for that matter."

Faith looked at him. "What?"

He nodded and kissed her. "Like I said, I wanted the one. I wanted my first love and just happened to have an interview with her," he joked.

She looked at him. "Seriously?"

He nodded. "Good thing I'm not on speaking terms with either of them anymore," he said as he gulped down the rest of his sweet tea. "Why do you ask," he joked.

"So, technically they're mine?"

"Nope. Don't even go there fiancée of mine. Those belong to me, for me to taunt you with whenever I want," he joked. He knew she was gonna start again. He also knew when she slid into his lap that she was feeling better.

"Why did you have to go put the jeans back on?"

"Because I know what you're up to. I also know exactly what you want right now, and it's off limits." She kissed him and slid into his arms, straddling him. "Faith."

"Promise me something."

"What?"

"That if it ever…"

He kissed her. "I don't want to hear those words Faith. It's not happening. I'm not gonna walk out."

She shook her head. "Stop reading my mind," she teased.

"I'm not. I'm reading the sexy body in my arms right now. Like I said to you. Even if I have to make you talk to me in the middle of a fight, I will. Even if it means taunting every inch of you until you beg for mercy," he joked.

"Starting when," Faith asked.

Chapter 6

He devoured her lips and she slid on top of him. "Faith."

"What?"

"Don't go there. Not now."

"Then tell me the real reason why you don't want to pick a date yet." He shook his head and kissed her, toppling her over onto her back and leaned into her arms.

"Because I want to make sure that you're okay. Good enough reason?"

"Okay as in know if we are or not. Making sure it sticks."

He kissed her. "Making sure that you have what you want instead of rushing everything. Babe, we're getting married whether you are or aren't. I just don't want us planning it all out and it doesn't stick. I want you to have everything..."

She kissed him. "I already do. All of that is just extra fluff Ridge."

He kissed her and shook his head. "What if we just find you a dress first and go from there."

She smirked. "Depends on where we have it." He kissed her, devouring her lips.

"Faith, where do you want to do it? The church or the house," he asked.

"Church."

"Reception at the hotel or your Mom and Dad's?" "I think hotel maybe."

He kissed her. "Go look for a dress. I can get my Mom to come, I can get your Mom. Whatever you want."

"And if I want you there?"

"You really think that's a good idea? I'm not supposed to see you in it until the wedding Faith."

"Who's gonna come with me then," she teased.

He smirked. "Leo's wife. Leo maybe. You'll be fine. I can pick you up after if you want."

She kissed him. "You sure?"

He nodded and kissed her. "Whatever you want for the wedding, we'll get."

"Ridge, it's your wedding too. What do you want? There has to be something."

"You. That's it. I don't care about the flowers, the food, the décor. None of it. All I want is you." She kissed him.

"You're gonna make me cry," Faith said.

He kissed her. "Now back to what we were talking about before all the wedding conversations."

"What was that?"

He shook his head and kissed her. "Movie." He smirked.

"Which one," she teased.

"The one you never managed to make it through." Faith shook her head.

"Really," she asked.

"The one I know you still won't make it through."

"All convinced and everything," Faith teased as he pulled her legs tight around him.

"Convinced. I mean, you barely made it through the first two," he joked.

Faith kissed him. "And," she asked.

"Are we watching yours too?"

"Okay," she teased as he pulled it up and pressed play. He walked downstairs and refilled the sweet tea glasses. He came upstairs, kissed her, and curled up on the bed with her. "Ridge."

"What?"

She leaned over into his arms and kissed him. "So, we're just bypassing the entire movie."

"Nope," she teased as she kissed him. He shook his head, slid her to her back and kissed her. "Ridge."

"What?" "I love you."

He kissed her, devouring her lips. When she went for the button of his jeans, he shook his head. "You aren't starting that Faith. The deal was that you keep your hands to yourself." She shook her head and brushed his hands away. "Faith."

She kissed him and went for the button again. He grabbed her hands and linked their fingers, pinning her to the bed. "What," she asked.

"The jeans are staying on." He kissed her and he kissed down her neck.

"Meaning what," Faith asked.

"Meaning you're all mine. If you can make it through the movie without attempting to get me naked, then you win," he teased.

"And if you don't make it through the movie?"

"That wasn't the deal. It's all on you," he teased as the kisses trailed down her torso.

"You aren't playing fair," Faith said.

"This isn't the fair game Faith. It's called me getting to taunt you and make your legs shake and your toes curl all night."

"And you think you're gonna win," she teased.

"Guarantee." He got to her hip and Faith's toes were already curling into knots. He nibbled at her inner thigh and her stomach was trembling.

"What," he teased as he kissed her inner thigh.

"You are so not fair. I can't even move and you're taunting intentionally."

He smirked and with one move. One move that had her legs shaking, her stomach trembling and her body starting to throb. "Ridge," Faith said.

"What?"

"Come here."

He shook his head. He kept going, nibbling and kissing and licking her body into throbbing even more. "Faith."

"What," she asked as she saw the scene from his movie that had caused all of it. "Come here."

He smirked. "Why," he asked as his fingers intensified all of it.

"Ridge."

"What?"

"If you don't get up here right now, I swear…"

He kept going and made it worse to the point that her body was almost shaking. "You were saying," he teased as he nibbled at her inner thigh.

"Ridge."

He kissed up her torso again, letting his fingers continue to taunt her. When he saw the light from the TV go out, he smirked.

"Giving up so easily. You barely made it through the first hour," he teased.

"Now," Faith said.

He kissed her and got up. "Where are you going?"

He slid back onto the bed a minute or two later. "What," Faith asked.

He handed her a blindfold. "What are you up to?"

He kissed her and put it on for her. "Ridge."

He smirked and she was reaching for him. "What are you doing?"

"Mine. I get to taunt you tonight. All night."

"Crap."

"Exactly," he teased as he kissed from her toes, up her leg, to her inner thighs. When she heard a buzzing noise, she shook her head.

"Ridge." She felt the vibration against her inner thigh as her toes curled into pretzels.

"Yes wife to be," he whispered in her ear as she pulled her legs around them, making the vibration stronger. "Crap," she said.

"What," he asked.

"I need you," she said.

"I bet," he teased. Faith went to kiss him and he nibbled back down her torso. He nibbled at her breasts and she shook her head.

"Ridge."

"What sexy wife to be?"

"Please." He shook his head and took the vibration away from her skin. Instead, his lips took over.

Her body trembled in his arms and her body exploded over and over again. When he kissed back up her torso, he devoured her lips and she reached for the button of his jeans. "Faith."

"Please."

He kissed her and before she knew it, the jeans were off. The blindfold was off and she had what she wanted. He plunged into her, deep, until her legs were so tight around him that he was past the point of being turned on. He needed her as much as she needed him. They kept going as her body climaxed over and over again like a rolling ball that never stopped. When his body couldn't hold back anymore, he exploded into her like a wild rapid. He collapsed into her arms and she could barely move. Her legs were curled tight around him and he all but refused to let her let go. "Ridge."

He kissed her. "What," he asked.

"I don't think we're watching the movie."

"I don't think you're gonna be able to keep your eyes open," he teased. She kissed him and he slid to his side, pulling her with him.

"I think you're right," she joked.

"About what beautiful," he asked as she slid him to his back and rested her head on his chest. He pulled the blanket up just enough to cover them.

"Sleep." He kissed her forehead and once her heart stopped racing, she was asleep in his arms. Getting up was no longer an option. He managed to grab his sweet tea, noticing the glass empty, poured Jack into it and gulped it down.

Just as he put the glass onto the bedside table, his phone buzzed. He slid hers to the charger and looked, seeing a message from his Mom:

> *Hi honey. Was gonna see if Faith wanted to look at dresses tomorrow. Her Mom and Dad decided to stay home. I can make an appointment in the morning. I was up looking at bridal magazines. Your Dad is currently laughing at me. Sweet dreams baby. Love you and Faith.*

He smirked. He knew that trusting Leo or Kellan with her safety was gonna be a big ask, but at least he'd be able to get a real workout in. "Sleep," Faith said. He kissed her forehead, put his phone on the charger and fell asleep curled up with the love of his life.

The next morning, Ridge woke up to the one sensation that he hadn't felt in way too long. He looked down and saw Faith, taunting him into waking up. It felt good. Too good. Way too good. "Faith."

She kept going until he pulled her up his body. "We kinda talked about this."

She slid into his lap, sliding him into her.

"Damn," Faith said.

"Hot and bothered much," he joked as they had morning sex on their bed. Hell. Their bed even sounded hot. When he leaned her back onto the bed and kept going, she smirked.

"Ridge."

"What sexy?"

"Good morning."

"And here I thought that you would be too tired to move," he joked as her body tightened around him. He teased just enough to get her even more turned on. "All mine," he teased.

She smirked and he kissed her, feeling her almost mew his name as her body climaxed and his followed. "I swear, I am so cutting you off," he teased.

"Really? So, you don't like the one sure fire way to wake you up?"

"Not what I was expecting." She kissed him and he saw the time.

"It's 7:30. Why are you awake," he teased.

"Because I somehow fell asleep at 11." He smirked, kissed her and went to get up when she pulled him back.

"Faith."

"Who were you texting?" He kissed her and handed the phone to her.

"Code is 2032."

She looked at him. "What?"

He smirked and kissed her, got up and went to freshen up in the bathroom. She went into his phone and saw the text immediately.

"Your Mom?"

He nodded. "I gather that you have plans to look at lacy things with Mom and your Mom. You should probably call her," he teased as he brushed his teeth.

Faith walked into the bathroom and sat on the counter. "Ridge."

"Yes beautiful," he said as he kissed her and got toothpaste on her lips.

"I was thinking."

"Oh crap."

"If we had it at my Mom and Dad's instead..."

He spit out the toothpaste, rinsed his mouth and covered hers. "Too early for wedding plans."

"Ridge."

"Fine. What," he asked as he grabbed his razor and shave cream.

"If we had it at their place, we could have it super small like you said. Just the people that we really want there. We could probably all fit around the dang dinner table." He kissed her.

"Talk to them about it today. I'm fine with whatever. Like I said. I just want you."

She kissed him and slid his razor from his hand. "Faith, I'm..."

She kissed him again. "I like it scruffy. It's spikey."

"While I appreciate the sorta compliment, still shaving." She kissed him and he shook his head. He put the shave cream on and shaved while she went through the ideas swimming in her mind about the wedding. When he rinsed the last of the shaving cream off, she kissed him again and he picked her up, wrapping her legs around him and carried her into the shower, flipping the hot water on. He slid her under the showerhead and smirked.

"Maybe you need cold water," he joked.

"Not funny," she teased.

He washed her hair for her as she planted kisses on his chest. "Faith, don't start. I'm awake. I can pick you up and make your legs shake all over again if I have to."

"Promises, promises," she joked.

He shook his head. He rinsed out her shampoo, slid conditioner in her hair and leaned her up against the tile wall. "You really wanna start this today when you have to go to work?"

She smirked and nodded. "Faith."

"Fiancée."

He shook his head. "Bend over."

"Ridge."

"You wanted to start this."

"But." He leaned her over the bench and started taunting her all over again until her knees were starting to give out. "You sure," he asked. She went to stand up and he turned her towards him, picked her up and wrapped her legs around his hips, pinned her hands to the wall, linked their fingers and the sex was off the rails. She was so turned on that she forgot where she was completely. He knew every single inch of her body and exactly how to get her past turned on. When her body climaxed the second time, he couldn't stop himself.

"All....your.....fault," he said as he kissed her with a kiss so deep they both got goosebumps. When she slid to her feet, he helped her to the bench and sat down beside her. "Yeah. I may have to work from home. I don't think I can walk," Faith joked.

"Good. Serves you right," he teased.

Faith smirked. "Ridge."

"Yes love," he said as he kissed her and managed to get up.

"What are we doing tonight?"

"You mean after you get home from dress shopping and your girl day?"

She shook her head. "Tonight."

"Dinner out, walk on the beach maybe." He smirked, flipped the water off and grabbed the two towels from the warmer. He wrapped one around his hips and walked over to Faith, wrapping the other around her. "Since I have to go hang with the Mom's, at least tell me something that you want me to wear."

"White preferably, nothing all poofy Cinderella style. Something that makes you feel beautiful."

"Sexy or no," she teased.

"Faith, if you walk down the aisle in something completely see-through, I'm putting my jacket over you. End of discussion."

"Backless?"

He shook his head. "You want that for the party after, fine, but no walkin around that wedding all naked," he said.

"Okay. That helps," Faith teased as he kissed her and walked into the bedroom. She smirked and followed him.

"What," he teased seeing her leaning against the door frame of his closet.

"When do you think," she asked.

"As in a date?" She nodded as he pulled on boxers and his jeans. "Stop Faith. Go get your phone and check and see a date."

When she smirked, he shook his head. "You really need to get that dirty mind checked out. I know that look Faith."

"Same look I gave you when you showed up that first day," she joked.

"Woman, get the calendar up."

He slid a shirt on and came into the bedroom. "September 21?"

He looked at her. "I thought you said November."

"September 21," she teased.

"Or October 19th."

"November 16th." He shook his head.

"What date did you want to do this so we actually have time to plan it?"

"We can ask at the church."

He nodded and kissed her, making a call to the church.

"And how is Ridge Sams," the secretary for the church said.

"I'm well. And you Miss Sara," he said.

"I'm good. What can I do for you?"

"Well, I was gonna see if y'all were able to do a little favor for Faith and I."

"Faith Cartwright?"

"Yes ma'am."

"What can I do for y'all?"

"Well, we're looking at wedding dates. I was gonna see what you had available."

"What are the dates?"

Ridge gave her the dates and there was only one that was left available. "The only option is October 19th unless she wants to change it to the 18th."

"Can we set the 19th?"

"Sure. I can even get the bishop to do the wedding ceremony. He's very close to your Mom and Dad and Faith's parents."

"Thank you," Ridge said.

"I'll get everything organized. You'll have a lot to do before then."

"Thank you. I'll pop by this afternoon."

They hung up and Faith looked at him. "October 19th." Faith marked it down. "Still need certificate, since we were both baptized at the church, we're good on that. There's one last class thing we have to do, but other than that we're fine."

"So, we're actually doing this. On October 19th."

"Let's just hope that there isn't a freaking hurricane." She kissed him.

"Now we need invites."

"More importantly Faith, you need clothes. Then a different dress if that's what you wanted," Ridge teased.

"And in that order?"

He nodded. "Walking around in a towel isn't gonna work when you're meeting them to try on dresses."

She kissed him. "You sure you don't want to have more

input on this dress?" He kissed her.

"Remember that dress you wore intentionally because you wanted to taunt me?" She nodded with a smirk ear to ear. "Nothing that sexy. That work?"

She nodded. "Really low cut, backless and not overly sexy. Done."

Ridge shook his head. "Woman, stop trying to taunt me and get dressed."

He kissed her and headed downstairs, padding his way down the steps, and walked into the security office. "I need y'all to take care of Faith. I don't care who goes," Ridge said.

"Where," Kellen asked.

"I can't go to the bridal place. I need one of y'all to go."

"I can take her there. Do you need me to stay," Kellan asked.

"Until she's back at the house, yes. They're having girl time. I want her to relax and enjoy the time. If she wants me to come after the bridal salon, I can. I just can't be there when she's looking at dresses," Ridge said.

"I never said you couldn't be there," he heard as Faith came downstairs in a dress and bare feet.

"I can't. Kellen can take you down and stay with you until you're home."

"You're comin to lunch. I talked to your Mom," Faith said as she leaned against the door frame and slid her heels on.

"Then I'll drive down and meet you when the dress stuff is done," Ridge said.

"Good," Faith teased.

He shook his head. "Determined fiancée you have there bud," Kellen joked.

Ridge shook his head. "Babe, what time is the appointment?"

"45 minutes," Faith said.

Kellen got up, got Faith, and walked her outside, helping her into the SUV. When Ridge came outside, Faith smirked.

"You coming with me," Faith asked as she opened the window. He kissed her.

"You're going with Kellen. You're good love. Have fun."

"And where are you going?"

"To do a workout. Just wanted to come say goodbye," he teased. She looked at him. "Run on the beach, check on the guys, come back and eat then get work done before I have to meet this sexy woman downtown," he joked as he handed Faith her bagel for breakfast.

Faith kissed him and she headed off with Kellen, and Ridge took off to get his workout in. She made her way downtown and got a text from Ridge:

> *I want you to feel beautiful. That's all. I don't care*
> *if it's a lacy suit, I don't care if it's a tutu. All I want*
> *is to see how beautiful you are. I want you to look*
> *in the mirror and feel the way I felt the first time*
> *that you kissed me. You're my world and you*
> *always will be. Forever doesn't mean a fancy*
> *$10,000 dress. It means you and me, hand in*
> *hand. The dress is just a bonus. I love you.*

Kellen handed her a box of tissues and she sniffled. "Kellen."

"Miss Faith."

"Can you do me a favor when we get there?"

"Sure."

"Can you check on him and make sure he makes it back to the house okay?"

"Sure, but you do know that he carries when he's on his run right?"

Faith looked at him. "What?"

"He did when you started getting threats. He has since he started guarding you."

Faith looked at Kellen. "I haven't seen it."

"I know. Trust me, he's more dangerous than anyone else that could come after you." Faith nodded and they had a quiet ride the rest of the way. Kellen got her Starbucks on the way through, and when they got to the bridal store, he parked and helped her out, locked up the SUV and walked her in.

When she got there, his Mom and hers were there waiting. Flowers were in a bouquet with a card at the table. "You two beat me here? Really," Faith teased.

After hugs and a quick visit, Faith saw the card in the flowers. "Y'all didn't have to get me flowers," Faith said.

"They weren't from us," his Mom said. She grabbed the card and her eyes started welling up.

"Baby," his Mom said.

"You do realize that your son is the all-time mushiest guy ever right?"

His Mom nodded and gave her a hug. "When he loves you, he never stops telling you. He never gives up," his Mom said.

"Everyone is far too mushy over here," her Mom said as they all had a group hug.

"Alright. Dress time," Faith's Mom said. Faith nodded and they all went to look at dresses. By the time they had her in the first dress, Faith was still in shock. It's like everything was hitting her all at once.

She came out and showed the Moms and when they were both in tears, she smirked. "And," Faith asked.

"You look amazing," her Mom said.

"It's not too much," Faith asked.

"Not sure it's good for...are you having the wedding at the church," her Mom asked.

Faith nodded. "Then you'd need something so your shoulders are covered."

Faith nodded. "We have a solution for that," the consultant said as she slid a lacy jacket over the shoulders. Her Mom shook her head.

"It's not really working," her Mom said.

"I mean, it's okay for the party, not really for the aisle," Faith said.

"I agree with you. I mean, it also depends on where the event is gonna be," his Mom said.

"Well, the ceremony is at the church, we're sorta in the air about the reception, but maybe at the hotel or we do it at the house," Faith said.

"You'll actually let Dad and I do that," her Mom asked.

"Maybe. We don't even know how many people," Faith said.

"We can do it at the house." Faith smirked. She went and tried on the next dress and she started liking the dress. She more than liked it. There was lace, sparkle, satin and flowy. It was a little much, but when she shook her head, they opted for the next one. It wasn't right either.

When they gave her one that had sparkle and was flowy and soft with a slit that he would complain about, she smirked. "Can we add a little bit of sparkle to the top," Faith asked.

"Most definitely. You look beautiful in it," the consultant said. Faith came out and showed their Moms and her Mom was speechless. So was Ridge's. They slid the veil she'd chosen into her hair and her Mom was crying.

"Baby," his Mom said.

"Do you think he'd like it though," Faith asked.

Her Mom nodded. "You look like an angel," his Mom said.

"It's flowy and stuff so it's comfy. I don't need another dress," Faith said.

"We can add an overskirt if you want it for the ceremony, but you're covered. It's relatively clear with that shimmer, but you should be fine. You can take the illusion part off for the party," the consultant said.

"Mom," Faith asked.

She nodded. "You don't need to look anymore," she said.

Faith looked at them. "You sure," she asked.

Her Mom nodded and Ridge's Mom got up and hugged her. "This mean that you're taking the dress?"

Faith nodded. "Well, since you don't need any alterations, it's an off the rack," the consultant said as she walked back into the dressing room with Faith.

"Did Ridge call?"

The consultant nodded. "He said that you needed the dress for October 19th. That means that you had to do off the rack. There's room since it's flowy for anything that may come. If you decide that you want to alter it, we can closer to," the consultant said.

"And what's the price," Faith asked.

"Already paid for," the consultant said.

Faith looked at her. "By who?"

"Your Dad."

Faith looked at her. The consultant got a photo of her in the dress and she sent it to her Dad. Faith slid out of it, got re-dressed and the consultant got the information for the dress. "I can order you a new one if you want with the extra sparkle. It'll be ready before the wedding."

Faith nodded. "Thank you," Faith said.

They filled out the paperwork, paid for the dress and when Faith came back into where her Mom and Ridge's Mom were, her Mom gave her a hug. "I swear, you are full of dang surprises," Faith said.

"Your Dad's idea baby."

"Now I need to get you two a dress," Faith said. They looked through the dresses and within a half hour, the Moms had dresses too. As they were paying for the dresses, Faith saw Ridge standing outside the store. She smirked and made her way outside, grabbing her flowers on the way through.

"Hey handsome," Faith said as he turned and saw her.

"Hey yourself sexy. How'd dress shopping go?"

"I found a dress. Mom cried, and your Mom cried then I found them dresses." He kissed her and Faith slid her arms around him.

"I need to ask you something," she said.

"What?"

"Kellan said..."

"I know. He told me. I'm surprised you didn't know."

"All that time on the beach?"

He kissed her. "In the towel."

She looked at him. "Seriously?"

"Babe, I told you before. If they want you, they have to go through me."

She looked at him. "I told you that. Nothing is gonna happen to you. You know that."

"Ridge."

He kissed her. "Yes fiancée."

"I love you."

"Good thing. I'd hate to see what that wedding would be if you didn't," he joked.

"And Mom and Dad want us to have the reception at the house."

He smirked. "We can talk about it later," he said as Kellen took off.

"Where are we heading for lunch," he asked as his Mom and hers came outside.

"The Belmond," Faith's Mom teased. Ridge walked Faith to the truck and they headed over to the hotel with her Mom and his following behind them.

"Ridge."

"Sexy."

"What would you think if we had it at Mom and Dad's? Is it too much?"

He kissed her hand as they pulled in. "Honestly, if they want to have it there, it means being more secure, but I still kinda want us to have the photos somewhere."

He kissed her. "Beach house?"

He smirked. "Or we do the photos at the house."

He kissed her. "We figure it out first. Did they say they could get the dress in time?"

She nodded. He shook his head and kissed her again, hopping out, getting her door for her and they walked into the hotel. He'd parked in the one spot that they could find at the door. "Babe," Ridge said.

"What?"

"You sure you're okay?"

She nodded and slid her arms around him. "Then why do you look all shaky?"

"I didn't know that you had something with you."

He showed her and Faith shook her head. "Why?"

"Because someone threatened your life. Someone tries to hurt you and I handle it. That's the deal love. I refuse to let anyone harm a single hair on your head." Just as he said it, his Mom and hers came in and her Dad showed with his Dad. He had no idea they were coming.

"Hey," Ridge said as he gave his Dad a hug and shook her Dad's hand.

"We decided to come hang with you two for lunch. How was dress shopping," her Dad asked.

"Dad, you know you didn't have to right," Faith asked.

"My only baby girl. Yeah I did," he said as he gave Faith a hug. Ridge guessed what she was talking about. All it did was get him irritated. Showing how he felt wasn't an option. They all went into the restaurant and sat down to lunch.

The longer they sat at the table, the more he got irritated. When his Mom rubbed his back, he looked at her. Faith slid her hand in his and he couldn't get past it. He needed to breathe and get air, but there was no time. When they finished lunch, Faith slid her hand in his and linked their fingers. After a hug goodbye to everyone, he got her door and slid into the truck beside her. "You okay," Faith asked.

"He bought the dress?"

"I didn't know he was. Ridge, the dress was less than 3. They wanted to do it. I attempted to put half down and he'd already covered it."

"And now the reception at their house."

She knew what he was really mad about. "Ridge."

"I can't. I can't believe that they're taking care of..."

She got him to pull over. "What?"

She put the truck in park, took the keys and slid his seat back, sliding into his lap. "I can't do anything about it. I can't."

She took a deep breath. "Ridge."

"I don't want it at the house."

"Ridge, we'd have…"

"I don't care."

"Babe, it's fine."

"Either we do it at our place or at the hotel. I don't…"

She kissed him. "I know. He went too far."

"Faith, he can't just disrespect me like that."

She kissed him and wrapped her arms around him. "We'll figure it out. I don't want you driving all mad."

He kissed her and wrapped his arms tight around her. "I'll talk to him Ridge. I promise you."

He nodded and kissed her again as he devoured her lips.

"Beach?"

He shook his head. She kissed him again and slid out of his lap as he slid the seat back up.

"Babe, I love you, but your Dad is starting to make me feel like I can't handle things myself. I'm not impressed right now," he said.

Faith slid her hand in his. "I know. I did tell him that he was overdoing it. He wanted to do something to contribute. That's what he chose."

"I don't want it there."

"I know. Like you said, we do it the way we want."

He kissed her hand. "I get that you're his only daughter, and I get that he wanted to do something special, but it was..."

She nodded. "I know Ridge. I'll talk to him."

He shook his head. "I'll do it," Ridge said.

They got back to the house and headed inside. She took his hand and went to walk him upstairs, but he walked into the security office. "Ridge."

"I'll be there in a minute."

She shook her head. "Come," Faith said as she walked him upstairs.

"Faith." She walked in and closed the bedroom door behind them and sat him on the chair.

"What?"

"Breathe. I get that you're mad, and you deserve to be. I love you. I'm not gonna go through another war between you and my Dad about this."

"Faith."

"Call him on speaker."

He shook his head. "It's between your Dad and I. Period." She sat on his lap and called her Dad.

"Baby," her Dad said.

"Ridge is a little upset."

"About what," he asked.

"About you buying the dress." She could hear in her Dad's exhale that he knew it was coming.

"I understand that. We offered the house so you had flexibility. It's up to the two of you to decide what you want. The dress was the least expensive part of what I know that y'all want for the reception. That's the only reason why. I'm not going to do anything else like that. Are you okay with that," her Dad asked.

"I'm just...It's not like I can't afford the dress for her."

"I never said you didn't. I promise. I fully expected the $20,000 charge on my card. I'm not going to interfere beyond this," her Dad said.

"I appreciate that you're helping. I do. It's just..."

"I know. I would've felt the same," her Dad said as the stress seemed to dissipate.

"Dad, thank you for the dress."

"You're welcome baby."

They got off the phone with her Dad and Faith kissed Ridge. "Are we okay," she asked.

"I guess," he replied still a little annoyed.

"Ridge."

"I don't want to have fights with him about it. I can pay my own way."

"Ridge."

He looked at her and Faith kissed him. "We're fine. This is what Dad does. What he's always done."

"He does realize that you can't be bought right?"

"Ridge, he tried to buy this house for me when I bought it. That's the way he is. If he can do it, he helps people so they can save their money. He doesn't even want me spending my money on the wedding. I told him that we were paying for the wedding ourselves. He knows now to back off and let us handle it. We're alright. I promise you."

"You do know that I'm never gonna be like that right? Buying someone's attention."

She kissed him. "If we have babies, we just might be there fiancée."

"I don't even go there unless it's warranted. I get that you're his baby girl and everything. I do. I just don't think that doing it without telling both of us is a little much."

Faith hugged him. "I love you, but my Dad isn't like that. He wasn't any different when you were around when we were little. Everything we could've ever wanted was handed to us. You know that."

He took a deep breath. "Faith, I don't like it."

"I know. We talked it out. It's done now."

He kissed her. "I don't want us like that if we have this baby."

She kissed him and nodded. She knew at that exact moment that they were gonna be alright. That him being raised differently from her, was more than she thought. He wasn't handed everything unless he was at the house with her. He worked for everything, but he also knew the meaning of a dollar. He was the only man in the world that made her feel safe when she didn't. The only one that understood her mind and her soul. The only man she'd ever met that would take a bullet for her and still be standing.

"Babe."

"What?"

"Do you at least love the dress?"

She smirked. "You're gonna cry like a baby."

"Is that a yes or no," he teased.

She nodded. "Our Moms both cried. It's beautiful."

"And?"

"Church appropriate. It's exactly what I wanted."

He kissed her. "Good. That's what I wanted," he teased.

Faith looked at him.

"And what do you want to do beyond that," she asked.

"We can do the classes in a weekend. Beyond that, we just need the marriage license and we're good. The rest of it we can figure out. The florist who dropped off those flowers for you is gonna do the flowers for the entire thing. Whatever we decide to do, we do," Ridge said.

"So, do you want to do it at the house or the hotel?"

"If we do it at their house, I'm handling it. I don't want your parents putting in for it. That's the only way," Ridge said as Faith nodded and kissed him. "You decide what you want," Ridge said.

"I liked that idea that you had about the flowers on the ceiling idea."

He smirked. "And?"

"Sparkly."

He smirked. "Never doubted that," he teased.

"I like the silver idea."

"What color dresses did our Moms get," Ridge asked.

"Platinum and pale grey. The dresses are beautiful," Faith said.

"At least that's another thing that I don't have to figure out," he teased.

"And I sorta made a decision. I'm gonna ask your Mom to be my matron of honor," Faith said.

He looked at her. "Seriously?"

"Either I ask her or your sister."

He smirked. "Faith, you ask who makes you happy. I was gonna ask Kellen," he said as Faith looked at him.

"Why?"

"Because he's the one that smacks me out of stupidity when I'm acting a fool."

Faith smirked. "And who's gonna be my wedding bodyguard?"

"Conner."

Faith smirked. "All planned out?" He nodded.

"We good," he asked.

Faith nodded. "I have a feeling that we're gonna be busy," she teased.

"Just remember something. Low stress. If you aren't feeling well, we go to the doctor."

Faith nodded and kissed him. "And if you start feeling like it's too much, tell me. No more stressing out. Where did you go this morning anyway," Faith asked.

"Run, checked on the guys at the beach, workout at the

house, a shower that somehow was really fast, and then had to run into town and grab something. Then I met this really sexy woman I know at that bridal shop," he teased.

"And what else do you want to do tonight," she asked.

"You want a run at that movie again?"

She smirked. "Or we start over with part one again."

Chapter 7

Faith got more work done that afternoon and then curled up on the sofa with Ridge. "What's wrong," Ridge asked.

"Tired. Just kinda hit me."

He kissed her. "Babe."

"It's not anything wrong. I promise you. I'm just exhausted." He kissed her, got up, handed Faith his laptop and carried her upstairs to bed.

"What are you doin?"

"Letting you rest," he teased. He leaned her onto the bed, resting her head on a pillow and grabbed his laptop, plugged it in and curled up on the bed beside her.

"Ridge."

"Wife to be."

"I love you."

"Love you too beautiful." He kissed her and Faith fell asleep beside him. He sent off a message to her doctor to see if it was normal to be that tired. When he got a reply back within a matter of 5 minutes, he opened it:

> *Right now, it could just be that she's tired, but if she's like this for a few days, I need her in my office. Either that or I come to the house. Try some water and electrolytes. Should help. If not, call me and I'll come to the house.*

He gently got up, went and got her the water bottle they always had for the gym and filled it to the brim with ice water. He came upstairs and put it on the side table and got back to work on planning out what she'd wanted for the wedding. He found a photo and contacted a friend who had connections in the wedding planning industry. When he got a reply to the email, he almost laughed:

> *It's about time you two got together. I actually just did a similar idea minus the silver accents at another wedding. I can do it since everything was silk flowers. I can get it done. Just let me know the date. I also have a connection with the caterer and the cake if that's what you want. Shoot me a date and let me know location.*

It's what he'd hoped to hear. He took a deep breath and replied:

> *It's gonna be at her Mom and Dad's house. Tent most likely. We'd need a pathway to get from the house to the tent, a big enough floor put in so nobody had to worry about high heels and tables. Not sure on guest list, but it'll be October 19th. I'll keep you posted on numbers.*

Faith snuggled up to him and he pressed send. "What you doin," Faith asked.

"Organizing all those ideas into a plan. Part of it is organized," he said.

"Ridge."

"Remember Kelly Cameron?" She nodded. "Wedding planner now."

"And you know her how," Faith teased.

"I saw her at the beach. Bumped into her actually. She was there with Eric Sampson."

"No way," Faith said.

"They're hitched supposedly. Anyway, she's offered to do the reception part."

"Meaning?"

"We need a guest list, cake and caterer plus whoever's doing the music."

"Ridge."

"She's gonna do the décor stuff and we..."

"We're doing it where?"

"You wanted it at your Mom and Dad's." She looked at him.

"And you did all of that when I was having a nap?" He nodded and kissed her.

"Ridge."

"Sexy."

"Thank you."

"For what? Getting it planned while you're sleeping?" She nodded.

"I don't know why I'm feeling like crap. I really don't." He handed her the water bottle.

"Doc said to drink water. Electrolytes. If you're still feeling like crap, she's coming here."

Faith looked at him and sat up. "All of this while I was resting?"

He nodded and kissed her. "Less stress on you."

"And what did you tell her?"

He went through the list of plans. The silver and wisteria ceiling, the sparkle on the tables, the silver tablecloths, and the dance floor. It's the way she'd explained it. When he'd sent photos of the ideas that he'd found in one of Faith's bridal books, it was perfect. She was gonna have the dream, and her Dad wasn't paying for any of it.

"Ridge."

"Sexy."

"Can you call the doctor," she said.

"Babe." She got up and ran for the bathroom. He got up and ran for the bathroom behind her as he saw her really sick. He called the doctor and carried her back to bed. "Babe."

"I'm okay."

"No, you aren't. Something's not right and you know it." When he got a text that the doc was on her way, he handed Faith the water. "Babe, you know something's not right."

"I don't know what it is, but my stomach hurts." He looked at her. "Don't go there Ridge." He kissed her, went downstairs to let the guys know the doctor was on her way there and went back upstairs.

When he saw Faith curled up in bed, he knew something wasn't right. "Babe."

"I'm just achy."

He shook his head and kissed her. "You sure you aren't…"

"Ridge."

"Are you?" She shook her head and within a matter of minutes, she was running for the bathroom again. "Babe, are you okay," he asked.

"Ow," Faith said. He ran into the bathroom and saw her curled into the fetal position.

"Baby," he said.

"Ow." He picked her up and carried her back into the bedroom, leaning her onto the bed. Not two minutes later, he got a text that the doctor had just arrived.

When the doctor came in, she looked at Ridge. "She started feeling worse. She was in the dang fetal position in the bathroom," Ridge said. She nodded and checked on Faith. Ridge didn't leave the room and refused to even step out to give her space.

"Ridge, give us a moment," the doctor asked. Ridge refused to leave. "I'm staying."

"Ridge, please," Faith said. He shook his head and left the room, pacing outside the door.

"Nauseous," the doctor asked.

"And stomach pain. Really sore. Cramping," Faith said. The doctor grabbed the soundwave that she had on hand. When Faith started worrying, the doctor turned it on and did a quick scan to check.

"It's not really gonna show much since it's early. Have you been spotting?"

Faith looked at her. "You think that I'm losing..."

"I don't know for sure."

Faith shook her head. "Go flippin figure. We're all excited and happy and then it backfires," Faith said.

"We're gonna have to do an ultrasound. Have you been drinking lots of water?"

Faith nodded. "Faith, you need to come to the office or the hospital. We have to find out. You okay to come," she asked.

Faith nodded. The doctor put her things in her bag,

opened the door and Ridge saw Faith getting up.

"What's wrong," Ridge asked.

"Hospital. I'm making sure that everything is alright. I can't do much here since it's early," the doctor said. Ridge walked into the bedroom, grabbed their phones, and picked her up, carrying her down the steps.

They walked out to the truck and Kellen shook his head. "SUV. I'll drive," Kellen said as Ridge slid her into the back seat and curled up with her. Kellen handed Ridge her purse and his wallet.

"Good move," Ridge said.

"You need your dang wallet and she needs her purse. I wasn't about to let you go through that crap," Kellen said as they headed to the hospital, following the doc.

They pulled into the hospital and Ridge hopped out of the SUV, helping Faith out. He picked her up and carried her inside. "Sir," the nurse said.

"They're with me," her doctor said.

"I have to sign them in," the nurse said.

"Follow us," the doctor said as they went back and went straight to a room. Ridge all but refused to leave the room. He filled in the paperwork and Faith started getting worse. The doctor got her checked out and she looked at Faith. "I knew," she replied.

"It happens. Honestly, I'm still stunned you two actually managed to get pregnant. That shot is almost foolproof."

"So, what's the next step," Ridge asked as Faith held his hand tighter than she ever had before. The doctor went through everything and it's like she was mouthing words without noise coming out. All of it was a blur. Faith was in tears and so was Ridge. "I'm staying in here with her," Ridge said.

"I know you want to, but we need to do this. You can't…"

"I'm staying."

"Ridge, she's going to be taken into a quick surgery. You can't."

He shook his head. "I'm staying until she goes in then," he said.

The doctor nodded and left them to talk alone until she could get them a surgical room. "Ridge."

"Babe, we're alright. I promise you that we are. We can try again like we said."

"I guess it's good that we never told our folks."

He kissed her. "I love you. You know that right?"

She nodded. "We'll be alright. One less worry."

She nodded and he kissed her again. "Tell me what you want."

"Can you just hug me," Faith asked.

He hugged her, holding her as best he could. "Ridge, if I…"

He shook his head. "We can do anything. Sky's the limit baby. Name it and we'll go."

"Beach."

He nodded and kissed her. "I'll get our stuff over there. No stress. Deal?"

She nodded.

"Jack." He shook his head.

"We don't need it Faith. Especially now."

She nodded. He kissed her. "We don't. It happened. I'm just glad we called the doc," Ridge said.

"Well, in about 10 minutes, they're gonna come in and get you. Just happened to have a cancellation. You doing alright," the doctor asked.

"How far along do you think I was?"

"Less than 2 months. We're just doing the procedure to make sure."

She went through all the post procedure steps and it's like it all fell on deaf ears. "Is she staying?"

"Until she's stable, then she can go home. Are y'all heading back to the house?"

"Beach," Faith said.

"Alright. If you need anything at all, I'm in the city today. Just call me and let me know you need me." Faith nodded.

By the time she was back from the procedure, Ridge's eyes were red and puffy. He'd let everyone at the house know they were heading to the beach and Kellen opted to trade off with Calvin. He brought the laptops down, brought down some clothes that the housekeeper had packed up for Faith and Ridge, and she followed Kellan down in Ridge's truck. When they got to the beach house, the guys traded places. They waited for the word from Ridge about Faith.

"Am I allowed to lay down with her," Ridge asked.

The doctor nodded. Faith slid over just a little and feeling his arms around her calmed her enough to rest.
"Everything okay," Ridge asked.

"She will be. I think we're gonna hold off on the shot for a while. Let her body calm. I'll check on her in an hour or so. Just know that she's not gonna feel well for a few weeks. If you need anything, I'm a call away."

"Thank you," Ridge said as the doctor grabbed another blanket and slid it over them. When his phone buzzed, he wanted to ignore it, but he checked it:

> *Everything is set at beach house. Housekeeper here. Clothes and laptops here. I brought the extra bottle of Jack because I know you well my friend.*

Calvin is at the big house. Staying at beach with you and Faith. If there's anything you two need tell me.

Ridge slid his phone back in his pocket. Seeing her hooked up to an IV and heart monitors was killing him. When she started almost trembling, he knew. "Not leaving your side. I'm right here," he said as he pulled the blanket up and held her to him.

"I screwed this up," Faith said.

He shook his head. "Babe, it happens. We can't think more into that. We can't put blame anywhere. Like I said, you're more important to me than anything in the world. I don't want you blaming yourself." She turned to face him. "Babe."

"It is my fault."

He shook his head and kissed her. "It's not. Just breathe. I've screwed up too baby. A billion times over. Doesn't mean we can't try again." She kissed him and curled back over so she was the little spoon again.

He didn't want her seeing him in tears. He was her protector and he couldn't protect her from it. He couldn't fix it. Hell. He couldn't fix anything. They'd been together a million times. Even when they'd found out she was pregnant, they were still together. They were still having sex in that bed and he was teasing. He was petrified that he'd messed it up. That it was his fault. That all of it had been too much. He slid out of the bed when he knew she was asleep and walked into the hall.

"What's wrong," the doctor asked as she looked in.

"This wasn't because we were messing around right?"

"Ridge, it happens. If the baby attaches in a bad position, it happens. It has nothing to do with you two sleeping together. It's not stress either. It just happens. We can't predict it and we can't do anything other than what we did today. I promise you. I know it's hard to wrap your head around it. I get it. It's not your fault and it isn't hers," the doctor said as Ridge nodded and brushed tears away. When Kellen messaged again, Ridge shook his head:

> *Heading down. Bringing you coffee. You alright? I thought she'd like comfy clothes. Bringing her joggers and your hoodie she always wears. Do you need anything else?*

Ridge replied:

> *Thank you for that. She's currently sleeping, but I'm going back in. I'm scared for her. I can't even quit crying. Maybe soup tonight or pasta. Something she loves. Thank you my friend.*

He put his phone in his pocket and felt hers beside it. He took a deep breath and sent Kellen the room number. He went back in and Faith was sitting up. "You okay," Ridge asked. Faith shook her head. He sat down on the chair beside her, not letting go of her hand for a half second.

"I want to go home," Faith said.

"You have to stay for a while. Once the sedation wears off, we'll see how you're doing. Best thing to do is rest," the doctor said.

"Do you want to lay down," Ridge asked.

Faith shook her head. "Who were you talking to?" "Kellen was checking on you. My hoodie and your joggers are on the way," he teased.

Faith kissed him. "Ridge."

He sat on the side of her bed. "What," he asked.

"Are we still okay," she asked as she scootched down on the bed.

He tilted the bed back a little and nodded. "Always and forever," he said.

"Please," Faith said.

He kissed her and curled back up behind her on the bed, wrapping his arm around her. "Babe, rest. You never have to worry about you and me. You know that right," he asked as Faith nodded.

"I love you," she said.

"And I love you beautiful." She nodded back off and when he saw Kellen, he shook his head. Ridge got up gently so she wouldn't wake up and got the coffee and clothes, thanking Kellen.

"She alright," Kellen asked.

"She will be."

"I just wanted to make sure y'all were alright. I threw an extra hoodie in there for you. It's calling for rain in a little bit."

"Thank you," Ridge said as Kellen nodded. He headed out, leaving them on their own and Ridge finished his coffee and curled back up in the bed with her.

They made it out just before dinner. Ridge was exhausted and Faith was in tears. He picked her up and carried her to the SUV, leaned her onto the seat and handed Faith her purse. Seeing her in his hoodie almost had him smiling.

"Thank you for bringing the hoodie," Faith said as Ridge hopped in beside her.

"Most welcome. You have homemade soup waiting on you at the house. Nothing huge. I got your laptop and your stuff brought over," Kellen said.

"Thank you," Faith said.

"Most welcome," Kellen said as he motioned for Ridge to look out the window.

"What," Faith asked.

"Rainbow," he replied.

Faith started welling up and Ridge snuggled her to him. "We're okay," Ridge said.

She shook her head. Kellen couldn't help but feel the pain.

Either could Ridge. There wasn't anything that either of them could do.

They pulled into the beach house and Ridge carried Faith inside, walking straight upstairs to their bedroom and laid her on the bed. "You okay," Ridge asked.

Faith nodded. "I will be."

He kissed her and wrapped his arms around her. "Do you want soup?"

Faith nodded. "I can smell the fresh bread. She always does it when I'm under stress," Faith teased.

He kissed her. "What do you need?"

"You." He hugged her and she slid her arms around him. "I screwed this up for us," Faith said.

"The doctor even said it's nobody's fault love. I promise you that."

"I still messed it up."

He shook his head and kissed her. "Babe, it's not your fault. Neither one of us even knew until a few days ago. It's alright."

"It's not," Faith said. He shook his head and curled up with her on the bed.

"I know you're worried and that you have a million questions. I asked her when you were sleeping if there was anything we did to cause it and she said no. Babe, we're alright. It happened. She explained a bunch of stuff about attaching too close to wherever. We're good love. I promise you," he said as he started welling up again.

By the time that they'd both managed to rest, the housekeeper came up with soup and fresh bread for them both. "Thank you," Ridge said.

"Most welcome. I figured that you two would be better off eating up here," she said.

Faith woke up to the smell of soup. "Thank you," Faith said as her housekeeper smirked and made her way down the steps.

"Eat babe. It'll make you feel better," he said.

Faith nodded and had some soup while he polished his off. "Better," he asked.

Faith nodded. "You do know that it's at least a step right," Faith asked.

"Meaning what sexy?"

"Meaning at least we got pregnant."

"That soup gave you a better attitude. You need another bowl?"

She shook her head. "Ridge."

"I love you. I always will, baby or not."

"And what else did the doctor say," Faith asked.

"That she thinks that you should be off that shot for a while. Just until your body gets past the thing today."

"And you told her no right?"

He shook his head. "Babe, we're getting married. Once your system is calmed down from this, you can go back on it if that's that you want. I'm not about to contradict your doctor."

"I'll talk to her. I don't agree with her."

By the time that Faith fell back asleep, the soup and bread were both gone, the drinks were gone and Ridge was getting more work done on the wedding plans. When he got a reply back that the DJ was handled, the floors were booked and the tablecloths were ordered, he took a deep breath. He had to write out a list of who he thought to invite. That's the moment that he realized that the only real friends that he had were Leo, Kellen, Callon and Calvin. The only guys he'd gone through literal hell with. There were a few friends of his Mom and Dad that were always around, but still, that was less than 25 people. He made a list for her, including her folks, her brothers and their relatives, her grandma and one or two friends he knew she still had. Altogether, it was less than 60 people, including 5 couples from work. He could live with 60. He took a deep breath, came up with an idea for the centerpieces, and after seeing a few suggestions from the planner, had the centerpieces done. The crystal vases on pedestals so people could talk, dangly diamond pieces dangling, her favorite flowers and even the ambiance she'd talked about. Fine. It wasn't the typical guy thing to do, but if it put a smile back on her face, he would've done everything in his power to make it happen.

He got a photo of each thing he'd planned and sent them all to her email with a note meant just for her:

> *There are things that you told me about, and*
> *things I remember you always wanted. From the*
> *lilac, lavender, giant white roses and sparkle to the*
> *wisteria ceiling. The silver tables to the dj. All of it*
> *is booked. The planner sent me the photos of what*
> *we discussed. I hope this puts a smile on that*
> *beautiful face. I even managed a guest list, though*
> *I know you'll be changing it.*

He attached the photos and sent the email. Fine. It had him more nervous than when he had got his college admission letter, but this was what she needed.

He gently got up, took the dishes downstairs, and saw a glass of Jack sitting on the counter with a piece of paper over it:

> *I knew you'd need it. If you want to talk, I'm in the*
> *security office. – K*

Ridge grabbed the glass, drank half of it, refilled, and came into the security office. "How you doin," Kellen asked.

"I don't know how I'm supposed to feel," Ridge said as he sat down with Kellen.

"Y'all know that it isn't your fault. You just need to let it sink in. That's all. It's hard as hell."

"And how do you know all of this," Ridge asked.

"Remember Ella?"

Ridge nodded.

"That's part of why we broke it off. She blamed me for stressing her out, I blamed her for being an idiot and drinkin before we found out. We played that back and forth for weeks. When it finally came down to it, I knew I wasn't ready and either was she. She walked off on me and I never heard from her again. After what y'all went through, I called her today. We actually talked," Kellen said.

"And?"

"We're goin out next weekend. Just for a sweet tea and a walk on Shem creek."

"Just take the girl out for lunch. Talk through lunch."

Kellen smirked. "Maybe. My boss might give me a few hours off that afternoon."

Ridge smirked. "Just go," Ridge joked as Conner came back in from doing the perimeter search.

"Go where," Conner asked.

"Are you good to do without me for 2 or 3 hours this weekend?"

"During the day? Sure. Why," Conner asked.

Ridge smirked. "Like I said. Lunch," Ridge teased as he took another gulp of his drink.

"You two alright," Conner asked.

Ridge nodded. "A long flipping day. I had sorta planned to go do wedding stuff with Faith and ended up in the stupid ER. Not my idea of fun," Ridge said as Conner realized that Ridge's eyes were red.

"What if you and Miss Faith go on a boat ride," Conner asked.

"No boat," Ridge said.

"My buddy Emmett has a dolphin tour thing goin on. He can take y'all on your own." Ridge nodded.

"Give her a couple days to settle, but yeah," Ridge said.

Conner nodded. "I'll ask him. Just let me know when."

Ridge took a deep breath, took another gulp of Jack, went and filled up his glass and came upstairs to see Faith on her laptop. "Babe, you're supposed to be resting," he said as he saw her eyes red and puffy.

"I can't. You did all of this," she asked.

"You saw the email?" She nodded. "The guest list is probably gonna be tweaked, but I got something to start with."

She motioned for him to come closer. He sat his glass on his bedside table and sat down on the bed beside her. "Yes love," he said. She kissed him. "So, you like it?"

"It's exactly what I wanted."

He smirked. "I remember all of the times you said you wanted a fairy tale. So long as it's not pouring rain, I'm happy," she teased.

"I also emailed your Mom and mentioned that we wanted to do it at the house if they were alright with it. Your Mom said yes," he teased.

Faith kissed him. "Thank you," she said.

"Babe."

"You didn't have to, but it did actually make me feel better."

"Now, all we need is food and cake."

She smirked and kissed him. "Surprised you didn't say surf and turf."

"I was considering it, but thought low country boil. Now, surf and turf sounds classier," he teased.

"Or we just have soup," she joked.

He kissed her. "Feelin better," he asked.

Faith nodded. "Honestly, seeing that email kinda put me in a better head space."

"We just have to pick a cake and dinner then we're done

for now," he said.

"Ridge."

"Sexy."

"What are you gonna wear," she asked.

"Up to you. Tux or suit," he said.

"Tux."

"Silver tie."

She nodded. "A Christian Grey tie," she teased as he smirked.

"Whatever you say beautiful," he teased. He kissed her and snuggled her into his arms.

"You do kinda have the guest list as I'd do it. A couple work people, but that's it. Dad's people."

"Fun," Ridge said.

"And you know that Mom's gonna want to throw a bridal shower."

"Promise me no bachelorette."

She smirked. "Don't need one. I have all I've ever wanted or dreamt of right here," she said as he kissed her forehead.

"Pretty lucky sexy woman of mine." She nodded as she curled up to him. "What?" She kissed him. "Baby, you know we can't mess around for a while right?"

"Just want to be close to you. That's all," she said as he kissed her.

He snuggled her to him and curled his arms around her. "How you feeling pain wise," he asked.

"Crampy and sore, but I'm okay," Faith said.

He grabbed her water and two of the tablets the doctor had given and handed them to her. She put one of the two pills back in the bottle and took the other. "You know that you can relax right? Nobody is expecting wonder woman right now."

"We didn't tell my folks or yours. I can't bail on work," Faith said.

He kissed her. "I'll talk to them."

"No."

"Babe."

"We."

"Now?" Faith nodded. She looked at him. "I need liquid courage," she teased.

"Not with those meds you don't," he said.

She shook her head. "We do it together," Faith said.

He nodded and she snuggled in close to him. He called his

Mom and Dad first. "Baby, everything okay," his Mom asked.

"Is Dad around?"

"Yeah. Why," his Mom asked.

"Speakerphone Moment," Ridge said.

"Lily's Mom and Dad are here too. That alright," his Mom asked.

"Yep. Speaker," Ridge said.

"Alright baby. We're all here," his Mom said.

"Well, we got some news earlier this week. We found out that Faith was pregnant," Ridge said.

"That's good news though. Why do you sound all upset," Faith's Mom asked.

"Well, we ended up in the ER this afternoon. I wasn't feeling well and the doc rushed me there. We lost it," Faith said.

"How far along were you," her Mom asked.

"9 weeks. I'm alright. We're at the beach house. Ridge is taking good care of me," Faith said.

"Baby," her Mom said.

"We wanted to tell you so you knew why she was a little MIA for the next few days," Ridge said.

"Are you okay if we pop over tomorrow maybe," Ridge's Mom asked.

He looked at Faith and she nodded as she started getting tired. "Just give me a shout before you head over. She's just gonna be resting," Ridge said.

"Alright. Thanks for letting us know," her Mom said.

"Most welcome," Ridge said.

"Love you," Faith said.

"Love you too baby," Ridge's Mom said.

They hung up and Faith kissed him. "And here I thought you were sleepy." She smirked.

"Thank you," she said. He snuggled her to him and she rested her head on his chest.

"Babe, I know it's not something that you wanted to ever have to say, but my Mom and yours have gone through it. I remember my Mom telling me when I was a kid," Ridge said.

"Still wouldn't have wanted this. I would've passed on this experience." He smirked and kissed her head. When they both conked out, he still felt like crap for the entire situation. He knew it wasn't his fault, but he couldn't help feeling guilty.

The next morning, Ridge woke up and shook his head. Faith's arms were around him and he didn't want to wake her. "Where are you goin," Faith asked.

"Coffee. Sit outside and watch the sunrise," he said as he kissed her.

"I'm coming."

He kissed her. "Babe, you don't have to. Rest."

"I'm comin with you." He kissed her, got up and handed Faith his hoodie. He slid swim shorts on, pulled on his other hoodie and kissed her, then went and freshened up. When he came back into the bedroom, she was sitting on the edge of the bed. "You okay?"

She shook her head. "I got dizzy."

"Stay here." He went and grabbed her ice water, running back upstairs. He handed it to her and she had the water. "I'll carry you."

She shook her head. "I'm okay."

"Babe, for me." She took another gulp of water and he picked her up and carried her downstairs.

He walked outside, sat her on the chaise and grabbed the beach blanket from inside, handing it to Faith. He went in and made the coffee and grabbed his towel and water bottle with his gun just in case. He had a really odd feeling. He put the towel on the table beside her, handed her the water, and got their coffees. He came back outside and she was curled up. "Warm enough," he asked. Faith nodded and kissed him. He curled up beside her, wrapped his arm around her and they just relaxed and listened to the waves. "Ridge."

"Beautiful."

"What would you think if we tried again."

"You mean now?"

"I mean when it's safe to."

He kissed her. "Practice is always good," he teased.

"Funny."

"And we still didn't make it…"

She kissed him. "Don't remind me," Faith joked.

He kissed her neck. "I love you," he said as he kissed her neck again.

"I know you do handsome fiancée," Faith said. He shook his head and gulped his coffee.

"Where's your phone?"

"In the house beside yours. Why?"

She looked at him. "Really?"

He nodded. The only other person that's awake right now is running on the beach. We're good baby."

"Then why did you bring out the really heavy towel?"

He kissed her. "Because of the guy two doors down."

She shook her head and curled up with him. "Thank you for the coffee."

"Welcome babe. Now are you actually feeling?"

"Sore, but better than yesterday. Honestly, I was probably just dizzy from the meds."

"Babe, you went through hell yesterday. Dizzy is the least of the problems."

He kissed her forehead and saw her cup was empty. "Refill?"

She shook her head and took a gulp of the water. "Babe, look out right down the middle. Do you see it?" Two dolphins jumped clearly into the air and he smirked.

"You and me." He nodded.

He curled her to him and Kellen came outside, handing Ridge the cell phones. "What's up," Ridge asked.

"Your phone was ringing," Kellen said as he headed inside. Ridge looked at the call display and saw his Mom's name. He kissed her and called his Mom.

"Good mornin," his Mom said.

"Hey. What are you doin up so early?"

"Your Dad went for a run with Faith's Dad. I couldn't sleep," she said.

"We're just watching the waves and having coffee. I couldn't really sleep either," Ridge said.

"You okay if I come by this morning?"

"Babe, you okay if Mom pops over?" Faith nodded. He knew she was exhausted, but he needed his Mom too. "Sure," he said.

"Alright. I'll get some food in me and head over. See y'all soon."

"See you," Ridge said as he hung up.

"She on the way," Faith asked. Ridge nodded.

"Then we have to shower." He smirked. "And eat." He brought his towel in with the coffee mugs, came outside and carried her back in, and up the steps to their bedroom. They had a quick shower, got dressed and came downstairs to eat when Ridge's Mom showed.

She came in and instantly hugged Faith. "You doing alright," his Mom asked.

Faith nodded. "Just tired and achy. I'm alright."

"Good. My goodness. What a few days you've had," his Mom said as she gave Faith a hug again.

"A very long 48 hours. Thankfully, Faith is alright," Ridge said. "Mom, coffee?"

"Please. Thank you baby," his Mom said as she sat down with Faith. It gave him just enough time to print out a copy of what the invitations would look like and get her idea of who else she wanted at the wedding. They all visited and when Faith's Mom came over too, he knew that it was girl time. He made sure Faith had everything she needed and went to head into the security office. "Ridge," her Mom said as she walked over to him.

"What's up," Ridge asked.

"How are you doing with the wedding planning," she asked.

"Kinda surprised her this morning. It's 90% done. Just have to fix up the guest list and get the food and cake done. Thanks again for letting us have it at the house."

"Most welcome. I know that buying the dress kinda rubbed you wrong. I'm sorry about that," her Mom said.

"It's fine. The rest of the plans are gonna be a surprise. I know there's a few couples that you two wanted to invite so I made room in the guest list."

"I appreciate that. How are you doing with what happened," her Mom asked.

"Part of me thought it was something we did, or stress or whatever. When it wasn't, and the doctor walked me through it, I had to try and explain it to Faith. She's still convinced it was her fault," Ridge said. Her Mom gave him a hug.

"That's all you could do Ridge. Thank you. Thank you for making her tell us." Ridge nodded.

"We sorta discussed it and realized we should. I didn't want her to get a million questions about why she wasn't at work."

"Good point. She's lucky she had you with her."

"I wouldn't have left her side for anything," he replied. They came back into the living room and Faith slid over a little so Ridge could sit down with her. His arm slid around her and it's like she melted into his arms.

Chapter 8

When Faith's Mom and Ridge's Mom finally headed out, Ridge carried her upstairs. "What," Faith asked.

"You've been yawning for a half hour. Your job, my love, is to sleep and heal."

"Then stay up here with me."

He kissed her. "Fine, but I'm getting emails done," he said. Faith nodded and kissed him, sliding into his lap.

"Faith."

"What," she asked.

He shook his head and she smirked. "I know what you're doing."

"Nope."

"Babe, you're supposed to rest." Faith kissed him again and he slid her to her back and leaned into her arms. "Faith, do you ever behave?"

"Around you? No."

He shook his head and kissed her, devouring her lips until she got goosebumps. "Ridge."

"Yes sexy," he said as her leg slid around his.

"You sure that I'm supposed to have a rest?"

"You aren't getting any until the doctor said you're free

and clear. End of discussion." She kissed him and he deepened the kiss until he could feel her heart pounding against his chest. "Faith, don't start."

"Don't start what?"

"You know what. I'm trying to behave myself. You start doing what I know you're trying to, you know I'm not sleeping in here."

"You wouldn't," she said.

"I would. This sexy woman all coiled around me like a sexy snake. Damn right I would." She shook her head and he kissed her again. The taste of her lips was turning him on. The taste of her kiss had his heart starting to race. "You need to rest," Ridge said as he broke the kiss.

"Nope," she replied as she pulled him back to her.

"Faith, don't start it."

"I like starting it," she teased as he felt the button of his jeans come undone.

"Faith."

"What?"

Ridge grabbed her hands and held her away from the zipper of his jeans. "Not happening. You don't want to start that."

"Says who?"

"Woman, don't taunt me like that."

She kissed him and pulled him to her with her legs. "Why can't I," she asked.

"Because we just…"

She kissed him. "I don't want to talk about it Ridge. I just want…"

"We can't."

"I can," she said as she kissed his neck and nibbled.

"Faith." She got a smirk that spoke volumes. "I'm getting up."

"No."

"Faith, you push one inch and you're done for."

"Let go of my hands then." He shook his head.

"I know what you're up to Faith. I'm telling you now, you go there and you aren't gonna get what you want."

"Yeah I will."

"Nope."

"Why?"

"Because you are behaving for the first time in your dang…"

She kissed him. "Mine," she teased.

"Faith." She kissed him and wriggled a hand free. "Don't touch." She nodded and completely ignored what he said. He grabbed her hand again, linking their fingers before she could get to the zipper. "We aren't doing this. We just aren't Faith."

"Ridge."

"Faith."

"I want…"

He kissed her. "I know you do. Just stop. Please baby. Just stop."

She kissed him and slid her hands free, holding his face in her hands. "You sure I can't talk you into it?" He shook his head.

"Too easily. Exactly why I'm going and sitting in that chair," he teased as he got up.

"Ridge." He shook his head. The fact that he was passed being turned on didn't go unnoticed.

She motioned for him to come closer and he shook his head. "Rest."

"Ridge."

"I'm behaving. Rest or I'm sleeping in the other room."

She looked at him. "Ridge." He shook his head and Faith got up, walked over and straddled him on the chair.

"Faith, go to bed."

"No," she said as she kissed him.

He shook his head. "Don't do it."

"Fixing it," she joked.

"I don't need your fixing wife to be. Go lay down." He felt her hand slide down his jeans and he shook his head. "Faith, stop."

"Mine."

"Not right now it isn't." When he felt her hand around him, he was done. Completely and totally done. Part of him thought it was intentional. A welcome distraction to everything that had happened, but when her hand moving up and down started getting him more turned on, he shook his head. "Faith."

She kissed him. "What," she asked.

"You need to stop."

"Nope." He kissed her, pulling her face to his until her heart was racing just as fast. He wanted to pounce. Hell. He wanted to take advantage of her, but he knew better. He'd had restraint. He had to maintain it. When his body couldn't hold back, his head went back and he felt warm on him. He didn't even look. He climaxed and felt her kiss his stomach.

"Crap. Faith."

"Mm," she said as she kissed his stomach.

"You do know that you are totally sleeping alone tonight right?"

"Why," she asked as she smirked.

He shook his head, got up and saw her with a Cheshire grin on the edge of the bed. "I swear, if I come out of that bathroom and you aren't in the bed, I'm kicking your butt," he teased.

"And if I'm all naked?"

"You're sleeping alone." He shook his head, walked into the bathroom, and cleaned up then looked at himself. She was taunting. She was teasing until she got her way. He knew it. He also knew that he couldn't sleep in that bed with her. He couldn't take that risk. He took a deep breath, zipped up and walked back into the bedroom seeing Faith in his hoodie and not much else.

"Faith."

"What?"

"I know what you're doing."

She smirked and patted the bed beside her. He shook his head. "Not happening."

"Why?"

"You know why. Get some rest. You need to sleep baby."

"And you need to get your butt over here. I sleep better with you."

He smirked and shook his head. "Nope."

"Ridge."

"You even start anything, I'm going downstairs." He kicked his shoes off and slid onto the bed behind her, snuggling her. "Happy now," he asked as she turned and snuggled tighter to him, sliding her arm around him. "Faith."

"What?"

He took a deep breath. "You need to rest. I get that you want something more than just me kissing you, but the doc said no. Leave it be. Please."

She nodded and kissed him. He tucked her in a little and she nodded off. When Kellen messaged that Leo was trying to reach him, Ridge went to get up.

"No," Faith said.

"I have to grab my laptop and cell. I'll be right back."

He got up, headed downstairs and grabbed everything, then came back upstairs. He logged into his laptop and saw the email from Leo:

> *Package arrived that you were waiting on. I put it in your closet. Is she doing alright? Do you need anything?*

Ridge replied back to him and looked up to see Faith

staring at him. "Babe, rest."

"I can't. Just come back over here." He kissed her and got up, sitting on the bed, and put his laptop and cell on the bedside table.

"Babe, you need sleep. I get that you don't want to, but you need to." She kissed him and slid into his lap. "What would you like," he asked.

"You."

"Faith."

"I love you."

"And I love you sexy. Out of my lap. Rest."

"Movie," she asked.

"Fine. I'll pick," he teased as he slid her out of his lap, grabbed the remote and flipped the TV on, picking a movie that he knew would put her to sleep.

When she finally nodded off, Ridge shook his head and kissed her head. He went back into his laptop and got his emails done. When he saw one from the jeweler that had made Faith's ring, he smirked:

> *Let me know when you need the wedding bands. I have a few ideas for hers that would go with the ring.*

Ridge replied back:

Photo? I'll need something understated for myself as well. Size 11

He closed up his laptop and finished watching the end of the movie. When he felt Faith move, he shook his head. Her leg slid over his and she leaned her head on his chest. "I thought you were resting," he teased.

"I was. I always sleep better beside you." He kissed her and slid his arm around her. "What was with all the typing," she asked.

"Email to the jeweler. He's making your wedding band and mine."

"Really? And what exactly are you planning for that wedding band?"

"For yours, something fine that matches your ring. He's making one for me that sort of goes with yours."

"Really," Faith joked.

"Babe, literally, all that's left to do is the cake and the food. I even talked to your Mom."

"She told me."

He kissed her forehead. "You really do need to rest."

"And you really do have to kiss me."

He laughed and kissed her. "No more funny business Faith. I mean it. You have no idea what was running through my head."

"Yeah I do," she teased.

"Not what I was talking about."

"I was," she joked.

"It's like your dirty mind just amplified. So bad," he teased.

"All your fault," she teased.

"My fault," he said almost faking being stunned.

"Yeah yours. You started all of this."

"You started trying to get me to watch that movie."

She smirked. "I remember."

"The appetizer," he joked.

"My legs were shaking for two hours," Faith teased.

"Then maybe we should just hold off on that discussion until the doctor gives you the okay," Ridge said.

"You sure you don't want to watch another movie," she teased.

He shook his head. "Really love. You have just gone through a whole level of hell and that's what you're talking about?"

She kissed him. "Around you, yes."

"Let me take care of you and quit. Just try and behave for the first time ever," he joked.

"Nope," Faith teased.

He shook his head and kissed her. "You're alright," he asked.

"No, but I'm trying to distract myself from thinking about it."

"Sore?"

She shook her head. "Just achy. Honestly, if she hadn't told me that I couldn't, I would go soak in the tub."

"Hot shower?"

She smirked. "Alone Faith."

She shook her head. He kissed her and got the heating pad that the housekeeper had brought for Faith. He plugged it in and handed it to her. "Thank you."

"Welcome. Honestly, I know you hate sitting in bed and resting, but you need to." She nodded.

"I kinda thought maybe we could go back out and sit by the water."

He smirked. "You sure," he asked.

Faith nodded. "It was kinda relaxing."

"That mean you're gonna behave," he teased.

She smirked. "Never know. We could go for a short walk on the beach."

He looked at her. "I don't know that it's a good plan."

"Ridge."

He took a deep breath. "Fine. You start feeling like crap, we're coming home."

She nodded and sat for a bit, hoping the heating pad would do its thing and ease the cramping and achiness. He rolled his jeans up and looked outside seeing the storm clouds. "Well, that idea is kinda out. It's about to start raining."

Faith shook her head. "Another movie," she asked.

He smirked. "Babe, do you want to sit up here or downstairs?"

"Up here, door closed."

He shook his head. "Stay here."

He kissed her, walked downstairs, and got himself a drink and got her a sweet tea. "She alright," the housekeeper asked.

"She needed the heating pad. Thank you," Ridge said.

"I'm making the pasta she likes for dinner. Just an oil and spices sauce."

"I appreciate it."

"And I put on a steak for you. The other stuff isn't much," she said.

He smirked. "I'll be upstairs with Faith if you need anything." She nodded and he headed back upstairs. He put his drink on the table by the bed and handed Faith a sweet tea.

"Ridge."

"Babe."

"Come here."

He smirked and sat down on the bed with her. "What," he asked.

"Come lay down with me."

He slid closer and she curled up with him. "Better," he teased.

Faith nodded. His arm slid around her shoulder and he flipped on a movie. "Which one are you determined to watch?"

"Gone with the wind."

He smirked and kissed her. "I'm surprised you can't recite the script by now," he teased.

She kissed him. "Ridge."

"Yes gorgeous."

"What would you think if we stayed the rest of the week," she asked.

"Since it's Friday you mean."

"Until Monday or Tuesday."

"If that's what you want to do. Just attempt to keep your hands to yourself alright?"

"Nope," Faith teased. He shook his head. Just as they got comfortable, her phone buzzed.

"Yep," Faith said.

"Are you alright if I pop by to check on you," her doctor asked.

"Sure."

"Have you stopped spotting?"

"Yes."

"Nothing at all?"

"No."

"Alright. I'm on my way."

They hung up and Faith messaged that they were at the beach. She curled up closer to him and he shook his head. "Faith."

She rested her head on his chest and he shook his head. "Yeah. I'm sleeping in the other room tonight."

"You do, I'm coming with you."

He shook his head and Faith smirked. "Woman, I'll stay in here, but you can't be doin what you did this afternoon. Promise me."

"I'm not promising anything. Ridge, we didn't..."

"You did."

"I'm not promising it." He took a deep breath. He let the guys know the doc was coming and within maybe 15 minutes, they said she was pulling up.

He paused the movie and got up. "Ridge."

"Doc is here."

Kellen walked her upstairs and she came in to check on Faith. "And how are you doing," the doctor asked.

"She was cramping so I grabbed her the heating pad. She's been a little antsy most of the day, but I tried to get her to rest," Ridge said.

"Good. Ridge, I have to do an exam. Are you staying," the doctor asked.

Ridge shook his head. "I'll be back in a few," Ridge said.

"And," the doctor asked.

"Just achy. Not sore at all."

"You weren't far along. It'll be a little while before you can get back to normal. Just know that you two are gonna have to use something. Your body needs time to recuperate. If the spotting stops completely, 3 or 4 days."

"Seriously?"

"Faith, I get that you're trying to get past it and leave it in the past, but you can't this time. You need time to let your body heal. Are you okay with it?"

"I talked to Ridge about it. We know it wasn't me or him. It wasn't anything we were doing. I just don't need to wait. I'm alright."

"Two more days and I check in then I'll let you know. That work?"

"No."

The doctor smirked. "Do you want to try for kids again," the doctor asked.

"We're getting married in October. We talked about kids. We both want them."

"Now or later?"

"I kinda want to go back on the shot," Faith said.

"Not happening for a while. Just make sure you're using something if you two are together. You need to give yourself time to heal inside." Faith nodded and the doc looked at Faith.

"What?"

"Nothing Faith. Nothing in that area."

"Fine," Faith said.

The doctor came out of the bedroom with Faith following her. "And how's the patient," Ridge asked.

"I'll come back in a day or two and check on her, but her body is bouncing back faster than I thought. She still has to rest, but light exercise is alright so long as you aren't overdoing it," the doctor said intentionally for Faith to hear.

"I get it," Faith said.

"Alright. I'll see you on Sunday night." Faith nodded and walked her out, thanking her. Ridge smirked as the housekeeper almost laughed. "And what are you two laughing at," Faith asked.

"You not overdoing it. I almost wanted to ask if we were talking about the same person," Ridge joked.

He kissed Faith. "You aren't funny," she joked.

"Yeah I am. Once the storm passes, we can go for a walk," Ridge said.

"Done," Faith replied. He came up with an idea that would either relax her, or get her dirty mind thrown into overdrive.

"Fire," Ridge asked.

He saw the smile come across Faith's face and she nodded. "Sure," Kellen joked.

Ridge kissed Faith and went and made the fire in the fireplace. She just watched and sat down on the sofa. Her housekeeper handed her the fluffy throw blanket and a sweet tea, then went upstairs. She cleaned the bedroom and came downstairs, putting Ridge's drink on the other side table for him. "Thank you," Ridge said.

"Most welcome. The pasta goes on in 20. Should be ready for dinner around 5:30," the housekeeper said.

"Thank you," Faith said.

By the time that Ridge sat down, Faith had a grin ear to ear. "What," he asked.

"Just thinking," Faith teased as he came and sat down with her.

"I know that mind of yours Faith. Stop."

She kissed him. "The last time you made a fire, I think appetizer happened," she whispered in his ear.

"The first time was at your Mom and Dad's during the storm when you were determined to get me to curl up in bed with you."

"It was pouring. It's not like there were many options."

"There were. You just didn't like me choosing another option."

Faith smirked. "I guess you couldn't handle me back then," she teased in a hushed voice.

"Oh, I could. I just opted to be a decent person instead of taking full advantage."

She kissed him. "I kinda like the way we did."

He shook his head. "Just sticking on that one topic." She nodded with a smirk. "Still sleeping in another room."

She shook her head and he leaned in and kissed her. "Come upstairs," Faith whispered.

"Nope. You're behaving for a few hours," he said in a quiet voice.

She smirked and kissed him. "Fine. I'm going to get my laptop," Faith said as she got up and went into her office, grabbing the laptop from her desk.

When she came back into the living room, Ridge was looking through emails on the sofa, getting comfortable. Faith smirked and sat down in his lap. "Faith."

"What?"

He shook his head and slid back just enough for her to get comfy like she had when the movie taunting had started. She got a grin ear to ear and opened her laptop. "Faith."

"Handsome," she said.

He shook his head. "Behave. Please," he asked.

"Nope."

He kissed her shoulder. "Faith, we can't do anything until

the doctor says you're okay. Leave it alone," he said quietly.

"So many other things we could do," she joked.

"And none of them are happening after earlier." She smirked and closed her laptop, leaning back into his arms.

"Ridge."

"Yes love."

"I love you."

"Nice sucking up. Answer is still no. I love you too."

She smirked. "Ridge."

"No." She turned to face him, putting her laptop on the table. "Faith."

She kissed him. "What," she asked.

"Still not gonna happen."

She slid on his lap, straddling him on the sofa. "Why?"

"Faith."

She shook her head. "You are such a buzzkill."

He kissed her and shook his head. "Behaving. You should try it," he teased.

Just as Faith was about to do something that would get her in more trouble with Ridge, her housekeeper said that dinner was ready. "Up," Ridge said. She kissed him and he shook his head, picked her up and walked over to the counter, sitting her on the chair. Faith got that grin again and he shook his head. "Stop."

"No. There's no reason why we..."

"Faith, eat your dinner." They both ate with Faith teasing him the entire way through it. When he got up and helped do the dishes, Faith smirked. He needed to separate himself. Get away from the temptation. When he finished with that, he sat down in the chair and double checked his emails:

> *Here's my suggestion so the rings somewhat match.*

The jeweler had outdone himself. He agreed and said he'd be there the following day to pay for them. Just as he pressed send, he noticed the housekeeper was gone. Faith slid into his lap and smirked. "Still not happening," Ridge said.

"Who were you texting?"

"Jeweler is making the rings. Anything else you need?" She nodded. "Faith." She kissed him and he shook his head, deepening the kiss until her body was tight against his and her hands were somewhat immovable.

"Upstairs," Faith said.

He shook his head. "You're behaving remember?" She leaned her body against his.

"You really want me to do this here," she whispered.

"You're not doing anything wife to be. You're sitting and watching a movie."

"Says who?"

"You really want to test me?"

"I want..." He kissed her. "I have ways to make you sit and watch that movie Faith. Ways to prevent your hands from going places they shouldn't be," he whispered as he felt her legs almost tremble.

"Bring it on," she teased as she whispered in his ear.

He looked at her. "Testing me?" She nodded and kissed him. He got up and took her hand. "Kellen, keep an eye on the fire for me," Ridge said as he grabbed his phone and walked her upstairs.

"What," Faith asked as he walked into the bedroom and closed the door. Faith almost started to get excited. "What are you gonna do," Faith said almost laughing.

"You really want to push that button."

She nodded. "Faith, she said no. Nothing until she gives the okay. Instead, you keep trying to taunt anyway. Why do you have..." She kissed him. He picked her up and devoured her lips until she was pawing at his clothes. "Faith."

"What?"

He leaned her onto the bed and kissed her again. "Stay there."

"Why?"

"Woman, sit."

He left the room and got himself a glass of Jack from downstairs, got a glass of ice water for Faith, then grabbed the box from his room, opening it and grabbing something. He got a grin knowing the look that he'd get for it. He walked back into the bedroom and she was sitting on the edge of the bed. "Faith." He handed her an ice water and she looked at him.

"What," she asked. He took a gulp of his drink and just looked at her. "Ridge."

He kissed her and she could taste the Jack. All she wanted was a sip. Something to make her forget what she'd just been through. "Why," he asked.

"Why what?"

"Why are you so determined to be together when you know the doc said we can't?"

"Because."

He shook his head. "You do realize that it's not gonna change what we just went through right?"

She nodded. "Still helps."

"You can't replace that with the two of us having sex."

"Never said we had to."

"And you aren't doing that either."

"Says who," Faith asked as he put his drink on the counter and shook his head.

"You have two choices. Three really."

"What?"

"Either you behave, or you and that headboard become attached."

"Funny," Faith replied.

"Did you think I was joking?" She looked at him. "I get that you want to get past it, but it's not gonna happen like this. We can't and you know it. I'm not here as a toy when you need a distraction Faith."

"I'm not allowed to want…"

"I never said you weren't. I just said that if you really needed a distraction, I wasn't gonna be it."

"I just want us. I want us back to how we were before all of this."

He shook his head. "Babe, I love you. I do. I want us back to the way we were too, but I can't do it. The doctor said we can't, and you being alright is more important."

"Can't we just be together? Curl up in bed and just…"

"After that little thing you did earlier, no."

"Ridge."

He kissed her. "Either that or you're keeping your hands to yourself. Period. You don't, I am seriously sleeping in the other room."

"I love you."

"I know. I love you too. Just remember what the doctor said. That's all I'm saying wife to be."

She kissed him again. He got his drink and sat down on the chair. "Seriously," Faith asked.

"Yep." He flipped one of her movies on and she grabbed the remote.

"Come sit with me," Faith asked.

"Are you gonna keep your hands to yourself?"

"Yes."

Ridge took a deep breath and got up, grabbing his drink, and laid down on the bed beside her. She curled up beside him and rested her head on his chest then pressed play. "What were you gonna do," Faith teased.

"You don't keep those hands where I can see them, you'll find out," he teased.

She looked at him. "Meaning?"

"Don't." He motioned for her to watch the movie and her arm slid around him. He took a deep breath. When she snuggled in closer, he shook his head. Her leg slid around his as he could feel the room start heating up. When he looked and saw her asleep, he shook his head. He watched the last of the movie, turned it off and tried to slide out of bed. When he couldn't, he shook his head. "Where are you going," Faith asked.

"Getting changed for bed." She kissed him and slid on top of him. "Faith."

"What?"

"We discussed this." She kissed him again and he slid her to her back, sliding into her arms. "What did I tell you?"

She looked at him. "Kiss me."

He kissed her, devouring her lips until she was pulling at his clothes. "Faith."

"Off."

"No." She looked at him and he took a deep breath. "This is why I said..."

She kissed him again. "Ridge."

"What?"

"Take the shirt off."

"Not happening."

He went to get up and she wouldn't let him. "Why," she asked. She kissed him again as he deepened the kiss and she wrapped her legs around him. That kiss didn't break, didn't stop, and only got worse. He remembered one detail. One. He slid his hands in hers, linked their hands and slid them over her head, holding her in place. He wasn't running the risk again. He could've done just about anything, but even he had to remind himself that she wasn't allowed to do anything. When he kissed down her neck, she tried to break free and he stopped her. "Did you think I was joking," he whispered as he felt her heart racing against his. He slid her hoodie off.

"Ridge." Within a matter of two minutes, she was going for his jeans again. He got her hands and linked their fingers again.

"Nope," he said.

"So, you're allowed to taunt me and I can't do anything?" He nodded as he kissed over her heart. "You aren't being fair."

He kissed her. "If you decide to move your hands, I leave the room."

She shook her head. "Ridge. Please."

He kissed her and held up two items, both of which put a smirk on her face and made her shake her head. "You're serious."

He nodded. "Choose one."

"Fine. I'll behave."

He shook his head. "I know better."

"Ridge."

"You want me? Fine. Feeling is flipping mutual, but I can't do anything either." Her arms slid around him and pulled him back to her. "What," he asked.

"Distract me."

He kissed her and shook his head. "Faith."

"What?"

He kissed her and her legs slid around him again. "You promise me that you aren't going to go there?"

"Can't promise anything, but I will attempt..." He kissed her again and the kiss just got even hotter than it was. Every time he deepened the kiss, they were both getting goosebumps. Feeling her in his arms, the taste of her kiss, the feel of her lips on his and he was getting hot and bothered all over again. "Let me," Faith asked.

He shook his head. She kissed him and he sat up. "What," Faith asked. He slid her joggers off and her legs slid back around him. When she went to undo his jeans, he stopped her.

"Faith."

"What?" He shook his head and he pulled her tight to him.

"Don't touch the jeans."

She kissed him and he looked at her. "What," she teased. He kissed her and the kiss went from light to deep to deeper to making out like their lives depended on it all over again.

When he started getting to that point where he either got up or handled the situation, he felt her hand on him, in his jeans. "Faith."

She kissed him and his body just tightened. "Mine," Faith said.

He shook his head and she smirked. "You aren't gonna do it," he said.

"Says who," she teased. Before she was able to move, his body had already found its release and she was only making it worse. "Ridge."

He kissed her, devouring her lips. "Move your hand." Instead of doing as he asked, she slid his shirt off, throwing it into the laundry bin. "Woman, you never behave do you?"

"Either I did or you..." He kissed her again and got up. He walked off, walked into the bathroom, and closed the door.

He slid his phone from the back pocket, took out his wallet and shook his head. He threw his jeans into the laundry and cleaned up a little. Just as he flipped the water off, his phone buzzed:

Come back to bed.

He took a deep breath, came out of the bathroom, and grabbed boxers, sliding them on and slid onto the bed beside her. "You alright," Faith asked as he saw her in sexy lingerie.

"I'm sleeping in the…"

"Ridge."

"You just proved my dang point woman."

"We can do whatever we want to. Who cares what she…"

"Faith."

She shook her head. "Fine. Sleep and nothing else."

"Good. Keep it that way until she clears you."

"Not gonna be easy."

He shook his head and took a gulp of his drink. "Tell me about it. I swear you are…"

"Yours." Faith smirked.

"Too tempting. Way too tempting. How long is the longest that you went without…"

She kissed him. "4 years."

He looked at her. "Seriously?"

She nodded. "21-25. Nobody would even talk to me when I

started working at my Dad's company. I was working in every sector until he figured out the best fit. I didn't have time to date."

Ridge shook his head. "Faith."

She kissed him. "I didn't. Then I just started dating here and there and bumped into Holden, then all of that stupid crap."

"You do realize that right about then I was away right?"

"Away where?"

"Military."

"Ridge."

"That was the year I actually came home. Mom lost her marbles when I came home. I ended up doing security then started the bodyguard stuff," he said.

"You never told me," Faith said.

He figured that he might as well just tell her. "I sorta had a breakdown and couldn't snap myself out of it. I needed to leave and they allowed me to discharge that year."

Faith looked at him. "You okay now?"

"You remember what happened in Jekyll. That was part of it." Faith shook her head.

The fact that it took her miscarrying, a storm, a fire, and her doing the one thing that left him not in control to pull it out of him was almost shocking. When it was fully out of his system, he finally calmed. "Ridge."

"Yep."

"I know that it was hard to handle, but I'm glad you're here."

He kissed her. "Me too. Just remember what I told you alright? Until all of the stuff with the threats is resolved, I need to keep your safety first."

She nodded. "By the way, we ordered the glass."

"What glass," he asked hoping that she'd say replacement glass that was bulletproof.

"You said the bulletproof glass was a better idea for the window facing the front."

He smirked. "Good."

"Ridge."

"Beautiful."

"Do you want to try again," she asked as he kissed her forehead.

"When we're ready." She snuggled up to him and he wrapped an arm around her. They were finally calm and watching the movie that he knew she loved.

Chapter 9

Ridge woke up the next morning and saw Faith completely out cold. He slid out of bed and freshened up, slid joggers on and headed downstairs. He made coffee and walked outside, drying off the two chairs outside. When he heard the swish of the sliding door, he smirked. "Came down here without me," Faith said.

"What are you doin up? You were out cold," he said.

"I can't sleep without you there Ridge."

He kissed her and she slid onto the chaise with him. "It's kinda nice out here after the storm," he said as Faith laid the blanket over them.

"It is. It's almost calmer," Faith replied. He kissed her head.

"And what are we doing today after we caffeinate?"

"Go see the doc, maybe go to the office and get the paperwork I need then a walk on the beach."

He smirked. "You sure," he asked. Faith nodded and snuggled in closer.

"Ridge."

"Beautiful."

"Did you hear anything else about that guy who was after my Dad?"

"I sent them off an email to be honest. I wanted to see if

there was any follow up. They should've nailed him down by now."

"Are we okay to go for a walk," Faith asked. He kissed her. He grabbed his phone and checked emails, seeing one from the detective:

> *We have an arrest warrant for him. It'll be over soon. Everyone flipped on him. We have enough to throw him in jail for years. Officers still posted in unmarked vehicles at the house and beach house for extra safety.*

Ridge smirked and showed her the message. "That's good right?"

"That's better than a good thing."

He kissed her neck and sent the email to her Dad. When he saw that her Dad had opened the email, he smirked. It was only a matter of time until his phone rang. He slid his arms around Faith and kissed her and her Dad called. He put it on speaker.

"Good morning Dad," Faith said.

"Mornin. Ridge, thank you for that email. At least we know who we're dealing with now."

"I found the connection and he was on our list. Honestly, I'm sorry it ended up being him. Didn't he used to own part of the company that you took over?"

"Yep. Thankfully, we had a restraining order against him.

Sort of explains why he was sending stuff to Faith's," her Dad said.

Just as they were finally relaxing, Ridge got her up and walked her inside. "Dad, I'll call you back," Faith said as she hung up.

"Kellen," Faith said. Kellen ran for the sliding door and came outside to see Ridge walking down the steps to confront Holden.

"And what do you want," Ridge asked.

"Going to see Faith," Holden said.

"Nope."

"Ridge, she's..."

"You're getting a serious butt whooping if you think you're going near her," Ridge said as he pointed the gun at Holden.

"And why's that? Because you claimed her already," Holden asked.

"Because she's my fiancée. Either go back to the hole you crawled out of or I'm sending you to the bottom of the ocean."

"Right. Like she'd be with a loser like you. I mean seriously Ridge. Did you think that I'd fall for that?"

"It's true. Either you walk back to your house and don't come near here again or the police will handle you," Kellen said as one of the undercover officers came around the back.

"Right. By the way. I saved those photos," Holden said as the officer came out and arrested Holden.

"You're being arrested for Harassment, blackmail, stalking, solicitation and breaking a restraining order," the officer said as they handcuffed Holden and hauled him away.

Ridge looked at Kellen. "About dang time," Kellen joked.

"Thank you," Ridge said.

"I know what you wanted to do. That's why I stepped in."

"Where's Faith?"

"In the house. It's fine," Kellen said. Ridge slid his gun back into the towel and came inside, seeing Faith on the steps. "Babe."

She ran into his arms. When he saw her eyes all red and puffy, he shook his head and picked her up as she wrapped her arms around his neck. He carried her upstairs, sat her on the bed and held her to him. "It's fine."

"You were about to shoot him Ridge."

"I was stopping him. That's it. I knew the police were in the front yard," Ridge said as she held on.

"Ridge."

He kissed her. "It's alright. He's gone. All of it's gonna be over."

"Ridge, you were pointing a gun at him."

"It was either that or he came in this house and went for you. That wasn't happening. I told you before. If he wants you, he has to go through me Faith."

"If he'd…"

Ridge kissed her. "I never would've let that happen and either would Kellen. He was out there with me. It's okay love." Not two minutes later, his phone rang.

"Ridge," her Dad said.

"Sir."

"Everything alright? Faith was losing it."

"Holden showed at the beach house. Kellen and I handled it and he was arrested by the police. I'm right here with Faith."

"Thank you."

"I'm just as shaky as she is right now. I don't know what the hell possessed him to show up here like it was nothing."

"What else did he say," her Dad asked.

"That he had photos saved. That was pretty much the nail on his coffin in my eyes."

"I'm coming to the house."

"You don't have..."

"I'm coming." They hung up and Ridge kissed Faith.

"Get dressed. Your Dad's on his way here."

Ridge got a quick shower, slid jeans and a t-shirt on and came downstairs to see her housekeeper plating eggs benedict for 6. "6?"

"Her Mom and Dad are on the way. Someone has to feed them," she said as Ridge thanked her. He got another mug of coffee and saw another pot. "Thought of everything this morning," Ridge said.

"Thank you for that this morning. I don't know what would've happened if he'd got in here."

Ridge nodded. "Kellen, Conner. Come get some food," Ridge said. They came back in and after a quick thank you, they went back to the security room. Faith came down a little while later and Ridge went up to help her.

"I'm okay," Faith said. He kissed her and carried her down the steps to the high-top chair at the counter. He sat her down and they went to start to eat when Faith's Mom and Dad showed. Kellen got the door and they came in and ran straight over to Ridge and Faith. "Are you okay," her Dad asked.

Faith nodded. "Scared the crap out of me, but yes," Faith said as her Mom hugged Ridge.

"That's what I'm here for right," Ridge asked as her Dad hugged Faith.

"Thank goodness you and Kellen were. Thank you," her Dad said as he gave Ridge a hug.

"Come have some breakfast," Faith said as they all sat down together and ate.

"You're alright," his Mom asked.

Ridge nodded. "Faith was a little worried, but it's alright."

"You with a gun in your hand isn't exactly a calming sight," Faith said.

He slid his arm around her and gave her a hug. "Well, I also got word this morning that the entire case is complete. They arrested Holden and Cameron, Zack, and Jack Anderson. We don't have to be on edge," her Dad said.

"At least that's something," Ridge said as he finished his breakfast and helped clean up.

Once everyone was over their worry, her Mom and Dad headed home and left Faith and Ridge to try and relax on the sofa. "We're not going into the office if that's what you're thinking," Ridge said. She kissed him. An all-encompassing kiss that had her sliding into his lap on the sofa. "Faith," he said as the kiss broke and he wrapped his arms tight around her.

"Don't ever scare me like that again."

He nodded and hugged her. "It scared me babe. I had a feeling that he'd make a move when all the other pieces were falling. I just didn't want you in the middle of any of it." She held on even tighter and he knew. Every ounce of stress from the past few days was pouring out of her. All of it.

He picked her up and carried her back upstairs. "Ridge." He leaned her onto the bed and curled up with her. "And they know that it's over right," Faith asked.

"They believe so."

"Ridge."

He looked at her. "What baby," he asked.

"Tell me that you don't have to keep carrying that..."

"Still holding onto it. I'll put it in the lock box, but it's staying near me."

Faith shook her head. "Ridge."

"It's been here since I walked in the door. Nothing is gonna change."

He kissed her. "Tell me that you won't do something ridiculous."

"Such as?" She looked at him. "Babe, do you remember when I told you I was security first and your man second?" She nodded. "You want it out of a drawer and in a closet, fine. It's staying in the house."

"Security office."

"Alright," he replied. She kissed him and her phone buzzed, making her jump in the air. She shook her head and grabbed her phone.

"Hi doc," Ridge joked as Faith put the call on speaker.

"And how's my favorite patient," the doctor asked.

"I'm alright. Had an insane morning, but I'm good. The cramping is almost gone," Faith said.

"Good. I'll be by later this afternoon around 4. That alright," the doctor asked.

"Yep. We'll make sure we're back from our walk," Ridge said.

"Alright. I'll see you this afternoon." They hung up and Ridge put her phone on the charger with his.

"Are you actually feeling better or just saying it because you're determined to get some?"

"Both."

He smirked and kissed her. "Babe, I love you, but you really have to get your mind out of the gutter." She kissed him and smirked.

"Walk on the beach?"

She looked at him. "Where we can walk wherever we want."

"Depends. Are you bringing it with you?"

"Have to."

"Fine," Faith said as he kissed her.

"Where is it now?"

"Drawer." She kissed him and slid into his lap. "Faith."

"What?"

"Don't you start that again."

"I'm putting my bikini on," she teased. She kissed him and slid off the bed, changing into her red bikini, slid shorts on with it and a tank top and came back into the bedroom. "Are you putting on swim shorts?"

"Faith." She kissed him. "Fine, but promise me that you aren't gonna intentionally run into the water and..." She kissed him. She texted her doctor and asked if she could go swimming. When she got a reply, she shook her head. "What," he asked.

"Can't go in the water until she gives me the stupid okay."

"You can go up to your knees."

She smirked. "Nice option," Faith joked.

He knew she was getting annoyed with all of the things she couldn't do. He slid his swim shorts on with a tee, grabbed the phones and a beach towel, hiding the gun. They headed downstairs and Kellen saw them. "We're heading off for a walk on the beach. If you need me, call," Ridge said.

Kellen nodded, opting to stay on the deck to keep an eye out. "Why is Kellen on the deck," Faith asked as they made their way down to the water.

"Because of what happened this morning. He's keeping you safe just like I am," Ridge said.

Faith shook her head. "I think it's a little much," Faith said.

"Babe, if it hadn't been for the two of us, who knows what would've happened this morning." Faith shook her head and went up to her knees in the water.

"Come in the water," Faith said. He walked over to her and splashed her. "You're doing that now?" He nodded. The two of them ended up in a water fight in the shallows of the beach.

"Faith," Ridge said as she tackled him to the sand.

"What," she asked.

"Any reason in particular that you're determined to knock me to the sand?"

"Yep," she teased as she kissed him. He flipped her to her back and kissed her.

"And what's that reason sexy?"

"Because I can," she joked.

He shook his head and kissed her. "Are we finishing the walk or avoiding the world?"

"Both."

He smirked and kissed her again, devouring her lips. "Come on sexy. Walk with me."

He pulled her to her feet, got his towel and everything in it and they kept walking as he brushed the sand off her backside. "Ridge."

"Sand," he teased.

"Keep smacking my butt like that and you'll get it back tenfold."

"Promises, promises," Ridge joked.

They played around with a new sense of calm. They were back to being playful and fun and relaxed. When they made it back to the house, two glasses of sweet tea were waiting. Ridge smirked and Kellen came back outside. "How was the water," Kellen asked.

"Warm and salty. Thank you for the sweet tea," Faith said.

"Most welcome. I thought you two might need something. Ridge, are you good if I go do that thing?"

Ridge nodded with a smirk. "What," Faith asked.

"He has a date."

"Good luck," Faith said as he nodded and headed off.

"This mean Conner is here solo," Faith asked.

"You, me, Conner and…"

"Good," Faith teased.

"And why is that? One less person to hear you screaming my name," he teased.

"Maybe. Maybe he's finally getting a life after being stuck beside us for however long."

Ridge shook his head and they had their sweet tea as they watched the waves. "Ridge."

"Yes beautiful."

"What are we gonna do for cake?"

He smirked. "Well, I sorta have the plan of how it's gonna look, but we did need to kinda decide on the flavor."

"And what design did you decide we're doing?"

"Silver satin look with the white roses and wisteria."

She looked at him. "I kinda love it," Faith said.

"And we had a few options for flavors if you wanted to go taste test."

"Which one did you like?"

"The white and chocolate swirl with raspberry filling and white buttercream."

She looked at him. "And when did you taste test?"

"I didn't. My sister had it for a birthday cake a long time ago and I always loved it."

Faith smirked. "We're going to taste test."

"And what did you want to do about food for the reception?"

"Part of me says small stuff instead of a big meal."

"Or smaller portions?" Faith nodded. "What did you think about the guest list," he asked.

"Everyone that's important. I'm good."

"So, 60 max?"

She nodded. "What do you want to do for the dinner?"

"Part of me says pasta with crab or something. Part of me says surf and turf," Faith said.

"I like the surf and turf idea. We could do crab cakes with it."

She looked at him. "Stop reading my mind."

He smirked. "Salad?" She nodded and he realized that they'd actually planned the food.

When Ridge heard the swoosh of the sliding door, he looked over and saw two seafood cobb salads. "What's this," Ridge asked.

"Cobb salad minus the tomatoes. I added in the crab meat," she teased.

Faith smirked. "My fave. Thank you," she said.

"Most welcome. Glad to see y'all are doin better," her housekeeper said as she headed inside. Ridge smirked.

"What," Faith asked.

"Like your extra Mom."

"Something like that," Faith replied. They had their lunch and relaxed for a little bit. "Still watching everywhere," Faith asked.

"My job remember," he teased.

"Ridge, you're off the clock for the next 10 minutes. Relax."

They relaxed and enjoyed the summer breeze and the saltwater scents of their beach. The one they'd grown up on. The one that they'd played on. The place where he'd kissed her for the first time. Where her parents had met up again. Where every good memory had started. It was calm and serene. No stress, no worry about random gunman attacking. Nothing. Faith finished her salad and walked over to Ridge and kissed him.

"What," he asked as she wrapped her arms around him.

"I love you."

"I love you back," he said as he kissed her.

"What would you think about going upstairs," Faith said.

"I think your doctor is coming and you have to behave."

She shook her head. "Over-rated," she teased.

He kissed her and got up, bringing the dishes inside with her right behind him. She had his towel, the phones, and his gun. He took the towel, handed Faith the phones and put his gun in the lockbox and put it in the safe. Conner nodded.

"Let Kellen know."

Conner nodded and Faith walked upstairs with Ridge. "And what exactly did you want," Ridge teased.

She slid her t-shirt off and undid her bikini. "Faith."

"What?"

"What are you up to?"

She walked over and slid his shirt off. "Come with me."

"Where?"

"Shower."

He shook his head. "Faith." She walked into the bathroom, dropping her shorts and her bikini bottoms. He shook his head, put her clothes into the laundry, pulled his shorts off and went and hopped into the shower with her.

He shook his head and Faith kissed him. "Really?"

She nodded and grabbed her shampoo, washing her hair. When she felt his fingers take over the scalp massage, she leaned up against him. "Faith."

"Not doing anything," she teased. "Just feels good."

He shook his head, kissed her and slid her under the water. "Ridge."

"What?"

"Now that we have the idiots out of the way, what..."

"If you say move it up, I'm kicking some butt."

She kissed him. "What if we go somewhere just you and me?"

"Such as," he asked.

"We can go to Myrtle beach or Pawleys or something."

"Or Bluffton to the resort."

She smirked. "I'll see if I can book something."

She kissed him and he grabbed her conditioner, combing it through her hair with his fingers. She sat him on the bench and slid into his lap. "Yes Faith."

"What you doin tonight?"

"Sleeping."

She smirked. "Movie rematch."

He shook his head. "Not when you just…"

She kissed him. "If she gives me the go-ahead."

He kissed her. "Up."

"Is that a yes?"

"We'll see," he said as he slid her under the water and stepped out.

He went and slid into is boxers then a pair of jeans and pulled his tee on. When she came out of the bathroom naked, he shook his head. "Faith."

"All yours sexy," she teased as she kissed him and walked into her closet to grab something to wear. He shook his head, checked his phone, and almost snapped. "What," Faith asked.

"Zack is out."

Faith looked at him. "How?"

"I don't know love. Hopefully, he stays as far from here as possible. They got a restraining order, so at least that's a good thing."

"Meaning?"

"Meaning I'm glad we have two security guys with us." She kissed him.

They came downstairs and curled up on the sofa while she waited on the doctor. She intentionally put her hair into a ponytail and he shook his head. "What," she asked.

"Nothin," he replied.

She kissed him. "Remind you of anything?"

He took a deep breath. "You're just begging to relive it."

She nodded and kissed him. "Talk to the doctor then." She smirked and he shook his head. "I've created a monster," he joked.

She kissed him and they watched a movie while they waited. When the doctor showed, Faith kissed him. "And how are you feeling," her doctor asked.

"Antsy and determined to get my life back," Faith teased. She walked upstairs with the doctor and she checked Faith over.

"You still cramping," the doctor asked.

Faith shook her head. "I'm fine. I'm just way too antsy to sit here anymore."

"Well, so long as you promise to use something for a while, you're okay to do whatever. If it hurts, stop. That's the deal." Faith nodded. "You need to give yourself time. You're mostly alright, but you need to take your time. Don't just jump into things."

"Bubble bath?"

"Fine," the doctor said.

"Thank you."

"Remember what I said. Protection for the next few weeks."

Faith nodded and came downstairs with her. "And how's the patient," Ridge asked as Kellen came inside.

"She's got the semi-all clear. Just remember what I said alright," the doctor replied. Faith nodded and walked her out.

"I don't know how you talked her into it," Ridge teased.

She kissed him. "I didn't need to," Faith replied.

He shook his head and she slid into his arms. "Just keep getting away with everything," he teased.

"Always" she joked.

He kissed her and her legs slid around his hips. "What," he teased.

"Movie night round 2," she teased as she whispered in his ear.

He shook his head and kissed her. "Faith, we're not discussing that."

She smirked and kissed him. "What did you want for dinner," Ridge asked.

"I want to go out. We don't have to watch…"

"Yeah, we still do."

"I want to go out and have dinner just you and me. That allowed," Faith asked.

"If you want. Name the place and we'll go," he said.

Faith smirked. "You know where."

He called Tavern and Table, reserved a table and they headed over. "In that good of a mood," Ridge asked as they headed over.

"That determined to get our lives back. It's done."

He kissed her at the light. "I love you. I do. Just remember that you're taking it easy."

She smirked. "If that's what you wanna call it."

He shook his head, pulled in and found a parking spot, paid for parking, and walked into the restaurant hand in hand with Faith. He got her chair for her and they sat down to dinner. "And," he asked.

"And what?"

"You aren't doing anything insane tonight. You know that right?"

Faith smirked. "Movie night and I get to see what was in that box of stuff you ordered."

He shook his head. "Faith."

"What?"

"You really have no idea what you're talkin about."

"Yeah I do. I know part of what…"

"Can I take your drink order," the waitress asked.

"Jack and coke please," Ridge said.

"Same for me," Faith replied.

"Dinner order?" Ridge looked at Faith. They both ordered their shrimp and she had one heck of a look on her face.

"What," Ridge asked.

"Just picturing what was in that box."

He shook his head. "Faith."

"What?"

"Not happening."
"Why?" He shook his head again and the drinks showed.

"Because I said so. They aren't yours."

"Do I get to know what's in it?"

"Eventually, but it isn't happening now."

She gave him another look. "Don't go there Faith. Just don't."

She smirked. "You know, I could just go in and…"

"Nope."

"Ridge, come on." Dinner came out a few minutes later and she was still trying to get the answer.

"Faith, stop asking."

"Tell me then."

He shook his head. "I love you, I always will. Just stop asking."

They finished dinner and walked down the boardwalk together. "Just give me a hint."

"You're like a dog with a dang bone woman. Stop."

"Ridge."

"When you stop asking we can finish our walk," he said.

"Come on."

He shook his head. "You'll know when I say you will."

She smirked as they walked the rest of the pathway. When he knew nobody was behind them or anywhere near them, he turned and looked at her. "What," Faith asked.

"Remember when I said that we were taking it easy?"

Faith nodded. "What about it," she asked as she sat down on the bench.

"I meant it. All of that stuff is on hold for a while."

"Why?"

He looked at her. "Faith, don't get me wrong. I love you and I love being with you. If you don't know that now, I doubt you ever would. Fact is, we can't just jump in with both feet right after that. We can't."

"Ridge, she said we..."

"We aren't jumping in full steam ahead to the way we were. I'm not doing it."

She looked at him. "So, now you're just gonna not..."

"Faith."

"We aren't..."

"I didn't say we weren't. I said that what happened before is not happening tonight. Not that far anyway."

She looked at him like he'd just kicked her when she was down. "Meaning what?"

"Meaning we aren't going for the entire meal if you know what I mean." She looked at him. "Take our time easing back into it."

"Why?"

"Because I don't want you to be in flipping pain. The doc said..."

"I don't care what she said to you."

Ridge shook his head. He took her hand and walked back towards the truck. "I'm the only one that decides what's too damn much Ridge."

"Then decide," he said as he kept walking and made his way to the truck. He opened her door, got in on his side and waited.

He heard a thud on his tailgate and turned to see Faith sitting out there. He shook his head, took a deep breath, hopped out, closed her door, and came around the back. "Why? Why can't we just go back to how it was before we even knew we were?"

"Because we don't have a dang time machine. We can't just keep going the way we were. Your body can't handle it after what happened."

"Ridge."

"Baby, I get it. You're determined to move on. Just take it easy for now until we know. I didn't say we never would. I said we ease our way back into it."

"I'm done Ridge. I'm done feeling like crap because it happened. I just want us back to the way we were."

"We are. That's the only part of it we have to ease our way back into. If you're feeling okay, we keep going. You aren't, we stop. It's for you baby. Just you."

She shook her head and looked at him. When she got up, he hoped that she would just get in the truck and come home, but she walked off. He took a deep breath, locked up the truck and followed, just to make sure she was alright.

"Stop following me."

"Faith, if I have to pick you up and put you in the dang truck myself I will." She kept walking and got all the way back down to the end of the boardwalk when he cornered her.

"What?"

"You want something, fine. You want things to go back to how it was before all of this, fine. You're in pain, I'm stopping."

He picked her up, carried her back down the boardwalk and put her in the truck, locked her door and got in, heading back towards the house. "I'm not fragile Ridge."

He didn't say anything. Not one single word. Saying the words that were on the tip of his tongue would've scared the crap out of her and made her disappear to Mom and Dad's house. She'd be gone for good and never come near her again.

He got back to the beach house, got her door, locked up the truck and walked into the house. Faith followed. When he walked upstairs to the main bedroom, he grabbed his bag and put what he'd brought into the bag and took it back downstairs. "What are you doing," Faith asked. He put the bag in the security room and got his gun case from the safe, putting it into the bag then zipped it up.

"Ridge."

He walked into the kitchen, got himself a drink and walked outside, sitting down on the beach with his Jack. He was past livid. Way past it. He needed to get the anger out somehow. When he heard steps behind him, he was about to snap when he saw Kellen. "What?"

"Faith said you went silent."

"Has nothing to do with you Kellen."

"Your stuff is in the security office. It does." Ridge looked at him and Kellen shook his head. "You gonna tell me what happened?"

"No."

Kellen looked at him. "Go for a run. Get it out of your system."

Ridge shook his head. "I can't."

"Ridge, you need to get it out of your system. Go swim. Run. Something." Ridge took a gulp of his drink. "You do realize that you're gonna completely snap right?"

"Either I leave and put her life in jeopardy or I stay and be pissed off," Ridge said.

"Then stay," he heard. He turned around and saw her sitting on the steps. He shook his head and walked down the beach.

When Faith got up to follow him, Kellen held her back.

"Give him a few to cool off. You don't want to be near him right now."

"He took his stuff…"

"I know. Give him space."

Faith shook her head and walked inside. She went up and slid into joggers and a hoodie and got a sweet tea, then walked outside and waited for him to come back. She grabbed a blanket and sat on the steps. When the sun started to set and he still wasn't back, she started to worry. When she saw someone walking down the beach, she hoped. When it wasn't him, she started to worry even more. She walked back inside and sat down on the sofa, watching the sliding door.

Ridge came back down the beach and shook his head. He was still mad. He walked past the beach house and kept going. When he realized that it was almost 9, he walked back and saw the plaque by the deck. The one that Faith had put there when she bought it to commemorate her parents. "It'll never be us," Ridge said silently to himself. He put the glass on the deck and sat on the bottom step, still away from her line of sight. When his phone went off, he shook his head. He stared at the screen, seeing the photo of them he'd taken when they were away. He ignored the call and it rang again. He took a deep breath and let it go to voicemail. When he heard the swish of the sliding door and 4 steps towards him, he didn't move.

"So, you're just gonna take off and not even answer your phone? Seriously?"

"Go inside Faith."

"No."

"Woman, go inside," Ridge said.

"Kellen, I'm not…"

"Miss Faith, please."

Kellen walked outside and saw him. "Walk help?"

Ridge shook his head. "Can you stay with her here tonight?"

"You mean since she'd go postal if you walked out? No."

"I can't be here."

"You proposed to Faith. You can't take that crap back. She's not gonna let you leave without her."

"I don't care. I'll leave and go back to the other house. Let Leo have…"

"Dude, go in and talk to her. Go," Kellen said.

"No."

"Dude, I get it. She is irritating you. You can't leave and not say a damn word. She loves you. She's been sitting on that damn sofa in tears waiting for you. Go and talk to her." Ridge gave him a look that was the equivalent of a grenade being thrown. "You don't have a choice. Go," Kellen said.

Ridge took a deep breath and sat there. Kellen got the

glass, refilled it, walked outside, and handed it to him and Faith came and sat back on the chaise, staring at him.

"Can you please just go inside," Ridge asked.

"No."

He shook his head. "Faith, I get that you want what you want, but it's not happening tonight. May not happen this damn week."

"I don't care Ridge. Come inside."

"No."

"Then I'm coming…"

"No."

"Ridge."

"Just stop." She walked down to where he was sitting, took the glass from his hand and sat down beside him.

"Talk."

"Faith, go inside."

"No." He took a deep breath, staring at the water. He would've walked to his Mom and Dad's if he could've.

"Ridge."

"Why can't you understand that I was doing what I was doing for you? You've never gone through that before. You don't know how you're gonna feel. You don't know anything past feeling fine now. I'm doing it because I give a crap. Maybe it's been too long since someone actually did Faith. Maybe that's why you don't see it. I'm not gonna have you in pain because you're a stubborn pain in my backside."

He got up and walked down to the water and sat down. An hour passed with her sitting there in tears. She finally brushed tears away, calmed down and walked out to him. He finished his drink and felt a blanket across his shoulders. "Ridge."

"Faith, just go inside."

"I get it Ridge."

"No, you don't. Not even a little bit. You wanted me here to protect you. You wanted me to make sure you were alright. I try to do that and you fight me on every damn step. I say that I'm your bodyguard first and you can't handle it. You push until you get what you want. We lose a damn baby and you push until you get to have your sex life back. Like that flipping matters right now. We lost a baby Faith." She tried to hold his hand and he wouldn't. "We lost a child. How can you expect me to forget that and jump back into bed with you? You're just gonna tell me that you won't use any protection like the doctor told you to. I can't keep doing this."

"Doing what Ridge?"

"I can't keep living in fantasy land. Like there's no pain or hurt. I can't." He got up, put the blanket on her shoulders and finished his drink, walking back inside and refilling his drink.

When Kellen tried to stop him, Ridge shook his head and took the bottle. He sat down on the sofa and put the bottle down, gulping down an entire glass to numb the pain. Faith walked back in, took the bottle, put it in the safe, took his glass and put it in the sink and sat down on the chair. Kellen shook his head, knowing a storm was brewing and about to cause a tsunami in a matter of seconds between them. "Faith, just go to bed."

"No."

"I'm sleeping down here."

"No, you aren't Ridge."

He shook his head. "I'm not playing a game with you. I'm not playing that stupid game that you're gonna do whatever to get your way. Not tonight."

Faith looked at him as her eyes started welling up. "I don't want to think about it anymore. I don't. The only thing I can do is try and move on. It hurts. It hurts that we lost that chance. It hurts that it was ours. You hurt as much as I do. I get it. I just need to move past it. That's the only way I know how to survive it. When you got hurt in Jekyll, it killed me. I was petrified that I'd lost the only man that I loved who never let me get away with anything. The only one that loved me for me. Now we lose the only thing that was us. You went and planned the dream wedding to make me feel better, knowing that you didn't. I can't lose you Ridge. I can't."

"Then stop trying to get on with your life and just be the woman I love. We don't have to have fifty shades level sex every damn ten minutes. You can't do it right after that. You have to take your time. You want to be in pain and have me not stop, find someone else to do it."

She looked at him. "Can you just hold me tonight then?"

He looked at her. "You don't want that Faith."

"Tonight, I'll take it." She got up and walked over to him, sliding into his lap and hugged him. He shook his head and leaned back, taking her with him. She slid her legs around him and kissed him. "I don't wanna fight with you. I don't," Faith said.

"I'm not doing it to hurt you Faith." She kissed him and he leaned her onto the sofa, curled the blanket over them and curled up on the sofa with her.

"I want my best friend back."

She kissed him and he kissed her forehead. "I never left," he replied. She kissed him again and he snuggled her tight to him.

"Come to bed."

"Faith."

"Just come upstairs and come to bed. I promise you."

He took a deep breath and they got up, walking upstairs.

Kellen breathed a sigh of relief. He locked up, did a quick perimeter check and came inside. He locked the doors, made sure everything was secure and sat down with a big glass of ice water.

Ridge walked into the bedroom and Faith curled up on the bed, pulling her hoodie off so she wasn't so hot in bed. She had a tank on with the joggers, determined in one way or another to just get Ridge to be calm and not take off in the middle of the night. When he wouldn't sit on the bed, Faith looked at him. "Ridge."

"Just get some sleep."

"Please." He shook his head. "Ridge, you need sleep and so do I. It's been a long day. Just come to bed and get some rest." He shook his head and looked out the bedroom window. "Do you want to go back to the house?"

"Just go to sleep Faith."

She got up, walked over to him, and stood in front of him, wrapping her arms around him. "Come," she said. He shook his head. "Ridge."

He looked at her. "I can't."

"Ridge, just come lay on the bed with me."

"Faith, go get sleep."

She walked him to the bed, pushed him on it and looked at him. "Talk to me."

He shook his head and Faith slid into his lap. "I love you. I get it. I just want you to lay down with me."

"Faith."

She kissed him. "Just lay down." He shook his head. She kissed him again and felt his arms wrap around her. "Please." He took a deep breath. "I'm sorry. I don't know how to fix this Ridge. I don't know how to fix what happened either. I'm not losing you because of it too." She kissed him again and he kissed her back. That kiss went on until they were curled up on the bed together. "You wearing jeans to bed," Faith asked.

"You trying something?"

She shook her head. She heard his shoes fall to the floor then saw his jeans slide to the floor. She pulled the blankets up and curled up in his arms. "That's all I wanted," Faith said. When she looked at him and saw his eyes welling up, she kissed him.

"I love you," he said.

"I know you do. I love you. I'm never letting go Ridge." Something popped back into place. She didn't know what it was, she didn't know what she'd done, but something between them clicked again. "We alright," she asked as she leaned her head on his chest.

"I am just having a hard time getting past it. That's all. I don't know how to," he said.

She kissed him. "Remember that we can still try again

when we're both ready. Not just me complaining. That work?"

"She told me at the hospital that when we're ready to get back to normal, it's not gonna be the same. That's why I didn't want to push. That's why I didn't want anything happening yet."

She took a deep breath. "When we decide we want to, we go from there."

"Can you handle that," Ridge asked.

"If it means having you with me, yes." They both nodded off not long later and Faith held on for dear life all night long.

Chapter 10

When Faith woke up the next morning to an empty bed, she almost lost it until she heard someone sipping coffee. She looked over and Ridge was sitting by the sliding door in her bedroom with his coffee. She got up and walked over to him, kissing him. "Morning handsome," Faith said.

"I brought you coffee," Ridge said as she saw the iced latte on her bedside table.

"What time did you wake up?"

"5."

"We didn't get to bed until 11," she said.

"I know. I snapped last night. I'm sorry," Ridge said.

"That's how you felt. Pushing me away didn't exactly feel good."

"Like I said, I'm sorry." She kissed him, put his coffee cup by her drink and slid into his lap. "What are you up to?"

"Kissing my fiancée good morning," she said as she kissed him again. When she felt his arms around her, he deepened the kiss until she got goosebumps. "Ridge."

"Yes," he said.

"You okay?"

He nodded. "I went for a run this morning and got the coffees. I just needed time to calm down."

"You coming back to bed?"

He shook his head. "Why don't we go back to the house today?"

Faith looked at him. "You sure?"

He nodded. "So long as we're going back okay, sure." He kissed her and went to get up. Her legs slid around him.

"Faith." She kissed him again and he picked her up and leaned her back onto the bed. "What do you want Faith?"

She looked at him. "I want us to curl up in bed and have our coffee together."

He shook his head and kissed her. "And that's why your legs are wrapped around me." She nodded. "Naked," he joked.

"Up to you," she teased.

He shook his head, kissed her, and leaned into her arms. "We're getting up," he said. Faith shook her head. He kissed the tip of her nose, unlocked her legs from around him and slid her onto the bed. "Drink your coffee," he said as he handed it to her.

She had her coffee and he sat down on the bed with her. "Ridge."

"Yes Faith."

"I missed this."

"The coffee?" She nodded.

He shook his head. "I had a feeling you'd want it." "

Can we go for a swim before we leave?"

"Depends. Are you gonna try putting that way too tiny bikini on?"

"It's the only one I brought," she joked.

He shook his head. "You're full of it and you know it. I bet I could find 10 other ones that actually covered you up more."

"Nope," Faith teased as she took a gulp of her coffee. She kissed him and got up, changing into her bikini. She slid an almost mesh cover-up over it and came into the bedroom.

"Seriously Faith." She brushed her hair, brushed her teeth, and came back into the bedroom and curled up on the bed with him. "Someday, I'm gonna get you one that actually covers your backside."

"Tan lines," she teased.

"You don't sit out there long enough for tan lines and you know it."

She smirked and kissed him, finishing her coffee. "Are you coming swimming with me?"

"Faith."

"Are you?" He kissed her and finished his coffee, pulling on swim shorts. "You start something in the water and I'm dunking you. You know that right?"

She smirked. "Maybe," she teased.

He shook his head, got the coffee cups, and came downstairs. Faith handed him the cell phones and they made their way down the steps. "So, are we heading to the house," Kellen asked.

"Someone is determined to go swimming for a while. I think we're gonna head back after," Ridge said as he put the cups in the washer. Kellen motioned for Ridge to come.

"You sure you're alright after last night," Kellen asked.

"I blurted all of it out on the beach. All of it. She knows how I feel. I know how she feels too. I needed to come to terms with it, and drinking didn't exactly help."

"You wouldn't put it down. I tried," Kellen said.

"I know. I appreciate it. I just needed to throw something or punch something."

"And?"

"Kicked sand."

Kellen smirked. "Calmer?"

"I will be. Maybe a swim will do me good."

Kellen nodded and Ridge went to grab his gun from his

bag. "Leave it. I'll be out there," Kellen said as he got a refill of coffee and sat out on the deck.

Ridge walked outside and saw Faith. "You coming with me," she asked.

He kissed her, picked her up and ran for the water, diving in with her in his arms, soaking her to the bone. When he surfaced, she shook her head. "Had to soak me."

He nodded and laughed then splashed her to soak her again. "I swear, you…"

He pulled her to him. "What," he teased.

"I guess you're feeling better," Faith said.

He kissed her and swam out further in the water. When he made it back towards her, he slid underwater then surfaced right in front of her. "About time," Faith teased.

He smirked. "And what did you want," he teased.

"You."

"I bet," he teased as she slid her arms and legs around him. He got to a spot where he was standing on the bottom with water up to his neck. "And," he asked.

"What?"

"You swear what," he teased.

"You splash me again, I swear, I'll dunk you."

"Hard to do when I'm taller Faith."

She kissed him. "I would."

"I bet you would." She slid her legs tighter around him. "What," he teased.

"Are we okay?"

He nodded. "We will be. I just needed time to calm myself down."

She kissed him. "Better," she teased.

"Depends on what else you're up to." She smirked. He shook his head and Faith nodded. "Faith. We're swimming, then heading back."

She shook her head and kissed him again. He shook his head and she smirked. "Ridge."

"What?"

"Are you swimming with me?"

He kissed her and she slid into the water intentionally. He dove under a wave and swam out as she caught up to him and dunked him. What she didn't notice was that her bikini bottoms got loose. She swam closer and felt one side of them completely undone. She looked at him. "Told ya," he teased as he swam even deeper out into the water. She went after him and by the time she caught up to him, he was making his way to the shore. "Ridge," Faith said.

"You just noticed," he teased. She shook her head and

chased him all the way up to the dock.

"Ridge."

He smirked and wrapped her up in the towel. "You seriously started this just to…"

He kissed her. "Yep." She shook her head and he smirked. "Come. Breakfast and we can head back to the house."

"Ridge."

"What?"

"Eat then we have plans."

"Where?"

She looked at him and he shook his head. "Not discussing it." She shook her head and they came inside to see Eggs Benedict waiting for them.

"You didn't have to do all of this," Ridge said.

"Yeah I did. You're both in a better mood today. Are we heading back to the house," her housekeeper asked.

Faith nodded. "Someone wants to go home."

"I didn't say that. I said we should go back. You have to actually go to work Monday and your stuff is at the house. That's it," Ridge said as they both ate.

"You sure there isn't another reason?"

He shook his head. "Nope," he replied as Faith shook her

head and finished her breakfast. "I'll stay and clean up a little and meet you over there. Is there anything special you wanted for dinner," her housekeeper asked.

"Let me take care of dinner," Ridge said.

"You sure?"

Ridge nodded. She agreed, they finished eating and Ridge helped clean up when he felt Faith's arms slide around him. "What," he asked. She took his hand and walked him upstairs.

"Faith."

"What?"

He shook his head and she walked him into the bedroom. "What would you like," he asked.

Faith sat him on the bed. "You."

"And?"

She slid onto his lap. "Before..."

He kissed her. "Get dressed."

"Why?"

He kissed her. "Because we're leaving."

"Ridge." He shook his head.

"Before..." He kissed her and leaned her onto the bed. "Get dressed." She slid the bikini bottoms off. "Faith." She took the bikini top off, throwing it to the floor. "I told you."

"And I say kiss me."

He kissed her, devouring her lips until she was trying to pull his swim shorts off. "I know what you're doing," he said as he kissed down her neck.

"I want you," she said.

"Faith." She kissed him and the kiss deepened until her heart was racing. That kiss led to making out and her untying the drawstring of his shorts. "Off," she said.

He kissed her and she peeled them off. "We have..."

"I don't care."

He reached for the drawer, grabbing one of the condoms he'd left just in case. He slid it on and Faith's legs tightened around his hips. "Slow," he said. Faith kissed him and he nibbled down her torso. When her toes started curling, he smirked. He loved how that looked. He kissed her hip and she was reaching for him. All he gave her was one hand. He nibbled her inner thigh and Faith's back arched. She knew where he was heading. When he kissed her at the apex of her thighs, her heart started pounding even harder. "You good," Ridge asked.

"Come here."

He shook his head and started teasing even more until her legs were almost twitching. "Not done yet," he teased. Faith pulled at his hand. When he did move up her torso, she pulled her legs around him.

"Ridge."

"Faith, promise me." She kissed him as his fingers continued to tease.

"Anything," she said as she waited for that full feeling again. The one she'd craved since she'd been in the hospital. The one she begged for. He devoured her lips, muffling her cries and gave her what she'd begged for. Slowly, he slid deeper and deeper. Her legs pulled him tighter to her and he couldn't fend her off. The sex was mind-blowing. Slow and torturous, but still insane. When her body climaxed once, twice, three times, he sped up. "Harder," she said.

He shook his head and Faith's legs pushed him further. When he climaxed and crumbled into her arms, she kissed him. "You alright," he asked.

Faith nodded and kissed him as he deepened the kiss until the goosebumps came out. "Holy crap," Faith said.

"What," he asked as he slid to his back and her leg curled around him as her head rested on his chest.

"I missed you. I really missed you."

"Faith."

She looked at him. "What?"

"You sure you're alright?"

"A little sore, but nothing that will stop me from walking," she joked.

He shook his head. "Happy now?"

"Nope."

He shook his head. "Never happy," he teased.

"Movie night." He laughed.

"Maybe take it easy."

She shook her head. "I want things back to the way we were. That's all. When we're together, I feel close again. I crave that closeness. That's all Ridge. It's like we're one. Like we clicked back together. I don't want us being apart."

"Faith."

"What?"

"I love you."

She kissed him. "And I love you fiancée."

They got up a little while later, showered and got dressed to head back. "Ridge."

"Yep."

"Can we stop off and get seafood on the way home?"

He smirked. "Already ordered it for delivery to the house. Saves us a little time," he said.

"Ridge." He looked at her as she came out in a mini skirt and a tank.

"Faith, put on actual clothes."

"These are clothes," she said with a smirk.

"Ones that actually cover your backside." She kissed him and slid on a skirt that was just slightly longer with a slit. "Woman, do I have to dress you?"

She kissed him. He handed her a pair of jean shorts and shook his head.

"I like the skirt better."

"And I know why. Driving Faith. Concentrating on the road." She smirked and kissed him. He freshened up, made sure he had his toiletry bag, put it downstairs in his bag and Faith followed as Kellen went up and grabbed her overnight bag.

"Are we allowed to leave," Ridge teased.

Faith kissed him and gave him a hug. "Now we can head out."

He shook his head, put the bags in the truck and helped her into the passenger side. Kellen organized flipping back to the other house and Calvin headed back to the beach house. Ridge and Faith stopped off at Starbucks, got coffees for them and for Kellen, handing him one before they headed back and got on the road. "Ridge."

"Yep."

"I was fine. If I was sore, I would've told you."

"Good."

She slid her hand in his and he linked their fingers. "You feeling better?"

He nodded. "You get why now right?"

She nodded. "I am stubborn."

"You just figured that out," he teased.

"I love you," she said.

"Love you back beautiful."

"Are we gonna have our movie night?"

"I swear, you are seriously having issues with that one-track mind," Ridge said.

"We can watch a normal movie and just hang out."

"Tried that when you were watching gone with the wind."

She smirked. "What's your option?"

"Sweet Home Alabama," he teased.

"I like it," Faith replied.

"Or Blind Side."

"Football brain," she teased.

When they got to the house, the seafood delivery was just showing. "Thank you," Ridge said as he gave the guy a tip. They took everything into the house and Ridge came outside and grabbed the bags. He took them upstairs and saw Faith sitting on the bed. "What," he asked.

She motioned for him to come closer. "What," he asked again as he came closer. Faith kissed him. "What?"

"Marry me."

"Kinda already am," he teased.

"Just us."

"Faith, we talked about this."

She kissed him. "You and I. City hall. We can do it our way."

"We're doing it our way."

"Ridge."

He kissed her. "What if we went and figured out the cake. Get your mind off it."

"Do the one we talked about. The chocolate raspberry."

"Faith."

"Can she drop it off here?"

He nodded. She looked at him. "Why are we rushing it now?"

"Because I literally thought 24 hours ago that we were calling it off."

He looked at her. "Why would you even think that?"

"Because it felt like it. You wouldn't let me near you, you wouldn't talk to me and you wouldn't even breathe near me. That's why."

He shook his head. "Babe, you need to know that when I start losing it, I can't have anyone near me. I need to calm myself and if that takes a few hours, so be it."

She looked at him. "Meaning?"

"My old way of dealing with it was punching the crap out of a punching bag. I know that you want things that sometimes I say no to. I do. If I say no, we have to leave that alone. We discuss it calmly."

She nodded. "I can't lose you Ridge."

He kissed her. "You're never going to."

He sat down with her and wrapped his arms around her. "You stomp your feet and throw a fit when you aren't getting your way. I get it. You get mad, storm off or do things that I say not to. When I'm mad, I'm silent and push everyone and everything away until I can calm myself. That's the way I've always been. When you went away to school, I snapped and refused to come inside. I sat on the porch swing for an entire day. My Mom thought I was losing my mind. I don't say things I don't mean. I don't intentionally hurt anyone unless I have to or I'm pushed. I shouldn't have said…"

"Ridge, I get it. You needed to say it. Hell. I needed to hear it. I was going too far."

He kissed her. "Just remember that I don't do things to hurt you. I knew what you wanted. I wanted it too, but what the doc said was ringing in my head. I couldn't. Sometimes I have reasons that you don't even know beautiful." He headed downstairs and she followed, sitting him on the sofa.

She kissed him and slid onto his lap. "So, now that we're home, what do you want to do?"

"You're getting work done." She smirked. He shook his head. "Actual work. The stuff your Dad pays you to do."

"He told me to take time."

"I bet. I don't exactly think that he thought that you'd be exercising your dirty mind instead of feeling better," he joked as he kissed her.

"Never know handsome."

He shook his head. "Behave."

She shook her head. "Not much fun," Faith joked.

He kissed her and snuggled her. "Behave for once in your life. Just until after dinner."

She smirked and nodded. At least she'd managed to get him out of whatever funk he'd been in. "And what else are we gonna do tonight then?"

"Eat dinner, clean up, sleep."

"Ridge."

"Maybe a movie. Depends on how much work you get finished," he joked.

"Funny. You can't really have that many emails can you?"

"I own the company. There's 50 of us that do security stuff Faith."

"Seriously?"

"You never even looked at the resume when I brought it to you."

"That was a couple insane months ago. I can't really memorize..."

"What was it?"

"Ridge."

"Say it," he teased. She smirked and kissed him. "And?"

"First off, I know you..."

"Faith."

"When you showed, I forgot all about a resume," she said.

He kissed her. "And?"

"If I hadn't known you, I still would've…"

"What?"

"I never remembered you like this."

"With muscles?"

She nodded with a smirk. "You hired me because you thought I was sexy."

"Partially. You do know more about me than anyone else."

"And because I'm sexier than I used to be as a scrawny teenager." She smirked and he shook his head. "What am I gonna do with you? Dirty mind from the first day we saw each other again."

"Your fault." He shook his head and got up. "Where are you going?"

He got her laptop and typed in the website for his company then handed it to her.

"What," Faith asked.

"My company," he replied.

"This is huge."

"4 offices. Luckily, you got the boss to help you out," he joked. Faith put her laptop down and slid into his lap. "What?" She kissed him. "Faith."

She slid her laptop from his hands and kissed him again.

"You're behaving until tonight. Emails." She closed her laptop, grabbed it, took his hand, and got up. "What are you up to," Ridge asked. Faith walked him upstairs to their bedroom. "Faith."

She closed the door and sat him back on the bed. "What," she asked as she slid her laptop onto the bedside table.

"You're getting work done." She slid on top of him and leaned into his arms. Within minutes, he had her pinned to the bed. "What are you up to Faith."

She kissed him. "Nothin," she teased as he felt her leg slide around his. He shook his head and kissed her with a kiss that turned her toes into pretzels, gave her butterflies and goosebumps at the same time and had her wanting him even more.

"What," he asked.

"Don't wanna wait until tonight."

He kissed her again with a kiss that had both of her legs wrapped around his hips. "You're waiting."

She shook her head. "No."

He nodded. "Like I said. We get work done then we can..."

She kissed him and tried to talk him into it to no avail. "Ridge."

"Nope. I know what you want. I have every day since I got here. You can wait until tonight," he teased.

"Ridge." He kissed her with a kiss that had her almost melting. Her heart pounded against his. She was almost trembling in his arms. "Ridge," she said as he kissed down her neck.

"Faith," he said.

"I need you."

"Then get some work done."

She shook her head and he nibbled at her breast through her shirt. "Come here."

He shook his head. She reached for him and he smirked. "What," he asked.

"I'm not waiting."

"Yeah you are," he replied as he kissed her and got up. He untied her legs from around him and stood up. "Work."

"Come here." He shook his head.

She grabbed his hand and pulled him back on top of her. "You can't just do that and leave the room," she said.

"Yeah I can," he teased. She shook her head. "And why is that?"

"You tell me." She slid his hand to the apex of her thighs and he smirked.

"You…"

She kissed him. "What?"

"You can wait," he teased.

She shook her head. "Ridge, stop teasing."

"I thought that's what you loved," he joked. She kissed him and he taunted her even more, still not giving her what she wanted. She pulled her lacy panties off and he shook his head. "Faith."

"You started it."

"And here I thought you lusting after your bodyguard started it."

She kissed him and felt his fingers starting to taunt her. "Ridge," she said as she was digging her nails into his back.

"What," he whispered as the goosebumps got goosebumps.

Her heart was pounding and with every touch of his hand, she was almost shaking. Just as her body was reaching its peak and the kiss was almost as hot as what they were doing, her body was borderline about to explode when he stopped. "Ridge."

He smirked and kissed her. "What?"

"Why did you stop?"

He devoured her lips again and kept going until her body exploded. When he kept going then stopped again, she was almost overwhelmed. "You gonna behave now," he asked. She kissed him with a kiss that could've turned gold into liquid and he smirked as her body climaxed again. "Now, what were you saying," he whispered as she went for the button of his jeans. "Faith."

"Now." He shook his head and she reached and handed him a condom from her drawer. "Now Ridge."

He kissed her and she undid his jeans. "Don't."

She pulled the zipper down and he stopped her. "Faith."

"Now. Right now, Ridge. Please." He shook his head and did as she asked.

Her body throbbed around him like he was one of the buzzing toys that he'd got to taunt her with. This time, there was no taking it slow. There was her pulling him to her until he couldn't say no. He devoured her lips and she tried more than once to lean him onto his back until he had her hands linked with his and pinned to the bed. They kept going and this time, she wouldn't let him take it slow. When she whispered harder, he shook his head and gave her exactly what she wanted. That morning had been the test. Now, it was playful. She couldn't move, and she didn't care. When he reached his climax, her body tightened around him and he smirked.

"All mine," he joked as he kissed her neck.

"Ridge."

"What?"

"I want you."

"Good," he teased. He slid to his back and she curled up to him. "Happy now," he joked.

"I don't know that I can walk."

"Good," he joked. Faith kissed him and they curled up together. "So, that's really why you hired me. Nice going sexy," he teased.

"You're lucky you even made it to your truck."

He smirked and kissed her. "And then seeing you out with what's his name that night."

"Holden?" He nodded. "You did kinda save me that night."

He smirked. "Had to. I knew what he was up to."

Faith smirked and snuggled him as he pulled a blanket over them. "And what was that?"

"Knowing what I know now? Probably taking photos of you without your knowledge, drugging your drink."

Faith looked at him. "You think he'd do that?"

Ridge nodded. "He put cameras in your beach house Faith. I wouldn't put anything past his stupid head. I've hated that man since we were in grade school. Fact is, he was shady in high school and he only got worse love. I wasn't letting him near you for anything."

She looked at him. "Ridge."

"Yes my love."

She smirked. "I love you."

"Love you too. Always." She kissed him and he snuggled her tight to him. "Are you gonna actually get work done?"

She smirked. "Could just stay in bed," she teased.

"Or we actually get work done and get it out of the way so we can watch that movie tonight." She kissed him and pulled him to her. He leaned her onto her back and kissed up her neck. "We're getting up like it or not wife to be."

He got up, went into the bathroom to clean up a little and came out, grabbing his boxers and his jeans. "Seriously getting up," Faith asked.

He nodded, leaned over and kissed her and handed Faith her joggers and his hoodie. "Really?"

He nodded. "Get work done sexy. You may get an appetizer tonight."

Faith shook her head and got up. "Fine, but tonight, I pick the movie."

He kissed her again and sat her on the counter. "If you actually get work done, we can negotiate on the movie." When Faith got that Cheshire grin, he shook his head. "Woman, quit."

She kissed him. "Fine, but I get to pick the movie."

"Maybe." One more kiss and he left her on her own, made

up the bed and walked back downstairs to see Kellen almost laughing.

"And what are you laughing at," Ridge asked.

"You two made up."

Ridge rolled his eyes. "This isn't high school Kellen. Cut it out."

"At least it wasn't another war. What's up?"

"Nothing. We're doing seafood tonight. Do y'all want any," Ridge asked.

"Sure," Kellen replied as Leo nodded while on the phone with his wife. "

You do know you could just take tonight off right," Ridge said.

"Hold for a sec babe," Leo said as he looked at Ridge. "You sure," Leo asked.

"Sure. Go take her to dinner and a movie. If y'all want to get a babysitter, I can see if it's okay with Faith if she stays tonight with you."

"Ask me what," Faith said as she came downstairs and slid her arms around Ridge's waist.

"You okay if Leo has his wife over here for a date night tonight?"

"Depends. She staying all night," Faith asked.

"If you're okay with it," Leo asked.

"Sure," Faith said as she slid something in Ridge's pocket. She walked into her office, laptop in hand and sat down to go through emails. Leo went and talked to his wife, planning out a date night together. Kellen did another quick perimeter search and Ridge grabbed what she'd slid in his pocket. When he saw black lace panties in his pocket, he shook his head.

He went and sat down on the sofa, going through work emails when he saw a text from Faith on his phone:

> *Like your present?*

He shook his head and replied:

> *Someday I'm gonna have to staple these to you.*

She replied back a minute or two later:

> *Crazy glue. When you're done emails, come in here.*

He shook his head and put his phone down, seeing an email that needed his attention. He went through it, managed a reply, and went through all of the attachments. When he saw that the person that wanted to hire some people on his team were from Charleston, he dug deeper. When he saw that they were friends with her folks, he almost wondered if it was her Dad's way of apologizing. He got a few of the guys that were available to handle it, forwarding them the information that they needed to discuss. He went through the rest of the emails, delegated what he could and saw an email that he couldn't ignore:

> *You really think that I can't still get to her? I can.*
> *Even if I have to knock you off to do it.*

Ridge did a full hunt to find out where the email came from and when he saw it, he was stunned. It wasn't Holden, it wasn't Cameron. He sent the information to the detective that had worked on everything. Within a few minutes, his phone rang.

"Sir," Ridge said.

"When did this email come in?"

"Yesterday. 2pm. Kinda odd," Ridge said.

"It's a good thing we have someone tailing him just in case. Thank you for this," the detective said.

"Most welcome. I guess we're ramping up security here."

"Might be a good plan. If anything happens, text me. You still have my personal cell, yes," the detective asked.

"Yes. Thank you again. We're at the house not the beach house."

"Were you at the beach when the email came in?"

"Yes. She'd just got out of the hospital."

"Alright. We'll get undercovers back at the house for backup."

"Thank you," Ridge said as they hung up.

He got through the rest of the emails, then saw one come in from Faith:

> *Now I got roped into a meeting tomorrow. Thanks. What are you doin out there handsome?*

He smirked, closed his laptop, and came into her office. "Hey," Faith said quietly as she smirked.

"You never ever behave," he said quietly.

She smirked. "Not a problem," Faith said as she hung up.

"When are you…"

She kissed him. "How are your emails now," she asked.

"Caught fire. Had to turn it off," he teased.

"I bet it did."

"Faith, you do realize that I have glue to make these stay on right?"

She kissed him again with a grin ear to ear. "I know. This mean that I'm in trouble?"

"I'm picking the movie."

"And?"

"If I have to, I have handcuffs you know," he teased.

"Promises…"

He picked her up and sat her on her desk. "At some point, you have to stop."

"Why?"

"Because you're supposed to. You aren't even phased by what…"

She kissed him. "I missed my man. That not permitted?" He kissed her to the point that she fully thought that they would be throwing everything from that desk on the floor and he would get her legs shaking all over again.

"No," he said.

"Why?"

He kissed her. "Because you have work to get finished. I'm going to make dinner, and you're putting these back on and finishing your work."

She shook her head. When he slid them on her, teasing as he did, Faith's toes curled. "Leave them. I can take them off with my teeth later," he teased as he whispered in her ear. She looked at him and kissed him. He picked her up, sat her on her desk chair and walked into the kitchen.

He put everything together for dinner, putting his favorite spices into the water to cook the seafood, got the butter ready, chopped everything for the salad and an hour later, felt arms slide around his waist.

"And what do you want," Ridge teased.

"Hungry. Do you need any help?"

He shook his head. "Pour yourself a glass of wine," he teased.

She kissed him and poured them each a Jack and Coke. "Faith."

"What," she asked as she handed Ridge a glass.

"Are you seriously drinking this," he said.

Faith nodded. He kissed her and shook his head. "I do know exactly what you're doing. I told you before. Jack isn't gonna get you any further," he teased.

"Could," she teased. He shook his head and sat her on the counter, away from where he was cooking. "Why are you intentionally trying to stay away from me right now?"

"Because I know what you're up to. You stay there and keep your hands to yourself."

"Now who has the dirty mind," Faith joked.

He shook his head, finished his drink, and finished making the food. When he brought it to the table, Kellen came out of the security office and had dinner with them. "This is freaking amazing," Kellen said.

"Thanks. We all sorta needed this after this week." When Faith's hand slid up Ridge's leg, he shook his head and put her hand back in her lap. When her hand moved back to his leg, he cleaned up the shells and went into the kitchen, putting them into the sealed bag. When he came and sat back down, Faith smirked. He shook his head and they finished off the salad and the last of the seafood. "I put a little aside to have tomorrow in the omelets," Ridge said.

"Seriously," Kellen asked.

"Or in the benedict."

Faith got up to get herself a refill and grabbed Ridge's glass, getting him a refill too. She handed the glass to him and he shook his head. "Thank you for this," Kellen said.

"You're welcome. Thank you for your help this weekend," Faith said as Ridge's arm slid around the back of her chair. Kellen helped Ridge clean up and Faith went and got them each a bowl of sliced fresh peaches. When Ridge came and sat down on the sofa with her, she smirked. Kellen went back into the security office and Ridge shook his head.

"You are seriously cruising to get it."

She got a grin ear to ear. "Peach," she asked.

"Faith."

"What?"

"I know what you're doing."

"You love peaches," she said.

He looked at her. "You kinda forgot the coke in my drink."

"Oops," she teased.

He shook his head. "Faith."

She looked at him. "What?"

"You really want that movie night?"

She nodded. He kissed her, got up and went upstairs. "Where are you going?"

"Back in a minute," he said.

He changed into his comfy beat-up jeans and a zip-up hoodie and came back downstairs. "Really," she said.

"You want to start that little game then I'm getting more clothes on." She kissed him as he sat back down a few minutes later.

She slid up tight to him and handed him the remote. "Which one are we watching," she asked. When he put on the first 365 days movie, she shook her head.

"Not…"

"Not fair? Really," he whispered.

He saw Kellen go to do a perimeter search and kissed her. "New rule."

"What," she asked.

"No taunting or teasing or you lose. You lose, my choice what to do."

"Ridge."

"What?"

"Starting now?"

He paused the movie. "Why," he asked.

She turned to face him and kissed him. "Thank you for tonight."

"Dinner?" She nodded. He kissed her. "Babe, I had to cook. You gave your housekeeper the night off."

"Still."

"You wanted dinner at home. We got it. You wanted movie night, you'll get it, but you still have to follow the rules." She smirked. "I know that look Faith. Hands to yourself or I tie them together." She kissed him until she started to get him all hot and bothered. "I know exactly what you're up to."

"Good. Only fair," she said.

He kissed her and turned her around. "Like I said, you start something, hands are gonna be tied."

"That go for you too?" He shook his head. She giggled and turned around as the movie started.

Chapter 11

He slid the blanket over her as she slid in as tight to him as she could. One move and she would be on top of him. He took a deep breath and she took a sip of her drink. She leaned back and watched the movie. When it got to the one scene she'd always got antsy at, she took another sip of her drink and her hand slid to his thigh. "Faith."

"Just getting comfy."

They made their way through the movie and when it got to the really steamy part, he kissed her neck. He brushed her hair to the side and kissed across her collar bone. When he saw her eyes close, he smirked. His arms slid around her, undoing the zipper of the hoodie. When he felt the lace of her bra, he nibbled at her ear and felt her lean into his arms even more. He smirked and slid his hand under the lace of the bra.

"Ridge."

"Um-hmm," he almost mewed into her ear.

"Um."

"What," he whispered as he felt the goosebumps and the tantalizing reaction they caused. She shook her head, taking a gulp from the glass. "What's wrong," Ridge asked.

"You know what," she said. His hand slid down from there and she shook her head. He kissed her neck again and he knew. He slid his hand out from the way too tempting bra and wrapped them around her waist.

When she felt his hand slide under the waistband of her skirt, her heart started pounding. He could feel her breath start to speed up. When his hand slid to the still uncovered apex of her thighs, he smirked and nibbled at her ear. "What did I say about you leaving them off?"

"The part about glue or something," she teased.

He looked up at the screen and his fingers started teasing. "Ridge."

He kissed her neck again. "Yes," he said as the goosebumps got goosebumps. He kept going until she couldn't handle it anymore. She went to grab the remote and he took it away from her. He kept taunting until she was almost throbbing. "Faith," he said as she shook her head and grabbed his hand.

"You're doing it intentionally."

"This mean I win?"

He kept going and she grabbed his leg. "Ridge."

He paused the movie. "Meaning?"

"You need to stop."

"Nope."

She went to grab his hand and he shook his head. "Faith."

"Give me two minutes." He kept going and felt her body start shaking.

"What," he teased.

"Upstairs." He stopped the movie, turned it off and walked upstairs hand in hand with her, walked into the bedroom and closed the door. He smirked. "What?"

"I even won on a do-over of round one." She kissed him and he sat her on the bed. He drew the curtains and the blackout curtains until the room was pitch black. "Don't move," he said.

He walked into his closet and grabbed a few things from his bag. First was the blindfold, then the other things she had no idea were there. He grabbed condoms from the drawer and slid the blindfold over her eyes. "Ridge." He slid the hoodie off and kissed her. "What are you up to?"

"You wanted to know and were all determined to get your way," he teased.

"Meaning what?"

He smirked and kissed her again as she slid her arms around his neck. She slid the blindfold off. "Tell me what you're doing." He kissed her again, devouring her lips and pulled her skirt right off. He leaned her onto the bed and leaned into her arms.

"Put it back on," he teased. She shook her head and he devoured her lips. When her legs slid around him, he smirked.

"Faith."

"What," she replied.

"You sure that you're ready for this?" He kissed her and she nodded. She kissed him and went for the button of his jeans.

"Faith." She kissed him again and he slid his hands in hers, linking their fingers.

"Tell me what you want baby," he said.

"You can't go around teasing people like that," she teased.

"That's gonna look like child's play."

He slid the blindfold back on and kissed her, kissing down her neck and unzipping the hoodie. She pulled away and slid the hoodie off. He kissed her and she went to slide the blindfold off.

"Faith."

"Not happening."

He kissed her, devouring her lips and slid into her arms. "You are no fun whatsoever," he teased.

She kissed him and he peeled his shirt off. "Now, back to what you were attempting to do," he teased.

She went for the button of his jeans and he shook his head. "Faith."

"What," she asked.

He kissed her, devouring her lips and slid her hands above her head. He shook his head.

"Determined to take over?"

"Partially."

"You do, you never find out what was in the box." He kissed her again and one leg curled around his. He kissed down her neck and she smirked. "Faith."

"What?"

"You can tap out. If you want to."

She nodded as he nibbled at her breast then down her torso. "Ridge."

"Faith."

"What are you doin," she asked. When he got to her inner thigh, her toes were curling. His fingers took over the taunting and she felt his warm breath against her. She couldn't see anything, but she knew that he was determined.

When the taunting started all over again, her body was almost trembling. He nibbled and licked and then nibbled even more until his fingers found just the right spot to get her body throbbing again. "Ridge," she said as he kept going but deeper then even deeper until he could feel her body starting to throb around his fingers. He grabbed the smallest of the items, turning it on and letting it take over. "Oh my god," Faith said as that feeling that she'd craved just intensified. "You were saying," he teased as he nibbled at her even more as her legs wrapped tight around him and her body clenched the buzzing from the inside.

"Ridge."

"Yep," he said as he turned it up ever so slightly.

She dug her nails into his back and he kissed up her torso. "Not fair," Faith said as it kept going and he still teased.

He kissed her and she was almost trembling in his arms. "Still want to know," he teased as he slid it away from her and tossed it into his bag.

"That's what you did intentionally?"

"That's the tiny one," he whispered as she grabbed his hand. He slid up behind her and kissed her neck.

"Now, did you want to see the bigger one," he teased. He felt her undo his jeans.

"You sure you want to try that?" She went to reply and he kissed her, devouring her lips. "Faith."

She turned to face him and he shook his head. "Really?"

She undid his jeans and he shook his head. "Faith, you aren't even through drinks yet," he teased.

"I want you."

"I bet," he joked. He devoured her lips again, did his jeans back up and grabbed the other item he had to taunt her with from his bag as his hand started teasing all over again.

"I can't…"

He kissed her. "Baby."

She went for his jeans again and he stopped her. "Faith, he teased. Her toes were curled and her heart was racing all over again. "Mine," he whispered as all it took was one Moment. One for her to almost crash around him. "Tapping out," he teased as she reached for him and he grabbed the last item he was letting her know about.

"Ridge."

"Wife to be," he said as he nibbled until her legs started twitching.

"I need you." When she heard buzzing again, he smirked and slid back up behind her and let the buzzing do its thing.

He slid it against her and had it on low intentionally. When he felt her body almost trembling in his arms, he kissed her neck. "Tell me if you want me to stop," he whispered.

"No. Don't," she said as he flipped on the other feature to the rabbit.

"Oh damn," Faith said as he smirked.

"Faith," he said as he kicked his jeans to the floor and felt her body throbbing. He found one of the condoms and slid it on. "Faith."

"Oh my god," Faith said as she leaned up against him and didn't feel his jeans. "Please," Faith said.

He slid the rabbit off, knocked it to the floor and she turned to face him. "You okay," he asked.

Her legs slid around him and pulled him tight to her. The minute he got close enough to slide into her, she tried leaning him to his back. He shook his head, devoured her lips and they had sex. Hot, intense, and exactly what she'd begged him for. That's what she'd wanted. She wrapped her legs tight around him until he could barely move. He kept going as Faith's nails dug into his back and her kisses only muffled her moans. When he climaxed, she wouldn't let go. "Faith."

She kissed him and slid him to his back. "What," she asked.

"What are you up to?" She leaned into his arms and he kissed her again, snuggling her to him and leaning her onto her back.

"I don't know that I can breathe," Faith said as she caught her breath.

"And?"

She smirked and kissed him. "I don't know that I could've handled more," Faith said.

"Wow. Did you figure out what they were," he teased.

"I may need that second one."

"For what?"

"For when you're not here." He smirked and shook his head.

"Remind me to keep that one hidden." He kissed her and went to get up.

"Where are you going?"

"Cleaning up," he teased as he kissed her, slid out of bed, grabbed the two items, hiding them away then went into the bathroom. He flipped the hot water on in the shower, slid the condom off and stepped under the stream of hot water.

He cooled the water down just enough when he felt arms slide around him. "Faith."

"What?"

"I thought you were tired."

She smirked and he turned to face her. "I am. Odd question. What was the blindfold for?"

"Since you wouldn't let me do it, I'm not telling," he teased as he leaned over and kissed her. When she sat down on the shower bench, he shook his head. "I know what you're thinking. Not happening Faith. We're going to bed."

She smirked. He shook his head, flipped the water off and

stepped out, wrapping a towel around his hips. "Are you coming to bed," she asked as she stepped out of the shower, wrapped a towel around her and sat on the counter.

"In a minute." She smirked. "Faith."

"What?"

"Stop while you can still walk," he teased. She motioned for him to come closer and he shook his head, leaning into her arms. "What would you like," he asked as he kissed her. When she undid his towel, he shook his head. "Faith."

"What?"

"You tapped out. You're getting sleep."

"Totally over-rated," she said as she pulled him to her. When she went to slide her hand to him, he backed away.

"Not tonight." He kissed her, slid the towel back on and went into his closet.

When he emerged 10 minutes later, she was in his t-shirt sitting on the bed. "I love you. You know that right," Ridge asked. Faith nodded with a smirk. "Do I need to take you shopping for pajamas?"

She smirked. "Kinda love this shirt."

"Why?"

"Your favorite one. Smells like you." He shook his head and kissed her then hopped into the bed on his side.

"Really," she said.

"Babe, sleep. You need to rest." She slid under the blankets and slid over to him. "Faith."

"What?"

"If you think that starting something is gonna help you sleep, you are not gonna like my reply." Her leg slid around his and she curled into his arms.

"You sure?"

He nodded and kissed her forehead. "You need sleep, and I probably have scars on my back right now," he said.

She slid a little further and he shook his head, flipping her to her back. "Faith, we aren't."

She nodded and he shook his head, kissing her until she had goosebumps on top of goosebumps and her toes were curling into triple knots. "Now, what were you saying about you don't need sleep," he asked.

She kissed him and when he felt her hand on him, he shook his head and she kept going until he was too turned on. "Still need sleep," Faith asked.

He kissed her, grabbed a condom from the drawer and shook his head. "Faith, you keep doing this and you're gonna need more than a few hours to sleep."

She went to dip her head down and he shook his head, pulling her to him. He pulled her hands away, flipped the light off and slid the condom on. "Faith."

"What?"

"You sure?" She kissed him and he linked their fingers, holding her hands above her head. "Faith." She looked at him.

"Come here."

She went to kiss him and he shook his head. Her legs slid around him and he shook his head. "What?"

He kissed her, nibbling at her lips. "Faith, roll over."

She shook her head. He turned her to her stomach and she slid backwards until her body bumped into his. "Two options," he whispered as her goosebumps popped up on her skin again. "Why are you shaking," he asked.

"Heart racing," she replied. He kissed from her backside up her spine so slowly, bending her forwards. "Ridge."

"Yes," he whispered as she felt the kisses make their way back down her back. She felt a hand against her. "I swear, you are too much," he teased as his hands started to tease her until he felt her getting that much more turned on.

"Ridge."

He kissed the base of her spine. "Faith."

"Please." When he saw her hand try to slide towards him, he shook his head and put it behind her back. She could feel his warmth near her, and it just got her more hot and bothered.

"You sure you want to go there," he teased.

Faith nodded. She felt him against her and the moment he got close to them having sex again, the teasing intensified. "I need you," Faith said.

"I bet you do," he joked. He slid into her and she almost gasped. Intense was an understatement. He taunted and teased and took it so slow it was almost too much for her to handle.

"Ridge," Faith said as her heart was racing and her breath was almost ragged.

"Faith," he said as he went deeper.

"Harder."

"Nope. My rules remember," he teased.

She tried getting her way and the taunting went into overdrive. "Please," she begged.

"What," he teased coming up with one thing that could completely drive her insane. He gave her what she wanted and threw a whole new level of taunting into it. When her body clamped down on him and crashed into orgasm, he sped up even more until he collapsed at her side. "Holy crap," Faith said.

"What?"

"Had to find a new way to make everything hotter," Faith

said.

"I have a million tricks you haven't even seen," he teased as she slid to his side and wrapped her arm and leg around him. "Sleep," he said.

She kissed him and he got up to clean up. When he came back to bed, she was out cold. He smirked, slid into bed, put the phones on the charger, finished his drink and slid under the blankets with her, sliding her into his arms. "I love you," Faith said as she got comfortable.

"Love you more," he replied as he fell asleep.

Ridge woke up the next morning, seeing her still out cold. He gently got up, slid on boxers and joggers, slid on a shirt, socks and sneakers, grabbed his phone and AirPods and walked downstairs to the gym and started doing his workout. He got in a 3-mile run, got all of his weights done, got the rest of the stretches and workout done and was doing more stretches when he saw Faith coming down the steps. She was in a satin robe and nothing else.

"Mornin sexy fiancée," he said as he kissed her and took her hand.

"Morning handsome. How was your workout," she asked.

"Good. You slept in," he joked.

Faith shook her head. "Gee. I wonder why?"

"You started it."

They walked into the kitchen and saw spinach omelets and bacon waiting for them with fresh croissants and peaches. "You went overboard again," Ridge teased as her housekeeper sat down with them and ate.

"I wanted to make something special for y'all. I actually had an idea about your wedding plans," she said.

"Which was," Faith asked.

"Your folks have a chef right?" Faith nodded. "What if I made the meals with them?"

"There's 60 people coming," Faith said.

"If you had a buffet style, we could get a big steak and slice it off instead of individual steaks. The lobster tails aren't hard to do. We can make the vegetables ahead and slice off the steaks right before the meal starts. Gives you one less thing to do for the wedding. My gift to you two," her housekeeper said.

"Are you sure it isn't gonna be too much?"

She shook her head. "As long as you two are alright with it."

"I appreciate the offer. It's very sweet of you to offer all of that. I sorta wanted you there with us," Ridge said.

She looked at Ridge. "So long as you two are happy, I am. I will be. I'll come out and have dessert with you."

Ridge smirked and Faith nodded. "So long as you're alright

with 60 people, okay," Faith said knowing how much it meant to her. She left Faith and Ridge to eat and went to get some laundry on.

"So, that thing last night," she teased.

"Which one of the things are we talking about?"

She looked at him. "Funny."

He kissed her and finished his omelet. "Faith, just remember what I said. You're not supposed to jump in headfirst until you're on overload. It's not like I'm going anywhere babe."

"I missed it."

"What?"

"You and me, that far down the rabbit hole."

He smirked. "There are so many things you still don't know," he teased.

"Such as?"

He smirked. "Alright then. Here's the deal. I give you a page and you choose which things you want."

"Meaning what?"

He kissed her. "You'll find out."

She shook her head. "Ridge."

"What?"

"Tell me what you're up to." He smirked, pulled up the store that he'd bought the toys from and handed it to her as he got up and did the dishes. He had a list. It wasn't a long list, but just enough to peak her interest.

"Ridge."

"Wife to be," he said as he put the last dish into the washer. She motioned for him to come closer. "What," he teased. She pointed one out to him and he smirked. "Faith."

"What?"

"Last night," he whispered.

"Really?" He kissed her. He took his phone back, slid it in his pocket and kissed her yet again. She got up and looked at him. "Ridge."

"What?"

She got that look. The one that said that getting actual work done wasn't gonna happen. "Don't you have a meeting downtown?"

"Probably. It's only 8." He looked at her.

"You do know that it takes an hour to get there in traffic right," he said. She grabbed her phone and called the office.

"Miss Faith," her assistant said.

"What time is my meeting?"

"11. Did you want me to move it up?"

"I'll be in around 10:30. Just the one meeting right?"

"It's a board meeting. Last time it wasn't over until 3pm."

"Alright. I'll be there. See you at 10:30," Faith said as she hung up.

"And," Ridge asked.

"I have to be there at 10:30 for a board meeting."

"Then you should probably get showered and dressed," Ridge teased.

"I have time."

He shook his head and kissed her. He pulled his shirt off and she watched his muscles. The ones that had held her tight the night prior. The arms that she'd curled up in one too many times. The ones that had carried her to bed, carried her into the hospital, carried her to what had always got them even closer. He turned and looked at her.

"What," he asked.

"Nothin. Drooling over my fiancée." He smirked and walked over to her. "What," Faith asked.

He kissed her, devouring her lips. "Tell me what you want Faith."

"Not to go into the board meeting." He smirked and took her hand. "What," she asked.

"Come." He sat her on the bed and slid his arm around her. "What's really wrong?"

"You sure that I'm what you want," she asked.

"Where did that come from?"

"Ridge."

"Where? You said you wanted us back to the way we were before this."

"That's not what I meant," she said.

"Meaning what then?"

"Do you really want this life?"

He looked at her. "You're serious?"

"Ridge."

"You're seriously saying that right now?" It hit him like a truck.

"Ridge, all I'm saying is that I don't know that I'm enough."

He took a deep breath, determined not to snap at her. "Why are you convinced that you aren't?"

"Because I'm not as..."

"Faith." She looked at him. He got up, kicked his joggers and boxers off, kicked his socks and shoes off and went and had a shower alone. When he flipped the water to cold, he just got more pissed off. She went to slide in and he flipped the water back onto hot. He stepped out of the shower, wrapped a towel around his hips and she shook her head.

"Ridge." He shaved, freshened up and walked into the bedroom, pulling dress pants and a dress shirt on. He put cologne on and went to leave the room when she grabbed his hand.

"What," Ridge asked.

"Come here."

"Faith, leave it alone," he replied. She walked him to the bed. "I don't know what you want me to say Faith."

"Am I enough," she asked.

"If you weren't, there wouldn't be a ring on your hand. I wouldn't even be in this room with you. You wanted more. You got more. I gave you what you wanted and you seriously ask me if you're enough? Why?"

"Because I worry that I'm not. That all of the stuff that happened last night isn't enough for you." He shook his head and got up. "Ridge."

He looked at her. "Don't say it ever again Faith. Never." He walked out of the bedroom and went downstairs, grabbing his laptop. He got his papers together and put them into his bag. When his phone buzzed with a text from Faith, he ignored it. How she'd said it with a straight face he didn't know. When it buzzed again, he looked:

*Come upstairs Ridge. Please. Please come upstairs
so we can finish talking about this.*

He took a deep breath and walked upstairs. "What," he
asked as she closed the door behind him, still in nothing
but a towel.

"Am I," she asked.

"Faith, you're what I wanted. If that isn't enough for you,
fine. I wanted you then, I want you now. I never stopped
that. Stop thinking that you aren't enough. I never
would've let things go that far. I wouldn't have been with
you if you weren't. Enough. Go get ready," Ridge said as he
got up. Faith grabbed his hand. "What?" She kissed him.
"What do you want Faith? Tell me what you want." She
kissed him again and undid the buttons of his shirt. "We
aren't doing this." She kissed him again and slid his suit
jacket off, undid his tie, and slid her towel off. "What are
you doing," he asked. She undid the button of his dress
pants and he stopped her. "Faith, you have a meeting..."
She kissed him and went to undo the zipper to his pants
and he stopped her. "We aren't doing this. Not now," he
said as he shook his head and walked into his closet. She
locked the bedroom door, walked into his closet, and sat
on the counter. "What are you doing Faith?"

"Come here."

He shook his head. "Faith, you have to..." She kissed him
and pulled her to him as she undid his dress pants again.

"Come here."

He shook his head and she kissed him. "What?"

She kissed him again and he looked at her. "You do realize that at some point you have to realize that I'm not leaving right? No matter how many damn times you try and push me away or do something because you think it'll make me happy, I'm still not leaving. You want me gone? Fine. Say it and I'll walk out that door Faith."

"I want you."

"Sex doesn't fix this. If it did, last night would've…"

She kissed him, wrapping her legs around him. "Now," she said. He shook his head again, left the closet and grabbed something. She whole-heartedly thought that he was really walking out. That she'd already screwed up too much. She went to slide off the counter and he walked back in. "What," Faith asked.

"Do you want this? You and me. No more doubt and worry that you aren't enough. Do you actually want this?"

She nodded. "I don't want…" He kissed her until her body was covered in goosebumps.

She heard the tear of a packet and they had sex with her on that counter, then bed, then the floor in their bedroom. He let her up for air just as his body exploded into her. "Promise me," Faith said.

"What?"

"That you never let go."

He kissed her. "I swear you are talkin crazy. You need to get dressed," he teased.

"And you need to say it."

"That I'm never letting go even when you push me away?"

She kissed him. "That you never ever let go."

"I love you crazy woman. Stop thinking that I'm leaving your side." He kissed her and they got up. "Go," he said. Ridge smirked and watched her get dressed. He cleaned up and got re-dressed then walked back downstairs.

"You two good," Leo asked.

Ridge nodded. "Pain in my butt sometimes, but yes."

When Faith came down the steps, she was in a summer dress and had her blazer with it. "Wow," Ridge said.

"Like?"

He nodded noticing that for once, it wasn't a mini skirt. "What," Faith asked.

"Nothin. Just noticing that it's not super short," he teased.

She smirked and walked over to him. "And you didn't even notice what else I wasn't wearing," she whispered as the goosebumps popped up on his skin. He shook his head.

"I'll drive you two in. I have a quick stop to make," Kellen said with a smirk.

"We'll be at the office most of the day anyway. I'll let you know when we're ready to head back," Ridge said.

Kellen nodded and they all headed off together. They grabbed lattes and made their way to the office in morning traffic. "And what's the plan for the afternoon," Kellen said as Faith's hand slid to Ridge's leg.

"Harassing my fiancée. Board meeting."

"Sounds like a fun day," Kellen teased as Ridge's arm slid around her shoulders.

"Oh, I forgot to tell you. Remember Sally. The one that did that tattoo? She called me to check in and see if you still wanted that other one you were talking about last time we all hung out," Kellen said.

"And which tattoo was that," Faith asked.

He smirked. "Did you really want me to get another one?"

Kellen smirked. "Depends on what it was," Faith asked.

Ridge pulled the photo up on his phone and showed her. When she saw it, her jaw dropped. "A shield? Seriously," Faith asked.

He looked at her. "And?"

"No other option?"

He showed her the second choice. It was a lot more elaborate. "Ridge."

"Those were the choices," he said.

She looked at him. "Don't you think maybe something a little less violent," she asked.

He kissed her. "I'll see. Did you want to come with me," Ridge asked.

Faith kissed him. "Maybe," she replied.

He kissed her and they pulled into the office parking not long later. Faith and Ridge headed up to her office with their bags in hand, walked past her assistant and he went and sat down on the sofa. "Were you serious about that tattoo?"

He showed her the idea that he had. "Compass?"

"And the numbers on the outside are the exact location where we met."

"When you showed at my house?" He nodded. "See, that I like."

"Over my heart."

She looked at him. "Really?" He nodded. "I do kinda like it."

"And you could get the numbers if that's what you wanted."

She smirked. "I have a better idea."

"What," he teased. When she pointed to her ring finger,

he smirked. "Oh really," he joked as her assistant knocked and came in.

"Good morning," Faith said.

"Morning. I thought I'd bring in your messages and the updates for the meeting. Mr. Cartwright said that it should be done before 2pm."

"And it's starting when," Faith asked.

"11:15. Did you need me to get you anything," her assistant asked.

"Ridge may need lunch, and I probably will."

"We have your seafood wrap ordered for you both," her assistant said.

"Great. I think I'm good. We got coffee on the way in," Faith said.

"Alright. I'll let you know when it's a few minutes before you have to head up."

Faith nodded and she headed out.

"Saturday," he said.

"What?"

"I can get an appointment."

She looked at him. "What do you think about the idea," Faith asked.

"It's up to you if you want one on that finger," he said.

Faith smirked. "What do you think?"

"It's gonna be painful regardless. I just don't know if your Dad is gonna be too happy about it," he joked.

"What if it was somewhere else," she joked.

"Do I get to choose?"

She looked at him. "Depends," she teased. He motioned for her to come closer. "Where were you suggesting," she asked.

His hand slid up her leg to her inner thigh. "Ridge."

He smirked. "Right here," he said as his hand slid against her.

"Nice try."

"Idea. What if you put it near where mine is. Nobody will see it." She looked at him. When she nodded he smirked.

"Really?"

She nodded. He kissed her and she slid into his lap. "Ridge."

"What beautiful?"

"I love you."

"That's kinda good since we're getting married and everything."

She kissed him. "What if we did it tonight instead?"

He looked at her. "You really want to do that?"

"Scared," she teased.

"Two hours out of your night. No movies."

She smirked. "Saturday morning. Early."

He kissed her. "What time is it," he asked.

"Why," Faith asked. He looked at his phone and smirked. "Ridge." He kissed her, devouring her lips.

"Really," she joked.

"Taunting you before you go to your meeting," he joked. She went to close the blinds and he reached over and locked the door.

"Ridge."

His hand slid up her leg. "And your legs are all silky. Damn," he teased.

"Just noticed?"

When his hand touched her, he smirked. "Faith."

"Fiancée," she said as she went for the button of his dress pants.

"Hands off Faith."

"Ridge."

"Nope."

"Meaning what," she asked as he kissed her and the taunting got more intense. "Ridge."

"Yep," he teased.

Her legs started trembling. She gripped his arm. "Too much," he whispered. Faith kissed him. "More?" He kept going as she nodded. "I can't," Faith said.

He smirked. "Up."

"What?"

She got up with shaky legs. He grabbed something from his pocket and walked her into her private bathroom. "Quiet," he said.

"Ridge."

"Bend over." She shook her head. "Faith."

"Ridge." He closed the bathroom door, slid his dress pants off enough to give him space, slid his boxers down and slid the hem of the dress up.

"Quiet," he said. Faith smirked. The sex was mind-blowing. He covered her mouth more than once until her body gave way. He kept going until he climaxed and her legs almost crumbled. "That what you wanted," he teased as they stood up.

She kissed him. "Yep," she teased. He shook his head, cleaned up and disposed of the evidence.

"Faith."

"What?"

"No more naked workday for you. No more after today."

"Why?"

"Because you're gonna end up pregnant before the doctor okay's you."

"And?"

He shook his head and kissed her. "You have a meeting sexy. You can't go in there like this," he teased.

Faith smirked and kissed him. "I could."

"No."

He shook his head and kissed her. "I love you, and I love that you're all hot and bothered around me, but you need to work."

She kissed him, walked into her office, and fixed her lipstick.

"Faith."

"Yes handsome."

He shook his head. "I swear, your Dad is gonna kill me."

"Maybe."

He shook his head, straightened up and sat down on the

chair. He knew her too well. He unlocked the door and not 5 minutes later, her assistant knocked at the door. "Five minutes," her assistant said.

Faith got her things together and kissed him. "Do you want me to stay here?"

Faith nodded. "I still want out of that meeting asap," Faith teased. He kissed her and she headed up to the meeting. He brushed her lipstick from his lips and sat down at her desk with his laptop. He got a meeting in, got paperwork done and her assistant came in with lunch for him.

"I got extras for you. Also, I grabbed another coffee for you. That meeting always runs long, so if you need anything let me know," she said.

"Will do. Thanks," Ridge said. She nodded with a smirk and he went back to getting work done. He ate, then called the tattoo artist back.

"Long time no talk," Sally said.

"I know. Ended up doing security for my now fiancée. How have you been?"

"Fiancée? Since when," Sally asked.

"Remember when you did the other tattoo and I told you about Faith Cartwright?"

"Well damn Ridge. Nothing like being with the queen bee of Charleston."

"So, I came up with the tattoo idea. Remember the one we thought about the compass?"

"Yeah," Sally replied.

"North will be co-ordinates."

Sally almost laughed at his idea." "Like around the side of the compass," she said.

"And Faith wants the co-ordinates too."

"Ridge, you do realize that's gonna take me at least 2 hours right?"

"Yep. What you up to Saturday," he teased.

"Fine, but you owe me large."

"Conner."

"Um. You sure?"

"I'll ask him. Still paying you though."

"Alright. 7am Saturday."

"And what time do you think you'll be done?"

"Both? By 11."

"Done," he replied.

"Alright, send me over the address." He finished his call with her and smirked. He knew Faith would have her phone on silent and texted her:

> *Booked 7am Saturday. How goes the meeting?*

When he got a reply 5 minutes later, he almost laughed:

> *Did I ever tell you how much I hate these yearly meetings? Dad's at the other end of the table and when I got up here, he asked why I had a big ole grin. I told him it was wedding planning.*

He smirked:

> *If he only knew how naughty his daughter was.*

He saw the dots and a reply:

> *Part of me wants to get out of here. We could just stay at a hotel downtown. Nobody would know. Be as loud as we want to.*

He shook his head and replied:

> *Baby, we'd have to buy noise cancelling earphones for the entire block.*

Within a matter of seconds, he got another reply:

> *Now he's giving me a dirty look. Love you.*

He smirked and knew better than to distract her anymore. He got a little more work done, then saw an email from the detective:

> *Zack has been arrested. He attempted to get into Mr. Cartwrights home on the beach. The top dog of the problem has been neutralized. He had*

worked for her Dad years ago. He started another business and ended up in the mix as he co-owned the business with Zack. That was the connection. All of them were held without bail and under monitoring. It's over. Thank you for all the hard work on your part.

– Detective Cameron

Chapter 12

By the time Faith was done her meeting, it was almost 3pm. He messaged Kellen that they were almost ready to go. When he replied that he was on the way, Ridge smirked. Faith came back down to her office and saw him at her desk, closing and locking the door behind her. "And," he asked.

Faith walked over, slid his chair out from under the desk and kissed him. "That bad?"

"That determined to get out of here. If I have to hear numbers one more time, I'm gonna scream."

He kissed her. "40."

"Ridge." He motioned for her to come closer. "What," she teased.

"The number of times that you..."

She covered his mouth and laughed. "I swear, you were the only good thing in that meeting. My Dad almost kicked my butt, but it's done."

He showed her the email from the detective and Faith looked at him. "Does this mean what I think it does?"

"This means that we're still making sure that the houses are secure, and you're keeping security at both houses. Just means a little more lax."

She kissed him. "No carrying?"

"It's in my bag Faith. I'm bringing it wherever I go."

"And if I said I didn't want you to?"

"I still would."

She kissed him. "Fine. Can we go home?"

He kissed her, devouring her lips. "Yep."

She shook her head and his hands slid to her face. "What," she asked.

"I love you."

"I love you too handsome husband to be." He kissed her again and they packed up and headed out as he got the text from Kellen that he was there.

They hopped in and Faith smirked. "I swear, my Dad almost kicked my butt in the meeting. He asked who I was messaging and I told him it was a business email."

He shook his head. "Lying to your Dad now too. Wow," he teased as Kellen laughed.

"Leave it at he remembered what it was like before he married my Mom. Your Dad was in the meeting," Faith said.

"I didn't even know he was in town."

"You do realize that he asked if you were at the office right," Faith asked.

"And?"

"I told him that you were in my office getting work done. He actually headed out when I came back downstairs to my office." He took a deep breath and he messaged his Dad:

> *Hey. Heard you were in the marathon meeting. Everything okay? By the way, we sorta decided on the big dinner Sunday next week. We can do it at Faith's. What do you think?*

He got a reply a few minutes later:

> *Sounds good. Everything's okay. Just stress. Mom's heading out to visit some old college friends. We're leaving tomorrow to head to Charlotte. You doing okay? Faith looked happy.*

Ridge smirked:

> *We're better than okay. Wedding is planned for the most part. Can't wait for you to see it. It's gonna be small, which means you have lots of time to dance with Mom. Have fun in Charlotte.*

She slid her hand in his. "You sure you want to do it next weekend?"

"You can show off your tattoo," Ridge teased.

Kellen almost laughed. "You're getting it," Kellen asked.

"We both are," Faith said.

"Seriously," Kellen asked.

"Saturday morning," Ridge replied.

"At least tell me what you're getting," Kellen asked.

"Compass," Faith replied.

Kellen smirked. "I sorta knew that was coming. The only time this one has ever wanted to stay in one spot," Kellen said.

Faith snuggled up to Ridge as they headed back. "What are we doing for dinner," Faith asked.

"Not up to me tonight. Why," he asked.

Faith smirked. "Steaks and spinach salad. I saw her cooking the mushrooms to go on top," Kellen said.

Faith smirked. "Good. I'm starved," Faith joked. He shook his head and they pulled back into the house. They headed inside and his phone buzzed. "Go. I'm going upstairs," Faith said as she went inside.

"Yep," Ridge said.

"So, I heard about the fancy new lady," the voice said.

"The part where I said to never call me again?"

"Come over."

"Goodbye," Ridge said as he hung up and blocked the call. He came back upstairs to see Faith reading emails on her phone. "What are you up to sexy?"

"Got a weird email," Faith said as she showed it to him:

> *You aren't gonna marry the guy who screwed half of Charleston are you? Not worth it. Trust me. He's that way for a reason. – S*

He saw the email address and she saw him clench his jaw. "Ridge."

He walked downstairs, handed the phone to Kellen and he shook his head. "Seriously," Kellen asked.

"I want it done. Period. I want her done." Kellen nodded and Ridge walked outside. He took a deep breath, livid, and waited for the anger to pass. When he felt arms slide around his waist, he turned and kissed Faith. He had her leaned against the wall, fingers linked, in seconds. That kiss deepened and when it broke, she looked at him. "Are you okay," Faith asked.

"Kellen's handling the email problem."

"Who is it?"

"An old girlfriend who I dated for all of a month. I broke it off when she was trying to push me into things I didn't want to do. She put me in the damn hospital twice."

Faith looked at him. "Ridge."

"I'm not talking about it. Leave it."

"Gunshots or knife?"

"One of each." She shook her head and kissed him.

"Baby."

"Faith, don't. I'm not having that conversation."

She kissed him again. "Okay," she said.

He held her tight to him and kissed her forehead. "I love you. You know that right?" She nodded. "And what she said was bull."

Faith nodded. "Ridge, was she telling the truth?"

"No. Not one bit of it."

She looked at him. "That way for a reason?" He shook his head.

"Faith, she's a pain in my backside and has been since I walked away from her. She has no idea what she's talking about."

Faith looked at him. "You sure," she asked.

Ridge nodded. "She's annoying as hell. I don't even know why she caused that much crap over something she obviously could care less about at the time."

Kellen almost laughed. "What," Ridge replied.

"We all know the real reason why she's mad dude. You're 6 foot 6. She wants it and she's missing it."

"Meaning?"

"The bigger the man, the bigger the…"

"Kellen, go do some work or something."

Faith almost fell over laughing. "Really? You too now," Ridge teased.

"It's true though," Faith teased.

"Fine. You're cut off too," he teased as he sat down.

"Ridge," Faith said.

"I love you, but you do realize that I didn't ask for her stupidity right? She pushed too far. I don't need more attention on her."

Faith kissed him. "I get it. I do. Just remember something okay? I'm not the one that sent the nasty email."

He nodded and kissed her, pulling her into his lap. "And," he teased.

Faith smirked. "All mine," she joked.

He shook his head. "You are bad. You know that right?" She nodded and devoured his lips as he picked her up and walked upstairs.

"What," she asked.

"You're putting on actual clothes," he teased. He sat her on the counter of her closet and kissed her. Faith's legs slid around him and he shook his head. "Don't go there Faith."

"Why?"

"Because we have dinner in maybe 15 minutes." She kissed him.

"And we have time husband to be," she replied as she slid her shirt off.

He shook his head. "Woman, I swear, you are in a mood today."

"The mood that makes me want you?" He nodded. "That's because I do handsome," she teased. He kissed her again and slid her skirt off. "Now, what were you saying about wanting to wait until after dinner?"

"Always did like dessert first," he teased.

He closed the closet door and Faith slid his suit jacket and dress shirt off, smirking when she threw it into the laundry bin. "Faith."

"What?"

"Put something on." She shook her head and kissed him. "I am. You."

He shook his head, kissed her, and went and grabbed the condoms from the drawer. "Ridge."

"Don't even say it woman of mine." He slid out of his dress pants and Faith got a grin ear to ear. "I swear, if you say what I think you are, I'm walkin out of here."

She kissed him and pulled him closer. "All…. mine…

forever," she said between kisses. When he pulled her legs around him, she held on and pulled him tight to her. "Husband to be."

Ridge kissed down her neck and almost purred into her ear. "Yes love," he said.

Faith kissed him. He slid her legs out from around him and was about to start the taunting all over again when his phone went off.

She shook her head. "Don't you dare," she said. He kissed her and slid his hand to her inner thigh and started teasing while he answered.

"Yep."

"You able to talk," Conner asked.

"What's wrong?"

"Sounds really odd, but someone has been taking photos of the house."

"Then go out and tell them it's private property," Ridge said.

"I did and they screwed off, but they keep coming back."

"Cop. Call the detective."

"Alright," Callon said as they hung up.

"I can't believe you," she said as her legs pulled him back to her. He kissed her, devouring her lips until he felt her hands on him.

"Faith."

"Off." He shook his head. "Not happening," he said as he moved her hands and they had sex with her on that counter. They went from the counter, to against the door, collapsing onto the bed in their bedroom as she shook her head and didn't let go of him.

"Faith."

"Handsome."

He kissed her. "I love you, but you are gonna have to feed me if you keep doin this," he teased.

She kissed him and snuggled to him. "Why can't we just go without the stupid..."

"Because your doc said no," he replied.

Faith shook her head. "Seriously?"

He nodded. "I'm not doing it until she says that it's alright. I promised."

She kissed him. "And if I said I didn't care?"

"You're still waiting wife to be."

He kissed her again and managed to get up. "Where are you goin?"

"Clothes. Dinner is almost done," he said. He cleaned up,

slid jeans and a tee on and walked into the bedroom.

"Ridge," she teased.

"Yes sexy wife to be."

"Come here."

He smirked and sat down beside her. She kissed him and slid into his lap. "What," he teased.

She kissed him again. "Movie night."

He shook his head. "Not happening. I need sleep."

She smirked. "Over-rated."

"You're that determined," he asked.

She kissed him. "We'll see," she replied. She kissed him again, slid out of bed, wrapping her legs around him and he shook his head, pinning her to the bed.

"You're just insatiable. You realize that."

"With you. Only around you. Never before," she replied. He shook his head and snuggled her tight to him.

"Marry me."

"Anytime, anyplace handsome," she replied as he kissed her again and she went for the button of his jeans.

"We're getting up." She shook her head. "Then I'll bring you dinner in bed," he teased.

"I'd rather have dessert first."

He kissed her. "I know. I love you baby, but we're eating dinner downstairs."

He kissed her, got up and went downstairs. "Did you need me to help," Ridge asked as he saw her housekeeper cooking.

"Ridge, you do know you don't need to help. You're all good," her housekeeper said.

"Still."

"If you can get drinks for you and Miss Faith, that will be your contribution." He smirked, got the drinks, and set the table.

Faith came downstairs not long later wearing his t-shirt and her shorts and he shook his head. "Had to do it? My shirt?"

"Not for long."

He took a deep breath and they sat down on the sofa. "If you want to eat, dinner's ready," her housekeeper said as Ridge got up and grabbed the food, bringing it to the table. They ate with Faith on the other side of the table from Ridge, and her leg taunting him as she tried to play footsie with him under the table. "Faith."

"What," she asked.

His leg slid around hers and she smirked. "Are you two

going to be down here tonight," her housekeeper asked.

"That was the plan. Early movie and getting sleep," Ridge said.

"Alright then. I'll leave y'all to have dinner. I'm heading out with the girls tonight. If you need me to stay," she said.

"You deserve to have a life too. Go and enjoy," Faith said.

"Alright. Enjoy your date night," she teased with a little smirk.

"And what exactly did you have planned tonight Faith," Ridge joked.

"A really good movie. Jack. Spending quality time with this guy I know."

Ridge shook his head. "And," he teased.

"And we're staying home alone. Just us."

He shook his head. She slid over to the seat beside him. "What," he teased.

"I made a decision."

"On what," he teased.

"Two kids. If we…"

"Faith."

"If it happens before the wedding…"

"Baby, I love you to the moon and back, but you need to stop. The doctor told you no. She said to wait. That means that we're waiting until it's safe for you."

"Ridge, there's no guarantee that it's even gonna be that easy. You know that."

"I also know that you and your insatiable appetite for movie nights will make that the easiest task in the planet," Ridge replied.

She kissed him. "Kinda counting on it."

Ridge shook his head. "Not happening until doc says so. Get used to it love. We aren't going there. You know that's what she said."

"And I also know that I want us to have a baby. We don't need to wait Ridge. You…"

He kissed her, tucking her hair behind her ear. "Baby, we're waiting. You're more important than anything else. A baby can wait. I promise you."

"And if I don't want to wait a few months?"

He shook his head and kissed her. "Finish dinner then we can discuss this baby idea," he teased.

They finished dinner and Ridge got up to clean up the dishes with Faith two steps behind him. "What," he teased.

Faith kissed him and sat on the counter. "I still think we

could. Ridge, I want us to live like there's no tomorrow. Do what we want to do. Be happy."

He kissed her and slid his arms around her as her legs slid around his waist. "I love you, but you need to stop. We're not going there until the doctor says that we're okay to go ahead. I don't want you in the dang hospital love. That's what she said would happen if you got pregnant. We have to do this the right way. That so bad?"

She nodded. He smirked and kissed her. "You can't pout your way out of this sexy." She kissed him and he shook his head. "Now, if you're done attempting to taunt me, we have a date with a sofa."

She kissed him again and slid his shirt off of him. "Babe, we still have people here. Not a..." She kissed him, nibbling at his lip and he picked her up and carried her up the steps to the bedroom, locked the bedroom door, and pinned her onto the bed.

"You want a baby that badly?"

Faith nodded. "Then you call and ask her and get the answer. That's the deal."

She kissed him. "Come to bed."

"Faith, you wanted a movie night. You call her and I'll set it up. Regardless of what you want, we're not getting you knocked up tonight. My decision."

"And if I say we are?"

He shook his head. "Then you're doing it solo."

He kissed her and she pulled him tight into her arms. "Ridge."

"Don't go there baby. Just don't. I know you want to, but we could just practice you know."

He kissed her and got up, headed downstairs and got two glasses of Jack. When he felt arms slide around his waist, he shook his head. "And did you call her," he asked.

"She didn't answer," Faith said as he turned and kissed her. He grabbed his cell phone and called the doctor.

"Ridge," the doctor said.

He put it on speaker. "So, Faith was wondering if she's okay to try again," he said as he looked at Faith.

"If you're determined to, at least wait until next month. Give your body time to heal after that loss. You need to. I know you're all determined, but you have to for your own health," the doctor said.

"I did try to tell her that," Ridge said.

He kissed her. "I don't want to wait that long," Faith said.

"You still have to. Come in for a checkup and we'll go from there," her doctor replied.

"Fine," Faith said as they hung up.

"Like I said," Ridge replied.

"Still want movie night," she teased.

"Then grab your blanket. I'll get the drinks," he teased as Faith got even more irritated.

"You do realize that she can't exactly stop us right?"

"I can," he replied as Faith shook her head. "What do you want me to say Faith? Tell me. I'm okay with you wanting to try, but until she gives you the go-ahead, you aren't pulling me into all of it. I don't want you in the hospital. I don't want you trying and succeeding them ending up in a hospital bed or almost dying. I won't go along with that. Now, either we're watching the movie or I'm getting actual work done Faith."

He went and sat down, poured a glass of Jack, and got comfortable on the sofa. One way or another, he was doing something that night whether it included her or not.

"Ridge."

"What baby," he replied hoping that she was off the rant.

She walked over to him. "After we talk to her..."

"And after she repeats what I said."

"We go from there."

She kissed him. "Until then, are you sitting and watching the movie or what," he teased as he slid her onto his lap.

She leaned into his arms and kissed him. "We're watching the movie."

"Really? You mean you're gonna make it through the movie this time," he teased.

"Meaning we're making it through the movie." He smirked, kissed her, and snuggled her tight to him.

"Good luck with that fiancée of mine," he teased as he kissed her again. She poured herself a glass of Jack and got comfortable.

"Ridge."

"Wife to be."

"You really should have joggers on or something," Faith said.

"And you really should keep those hands to yourself," he teased as he slid his arms around her. Faith shook her head and snuggled in tighter to him. He shook his head and pressed play on the movie.

"Ridge."

"Yes," he said as he kissed her neck.

"I love you."

"Good. I love you back." When it got to the first scene that had always got her hot and bothered, she made it through, but slid her hands to his legs. "Faith."

"What," she asked.

"Hands." She smirked and leaned back against him. "I love

that you think you're gonna win tonight," he whispered as he kissed down the back of her neck.

"And if I let you win," she asked. He shook his head and kissed down her shoulder. "Ridge."

"Um hmm."

He kissed up her neck and nibbled at her ear. "I know what you're doing." "Good," he replied.

He pulled the blanket up as she watched. "And what lingerie did you slip on to attempt to win?"

He went to look and she shook her head as he peeked and saw the black lace. "Nice."

"That was my plan," she teased.

"Not gonna work." He kissed her neck and his hand slid down her torso.

"Ridge."

"Yep."

"What are you up to?"

"Nothin. Making sure that I win tonight." She shook her head and when his hand slid across her hip, she shook her head.

"You do realize that you're cheating," Faith said.

"I said that if you ended up turning the movie off, I win.

There was nothing that said I couldn't taunt you into turning the movie off." When he felt her body almost hum in his arms, he smirked.

"Ridge."

He kissed down her neck. "Yes," he whispered as goosebumps popped up on her skin. The taunting deepened until her legs were almost shaking.

"I think."

"What," he whispered as her goosebumps got goosebumps. His hand quickened until she was almost trembling in his arms. "Bed," he asked.

"Movie first," she said. The taunting continued and got more intense. When he felt her nails digging into his legs, he kissed her shoulder. When she turned to face him and devoured his lips, he paused the movie. "Take them off."

"Nope."

"Ridge."

"No." She went for the button of his jeans and he grabbed her hands. "Say it."

"Upstairs." He turned it off and she went for his jeans again.

"Faith."

"Now. Here." He shook his head and picked her up, carrying her to bed in his old bedroom.

"What are we…" He kissed her and closed the door.

"Why," Faith asked.

"Because that whole blindfold thing wasn't what you liked," he teased as he kissed her.

"Ridge."

"Yep," he teased.

"Take the jeans off."

He smirked and slid her shorts off, then the shirt. "Please," Faith said.

"I still have work to do," he teased. Faith kissed him, pulling him to her. He leaned into her lap and devoured her lips.

"Can't we just run away together," Faith asked.

He smirked and peeled the lingerie off little by little. "Ridge, this isn't fair."

"And?"

She kissed him. "Come here," he said as he took her hand and helped her up.

"What," she asked.

"Turn around," he whispered as Faith shook her head.

"What are you up to," Faith asked.

"Bend over."

She shook her head. "You'd better not be doing what I think you are."

When she felt warmth against her, her knees almost gave way. "Ridge."

She felt teeth, nibbling against her and making her legs crumble. "Faith," he said as his fingers continued the taunting.

"Do it again." He intensified it, and everything just got harder to resist.

He turned her around and leaned her onto the bed as he taunted until her body was throbbing. "Still think you can resist?"

She reached for him and he pulled back as she heard the faint noise of buzzing. "Ridge."

"Yes sexy." When the buzzing got closer to her skin, he smirked.

"I need you."

"I know," he said. The buzzing got to her skin and her toes were almost curling.

"Ridge."

"Yes baby."

"I want you." He felt her grab for the belt of his jeans and he smirked. He kept taunting until she was exploding not once, not even twice. The warmth of his lips against her hip was enough to push her over the edge, but when the other buzzing things came out, he had a grin ear to her and Faith pulled him to her.

"No more," she said.

"One more," he teased.

"You. Now." He grabbed the last toy from the drawer and she grabbed his arm.

"Oh my god," she said. He kissed up her torso and she caught his belt loop. She undid his jeans and slid her hand down his body until she was past hot and bothered.

He was turned on just seeing her body react to his taunting. The feel of her hand on him was starting to make it all worse. He grabbed that little packet from the drawer and she tried to push it away. He tore it open, slid it on and Faith pulled away from him.

"What," he asked.

"Jeans off." He kissed her and she reached for him when he pinned her to the bed and slid her legs around him.

"What did you want now," he teased as he grabbed the buzzing toy to make it all more intense.

"Ridge," she said as she almost squirmed as the buzzing intensified.

"Yes baby," he said as they had sex. Even when she could barely move, she pulled her legs tight around him.

"Ridge." He kissed her as the buzzing kept going. Her body was throbbing so tight around him that he almost couldn't hold back.

"Flip over," he said. Faith shook her head. He turned her to her front and he kept going, making the intensity even worse. He taunted in every single way that he knew how until she crumbled underneath him.

"I can't move," Faith said.

"That was the plan sexy," he teased as he kissed her neck and crumbled onto the bed beside her.

"I can't even see," Faith said.

"Intentional," he joked. She caught her breath and turned towards him.

"I'm still shaking," Faith said. He pulled the blanket over them and she kissed him. "What am I gonna do with you," Faith asked.

"Depends. You ready for the main course," he joked.

"New appetizer," she teased.

He kissed her neck. "Something like that."

"Can we go to the bedroom?"

"And why is that?"

"Because I want to see you." He kissed her and lit the candles in his room.

"You were saying," he asked. Faith kissed him and he slid his arms around her. "Now, about that whole light thing," he teased.

By the time they got to bed, it was almost 1am. Neither of them could even move, but they were back in their bed. The candles were out, but the spark between them was still burning white hot. He kissed her again and curled her to him.

"Ridge."

"Yes beautiful."

"What about dessert?"

"When you make it through the movie, you get dessert," he teased.

Faith kissed him and they fell asleep. They curled up among the blankets and nodded off. When Ridge's phone buzzed at 2am, he shook his head. He grabbed it and saw a message from Kellen:

> *Weird car at gate. Got license plate. It says that it's her Dad's security, but the guy is way too shady. Not sure what you want me to do, but I called the detective.*

Ridge gently got up, pulled his jeans on, and walked downstairs. "Are you sure it's her Dad's security?" Kellen nodded.

"I checked the plates. We never received anything that said they were coming for extra backup. The cops are out there in unmarked cars, but this one is odd," Kellen said.

"Did you contact her Dad's security?"

Kellen nodded. "No reply as to who it is."

"Hoodie?"

"Ridge."

"Is there a hoodie down here?" Kellen handed Ridge the black hoodie, he pulled on sneakers, grabbed his handgun, and went to find out who it was.

He made his way down the pathway and got a photo of the driver, then walked over, staying in the shadows. When he knocked on the window, it rolled down and he was face to face with a handgun. "You want to tell me why you're outside my fiancée's house," Ridge said.

"Who are you," the man asked.

"You answer me first."

"Protecting my boss's daughter."

Ridge looked at him. "That's why I'm here. Nice try though. Nobody told me you were coming. What's your name," Ridge asked.

"What's yours," the man asked.

"Ridge Sams." When the guy took off in the truck, Ridge got the plate and called her Dad's security.

"Ridge," his head of security said.

"Did you send someone over here as backup?"

"No. Why," he asked.

"Because there was a guy here claiming that y'all sent him. He took off when I told him my name."

"Plate?" Ridge gave it to him and headed back up to the house. "We don't have anyone on staff with that plate. I'm getting the information. It says Holden Whittaker owns the plate."

"Then you're handling him or I'll rip his throat out," Ridge said.

He went back into the house and handed Kellen his hoodie. "And," Kellen asked.

"Holden was behind it, not her Dad. Sam at her Mom and Dad's is handling him. If I do it, I'll be in jail for ripping his throat out," Ridge said as he shook his head.

He kicked his sneakers off and went to walk back upstairs when he saw Faith at the top of the stairs. "What did Holden do," Faith asked.

Ridge shook his head. "Come back to bed," he said as he walked upstairs and walked her back into the bedroom.

"Are you gonna tell me," Faith asked. He shook his head,

kicked his jeans off and slid back into bed.

"Come here," he said. Faith put her t-shirt on the chair and slid back into bed with Ridge.

"And?"

"He sent someone down, told them to say they were your Dad's security and were watching the house. I confronted the guy at gunpoint and he took off. He's gone," Ridge said.

"Ridge."

"It's handled. Kellen told me and I handled it. He's gone."

Faith looked at him. "And I'm supposed to be able to sleep after that?"

"Holden was the guy's boss. Your Dad's security checked."

When she curled into his arms, he knew she was worried. "Even when we think things are over, they aren't. That's another reason to wait," he said as he kissed her forehead.

"Faith."

"What," she said.

"You okay?" She nodded and wrapped an arm around him, leaning her head onto his chest. He watched her eyes close and felt her nod back off. He kissed her forehead again and fell asleep.

The next morning, Ridge woke up and Faith hadn't moved

a muscle. When he went to get up, Faith smirked. "Good morning beautiful."

"Surprised that you're still in bed," she said.

He kissed her. "Getting up for a workout. You coming with me?"

"I had another idea," she teased.

He kissed her and got up. "I know what you're up to. Still going to do a workout first."

"Ridge."

"You can come with me." She got up, slid his t-shirt on and walked into his closet, watching him get changed.

"And if I want you to stay in bed with me?" He kissed her and pulled his joggers on. "Well?"

He picked her up, wrapped her legs around him and carried her to bed, leaning into her arms and pinned her to the bed. "I love you. You know I do."

"Ridge."

"Workout then I'm yours the rest of the morning until we head to your doctor's appointment."

She kissed him. "Then stay in bed."

He shook his head and kissed her. "An hour. Hour and a half max. Promise," Ridge said.

He kissed her again and she wouldn't let him get up. "Come with me."

She shook her head. "You are such a party pooper," she teased. The fact was, he was pissed.

He got up and went downstairs to start warming up while she got dressed. When she made her way downstairs, Kellen put out the two water bottles.

"Thank you," Faith said.

"Most welcome," Kellen replied.

"What actually happened last night," Faith asked.

"He handled it. The officers did a full follow-up. They're handling it."

"You sure?"

Kellen nodded. "Ridge scared the idiot off. I promise you. It's handled."

Faith nodded and walked downstairs. She stretched out and intentionally tried to distract Ridge. "Yes baby," he teased.

She kissed him and he finished his warmup. "I love you," Faith said.

"Love you back. What's wrong," Ridge asked.

"Nothing. I just wonder why he'd send someone here to cause trouble," Faith said.

"Babe, stop worrying about it. I handled it. I promise."

"Ridge."

"He's not coming back Faith."

He hopped off the treadmill and kissed her. "You're fine. We're fine. Don't worry about all of it. He's not coming near you."

She kissed him. "Okay," she said.

He kissed her again and went and started the rest of his workout. "If I said that I wanted to go to the beach?"

"Babe."

"Just for today."

"We can talk about it." He started in on his weights and kept going until he finished all of it. Faith sat on the step with her water and watched. "What," he asked when he sat up.

"Something isn't right."

"Meaning what," he asked.

"Meaning why is he doing this now?"

Ridge wiped the sweat from his face and kissed her, grabbed his water, and took her hand, walking her up the steps to the kitchen to see Eggs Benedict with lobster waiting for them.

"Thank you," Ridge said.

"Most welcome. Enjoy," her housekeeper said as she went to clean up the bedrooms.

"Ridge."

"Babe, I get it. I don't think going to the beach when his house is a few doors down is a good move. Once the police handle it and we get the call back from the detective, we can go back down."

"I still want to go."

He kissed her. "I know baby. We can go hang with your folks if you want to. Might be a little bit better."

She looked at him. "We're doing the dinner this weekend." He nodded with a smirk. "Oh, I know. After dinner, we can come back here and relax since you have work on Monday."

"Are you gonna come to the office?"

He smirked. "Don't I always," he joked.

Faith kissed him. "Ridge."

"What," he asked as he finished his breakfast.

"I may have to go to a couple stops on that book tour. The one for that guy who has been procrastinating with his book. I wanna make sure he actually shows up. Will you come," she asked.

"Determined to get out of town?" She smirked.

"Determined to be away from everything for a while." He kissed her.

"If that's what you want, fine," he said as he kissed her shoulder.

They finished breakfast, cleaned up and Faith took his hand and walked him up the stairs. "Babe, you do realize you actually..."

She kissed him and he picked her up, wrapping her legs around him. "And what do you want," Ridge asked.

She smirked. "Come to bed."

"Babe."

"Bed." He shook his head and leaned her onto the bed.

"Faith."

"Yes handsome."

"Tell me what you actually want," he said. She kissed him, enveloping his lips with hers until the kiss deepened. "Tell me," he said as the kiss broke and her shirt slid off.

"You," she replied as he devoured her lips and peeled her clothes off. Before he managed to say anything, she was pulling at his clothes.

"Stop," he said.

"Why?" He went to grab something from the drawer and saw that the condoms were gone.

"What did you do," he asked.

"Not using them." He shook his head, got up and went into his room and grabbed them from the inner pocket of his bag. He walked back into the bedroom and saw Faith walking into the bathroom.

"Faith."

"What," she asked as she turned the hot water on and stepped in to the shower.

"You gonna tell me the reason why you tossed them all?"

"You know why." Ridge shook his head and walked out of the bathroom, grabbed his change of clothes, and showered in the other bathroom. He finished his shower, dried off and freshened up and got dressed. He grabbed his phone and walked downstairs, going into the office and checking emails.

When Faith came downstairs, she motioned to Leo and Kellen that she needed to talk to Ridge alone and they vacated the office. "What," Ridge asked.

"There's nothing..."

"Woman, I'm not talking to you about this again. You want something you can't have. You get what you want. Enjoy it," he said as he went back to doing emails. She closed his laptop and slid it out of the way. "What?"

"I don't want anything coming between us Ridge. If I say that I'm ready, then we try."

He shook his head. "When you're done acting ridiculous, go and see the doctor. She'll prove that I'm right."

"Ridge."

"I get it Faith. I do. All I'm saying is that you need to wait and let your body catch up to your head." She slid into his lap. "Faith."

"I don't want us fighting about it."

"Then don't throw them out."

She kissed him. "We don't need them."

He shook his head. "Faith, just stop."

He sat her on the desk and got up. "Ridge."

"We're going. Now," he said.

Chapter 13

He grabbed his wallet and his cell off the charger and messaged the doctor that they were on the way. "Are you coming," Ridge asked.

She took his hand and walked him into her office, closing the door behind them. "Ridge, just stop."

"You're the one that threw out the only thing protecting you from getting pregnant. We're getting married Faith. Concentrate on that instead of all of the pregnancy stuff. We have time to do all of it. We haven't even got the damn cake and food yet. There's nothing wrong with waiting Faith. Nothing. There's no reason for you to rush all of it."

She kissed him. One kiss that was followed by sitting him on the sofa in her office. "What," he asked.

"I just don't want anything getting in our way of what we want."

He shook his head. "We're getting up and going to your appointment. Leave it at that until she gives you an answer."

Faith shook her head. "Ridge, just..."

"Up." She got up and he took her hand and walked her out to the truck, helped her in and hopped in on his side, heading to the doctor's office. "Faith, I get that you want it now. I do. Just stop."

"You scared me last night."

He shook his head. "Changing the topic?"

"You're getting mad, so yeah."

He shook his head. "I haven't heard a single word since he was arrested. The cops found him and threw him in cuffs. We're good," Ridge said.

"And?"

"And what?"

"And is it over?"

"When you have a ring on that finger, and he realizes that he has no chance at all, that's when it'll stop."

Faith looked at him. "I just don't get why he did that last night."

"Babe, it's done. He's handled. I'm not putting up with his crap. If he shows up here, he's leaving on a gurney."

"Ridge."

"I mean it." They pulled into the doctor's office not long later and headed in.

The doctor did a full check up on Faith and when she asked if she could try for kids, the doctor looked at her. "I did tell you before that you had to wait for a while. A week isn't gonna do it. Give it another 6 weeks. I don't want you to end up having another miscarriage. You have to give your body time to recuperate. When your body is ready, you won't have an issue. That's all that I want for you. Medically, I can't stop you from taking the chance. All I can say is that it's not a good idea yet. It's too soon."

Faith nodded. "Fine, but I still want to try."

"Faith, give your body time, like the doc said. Deal," he asked.

Faith looked at him. "No."

The doctor headed off and left them to talk. "Babe."

"Ridge, I want to try."

"And I want you to be able to have a baby without having to rush to the hospital when you collapse. I don't want you going through that again. It doesn't mean we can't be together Faith. Just stop." She shook her head. "What," he asked.

"I get it, but it doesn't mean that I don't want us to try."

"We will when you get the all-clear. Promise," he said.

Faith kissed him and they headed out not long later. He took her to get coffee then went for a walk at waterfront park. "You have a million dreams baby. I know you do. When it's time, we will have babies. As many as you want. Until then, we keep practicing. We'll be fine."

"Ridge, I just want to do whatever we want. That's it. I love you. I want us to be able to do whatever we want whenever without having to get protection. I just want the old…"

"Faith, we used them when we first met. There's no reason for you to hate them now."

"Ridge."

He kissed her. "If I have to then I will. My problem. When you're ready for more than practice then we try. We're waiting until the doctor says so." She looked at him and he slid his arms around her. "We have time baby. Just think about what we can do until you are," he whispered as she got goosebumps.

Faith turned and looked at him. "What," he asked.

"Think so do you?"

"Maybe finish appetizers. Never know," Ridge said.

"Finish?"

"You tried to tag out Faith. You said no more and stopped me."

She kissed him. "Appetizer and entrée." He looked at her.

"I don't know that you can make it through."

"Really," Faith asked.

He kissed her and nodded. "Come on wife to be," he said.

"Where?"

"Truck." He walked her back to the truck, helped her in and hopped in, heading back towards the house while they could before the traffic started.

"This mean that we're actually doing the movie night," Faith asked.

"This means that whether you like it or not, the blindfold is staying."

"Nope."

He looked at her. "Yeah it is. You really want all of it all over again then we're gonna be doing something different."

"Such as," Faith asked.

"You'll see tonight. The word mercy isn't even gonna be in your vocabulary."

"Do we need safe words?"

"Red."

"Really?" He nodded and Faith couldn't help the silly grin the crossed her face. "What are you up to," Faith asked.

"You won't need to walk tomorrow anyway," he teased.

"Ridge."

"What?"

She shook her head and he slid his hand in hers, linking

their fingers. "You being serious?"

He smirked. "Maybe," he teased.

Faith shook her head. "Ridge."

"What?"

"Seriously?"

"No promises," he teased. They got back to the house and Faith was still kinda stunned.

He got her door for her and Ridge smirked. "You were being serious."

He kissed her and came inside. He locked up behind him and Kellen came out of the office. "Were you waiting on a package," Kellen asked as Faith smirked.

"Bag."

Kellen looked at her. He did a check of the box and handed it to Faith. "And what is that," Ridge asked.

"If you can do it, so can I," she teased.

"And what did you get?"

She kissed him, took his hand, and walked him upstairs. "Faith."

She handed him the box. "And what is this?"

"Sorta for you, sorta for me."

He opened it and saw the lacy lingerie. "Really," he teased.

"Like?"

He nodded. "And what else did you buy?" When he saw the box, and what was on the box, he looked at her.

"Faith."

"Kinda like the idea," Faith said.

He took it out of the box, handed her the lingerie and kissed her. "Ridge."

"Nope."

"I got…" He kissed her and put it in his drawer, plugging it in to charge it.

"Ridge."

He kissed her. "What?"

"Give it back."

"Needs to charge." Faith shook her head and he picked her up and carried her to the bed, leaning her onto it.

"What," she asked.

"And you thought that either you'd need it or…"

"Am I not allowed…"

He kissed her. "The answer is no. You won't need it unless it's a back massager."

"Says who?"

"Only one night you'll need it. You may not need it though."

"And why's that," Faith teased.

He kissed her. "Only one night that we're apart. If you have someone else here, you may not want…"

"Ridge."

"I mean, unless you trade me in for a bigger pain in your backside, you won't. Anyone else, you will." When she shook her head and almost laughed, he knew. "Considering it?" She nodded and kissed him. "Really? And you seriously think that I believe that?"

She smirked. "You think I can't do anything with it other than that?"

"Depends on what you're thinkin. I know exactly what to do to show you if that's what you want."

"On you," Faith said.

He shook his head. "Not happening Faith. Don't even go there."

She smirked and he got up. "Fine. You have fun and I'll go get lunch," he teased.

"Ridge."

He smirked. "What?"

"Come here." Faith kissed him as he leaned into her arms.

"What would you like," he teased. Faith kissed him and he shook his head.

"You have no idea what you're in for."

"Oh really," Faith teased.

"You that determined to find out what we're doin tonight," he teased.

"I have a few ideas," she teased.

"You still have to make it through the movie sexy. You haven't made it through yet."

"You do realize that taunting me while we're watching it isn't playing fair right?"

"Like I said, my rules."

He kissed her and got up and pulled her to her feet. "Come on beautiful. You get work done and I'll get my emails done so we can relax."

"Ridge," Faith said as she stood up.

"What?"

"We need another movie," Faith teased. He shook his head.

"You haven't made it through that movie yet baby. We'll find another one when you get through the movie," he teased. Faith shook her head and got up, taking his hand as they headed back downstairs to attempt to get work done.

She went into her office, and Ridge went in to go over everything from the night prior. "And," Ridge said as he came in and sat down.

"Well, whoever it was, has been arrested. They got confirmation that Holden was behind it all. I'm not exactly impressed that he got this close," Kellen said.

"Me either. I thought the police said they had some unmarked cars out there," Ridge said.

"There were supposedly."

"I didn't see any," Ridge replied.

Kellen shook his head. "I didn't see any when I did perimeter checks either," Leo said.

"Then they're full of it. We need to get in touch with the PD and make sure the info they gave me is the truth."

"It's up to you," Kellen said. Ridge called the officer he'd spoken to.

"Mr. Sams," the officer said.

"I need to get some information on the case. Do they actually have these people in custody," Ridge asked.

"Yes. The only one that was out was Zack Fairchild. He was brought back into custody after an attempted break in at the beach house. Why do you ask," the officer asked.

"Because I was told there would be unmarked police cars at the house and the beach house last night and nobody was here. Holden sent someone to the house to keep an eye on my fiancée. It took y'all over a half hour to get here. The undercover officers should have seen it instead of me running out there at 2am to handle it," Ridge said.

"Understood. I'll get the information and get back to you. It even says on the file that they were supposed to be there," the officer replied. Ridge hung up with him a little while later and got up and got himself a drink.

When Faith messaged him to come to her office, he was still pissed. He took a deep breath and walked into her office, Jack in hand. "What happened," Faith asked.

"Nothin. What's up?"

"Ridge."

"It's fine."

"No, it isn't. Tell me what's going on." He took a deep breath, a gulp of his Jack and looked at her.

"There were supposed to be unmarked cop cars last night. There weren't any. It took them a half hour to get to the damn house."

Faith looked at him. "I'm not impressed," Faith said.

"Either am I," he replied.

"What's the plan," Faith asked.

"Telling them off. Getting extra security here. Honestly, I'm just kinda stunned that they're actually lying to me. I don't even know if they have them all in custody or not." Faith looked at him. "Beyond the stupid police crap, what's goin on," he asked determined to get his mind off of it.

"Well, I sorta have to go into the office all week."

"And?"

"And I have to go out of town for two signings."

"Where?"

"Los Angeles and Houston."

"And? What's the problem."

"It means that I'm not here for a few days."

"It means a tiny bit of a vacation or break from Charleston. When do you have to go?"

"Two weeks. Right after the dinner with the family."

"Private flight?"

Faith nodded. "I was going to offer a seat to the author."

"You sure?"

"Not even a little, but I kinda want him on a separate plane. Money wise, it's better for him to be on the plane with me."

"And your security staff."

"Meaning what," Faith asked as Ridge sat down on the sofa and she came and sat down with him.

"Meaning Kellen would come with us. We're good. Whatever you want to do we can handle," Ridge said.

"I'm getting my assistant to get a suite at both of the hotels. That work?"

"Kellen would need a room next door." Faith looked at him. "And why is that?"

"Because someone is very noisy at night."

"Ridge."

"Faith." She shook her head.

"Do you want me to book it?"

"Just make sure the author is at the other end of the hallway," he teased.

Faith shook her head. "You never ever..."

He kissed her and pulled her into his lap. "Never what?"

"You are so bad."

"Learning from the master," he joked.

One more kiss and Faith slammed the office door shut. "You have work to do Faith."

"And?" He shook his head and kissed her as she went to undo his jeans.

"You never behave."

"Not around you. You're the bad influence," she joked. He kissed her again and she got the button and zipper undone on his jeans.

"Faith, no."

She nodded and he shook his head. "Not happening."

"Ridge."

He zipped his jeans back up and did the button up. "Why," she asked.

"Stay here. Back in two minutes."

"Ridge."

"Either I get them or you come upstairs. Those are your options.

She kissed him and undid his jeans. "Faith."

When he felt her hand on him, he shook his head. "Don't you start that again."

When she ignored him and made her move, he couldn't even look. "Faith."

"What," she asked as he felt her tongue against him.

"Faith, not happening. Up." He saw her head shake from

side to side as she kept going. "Faith, stop."

She sped up. "Faith." When his body couldn't hold the pressure back anymore, his body exploded. Hell. He hadn't felt like that since...since Jekyll.

"Mine," Faith teased.

"You do realize that the more you attempt to taunt me, the worse you're gonna get it tonight right," he teased.

"Well, about that. There was something else in the box."

"Which would be?"

"Something I wanted..."

"Faith." She turned to face him and he saw her face blushing.

He shook his head. "Faith, you have no idea what you're..."

"I put it on your bed."

He shook his head. "Faith."

"What?"

"That's really what you want?"

"You don't even know..." He kissed her, devouring her lips, zipped and buttoned his jeans and took her hand, walking her up the steps to the bedroom. He closed the door behind her and saw what she'd left in his room on the bed.

"Really?"

"You started it." He saw the one thing he thought she'd never ever even think of.

"This is what you want?"

"You have the remote."

He smirked. "Then we're going out for dinner."

"Ridge."

"Somewhere fancy."

"Meaning what?"

"Peninsula Grill."

"Ridge, that place is past being fancy."

"Good," he replied.

"This means I'm wearing a dress right?"

"And you're wearing something under it or you're in serious trouble."

She kissed him. "Do we have to bring Kellen?"

He shook his head. "We're going tonight," he said as he took the toy and charged it. He grabbed his phone, got a last-minute reservation and took her hand.

"Go get changed," he teased.

"What color," Faith teased.

"Leave it at the more you think you're taunting me, the more that little thing you bought will go faster."

She looked at him. "Meaning what," she asked.

"You bought it. Making sure you get the full effectiveness."

He smirked, plugged it in and watched her walk into her bedroom. He grabbed the condoms from his drawer, putting some downstairs in her desk drawer, put half the package in her bedroom drawer and slid the other into his suit jacket. He put his suit on the bed, put his boxers, shirt, and tie with it, grabbed a condom from the drawer and saw her stepping into the shower. He kicked his clothes off and slid in behind her. He knew better. He put the condom on, determined to get her back for her office antics. "You are so in for it," he whispered.

"Think so do you," Faith asked. He kissed her, devouring her lips and picked her up, leaning her against the wall of the shower.

"What," Faith asked as he smirked.

"You really thought that was the end," he teased.

"Meaning what," Faith asked as he slid inside her.

"Ridge."

"Tonight is gonna be way too much fun," he almost purred into her ear.

"And why is that," Faith asked as her heart started

pounding and her breath started getting heavy. All it took was him walking her to the bench. That's it.

"Bend over," he teased.

"Ridge."

He kissed her, slid her to the floor of the shower and she did as he asked.

"So, you really thought that doing that would get me all turned on?"

Faith smirked. "I was partially right."

He kissed up her back and his hand started the taunting. "Ridge." First his fingers, then the feel of his kiss on the back of her neck and down her spine. "I know what you're trying to do," Faith said.

"Trying? You think that's trying? That's just warming you up," he whispered as she felt his warmth against her backside.

"Ridge."

"Yes sexy."

"I want you."

"Oh, I know."

Her body shuddered as his fingers intensified the taunting. "Ridge." He knew that she was almost at that point. The one where she would either crumble or go to a whole new level of intensity. He backed away and she shook her head. "Please," she said.

"As you wish sexy wife to be," he whispered as his body slammed into her and the sex was deep and throbbing and intense. They kept going until her body couldn't take anymore and she was trembling. He sat down and pulled her on top of him until she couldn't take it. His body let go and he held her tight to him.

"And you actually think I'm gonna be able to walk into that restaurant?"

He smirked and kissed her back. "Like I told you before, you have no idea what I have planned Faith. There was one other thing that could go with that little buzzer you bought, but I doubt you can handle it."

"Meaning what?"

"Meaning you really need to look at that little thing you bought."

She smirked. "Are you gonna tell me?"

"You'll know," he joked. She turned to face him and kissed him.

He helped her up, they showered, and he stepped out, sliding a towel around his hips, wrapping the other around her. "What are you gonna wear?"

She smirked and showed him the fancy red dress. The neckline was almost too low, the side slit was almost too high and she had found her favorite stilettos to wear with it. "Faith."

"What?"

"When did you get that dress?"

"A long time ago. It made me feel sexy." He smirked.

"Alright then," he teased. He kissed her, pulled his boxers on then his dress pants and saw the barely anything lingerie she put on. "You are so bad," Ridge said.

"Meaning?"

"You're gonna end up in my suit jacket."

"And," Faith asked.

He shook his head. "Fine. You go put on your sexy lingerie and I'll finish getting ready," he teased.

Faith motioned for him to come closer. "I know what you're up to. Don't think I don't sexy." She kissed him and he finished getting ready, intentionally putting her favorite cologne on. He did his hair, slid his dress shirt and tie on and walked downstairs. He sat down, talking to the guys, then slid his shoes on.

"Where are y'all headed?"

"Fancy place downtown. Peninsula Grill. We will most likely be late," Ridge said.

"I'll drive you down. Parking is crap right now," Kellen said.

"Then you're gonna need ear plugs," Ridge joked.

"I get it. I'll keep my eyes to myself," Kellen teased.

"Fine. We'll probably be there for a while." Kellen nodded and Ridge charged his phone and walked upstairs. He saw her little buzzing toy was fully charged and walked into the bedroom. He made sure he knew how the remote worked and came up behind her as she was freshening up. "What," Faith asked.

"Bend over."

"Ridge." He smirked. "Now?"

"Not turning it on yet if that's what you're asking." She did as he asked and he slid it into the lacy nothing panties. When she got a smirk ear to ear, he kissed the back of her neck.

"Ridge."

"What?"

"You sure you know what you're doing," she teased. He nodded and kissed her neck, zipping up the back of her dress.

"Need a quick test," he teased.

"Of what," she asked. He pressed one button and she almost jumped.

"Yep. It's workin."

"Ridge, I swear…"

"Mine," he joked.

"You are seriously trying to make my knees buckle."

"You started it sexy," he whispered as he kissed her neck. He walked into the bedroom, grabbed the necklace that he knew was perfect for the dress and walked over, sliding it around her neck. "How'd you know this is what I wanted to wear," Faith asked.

"Goes really well with the ring," he teased. He kissed her neck and went back downstairs, grabbing his bag and handing it to Kellen. He grabbed his phone, her purse and slid her phone into it. He smirked, sliding the remote into his pocket. Kellen slid the bag into the back of the SUV and came back inside.

Faith came downstairs a little while later and he couldn't help the grin. "You ready beautiful fiancée of mine?"

"Depends," Faith replied as he kissed her hand.

"On?"

"Are you driving?"

"I'm driving you over. Gives you two time to talk," Kellen said as Ridge shook his head.

"Party pooper," Faith said.

"I would've but someone decided to give us some extra alone time." Faith looked at Ridge. When she saw the smirk, she shook her head. "Alright then. Let's go," Faith replied. Ridge walked her outside, got her door for her and slid in beside her. Kellen hopped in and they headed to the restaurant.

"Ridge."

"Yep."

"What if we decided to stay downtown tonight?"

"We can if that's what you want," he replied.

She looked at Ridge and smirked. One look to Kellen and he nodded. "And what was that," Faith asked.

"I had a feeling you'd say that. My bag is in the back."

"I can get a bag from the house for you," Kellen said.

"Okay," Faith said. They made their way downtown and he smirked. "What," Faith asked.

"Nothin," Ridge said. She couldn't help the little laugh. "Tell me when you want the game to begin," he whispered.

"Which one?"

He kissed her. "You know." She smirked. He shook his head. When she felt a slight buzz, she shook her head. Fidgeting was the least of her problems. "What," he whispered.

"Not here." He kissed her shoulder. Her phone buzzed as

they made their way to the bridge to head downtown.

"Yep."

"The rooms have been booked. Are you two alright heading out on Sunday night," her assistant asked.

"As long as it's after 8pm. Ridge and I are flying out alone."

"Alright. I'll get the arrangements made. I booked the author and his wife on a regular commercial flight."

"Thank you," Faith said as she hung up with her assistant.

"And?"

"Just you and I on the flight. Happy now?"

He smirked. "Yep." He kissed her and they pulled up to the restaurant not long later. He hopped out, helped Faith out of the SUV, and Kellen nodded. He got the room key for the suite that Ridge had booked, came back, and had it brought to the table for him and headed back to the house.

"Right this way sir," the waitress said as they made their way over to a back corner private table. "What can I get you from the bar," the waitress asked.

Faith ordered wine and Ridge ordered a bottle. "We're both having wine? Really," Faith said.

"You'll need it," he whispered as she got goosebumps. The wine showed a short while later and he poured them each a glass.

"Have you had a chance to look over the menu," the waitress asked. They both ordered and Faith got a smirk.

"What," he teased.

"Nothin," she said.

"Now, about that little game that you are determined to have," he teased.

"What about it?"

He slid his hand into his pocket and turned the buzzing on gently. She grabbed his leg. "What?"

"Ridge."

He kissed her. "And that's just the beginning," he whispered as she got goosebumps.

"Meaning what," Faith asked as he turned the tiny side on that she hadn't noticed was part of it.

"Where did that…"

"Like I said, you missed that part," he teased. Faith took a sip of her wine and he turned the buzz up just a little.

"Ridge, you are so not playing fair."

He smirked. "You did start this."

"Okay. Break."

He smirked. "More wine?"

She shook her head and kissed him. "Thank you," she said.

"Most welcome. You do realize that this specific dress is illegal right?"

"I wore it for you."

He kissed her again. "So, my sister is in. She's at my Mom and Dad's."

"Meaning your sister and my brother get to face off again," Faith teased.

"Something like that. I told her to be on her best behavior."

She smirked and kissed him. "And," Faith asked.

"What?"

"Do you think she can actually do it?"

"Behave? I mean, you can't. That I do know. I don't think that she's gonna do anything stupid."

Faith nudged him in the ribs. "I can to."

He shook his head. "No, you can't. Any more than I can when you're attempting to taunt me."

"Attempting? I succeeded," she teased. He slid his hand into his pocket and pressed the little button as the buzzing started again.

"You were saying."

She grabbed the edge of his jacket. "You have no idea what I have planned tonight," he whispered as their appetizer arrived and he almost smirked. He kissed her neck and Faith shook her head, he turned the buzzing down and they had their soup then once the dishes were taken away, he turned it back up and turned on the other part that he knew she had no idea about.

"Ridge."

"Yes beautiful."

"Off."

"Why?"

"Because if you don't I swear, I'm knocking the food to the dang floor."

"I'm not doin anything," he teased. Faith shook her head and he saw that she meant it. He turned the biggest part of the toy off and amped up the buzzing.

"Ridge."

"What," he teased. She grabbed his hand and dug her nails in.

"Not yet," he whispered.

"Off." He kissed her shoulder and turned it off. Just long enough for them to eat their entrée then she was all his. As soon as she finished, the taunting started all over again, and all it took was the flick of a button in his pocket. It kept going until he kissed her and she almost moaned his name. "Still think you can outdo me," he whispered.

"I need you right now. I don't care about the damn restaurant," she whispered.

"You mean this," he said as he flicked the button for the thrusting part of the way too hot toy.

"Ridge." He got the check, paid and the waitress left them to finish their wine.

"You have no idea what you're getting tonight. No movie," he whispered as she white-knuckled his hand.

"I need it off." He kissed her and flipped the thrusting part off and turned up the one spot that he'd noticed she'd got as part of the toy.

"Ridge, you aren't funny."

"You sure," he whispered.

"Crap."

"What," he asked.

"Ah," she said as he could hear her heart racing and her breath hitching.

"Didn't realize it did you," he whispered. She grabbed his hand. "What," he teased. She slid it under the bottom of her dress and he knew. He was turning the little buzz off, but it was going right back on at the hotel. They had their wine as Faith got a smirk ear to ear.

"Fine. Payback," Faith teased.

"That wasn't even on medium," he joked. They finished their wine and he helped her out of the booth and walked her out to the SUV.

"And how was dinner," Kellen asked.

"Really good," Faith teased.

"Your key," Kellen said as he handed the other room key to Faith.

"Where," Faith asked.

"Your favorite," Ridge whispered.

"I put your bags in the room for you. Just let me know when you're ready to head back," Kellen said.

"Thanks my friend," Ridge said.

"Most welcome," Kellen said as they pulled up to the hotel. They hopped out and made their way to the elevators and up to the luxury club suite. They walked in and Faith saw the roses.

"Ridge."

"What?"

"Don't say what. When did you manage all of this?"

"I know my woman. That's it. I had the hotel booked right after I got the restaurant reservation."

"This is beautiful," Faith said. He smirked. "What?"

"Nothin," Ridge said as he slid his hand into his pocket and round 1 of taunting began.

"Ridge, I know what you're up to." He turned it up even more and she almost jumped. He smirked and sat down on the sofa. "Ridge, I swear, cut it out."

"Come here then," he teased as he got a smirk ear to ear. She walked into the living room area of the suite and slid into his lap.

"Off." He shook his head.

"I'll take it off."

"But that's half the fun sexy," he teased as he pulled her to him and kissed her. He heard her breath hitching and felt her heart racing.

"Turn it off."

He shook his head and kissed down her neck. "Ridge," she said as he turned it up even more. Before she could say anything, he kissed her again and she untied his tie.

"What," he teased.

"Aah," she said as her breath hitched.

"Really...hmm."

"Ridge, off."

He smirked and kissed her. "Not even 5 minutes," he teased as his hand slid up her leg.

"Ridge." He kissed down her chest and he turned the intensity down just a little. She shook her head and went to peel the lace panties off when he stopped her and pinned her hands behind her back. "I can't," Faith said.

"Now it's my turn," he teased.

"I need a breather."

"The woman who was all determined to get me hot and bothered and now she needs a breather."

"Ridge."

He kissed her, devouring her lips and turned it off, sliding the toy and the panties right off. "Better," he teased. She kissed him and undid his dress shirt. "Tie," he said.

"What?"

"Faith, give me the tie." She handed it to him and he intentionally tied her hands.

"What are you doing?"

"You said you wanted the appetizer and entrée all in one. That was your comment," he teased as he nibbled down her neck then down the neckline of the dress. "You really shouldn't walk around all naked like this," he teased.

"Meaning what," Faith asked as she felt him nibble and kiss her breasts.

"Meaning you're lucky you weren't on my lap before we even got dinner."

She kissed him and he smirked. "What," Faith asked.

"Determined to win or lose," he joked.

"With what?" He kissed her, picked her up and sat her on the bed. He untied her hands.

"What are you up to handsome?"

"Dress, off." He undid the dress, slid it off of her and saw the way too sexy lingerie.

"Baby."

"What?"

"Damn. You got this to get my attention?"

"Yep," Faith teased with a smirk ear to ear.

"Gonna look just as sexy on the floor," he teased. Faith looked at him and he kissed her.

"Ridge."

"Yes," he teased as he kissed down her neck and hung up his suit jacket, her dress, his shirt and then slid her heels off.

"What are you up to," Faith asked.

"Making sure you're comfortable," he joked.

"And you're all dressed." He kissed her and grabbed a few things from his bag, flipping the lights off and drawing all of the blackout curtains. "Really," Faith asked.

He kissed her and went and got them each a drink, putting it beside the bed along with a glass of ice. "And what are you doing," Faith asked. He kissed her and devoured her lips, sliding her further onto the bed so she was up near the headboard. "Ridge."

"What?"

"I love you."

"Love you back sexy. By the way, I found the other stuff you bought."

"What?"

"That other thing you bought thinking I wouldn't notice. Fully charged," he whispered as she got goosebumps again.

"Ridge, I know…"

"What? You second-guessing that purchase," he teased.

"Sorta."

He kissed her again and leaned into her arms. "What do you need," he asked with that grin ear to ear. She grabbed her glass and took a gulp. "What," he asked.

"Breather."

He kissed her and slid her legs around him. "Really?"

She nodded and he slid the blankets down. "Faith."

"What?"

"I have an idea."

"Oh crap."

He kissed her and got up. He walked into the massive bathroom and saw the huge tub. He drew them a hot bath and kicked his dress pants off. "Faith."

"What," she asked.

"Come here."

She got up and walked into the massive bathroom seeing a tub filled with water. "What's this," she asked.

"Slide in. I'll get the drinks." He got the drinks from the bedside table and heard the relief of her sliding into the tub. He smirked, kicked his boxers off, making sure he had condoms nearby and walked into the bathroom and slid into the tub with her as Faith slid across the tub and into his lap. "Better," he asked. Faith nodded and kissed him.

"Thank you for dinner," Faith said as she kissed him.

"Welcome beautiful. You do know that we don't have to do anything tonight if you don't want to right?"

She kissed him. "One night where we aren't worrying about keeping quiet, where we can do whatever we want to? Not likely," she teased.

"Meaning you're ready for anything," he joked.

"Meaning you better be."

Chapter 14

They snuggled, had their wine, and she did her best to taunt him. He shook his head. "Faith."

"What?"

"You really think that you can get me all hot and bothered with that," he asked.

Faith nodded. "Pretty sure," she said as she put the drink down and slid over into his lap.

"Really?"

She nodded and kissed him as he felt her hand. "Faith."

"What?"

"I know what you're doing. Not workin."

"Really, because it sorta seems like it is," Faith said as he kissed her and she slid in closer.

"Faith."

She slid into his lap, pulling her legs tight around him. "What?"

"Not happening." She kissed him and he shook his head. "Up."

"Why?"

"If you're all hot and bothered already, then you're getting up. Go on," he teased as he calmed himself down.

"Ridge." He kissed her, got up and wrapped a towel around him, then wrapped one around Faith. "Ridge."

He took her hand, walked her into the bedroom and kissed her. "What," she asked.

He grabbed his phone, pressed something on the screen and pulled her into his arms. "What," she asked as she heard music.

"Dance with me," he asked.

"Ridge." He kissed her and pulled her into his arms. He danced with her to slow song after slow song, making it the most romantic night. "Ridge."

"What," he teased.

"What are you up to?"

"Am I not allowed to be all romantic with my woman?"

"Ridge."

He kissed her. "What?" She smirked.

He kissed her again and Faith shook her head with a grin ear to ear. The guy who was all physical was now the romantic? "What," Ridge asked seeing the look on her face.

"I love you. You know that right," Faith asked. He nodded and kissed her again.

"I also know what you want," he teased. She kissed him

and he picked her up and sat her on the bed, leaning into her arms. "Now, you were saying," he teased.

"Ridge."

"What?"

"I liked the romance."

"The last time we danced together, we were at prom. The only time."

She looked at him. "You remember that?"

He pressed a button on his phone and heard the song. "Remember?"

Faith looked at him. "Really," she asked.

He smirked. "Did you think I could ever forget it?" She kissed him.

"Thank you."

"Do you remember what happened during that song?" She smirked and kissed him, sliding her legs around him.

"Yep."

"You were drunk Faith."

"And you kissed me." He leaned in and devoured her lips.

"You know what I wanted to do?"

She kissed him and undid his towel, then untied hers. "I

have an idea," she teased. He kissed her and slid her onto the bed, flipping the light off. "What," Faith asked.

"Only an idea," he teased as he kissed her then kissed down her neck.

"Ridge."

"What?" He kept going, kissing down her torso, nibbling at her breasts until he knew her toes were curling. "Ridge."

He smirked. "What," he asked as he kissed her hip.

"I love you." He kissed her inner thigh and he could feel her breathing hitch and deepen.

"You all good," he teased.

"Ridge, you..."

"What?"

When she felt his warm breath against the warmest part of her, she shook her head. It didn't take much to get her turned on. The feel of his tongue against her, his lips, his teeth nibbling just enough to turn her toes into pretzels. All of it was getting her turned on. "Ridge."

"Yes sexy." His fingers took over and she was reaching for him.

"I need you."

"I haven't even started yet," he joked as he stopped and grabbed something from his bag.

"Ridge."

He flipped on the first of a few things that he'd brought to taunt her. "Yes my love," he said as he slid it against her inner thigh and then up to the apex of her thighs until her legs were almost shaking.

"Ridge."

"Yes beautiful," he said as the buzzing hit the one spot that made her toes almost contort into triple knots. When he leaned in and kissed her, she was almost moaning. "Just remember who started this," Ridge teased as she kissed him until they were making out and giving her goosebumps on top of goosebumps.

"Faith."

"Aah."

"More?" He saw her nod and he turned the speed up until she was grabbing at him.

"Ridge, come here."

"Nope."

"Ridge." He turned it up one more notch until she felt him kiss her neck.

"Off. I want you," Faith said.

"Not yet."

"Ridge." He kissed her and devoured her lips as the toy

just got more intense. "Ridge."

"What," he asked as he flipped the other button on and Faith was almost moaning his name. "So that's what it does," he teased.

"Oh my god. Ridge."

"What," he whispered.

"I want you. Now," Faith said. "Oh baby. I know. You haven't even made it through the appetizers," he whispered as she clamped on his arm.

"I need you."

"You sure you want me to turn it off?" When he felt her body almost trembling, he slid in behind her and her hand clamped onto his arm as her body crashed through another orgasm. "Really. I must remember this little thing next time I decide to taunt you."

"Ahh."

"Hmm. Yeah I like this one," he whispered as her body leaned against his. He slowly turned it down and she thought she'd get a breather. When he grabbed something else, she tried to get him to sleep with her. "Round two," he whispered as she felt another buzzing against her skin.

"Please." He kissed the nape of her neck and she leaned against him. "Please Ridge."

"Tell me what you want," he whispered as her nails dug

into his thigh.

"I need you." He kissed her shoulder and she shook her head. "Please." He slid the toy into the one place that was already tender and grabbed a condom from his bag.

"Crap."

"Already," he whispered.

"I need you."

"How badly," he whispered as he turned the speed up.

"Ridge." Her entire body was almost humming and throbbing around the buzzing that he was taunting her with.

When he felt her body climax again, he smirked and threw the buzzing toys into his bag, putting the condom on. She went to turn around to face him and felt his fingers take over. "You are so not playing fair," Faith said.

He smirked. "Just the way you like it," he whispered as he saw her goosebumps come up again. She turned to face him and he kissed her, devouring her lips.

"Now," she said.

"Not even..." She pulled his hand away and leaned him onto his back. "Nope," he teased.

"Ridge."

"Not yet." She leaned into his arms and kissed him and he

leaned her onto her back. "You really have no idea do you," he whispered.

"Meaning what," Faith asked as he went back to taunting her.

"What I have planned."

"Meaning?"

"You know that thing you were playing with at dinner?"

She nodded. "We could just bring that…"

"Ridge."

"That little, tiny part that you didn't know what it did." She looked at him as the taunting intensified. She pulled him on top of her and slid her legs around him as he took every buzzing toy away and made love to his fiancée.

Her body was throbbing and they kept going until he couldn't hold back. Until his body said it'd had enough. He felt her body reach its peak and he gave in. He found his release the moment her nails were digging into his back. "I guess it was a really good idea to be away from all the other…"

She kissed him and he slid to his back. She collapsed onto his chest. "I love you," Faith said as he felt her body still throbbing. He pulled the blankets up over them and she nodded off. She was more than spent. He was actually stunned that she'd lasted that long.

He got up a little while later, cleaned up, putting everything away, and slid back into bed with Faith, putting the phones on the charger he'd brought and putting condoms on the bedside table. He knew her just that well.

"Where did you go," Faith asked as he slid her into his arms.

"Cleaned up and charged the cell phones. Why," he teased.

He felt her leg wrap around his. "Ridge."

"What?"

"Marry me."

He smirked. "Kinda beat you to it baby." She kissed him and he leaned her back onto the bed. "Sleep love. You need sleep."

She kissed him again and nodded. "I love you."

"Love you back," Ridge replied as he curled up to her, wrapping his arm around her and pulling her against him so she was his little spoon.

When Faith woke up the next morning, he still had his arms around her and she felt his spiky kisses against her shoulder. "About time you woke up," he teased.

"What time is it," Faith asked.

"8. I have just enough time to taunt you all over again and still get you to church," he teased.

"Ridge."

"What," he teased as she turned to face him.

"I think we might miss..."

"Nope." She kissed him.

"Breakfast is on its way up."

"Ridge," she said.

"What?"

"We aren't..."

"We have to. I promised."

She shook her head. "When is breakfast coming?"

"20 minutes." She smirked. "I swear, you are worse than a horny teenager in the morning," he teased. She kissed him and he shook his head. "What am I gonna do with you?"

"Marry me. Have babies with me. Forever and a day."

He kissed her. "You already have my forever. You always did," Ridge said as she kissed him. When the kiss turned deeper, he knew. The shower wouldn't be enough, and it wasn't big enough anyway.

He grabbed a condom from the counter. "Ridge."

"What?"

"I don't want to use..."

He kissed her. "This or we don't do anything." He slid it on and Faith kissed him.

"I don't want…"

He shook his head. "Faith, stop. I told you before that either we use something or we aren't gonna do anything."

"I want…"

He kissed her, determined to silence the complaint. Her legs wrapped around him and they had sex that morning in bed. The fact was, the minute she complained about the condom was the minute she'd turned him right off, but he could fake it just long enough. When they came up for air, he got up. He had a quick shower, pulled his boxers on and there was a knock at the door.

He got breakfast and brought hers into her. "Are you sitting with me," Faith asked.

"Come sit in the living room," he said.

Faith slid his hoodie on and walked into the living room.

"Are you talking to me," Faith asked.

"We did talk about this right? Where I said we weren't going without it until the doctor said okay."

"I just want us to be able to do whatever we want." He shook his head.

"Faith, I'm not having the fight again. If you want to be together and sleep together, we're using it. That's the deal," he said. Faith shook her head and noticed that he'd got her eggs benedict.

"Ridge."

"What?"

"I love you."

"I love you too," he said. They finished eating and she got up and went to go shower.

"Come with me," Faith asked.

"Go ahead. I already showered."

She grabbed his hand. "What?"

"Come." He kissed her and flipped the water on for her as he freshened up and got ready for church. He got all the clothes put into the bags, leaving out her heels, dress, and lingerie. He got everything done then sat down on the sofa and called Kellen.

"And how was your night," Kellen said.

"Fine. We're heading to church then coming back to the house. You good to come get us," Ridge asked.

"Why are you all uptight again?"

"Yes or no Kellen?"

"Yeah, but what happened that got you in a crappy mood again?"

"Doesn't matter. I'll see you at 12:30."

"I'll be there," Kellen said. He hung up with Ridge a few minutes later and Faith came into the bedroom.

"Come here," Faith said. He slid his phone in his pocket and walked into the bedroom.

"What," he asked.

"I love you. You know that right?"

"Faith, we can talk about it later. We have to get to church."

"Ridge." He shook his head. She put on a little makeup, put her hair up and came into the living room with her toiletry bag. "We need to talk before we go."

"Why? We discussed this Faith. You don't want to use them then we aren't sleeping together. No more movies, no more toys. Nothing."

"I just don't want to have to keep using them." He shook his head, handed Faith her phone and put her things with his bags. Kellen messaged 20 minutes later that he would get the bags and take them over to church and they headed downstairs. Ridge checked out of the suite and they hopped in the SUV. When they got to church, she held onto his hand. She wasn't about to let go.

They sat down and Faith nudged him. "What?"

"I love you. I just don't like them."

"Fine. Don't." The service started a few minutes later. By the time the service finished, he was even more pissed. They headed out and Faith was determined to hold his hand. They got into the SUV and headed back to the house. "I got you both your coffee," Kellen said as he handed the iced lattes to them.

"Thank you," Ridge said.

"Most welcome. Everything alright?" Ridge glared at him.

"You could at least talk to me," Faith said.

"Don't start."

They got back to the house and Ridge took his things upstairs. Faith followed him. "Can you at least talk to me," Faith asked.

"We talked to the doctor. You agreed to what she said. Why change your mind now?"

"Because I want you. I want you without the stupid..."

"What?"

"You know what. If we're getting married, there's no reason why we should even wait."

"Then go tell the doc that and see what she says. If you aren't gonna listen to her, I'm sleeping in another damn room."

"Ridge."

He shook his head and put his bag in his old bedroom. "You can't be serious," she said. He put his things away and she walked in behind him. "Ridge."

"What?"

"I want us to try again."

"Then do it by yourself."

He walked back downstairs and got his water from the fridge. He walked back up to his room, got dressed into workout gear and went and worked out alone. He overdid all of it and he knew it. When his arms started to ache, he forced himself to stop. He stretched out and saw Faith sitting on the steps in her shorts, bikini, and t-shirt. "What?"

"Talk."

"Nothing to talk about Faith. You wanna ignore the doc, you tell her why. I'm not playing that game with you."

"Last night..."

"Last night was the last time. You don't wanna use them, we aren't sleeping together. Nothing. Period."

He went to walk past her and she stopped him. "Fine." He shook his head and walked past her, walked upstairs, grabbed his protein shake and headed upstairs to shower off all the sweat.

He walked into the bedroom, closed the door, went and

hopped into the shower and tried to wash the anger from his system. They'd had the same fight over and over. Whatever her reason was for trying to get pregnant, he had no idea. All he did know was that she was driving him up a damn wall. He knew that night wouldn't be easy. He probably wouldn't even sleep. He hadn't when he tried to not be around her. He'd always ended up back in bed with Faith, falling asleep to the scent of her shampoo that he'd loved. He shook his head. He had to shake the feeling off if it was the last thing he did. She wanted to be pregnant when they got married, he'd do it. He just wanted the doctor to give the okay. That's it. He didn't want her going through another miscarriage. He didn't want that on his conscience. He could fight himself all day and night, but he knew that she wasn't gonna let him separate himself from any of it. She wanted him. That's it. Hell. He wanted her just as much. He wanted to take advantage of every second. Make her feel like she had the night prior when she was begging for him. She felt so good. Like they were perfectly matched. He loved her to the end of the world, but he couldn't keep fighting her on everything.

He finished showering and took a deep breath, cooling the water to cool him off and make the steam shooting from his ears calm. He stepped out of the shower and grabbed a towel then saw her sitting on the countertop. "Faith, I'm not doing this."

"Ridge."

He shook his head, walked past her, and walked into his closet. He slid into shorts and boxers and a tee and walked downstairs. He grabbed his laptop and went and sat down outside on the patio. Faith saw him go outside, grabbed her laptop, and went outside to sit with him.

"Are you talking to me," Faith asked.

"I'm not having the fight again Faith. You want to go through all of it again then do it without me."

Faith looked at him. "I just want to be with you Ridge. That's it. I love you. Yeah, I want to have a baby with you. I just want us to be us again. Please."

He shook his head. "Faith, the doc says no. Until she gives you a go ahead, we're using something."

"I don't wanna lose you."

"Faith, I'm mad, not stupid. All I said was that until you accept that we're not going without for a while or I'm not sleeping in there with you, and I'm staying in my own room."

"You stay in there then I'm staying with you."

"And?"

"Ridge."

"Are you dropping all of the complaining?"

"Ridge, I want us. I don't want to lose you in all of this. I just…"

He kissed her. "Figure it out Faith. We've had this fight too many times already love. I'm not going through it again. I want us to be together and have a future with babies, but not until I know that we don't have to go through a miscarriage ever again."

Faith looked at him. "I love you Ridge. I just want to be able to do what we want instead of having a roadblock. If we want to have a baby, I don't want that getting in our way. I want to forget the miscarriage and the hospital."

He looked at her getting welled up. "So do I, but we have to wait. It doesn't mean that we can't be together Faith. It just means we make sure that you're healthy enough to try when we decide to."

"And?"

"And I'm not putting you in that situation again." She nodded. "Babe, I've loved you most of my damn life. I'm not leaving. All I'm saying is that I want us to be safe."

"Okay."

"No more fighting about using them. Nothing. Promise me." She nodded and he slid her laptop out of her lap and put both laptops on the table, pulling her to him. "No more stupid crap Faith. None. I get that you're frustrated, but just be happy that we have each other. That you're okay and healthy. When it's safe, we can try. I promise you I'll try as much as you want to."

Faith smirked. "Oh really?"

He nodded. "This mean we can practice tonight," she

teased.

"I love you. We'll see," he teased.

Faith snuggled him. "I can lose babies, I can lose everything, but I'm not losing you," Faith said.

"Exactly," Ridge said as he kissed her.

She curled up beside him on the chaise and looked at him. "What?"

"What's going on with the cop stuff? I thought I heard you complaining about something."

He shook his head and kissed her. "It's fine."

"Ridge." He shook his head again and grabbed his laptop, going into his email. When he saw the follow-up from the detective, he shook his head:

> *All of the men you mentioned have been arrested. Holden and Zack are both out on bail. The man who was arrested last is being held. They wouldn't allow him to get bail after everything that happened. If Zack or Holden contacts you or your fiancée, or her parents, it's violation of a restraining order. The woman who was party to Holden's threats was also arrested. Beyond that, it's handled. The case is going to court within the next 4 months. I'll keep an eye out. The man caught by your home was found and he had been employed by Holden, not her Dad. I'll keep you updated.*

Ridge shook his head and Faith looked at him. "Great. Holden of all stupid idiot people," Faith said.

"I kinda thought that was the deal. I'm just not exactly impressed."

"Ridge."

"Yes sexy."

"We good?"

"I don't want us fighting about it again okay?"

She nodded and kissed him. He kissed her forehead, hugging her until Kellen came outside. "What's up," Ridge asked.

"Did you get the email?"

Ridge nodded. "We have one other small issue." Ridge kissed Faith and got up, grabbing his laptop, and walked inside behind Kellen.

"What?"

"Holden called her phone. Twice. I managed to get into her phone and blocked his number and email from accessing anything in her phone. I just have a feeling."

"Make sure that they do regular checks at the beach and double up on checks here. If anything seems fishy, let me know and I'll get her out of here." Kellen nodded.

"Get who," Faith asked as she put her laptop down and

slid her arms around Ridge's waist.

"You. Holden already broke the restraining order."

"How?"

"Your phone."

Faith looked at Ridge then at Kellen. "What?"

"He called your phone twice and texted 3 times just this morning," Ridge said.

"How on earth did you two…"

Ridge looked at her. "To make sure you're safe, we backed up both our phones so we could track incoming stuff. I've got just as many stupid texts from them as you did."

Faith looked at him. "So, now what," Faith asked.

"We sent the info to the police. They're probably gonna re-arrest Holden for whatever," Ridge said.

Faith looked at him. "What?" She took his hand and walked him into her office, closing the door.

"What?"

She kissed him. "Faith."

"I am a little irritated that you didn't tell me about the phone stuff."

"And yet, you kissed me."

"I was mad, but honestly, I'm glad you guys handled it instead of me seeing it and flipping out."

"And that's not just because we finally quit fighting over the other thing?"

She shook her head and kissed him. "Faith."

"I'm just glad that you did it. Honestly, I hate him," Faith said.

"And?"

"Thank you."

He kissed her. "You good now?" Faith nodded. "The truth Faith."

"Irritated that nobody told me about having access to my texts, but I understand why," she replied.

He looked at her and sat her on her desk. "Faith."

"What?"

"You're really gonna just let that go when we did it intentionally without you knowing?"

Faith looked at him. "My Dad suggested it, but never got around to it," Faith said.

He shook his head. "Way too dang calm," he said.

"I knew you were. I knew a long time ago."

"And?"

"I had a feeling Ridge. There's no point in getting mad. The texts that Kellen saw might've been a little racy for his eyes if he saw the ones between us."

Ridge shook his head and looked at her. "You do know that you're in for it right."

"Why? Because I knew or because of the racy texts?"

"Both."

She kissed him. "And? What are you gonna do about it husband to be?"

"Maybe you sleep in that big ole bed without me."

"Or not."

He shook his head. "Or maybe you don't get any mercy."

"Ridge."

"Or I tie your hands tonight."

She looked at him. "You wouldn't dare," she teased.

He nodded. "I'll think about it this afternoon."

She smirked. "I bet you will. You gonna come swimming?"

"You go ahead. Just be prepared for that bikini to vanish."

She kissed him. "Promises, promises."

Faith kissed him and slid off the desk, running upstairs to the bedroom. He shook his head and walked back to talk to Kellen. "She pissed," Kellen asked.

Ridge shook his head. "Not even a little," he teased.

"And," Kellen asked.

"And she's fine. She sorta saw it coming."

"I did see other messages that came up between the two of you, but I didn't read them," Kellen said.

"Appreciate it but leave it. I'm gonna go for a swim for a bit. If you need me let me know?"

Kellen nodded and Ridge walked upstairs. Just as he did, he looked outside and saw her sliding into the pool. He shook his head and kicked his shorts and boxers off, slid his swim shorts on and pulled his t-shirt off, grabbing pool towels on his way outside.

When he got out there, she was leaning against the edge of the pool and watched him walk towards her. "What you doin over there sexy," Ridge asked.

"Waiting on you," Faith teased. He kissed her and slid into the pool.

"And what else," he teased as he slid up behind her and leaned his body against hers. In the back of his mind, putting condoms in his pocket of his swim shorts was the best idea ever. He slid one on, intentionally being prepared. "What," Faith asked.

His hand slid over her hip and into the front of her bikini

bottoms.

"Nothin," he whispered as he saw her toes almost curling. "Now, you were saying," he teased.

"Ridge."

"Yes."

"If I said that…"

He kissed her neck and untied the bikini bottoms.

"What?" When he started taunting even more and she felt him against her, she wanted to turn and face him, but he kissed her neck and linked their fingers as they had sex in the pool. It was almost as hot as the two of them having sex in the ocean, but better.

"You were saying," Ridge asked as the water started splashing around them.

"Aah."

"What," he whispered as he got deeper and harder until she was almost clamping down on his hands. "This what you wanted this morning," he asked.

Faith nodded and he kissed her neck. "Turn around," Ridge said. As she did, her legs clamped around him and he pinned her against the wall of the pool.

"So much easier when you aren't picking fights," he teased as he kept going until he knew that he couldn't hold back.

"Aahh. Ridge," she said as her body shuddered around his.

"Much better," he teased as she kissed him and he slid them both underwater.

"Now what," he teased.

"I thought you said we couldn't without..."

He slid it off and put it into his other pocket. "We didn't."

She kissed him. "I love you," she replied.

"You'd better."

She slid her legs tighter around him and he kissed her again. "Faith."

"Yes sexy fiancée," she replied with a grin ear to ear.

"You sure you're good?" He slid his swim shorts up and handed Faith her bikini bottoms.

"Better than good. I have just about everything I could want," she replied as she kissed him.

"Babe."

"I know. When it's time, we can. What do you want to do tonight handsome?"

"Movie."

He smirked. "You sure?"

She nodded. "Could work. Might need to change things up

tonight though."

"Meaning what," she asked.

"Meaning that thing you loved from yesterday."

She looked at him. "You wouldn't." He smirked. "Ridge."

"During the movie."

Faith shook her head. "And you really think that's a good idea?"

He smirked. "I figured out a few things about it. Wanted to try that out," he joked.

Faith kissed him and he walked into the deep end. "What," Faith asked.

He kissed her. "Just getting out of the sight line of the camera," he teased.

"For what..." He kissed her with a kiss that could've boiled the water around them. Her heart pounded against his chest and her breath hitched. "Ridge," she said as they came up for a split second of air.

"What," he asked.

"What are you up to?"

"No more fights. No more worrying, no more drama, no more ignoring what I say. Deal," he asked.

"Depends on what you're saying." He hopped out of the

pool, helped her out and leaned her onto the chaise. "Ridge."

"Yes or no Faith?" She nodded and he kissed her again. He pulled the towel around her, picked her up and walked upstairs.

"What," Faith asked. He closed the bedroom door and pinned her against it.

"Mine," he teased as she nodded. He kissed down her neck and walked to the bed, leaning her onto it and throwing the towel to the floor.

He leaned into her arms and Faith fumbled to pull the bikini top off. "Faith."

"What?"

"Turn over." She looked at him and shook her head. "No."

He turned her so she was face down on the bed. "What," Faith asked.

"Just stay there."

"Why," she asked.

"Because." She fully thought that Ridge was about to start taunting her all over again, but he had another plan. One she wasn't expecting at all. She was wound so tight, he thought she'd snap sometimes, and there was only one cure for that. He went into the drawer and she fully expected to hear the tearing of a condom packet, but she didn't. "What are you doin," Faith asked.

"Woman, just sit and relax." He smirked and opened the little bottle, rubbing some massage oil into his hands. When she felt the warmth against her back, she smirked. "What's that," Faith asked. He kissed the back of her neck. When he started massaging her neck and shoulders, she almost melted into the bed. "Ridge."

"Yes beautiful."

"Thank you." He smirked and got her neck and shoulders relaxed in minutes, until she turned towards him again. "Faith."

"What?" He shook his head and she grabbed a condom from the drawer and handed it to him. "It's a massage Faith."

She motioned for him to come closer. He leaned forward and she kissed him. "Yes wife to be." She kissed him and he slid his hands around her body. "Had to go and make this all sexy," he teased. Faith nodded.

He leaned into her arms and he kicked his shorts off, sliding on the only thing he was willing to let be in between them. When her legs slid around him and he felt the silky-smooth legs, and his hands slid to her backside, pulling her to him. "Ridge."

"Yes sexy."

She kissed him and he smirked. "Love you too." He leaned into her arms and she wrapped her arms around him. For the first time, there was no toy, no taunting, no over the top insanity. It was just Ridge making love to the only woman he'd ever loved. It was just as passionate as it always had been, but it was just the two of them curled up together.

That's all he'd wanted when he was a teen. To be with the woman he'd been crushing on since they were little kids. The woman he'd loved most of his life was his, fully and completely. He devoured her lips until he felt her nails almost digging into his back.

"Baby."

"What?"

"I love you." He kissed her again as he went deeper. When she was almost moaning his name, he refused to let go. He went harder, faster and he felt her body start throbbing around him as she held on tight to him.

"Ridge." His body gave in. It was intense as all get out and he wasn't letting her go. They curled up together among the blankets and he kissed her. "Happy," he asked.

Faith smirked. "Best afternoon we've ever had. I hate fighting with you."

"But you like making up," he teased.

Faith kissed him. "Only with you fiancée."

When they finally came back downstairs, fully dressed, Faith heard something sizzling. "What's that," Faith asked as he walked into the kitchen.

"No way."

"What," Faith asked.

"What are you two doin," her housekeeper joked.

"Tell me that isn't what I think it is," Ridge asked.

"Cornbread. I made that stew that you told me that you used to love. I figured you needed cornbread to go with it. How are you two doin," the housekeeper asked.

"Good," Ridge said as he snuggled Faith into his arms and kissed her.

"So, I was kinda thinking. You know how you said that you wanted to help with the food for the wedding," Ridge asked.

"Yes."

"Well, we decided that we wanted you with us at the wedding," Ridge said as Faith looked at him.

"Why," her housekeeper asked.

"Well, I was thinking that you're kinda the extra Mom. We want you there in more than just the kitchen."

"You sure," she asked.

Faith nodded. When she got teared up, Ridge gave her a hug. She nodded and hugged her.

"And I came up with an idea for the food," Ridge said.

"Meaning what," Faith asked.

"Grill outside. Steaks and lobster tails. What do you think," Ridge asked.

"And the steamed veggies on the buffet?"

Ridge nodded. Faith looked at him. "Really not formal," Faith said.

"Laid back food, fancy reception."

Faith nodded. "I like it."

"Well," Ridge asked as her housekeeper gave her a hug.

"Security will be here, but the guys and wives will be with us at the reception. Your Dad's security is watching the house and the beach house while we're at the reception."

"Do I get to know what's actually goin on with it all?"

"When we get there, you'll see it." Faith smirked.

"I got a reminder on my phone this morning. We only have a month and a half left."

"And tomorrow, we're having the big ole family dinner," Ridge replied as he smirked.

"Meaning no movie tomorrow."

"Meaning behave for one night and we have the rest of our lives to make up for it."

"Not soon enough," Faith teased.

He kissed her and they relaxed. They curled up on the sofa and Faith smirked. "What," he asked. She shook her head and got up. "And where are you going?"

"Grab the laptops," she said as he grabbed them and came outside.

"Enjoying the rest of the day out here," he asked.

"Where are the cameras?" He pointed them out and Faith kissed him. He picked her up and devoured her lips, leaning her up against the wall under the camera. "And what did you want," he asked.

"You really aren't gonna run off and elope before then with me?"

"Nope. Too much work put into the wedding," he teased as Faith kissed him.

"You sure you don't want to take off to an island somewhere?"

He kissed her again. "Woman, why are you so dang determined to avoid all the wedding stuff? Weren't you the one who wanted to do it so quickly?"

She smirked. "I love you Ridge. I just want the whole thing out of the way so we can go be alone. Really alone."

"We're still gonna need security."

She shook her head. "No more security. I just want us to

be alone," Faith said.

He smirked. "Sorta like the hotel?" She nodded.

"What if we just went and stayed at the beach?"

She kissed him. "As soon as we're done dinner, we go. That work?"

Faith nodded. "I have to go to work on Monday," Faith said.

"Oh, I know. Here's the deal wife to be. You're wearing actual clothes to work."

"Party pooper." Faith kissed him.

"I mean it."

"I know," she teased as he held her that much tighter.

"Good thing that doesn't include now," she whispered. He shook his head.

"You are seriously turning into a horny teenager."

"Around you. Just you," Faith said.

"Oh really?" She nodded and he kissed her again. "I remember a time where I swear I never thought this would happen," he said.

"And now?"

"You couldn't get rid of me if you tried. Not in a million years." She kissed him and he carried her to the chaise as they curled up together in the summer breeze.

"Ridge."

"Beautiful," he replied.

"What are we doing about a photographer?"

"Already booked. A friend of your Dad's offered. We have everything we need," he teased.

"And you booked the cake?"

He nodded and kissed her. "All you have to do is pick a wedding song," he teased.

"You know what one," she replied.

"Our prom song?"

She nodded. He looked at her and she kissed him. "That was the only thing we hadn't done? Seriously," Faith asked.

He nodded.

"And where are we going for our honeymoon?"

"Well, we could go to Savannah or the Caribbean, or we go to the Sanderling Resort. It's not exactly extravagant, but it's a beautiful spot."

Faith looked at him. "What if we do both?"

"What?"

"Savannah then the outer banks. We can go anywhere."

"You just want us to be alone?"

She nodded. "I have one other option. What if we went to Ireland," he asked.

"Why there," Faith asked.

"You and me, no stress, no watching our backs, just enjoying everything."

"You sure," Faith asked. He nodded.

"You really want no security, that's kinda the place."

"Where?"

"Westbury was the place I always wanted to stay. I went quietly with friends before and wasn't about to stay there. It was too fancy for them. It's perfect for our honeymoon though."

"Ridge."

"What?"

He kissed her. "Dad could fly us there."

"Faith."

"He'd probably offer. Why not," she asked.

"Because he already…"

Faith kissed him. "As a gift."

He shook his head. "You two, dinner's ready when you are," her housekeeper said.

Faith looked at him. "Ridge."

"No."

"No what?"

"No, he's not lending us his plane to get there. If we go, we're going my way."

He got up, helped her up, grabbed the laptops and they headed inside to eat. "You do realize that he's not the big bad wolf right," Faith said.

"I don't want him paying for anything else Faith. I just don't."

She nodded and he kissed her. "I get it," she said.

"I can get us a fancy seat in first class instead." She kissed him and they sat down and had dinner. The guys came in and ate and once they were done, Ridge called and checked on the guys at the beach house.

"What's happening boss man," Conner asked.

"Checkin on y'all. Everything alright over there," Ridge asked.

"We actually saw that Holden guy. He attempted to come inside, but we removed him. That's handled. How are you and Faith?"

"Coming out there after dinner tomorrow. You good with that," Ridge asked.

"So, in other words, we be scarce when you get here?"

"Thank you."

"Most welcome. See you tomorrow."

When Faith looked over at him, he had a smirk ear to ear. She also knew full and well what that smirk meant. "Ridge."

He walked over to her and leaned into her arms. "Yes love."

"I know that grin."

"I bet you do," he teased as he kissed her. "

And what news did you get?"

"Holden was arrested on your property."

"What?"

"He attempted to break in and the guys cuffed him until the police showed. It's done."

"Meaning?"

"Meaning we don't have to worry about the beach tomorrow night."

Faith kissed him and Ridge's arms slid tight around Faith. "And?"

He kissed her. "You should probably nail down the dinner idea then meet me upstairs," he teased as he whispered in her ear and kissed down her neck.

"And what might you be doing upstairs?" He kissed her, devouring her lips until her legs were wrapping around him.

"Upstairs first," she said. He shook his head and kissed her.

"Go. I'll meet you upstairs."

She kissed him and he got up. "Fine, but I swear..."

He kissed her again. "Grab yourself a drink. You'll need it," he teased as he took her hand and helped her up. He grabbed himself one heck of a strong drink and walked upstairs. He went into his email and saw a message from Holden:

> *She's mine. I heard about the wedding. Too bad you won't make it.*

He took a deep breath, sent the email to the detective, and took a gulp of his drink, kicking his jeans off. He grabbed the toys from his bag, put them in the drawer and made sure he put condoms nearby. He went to her drawer and laid out the lingerie and the silky blindfold she'd objected to more than once. He smirked and had a hot shower and when he stepped out, she was in front of him. "That was fast," he teased.

She kissed him and he picked her up, sitting her on the bathroom counter. "And what was the decision for tomorrow?"

"Roast beef dinner. Peach cobbler for dessert with her fresh ice cream."

He smirked. "And then you get me all to yourself again," Faith teased.

"Nice," Ridge said.

"And what were you doin," she asked as he dried off and wrapped a towel around his hips.

"Getting things organized," he teased.

"What kind of things?"

"Go look on your bed," he teased. She looked at him instead, sliding her legs around him.

Chapter 15

"Faith." Her arms reached up and wrapped themselves around his neck.

"Come here then." He leaned down and kissed her, devouring her lips until her toes were in knots.

"Go into the bedroom and put it on. I'll meet you in my old room."

"I know what you're up to husband to be."

"Good," he replied. He kissed her again with a kiss that had her covered in goosebumps. He helped her off the counter and she walked into her bedroom, seeing the lingerie there and the little thing she'd bought that he'd taken full advantage of.

"Oh, hell no," Faith said as he laughed in his bedroom. When she saw the note beside it, she almost laughed:

My way or nothing sexy wife to be.

She slid into the lingerie and followed his way too detailed directions. She shook her head, slid her satin robe over it and walked into his bedroom, seeing him in black joggers and nothing else.

"And," he asked.

"I'm not doing the blindfold." He smirked. It had always been a long shot.

"I knew you wouldn't," he teased.

"Why," she asked.

"You want to see what's coming." She nodded and he kissed her as he picked her up and sat her on the shorter counter. He kissed her again, devouring her lips and deepening the kiss until he felt her legs tighten around his. When his hand slid into his pocket, all it took was his finger bumping against the remote and her heels rubbed against his leg.

"Warn me."

He shook his head. He kissed her again and wrapped his arms around her. "Your favorite," he teased.

"Still prefer the real thing," she replied.

He kissed her again. "I know," he whispered as he closed the bedroom door and flipped the light off.

"Ridge."

"Yes sexy," he whispered as she felt her robe slide off. His hand slid into his pocket and turned it up higher.

He felt her nails dig into his arms. "Ridge."

"Just warming you up," he whispered as he kissed down her neck.

"I can't," Faith said.

"Can't what?"

"Stop." He turned it off completely. He kissed her and slid

it away from her body, throwing it into his bag. "You were saying," he teased.

"What are you planning?"

"You have a choice. 1, 2, or 3?"

"Do I get a hint?"

He smirked and kissed her. "Nope," he said as the lacy panties slid off along with the heels she'd put on.

"3," Faith replied as he picked her up and sat her on the bed.

"You absolutely sure?"

"You aren't giving me a hint."

"One is a little deeper than the others."

He felt her legs shake and smirked. "I want you first." He smirked and leaned into her arms, kissing her.

"Faith."

"What?"

"You sure you're ready for this?" She kissed him nibbling at his lip and nodded. When she felt something warm against her thigh, she almost hoped it was him. She felt his fingers against her, teasing her.

"Ridge." He deepened the kiss and he kept going. She almost moaned into his mouth.

"Aah." He kissed her and kept going. When she felt a buzz against her, she almost dug her nails into his arm.

"Ridge."

He kissed her again. "Yes love," he whispered as he smirked.

"I know what you're about…."

"You mean what I did," he said as he kissed her again and her body started trembling. He leaned her backwards onto the bed and she felt the fluffy pillow. "Ridge."

"Yes wife to be." He kissed down her neck. "Aah." He nibbled at one breast than the other as he turned the speed up on the throbbing, pulsating toy.

"Oh my…"

He kissed her again and smirked. "What," he asked.

"When did you…"

"The only one I hadn't opened," he whispered as he kissed back down her torso. He kissed her hip, her thigh then her inner thigh.

"Ridge."

"Baby," he teased as the toy slid to the floor and his fingers took over the taunting as he teased, kissed, and licked the apex of her thighs.

"Ridge."

"Baby," he said as he nibbled at her inner thigh again.

"Please."

"1 or 2?"

"You."

"Faith."

"1." He smirked and kept taunting as she felt something else slide up her leg.

"Ridge, tell me." He kissed her inner thigh and felt the buzzing return and increase in intensity. "You are so not playing fair," she said as he slid up her torso and devoured her lips.

"Aaah," she said as he kissed her. He deepened the kiss until her body was almost twitching. "Ridge, please," Faith said as he slid the buzzing away and threw it onto the floor.

"You have one left sexy." She shook her head and reached for the drawstring of his joggers.

He smirked. "Nope."

"Ridge, please," she said. He kissed her again and snuggled her to him.

"The last one," he teased.

"I can't take anymore. I want you," Faith said as she kissed him again and he felt her hand against the waistline of his joggers. "Faith."

"What?"

"Lay back." She shook her head and devoured his lips as he pinned her to the bed. When the last one came out, he smirked. She'd picked the two most intense things first. The last one was something so tiny that she could have her way at the same time.

"Oooh," she said as she felt the intense feeling. He smirked and kissed her.

"You were saying," he teased as she heard the tear of the condom wrapper.

"Ridge."

"Yes baby."

"I…" He kissed her and slid her to her stomach. "You what?"

"I can't…"

He smirked and kissed down her spine. "Too much," he teased.

"You." He gave her what she wanted. The toys disappeared and he was hers.

They kept going then she flipped him to his back and kept going as he nibbled at her breasts. "Ridge."

"Wife to be."

"I'm never letting you walk away."

"Good. I never will," he said as he flipped her onto her back and kept going until neither of them could hold back. They collapsed together onto his bed and he smirked.

"I love you," Faith said as he took a deep breath.

"I love you too beautiful. Always have."

He snuggled her tight to him and Faith leaned her head on his chest. "And," he teased.

"I don't think my legs could move even if I wanted them to."

He kissed her. "Good." She shook her head. He grabbed his drink, taking a gulp and handed Faith hers.

When he saw her fall asleep, he smirked and kissed her forehead. He slid the condom off and went to get up, but she wouldn't let him. "Two minutes," Ridge said as Faith kissed him. He slid out of bed, cleaned up and came back in to see her sexy naked body curled up among the blankets. He took another gulp of his drink and slid one of the ice cubes out. He leaned back onto the bed and she slid towards him. "Ridge."

"Yes beautiful."

"I love you."

He smirked and kissed her. "I love you too." He kissed her neck, down to her shoulder then his hand slid over her hip and when she felt the cold against her, her back arched against him. He went to move his hand and she held it there as he started teasing her all over again.

"Really," he asked.

Faith's hand slid down his hip until he felt her hand against him. "Mine," she teased.

He leaned over, grabbed another condom, and grabbed something else in the drawer. "What," Faith asked.

"Nothin," he teased.

He slid it on and the taunting began. "Didn't really think that you'd last this long," he teased.

"Ridge."

"Yes sexy," he teased as the taunting started again.

"You sure?" Faith nodded and leaned against him. One hand pulled her tight against him and the other started the teasing with the toy somewhat attached to his hand. "Since when did you hide that in there," Faith asked as they started having sex all over again.

He went deeper and deeper until he could feel her body clenching around him. "Aah."

"More," he asked. Her fingers linked with his and she nodded as it got harder, faster, and more intense until he couldn't hold himself back.

"Faith."

"Now." His body exploded as hers collapsed around him. She felt way too good. Even with a condom on, that he'd always hated, he still craved her like a kid craving sugar. He curled up with her, got rid of the condom and pulled joggers back on. He fell asleep with her in his arms. The place he wanted her to be for the rest of their lives.

The next day, they got up and ready and the more he was determined to be away from her folks, the more she wanted to be there. "Ridge, we can't just show up at dinner."

He kissed her. "Yeah we can."

She shook her head, slid her dress on and Ridge slid a dress shirt on with his casual pants. "Do we really have to go so early?"

She nodded and kissed him. "By the way, if you start wanting to go, tell me and meet me in my room."

"We aren't doing anything with your parents in the house."

She kissed him. "My room has its own bathroom remember?"

He shook his head. "You are horrible."

She kissed him again. "Nothing wrong with it handsome." He handed her the condoms and she slid them into her purse.

"You decide you need something, pat your purse."

Faith kissed him and they headed over, no matter how much he complained. "And we're taking the SUV why," Faith asked.

"Because if I need to get out of there, you'll know where I am."

"Purse?"

He nodded. He kissed her hand at the light and Faith smirked. "What?"

"Nothin," she teased.

"Do you know that in a matter of a couple weeks, we're gonna be in church saying the I do's?"

"3 weeks."

"That means tomorrow is your birthday."

"And Wednesday is yours handsome."

"And what did you want for your birthday," he teased.

"You."

"Done. What else?"

"Just you."

He shook his head. "You already have me, wife to be."

"And what do you want?"

"You."

"Ridge."

"All I want is you. All I ever wanted was you."

They got to her Mom and Dad's and he shook his head. "Ridge."

He kissed her as soon as the car stopped. "You know I hate being in this house."

She kissed him and slid his seat back, being beyond thankful for the blacked-out windows.

"What are you doing," Ridge asked.

She slid into his lap. "I love you. You know that right?"

He nodded. "Why," Ridge asked.

He kissed her, devouring her lips. "Because I don't want you two fighting."

"We aren't. I promise you."

She slid condoms into his hand. "Not out here."

"I'll meet you upstairs."

Ridge shook his head with a smirk. "Faith." She slid her hand down the front of his dress pants and he shook his head.

"Not out here."

"I was just warming you up," she whispered.

He shook his head, slid her hand away from him and he kissed her, sliding out of the SUV. He got her door for her, locked the SUV up, and they went inside hand in hand.

"You're here," her Mom said as she came over and gave them both a hug.

"Sir," Ridge said as he shook Faith's Dad's hand.

"Your folks are already here. We're all outside by the pool," her Dad said. Ridge nodded and walked outside to say hi to his Mom and Dad.

"Baby," his Mom said as she got up and came and gave Ridge a hug.

"And how's my baby boy doin," his Dad asked.

"Good. Almost done with all the wedding stuff. I can't wait until it's over."

"Why," his Mom asked.

"I just want her to see everything I did. She deserves the world," Ridge said.

"And," Faith asked as she came outside with her folks.

"You always will," Ridge replied as Faith came in and curled up with him.

"And what are you two doing for Faith's birthday tomorrow," her Dad asked.

"Taking her to the beach. As soon as she's finished work,

we're having a surprise date night."

"And what are you gonna do for your birthday," his Mom asked.

"We're going out to Bluffton for the night. A little vacation before the wedding,"

"I guess that means that we're celebrating your birthdays tonight," her Mom said.

Ridge looked at Faith and she smirked. "What," Ridge said as Faith linked their fingers.

She smirked. He shook his head and slid his arm around her as she snuggled in closer to him. "I have to run inside for a minute. I just want to check on the roast," Faith said as she nudged Ridge.

He excused himself and went inside with Faith. The minute they were through the door, she took his hand. "What are you up to?"

She walked him upstairs to her old bedroom, locked the door and kissed him. "I didn't know we were going anywhere," he teased.

"Away from everyone and everything," she joked as he kissed her. He picked her up and sat her on the counter in her bedroom.

"Faith."

"What," she asked as she slid her hand in his shirt pocket.

"Not here."

She nodded and kissed him, sliding her legs around him. "Tell me you didn't."

She kissed him and he shook his head. "Not in here."

She smirked and he picked her up and walked her into the bathroom, sitting her on the oversized counter and closed the door.

"Not here Faith."

She kissed him and undid the button of his jeans. "Seriously. We can't do this with them downstairs."

"Then don't be noisy." He shook his head and she kissed him. "And if I said we weren't?" She looked at him with a smirk. He kissed her and she snuggled her legs around his hips.

"Now. Before they realize…"

He grabbed the condom from his pocket and she kissed him. "Faith, remind me when we have kids to keep a close eye. If our kids are as bad as you…"

"And just another reason why you love me," she replied as he kissed her and they had sex on that counter. On it, over it and with her pinned against it. When he almost collapsed against her, she smirked and stood up.

"You do realize you were supposed to behave right," Ridge asked as they caught their breaths.

"That was behaving."

"Going commando at your Mom and Dad's isn't behaving."

She kissed him with a smirk ear to ear. "And you love it."

He kissed her, cleaned up and freshened up. "You do realize that they probably…"

She kissed him. "Still mad?"

"No."

"Then it worked."

Ridge shook his head and kissed her. "Fine. I'll meet you downstairs." She nodded with a smirk ear to ear. He kissed her again, walked back into the bedroom and slid something onto her bedside table. He sent her a text to check her side table and made his way back downstairs.

"Everything alright," his Mom asked.

Ridge nodded. "Faith needed to talk. Nothing out of the norm," he teased.

"I am glad that you two finally found each other. She's been a whole new woman since you two met," her Mom said.

"We're good for each other. Always have been," Ridge teased.

"So, what's the real plan for tomorrow," her Dad asked.

"Fancy restaurant downtown. I opted for High Cotton. I ordered flowers and a few surprises that I know she actually wanted. We both kinda already have everything we could need," Ridge replied.

"Well, we got you and Faith each a gift from all of us. We kinda decided together to do it that way this year. If it weren't for you two, we wouldn't really be family," his Mom said.

"She's the best woman I've ever known. I just want her to have it all," Ridge said.

"And where's the plan for the honeymoon," her Dad asked.

"We decided on two places, then the second half later in the year. She wanted to go to Ireland, so we're doing that part then coming back here and going to the outer banks. Sort of a vacation after the vacation."

"If I may, you're welcome to use the jet if you want. Saves the stress and drama of a commercial flight," her Dad said.

Ridge knew it was coming. "I appreciate that. I haven't really decided what the plan is, but I booked a suite at a hotel in Dublin," Ridge said.

"I do have a penthouse flat there. You're welcome to stay there if you want," her Dad offered.

He took a deep breath. "Once I figure it out, I'll think about it. Thank you for the offer," he said as Faith came out with a drink for Ridge and one for herself.

"Thank you for what," she asked as she handed Ridge his drink and sat back down curling up with him.

"And," her Dad asked.

"When are the guys coming," Faith asked.

"They're on the way. What about your sister," her Dad asked.

"She said she's coming. Hopefully no world war three at the table," Ridge joked.

Just as he said it, his sister and her brothers arrived, bickering as they made their way outside. "About time y'all showed," Ridge said as he got up and gave his sister a hug and Faith got up and hugged her brothers and a girlfriend she didn't know.

"Faith, my girlfriend Hallie," her brother Jack said.

"Nice to meet you," Faith said. They all sat down and talked until the housekeeper came out to let them know that dinner was ready. Ridge was beyond ready to just leave, but Faith wanted to enjoy it all.

They had a relaxing dinner, everyone gave Faith and Ridge their birthday gifts and when her Mom and Dad's housekeeper came out with two cakes, one for Ridge and one for Faith, she smirked. It was a relaxing dinner as they finished the food and the dessert then started reminiscing. "So, do you need us to do anything for the wedding," his sister asked.

"I appreciate it. We sort of have a bunch of big plans for it, but somehow your brother seems to have planned it all as a surprise. I literally have no idea what to expect short of my dress. I know you were kinda hoping I'd stick with that first one from when we all went out to look, but I kinda cancelled the order. I found something I liked a lot better. Suits the smaller wedding better," Faith said.

"I had a feeling the one we got was a little too much," her Mom said.

"The other one is very much us. It's comfortable and really pretty," Faith said.

"All I know about it, is that it makes her feel beautiful. That's all I could ask for. That's all I wanted for her," Ridge said.

"Well, I can't wait to see it all together," her Mom said. They finished chatting and opened the birthday gifts from the family and after finding checks from their folks and surprises from the rest of the family, they finally headed out and went straight over to the beach house.

"Is it bad that I wanted out of there as fast as possible," Ridge said.

"What did Dad say this time," Faith asked.

"Offered his penthouse in Dublin and the jet."

Faith smirked. "I did warn you he was going to. He just wants us safe."

"And me taking full advantage of his daughter under his roof isn't gonna work love. Sorry."

"At least let him lend us the jet to get there and back."

He shook his head. "We talked about that."

"And I still say that you could take him up on the offer. The penthouse, I get."

"Maybe."

She smirked. "You do know that he's not doing it to get back at you right?"

"I still can't believe you told him about getting a different dress."

"It's our wedding. Our choice what we want. I kinda think that maybe him getting the dress was a little too much. I agreed with you."

He smirked. "Oh, I know." He kissed her hand and they made their way to the house.

When they arrived, flowers were on the counter with a card for Faith. "What's this?"

"The first present from me for your birthday," Ridge said as he kissed the back of her neck.

"I can't wait for the second one," she teased as he unzipped the back of her dress and kissed down her back.

"Ridge." He picked her up and carried her up the steps to

the bedroom and saw the candles.

"And what's all of this?" Ridge kissed her and slid the dress off. "What," Faith asked as she smirked.

"Nothin," he teased as Faith sat down on the edge of the bed and motioned for him to come closer. "Wife to be, what else could you want for your birthday?"

"I have a few other things on that wish list," she teased.

"Any of them involve sleep?"

She shook her head. He kissed her and shook his head, walking into the guestroom. "Where are you going?"

"You coming to get your present or not?" She slid her satin robe on and followed him, kissing him as he closed the door.

"What are you up to?"

He kissed her and slid his arms around her as he smirked. "What?"

"Remember last night?"

She nodded. "You sure you want that upgrade?"

Faith looked at him with a smirk. "Depends."

He kissed her and he leaned her onto the bed. "What?"

"You want your birthday gift now or tomorrow?"

She got a grin ear to ear. "Tonight, and tomorrow."

He smirked and shook his head.

"You sure?"

She smirked. "Depends. What do you want me to do for your birthday?"

He smirked. "There's a lot of things. Sleep, walk on the beach, picnic maybe."

She smirked and shook her head. "The exact opposite of tonight?"

"We'll see," he teased. Faith kissed him and he leaned into her arms. "Faith."

"What?"

"You have 4 options."

"And what are they?"

"Choose a number. Just try to keep it down tonight."

She smirked and he kissed her. "Before we do that, can we get a drink?" He handed Faith a glass of champagne that had been perfectly chilled.

"And?" She kissed him and he smirked, taking a gulp of the Jack that Kellen had put on his bedside table. He kissed her and grabbed a few things from his bag. "What are you doing," Faith asked as he put the condoms in the side table.

"Nothin. You sure you're up for it?"

She nodded and undid his shirt. "Come here."

He shook his head and kissed her as Faith slid onto his lap. "Ridge."

"Yes sexy."

"I want my man."

"Do I know him?"

She shook her head and kissed him. "Funny." She kissed him and he untied the belt of her robe. "If you change your mind you tell me."

She smirked. "Not going to," she replied as he leaned her onto her back and he flipped the light off.

"What in the..."

He kissed her neck, then down her torso. "What," he asked.

"You blacked out the window?"

"Just for tonight," he whispered.

"Why?"

"Because it's a lot more fun when you can't see what I'm about to do."

He pinned her on the bed and kissed her. "Why is it that you can do whatever you want and I can't?"

He kissed her. "Faith, I love you, and I always have. My

game. You wanted to play and we are. You refuse to behave, so I always win."

He kissed her again and she went for the button of his dress pants. "Faith."

"What?"

"No." She shook her head and he kissed her and she felt something cool around her wrists. "And what is that?"

"Go ahead and attempt that move again." He kissed her and got up.

"Where are you going?"

"Nowhere love." He slid out of his dress pants, kicked his boxers off and slid into his baggy comfy jeans instead and saw Faith almost laugh.

"What?"

"That's one way to get your way," she teased.

"Faith."

"What?"

"You sure?"

"I am most definitely sure, but if I need two seconds to breathe…"

He kissed her and leaned into her arms. "You were saying," he teased as he kissed down her neck.

"Ridge."

"Two what?" He kissed down her torso and was about to start taunting all over again when his phone buzzed.

"Don't you freaking dare," Faith teased as he kissed her and slid the phone off the counter.

"Yep," Ridge said.

"Slight issue. Holden got out."

"What? He tried to..."

"I know. Locked up and alarms are on. Doing a perimeter every hour. Leo got Conrad and Sammy to come help at the house and I'm down here with you and Miss Faith." "Thank you," Ridge said as he hung up. "And what was that?"

"Work. Now, where was..."

"Ridge."

"Moment is kinda gone."

"Hands."

He smirked and kissed her. "That, I'm leaving where it is."

Faith shook her head. "Ridge, you aren't funny."

"Best way to prevent you from doing something when I say no," he teased.

"Or you could just trust that I won't." He kissed her and

Faith's legs curled around him.

"What was it?"

"Nothing." He knew she wouldn't fall for it, but he wasn't ruining the entire night.

"Come here."

He leaned on top of her and untied her hands. "What would you like sexy," he asked as her legs curled around him.

"Tell me."

"No."

She went to grab his shirt and felt his skin. He went to get up and she stopped him. "Tell me Ridge."

"Holden got out."

That's all he had to say to ruin the mood of the entire evening. He put everything away, got the drinks, handed Faith her robe and pulled on a hoodie, walking into her bedroom, with the condoms in his hoodie pocket.

"When," she asked.

"Probably when we were eating dinner. I'm not gonna be in bed. I'm letting you know now," he said.

"You do know that you need sleep right?"

He nodded and gulped down the half glass of Jack in one

gulp. "Ridge."

"What?"

"Do you have it?"

He nodded. "Hoodie pocket. Why?"

"I thought..."

"One house to the other. It's coming with me."

"Take the hoodie off."

"No. You can have your present tomorrow night. You need rest. You have..."

She kissed him and slid into his lap. "Take the hoodie off." He shook his head, took the gun out, put it on the counter and slid the condoms onto the bedside table. She pulled the hoodie off of him.

"What do you want love?" She wrapped her arms around his neck, wrapped her legs around him and kissed him in that exact spot. "Here?"

She nodded as she handed him one of the condoms. "In the middle of all of this?"

She kissed him and undid his jeans. "Faith."

"What?"

"You that..."

"Worse." He slid the condom on and pulled her to him.

"Not in the chair." He picked her up, walked her to the bed and leaned her onto it, kicking his jeans off. "Faith."

"What?"

"You sure?"

"I want my fiancée. Now."

He kissed her again and felt her slide his hand down her torso. He started teasing and it was almost a turn on for him. "Ridge," she said.

"Yes baby," he said.

"Yours." That's all that needed to be said. The sex was almost indescribable. It was white hot, intense, deep, and felt like they had no cares in the world. He kept going and taunted as he pounded into her. It was hotter than the moments that he'd taunted her with. Hotter than seeing her writhing in pleasure every time he got her body to climax. She was his. All his. They kept going until she was almost screaming his name, only being muffled by his kiss. Even when he exploded his orgasm, she wouldn't let go, and wouldn't detangle her legs from around him. "Faith."

"What?"

"I love you."

"I love you back fiancée. Forever." He leaned to his side and kissed down her neck.

"Don't you dare move," Faith said.

"Two seconds."

When he came back, Faith had something in her hand. "What's that?"

"Round two."

He shook her head. "So, all of it was a ploy to get me in here?"

"Nope. Just figured since you chose to be in here instead, we could keep going."

"Then I'm getting us refills." She shook her head and motioned for him to come closer. "What love?"

She kissed him and he slid the little buzzing toy from her hand. "Nope. Give me two seconds." He messaged Kellen to bring the bottle of Jack to the bedroom door. When he got a reply with a laughing emoji, he smirked. "What?"

He heard footsteps, grabbed the bottle from Kellen, relocked the door and poured himself another glass.

"You sure?"

"Give it back."

"This," he teased as he flipped it on and started taunting.

"Ridge."

"What?"

"I love you." He kissed her again, turning up the speed

until her legs were twitching.

"Still," he teased as he nibbled at her breasts.

"Ridge." His fingers continued the taunting as he grabbed something he'd left in the bedside drawer. "Ridge," Faith said as he felt her warmth around his fingers.

"Damn," he said.

"What?" He kissed her and intensified it even more.

"Aah," Faith said as she almost white-knuckled his arm.

"More. Gotcha," he teased as the one thing that she didn't expect happened. The one thing he'd always thought would be too much was what she needed. He turned it on high and continued to tease as it slid against her. "Ridge, I want…"

He kissed her again as he got even more turned on. He kept teasing, sliding another condom on and took over, as he had sex with her again. That feeling was becoming an addiction with her. The feel of her legs tight around him, her body pulsating and throbbing deep around him. It was something he refused to live without ever again. When he climaxed again, he smirked and Faith was breathless. "Still more," he whispered as Faith shook her head.

"Turn it off." He did, putting it to the side as she pinned her body against his. Her body still throbbed and if he'd touched her, it would've sent off shockwaves. "Happy birthday fiancée."

"Don't move," she begged.

"I have to." She shook her head and he snuggled her tight to him, pulling the blanket over them.

"Ridge."

"Yes love."

"Don't ever let go." He kissed her neck again and slid out of her.

"Two minutes," he asked. Faith nodded and he got up, cleaned up, pulled boxers and joggers on, and grabbed the Jack and his handgun from the bedside table.

"Where are you going?"

"Nowhere. I'm getting back in bed with my way too sexy and very horny fiancée." She smirked and he snuggled her to him. She turned to face him and kissed him. "Good answer," she teased.

"I figured you'd say that," he teased as they curled up in bed and fell asleep not long later.

The next morning, Ridge was wide awake at 5am. He gently slid out of bed and went downstairs to talk to the guys.

"And," Ridge said poking his head into the security office.

"Mornin. So, we got it handled. We got the extra guys to come keep an eye on the house. Two are at the house, two more here with us. Honestly, I had one of the guys watching Holden's place specifically. Right now, the restraining order includes her properties. He's not allowed out of his own property. No beach. He won't last long and we all know it. Just be careful if you decide to go for a swim," Kellen said.

Ridge nodded. "Just keep an eye out. I'm gonna try to get her to go back to the house tonight. It's too close for my liking," Ridge sad.

"She's safer here than anywhere right now. Are you two heading into her office?"

Ridge nodded. "I'm going for a run, then we're coming back and getting ready to head in."

Kellen nodded and Ridge went upstairs, pulling a shirt on, getting his handgun from the drawer and pulled his sneakers on.

"Where are you going? It's not even 6."

He leaned over and kissed Faith. "Run then home and we get ready to head to your office."

"Do you want me to come with you?"

He smirked and kissed her. "I love that you want to, but you need to get rest. I'll be back in an hour love." He kissed her again and got up, heading off. He went for a run and when he went past Holden's, he saw Sammy keeping an eye.

"Really," Ridge asked.

"He's not getting near her," Sammy said as Ridge laughed and headed off. When he managed to get back, Faith was sitting on the back porch with breakfast.

"Really," Ridge said.

"We're eating. I'm starved after…"

He kissed her. "Gotcha."

He smirked and sat down with her. "And you cooked?"

She nodded. "The spinach omelet you love and the bacon. What took you so long anyway," Faith asked.

"It's called a run. Ran back through the water."

Faith kissed him and heard someone clearing their throat. He looked and saw her Dad. "Good morning," Ridge said.

"Morning. I wanted to make sure that you two are doing okay. Your Mom wanted to come down to the beach last night too after y'all left. Everything okay," her Dad asked.

"Definitely. Slept like a baby and now, meetings at the office."

"Well, about that. All your meetings were pushed to Friday. I had one other gift for you that I didn't want to give you in front of everyone," her Dad said.

"Meaning what," Faith asked. He handed Faith an envelope. Ridge hated that. He knew what was in it, and he also knew that he didn't want whatever it was. She opened it and saw the card, read it, and saw the information on the plane.

"What's this," Faith asked.

"You two have the jet to and from. Whenever you want to leave, just give them a heads up. One less thing to worry about," her Dad said.

"You really didn't have to," Ridge said.

"Our wedding gift. I promise that's it," her Dad said. He knew better.

"I guess we have the flight figured out then," Ridge said determined not to make a mess of her birthday.

"If you two want a vacation, you can take the jet wherever you want. Faith got a promotion at work."

"What," she asked.

"You're now running media. Music and Lit. Your brothers are staying where they are, but you tripled what I thought was possible. I wanted to tell you last night," her Dad said.

"This is amazing Dad. Thank you," Faith said as she got up and hugged her Dad.

"We're gonna announce it on Friday morning at the board meeting. It's at 10. You'll be there right?"

Faith nodded and hugged him again. "Thank you."

"Proud of you," her Dad said as he finished his run and headed home.

"Happy birthday," Ridge said.

"Don't be mad."

"Like I said, saves time on booking flights."

Biting his tongue was becoming a regular affair. She leaned into his arms. "Ridge."

"Yep."

"You're gonna start bleeding if you don't quit biting your tongue."

"Faith, it's your birthday. I'm not having a fight with them."

She kissed him. "Too much?"

He nodded. "It's fine. I'm leaving it alone. That's their thing. Fine. Means more time to taunt his daughter on the plane," he teased.

"Let's not tell them that part," Faith teased.

He kissed her. "And now that you don't have to go in, what do you want to do today."

"I think a swim, bed, swim then more bed then dinner."

"Skipping meals," he teased.

Faith kissed him. "I want us alone all day. We can go for lunch or whatever you want."

"It's kinda your birthday. You choose," Ridge said.

"Swim then we take our time getting ready and go to Savannah for the day."

He smirked. "We're gonna have to be back before 5."

"Why?"

"Dinner reservation. You have to get changed," he teased.

Faith looked at him. "Where?"

"You'll find out tonight. You know how much you love putting on fancy dresses," he teased.

Faith smirked. "Okay," she replied.

"This means get in the house and get ready. Swim tonight."

She smirked. "Nope."

"Faith."

She slid his hoodie off, revealing the bikini.

"Woman."

"I'll wait for you," she teased. He kissed her, walked into the house, put the dishes away and changed into his swim shorts, giving Kellen the hint, and slid the handgun into the beach towels. He came outside, put the towel on the bottom step and picked Faith up, running out into the water and dunking both of them. Faith splashed water at him and the two of them were back to having fun like two kids. They kept playing around as Faith tried to dunk him and he dunked her instead. They played around and when Faith jumped into his arms and wrapped her legs around him, he couldn't help but laugh. "Trying to dunk me?"

She kissed him. "That too," she teased.

He kissed her and devoured her lips, walking deeper into the water. "What," Faith asked.

"I love you. More than you even know."

She snuggled him. "I love you back," she replied.

"Am I allowed to take you out of here now?"

She kissed him. "You sure you aren't mad about..."

He kissed her. "No more worrying."

Faith nodded. She kissed him again and they headed back towards the shore when Ridge saw Holden. Kellen and Sammy took over as Ridge grabbed the towels and walked Faith inside.

"What's wrong," Faith asked.

"Restraining order." Faith looked at him. "Come on birthday girl."

Chapter 16

After a surprisingly fast shower, they got changed and Ridge took her down to Savannah. "Why here," Faith asked.

"Because we're away from the drama. Besides. I know you're addicted to those Byrd's cookies."

"True," Faith said as they wandered over to the shop and got some to bring home.

"You okay?" Faith nodded. "I know something's wrong baby. Just say it."

"When did he get out?"

"Last night. I got a message that he was out. We tripled up security until he learns to back away."

Faith looked at him. "What?"

"Three weeks until the wedding and that happens?"

"Babe, we're away. We can get our minds off it." She looked at him. "Ridge."

He kissed her. "Come." He walked her off to a café to eat lunch and get her mind off it.

"Why didn't you tell me?"

"Babe, Kellen told me at 1am. You were asleep. I doubled up security for the houses so we were safe. What's wrong with that?"

"I didn't realize it was that late."

"Like I said, I'm keeping you safe. First job," he said.

Faith kissed him. "Thank you."

"I'm not letting him come near you. I didn't want you hurt or to even see it."

She nodded. "Are you still mad about Dad's present?"

"Faith, I can't tell him no. I tried, and he disregarded what I said. I can't do anything about it now."

She kissed him again. "Ridge."

"Yes beautiful."

"I love you."

"Love you more fiancée of mine."

They walked around the shopping area, went and got a sweet tea and relaxed a while at Forsyth park then headed down to River street and walked around a while. "If you want to go back..."

"Ridge."

"What?"

She kissed him. "I love you. Thank you for the distraction."

He kissed her and wrapped his arms around her. "Tell me what else you want to do."

"Drive the back way home."

"You want to stop at Sheldon Church?"

She nodded. He smirked, kissed her, and took her to Wormsloe first. "How'd you know," Faith asked.

"Because I know my woman. Walk?"

She nodded. They paid and headed through the pathways. "Babe, you do know that nobody could hurt you on my watch right?"

She nodded and kissed him. When they finally started making their way back, they took the back route like she wanted. They cranked the tunes they loved, sang, and laughed the entire way back. When they got back to the house, presents were sitting on the table and a bottle of champagne with two glasses was sitting on the side table.

"Ridge."

"Happy birthday baby."

"What did you buy?"

"Open the little one first."

She shook her head, kissed him and he handed her the box. She opened it and saw the bracelet. It had three charms on it. One for their birthday month, one with the date they had their first date, and one for their wedding day.

"Ridge."

"And?" She kissed him.

"Thank you."

"I wanted to surprise my girl," Ridge said.

"You don't have to do all of this."

"Open this one," he teased as he handed her another box.
"I know that look Ridge."

He smirked. That one was a gift for both of them. She
opened it and saw the box. "No, you didn't," Faith said.

"You're the one that wanted to play along."

She shook her head, pulling out handcuffs. "Ridge."

"Like I said before. You need to behave," he teased.

"I swear, you are so bad," Faith said.

He handed her the next one and knew she would laugh.
She opened it, fully expecting to see a toy of some kind
and saw a dress and heels.

"Ridge."

"What?"

"When?"

"When you were looking at dresses." She smirked, seeing
a black and white dress that was just as sexy as anything
she owned, and heels to match.

"It's beautiful."

"Did you think I put a toy in there?"

She smirked. "Either that or something else that's too naughty."

He kissed her. "I mean, I could take some of this back," he teased.

Faith kissed him. "Two left," he said. She opened one and saw a new iPhone.

"Ridge."

"Fully loaded and extra security on it."

She smirked. "Of course you did," she teased.

"Making sure nobody can hack it. That's all." She kissed him. "Open the last one sexy." She shook her head, sat him down and slid into his lap as she opened it. First, the card:

> *To my forever and always. You've been my dream my entire life. These are just something to remind you that I love you. Some to make you blush, some to make you reminisce, and some to show off the gorgeous woman I'm marrying. I love you. — Your husband to be.*

She looked at him. "Ridge."

He kissed her shoulder. "Yes love."

She kissed him and wrapped her arms around him. "I love you."

"Love you back beautiful." She opened the box and saw the lingerie that was way too sexy, sexy pajamas and a little box. "You didn't."

"Better," he teased.

She saw it and smirked. "Ridge."

"What?"

"Seriously?"

"To go with the dress." She shook her head and kissed him.

"Ridge, you are certifiably..."

"Sexy?"

"I'm not doin it." He nodded. "Why?"

"Because we're having fun tonight."

He kissed her and she shook her head. "You are the one that needs to behave." He kissed her again.

"Come on sexy. Let's take all of this upstairs and get ready." They took everything upstairs, put it away and Ridge went to hop into the shower. When Faith slid in behind him, he smirked. "I know exactly what you're up to Faith."

He turned to face her and she kissed him. "Thank you for all of this today," she said.

"I promised you way back at the beginning that you were safe. You know that right?"

She nodded and kissed him. "But, for today. All of the day trips. Thank you."

He nodded and kissed her. "I get to surprise my woman once in a while, and not just in bed," he said.

She smirked. "And I get to surprise you on Thursday."

He nodded and kissed her. He washed up and Faith washed his back for him. "What," he teased.

"Where are we going for dinner?"

"Your favorite fancy restaurant."

"Ridge."

"Hall's." She smirked and kissed him. They finished their shower and he wrapped her up in a warm towel, grabbed the other and dried off.

"You sure you want me to wear the fancy one?"

He nodded. "And the other thing."

She looked at him. "No."

He nodded.

"Ridge."

"You wanted to. Private dining room."

They both got changed. He intentionally put on her favorite cologne, the black dress pants that she loved and his dress shirt. When she came out of her closet in her lingerie, he smirked.

"Faith."

"Not until we leave." She did her hair, put on her makeup, and slid into the dress.

"And," Ridge sked.

"I love the dress," she said as he zipped the back up for her.

"And it looks amazing," he said as she slid her heels on. When she slid the remote in his pocket, he smirked.

"Nice," he teased.

"Are we going to the hotel or back here?"

"Back here, but you can't be noisy," he teased.

"And is there a reason why?"

He shook his head. "Yeah there is. Your presents aren't done."

"Found another movie," she teased.

He shook his head. "Something else that will keep you awake all night long," he teased.

"I thought that's why I was marrying you," she teased as she kissed him. She grabbed her purse, sliding her phone and wallet into it and they headed downstairs. Kellen was waiting in the SUV.

"We aren't driving ourselves?"

Ridge shook his head. "You may want my eyes on something other than the road," he whispered as she got goosebumps and hopped into the SUV with him right behind her.

"Are you two ready," Kellen asked as Ridge nodded. It was his way of asking if Ridge had brought his handgun.

"And what else did you plan for tonight," Faith asked as he slid her closer to him.

"A few things. Fun things. Way too naughty things. Things that will make your toes turn into permanent pretzels," he whispered as he kissed the edge of her ear.

"Ridge."

"Mm."

"Are we going back tomorrow?"

He shook his head. "You won't be walking much," he teased quietly so Kellen didn't hear any of it.

"Promises, promises," Faith teased as they made their way over the Ravenel Bridge.

"I was thinking the other day. Why aren't you inviting any

of your friends to the wedding," Ridge said.

"You know me. I never have time to keep in touch with anyone short of your folks and mine. A lot of my friends moved away. The few that are here are 3 kids in and wondered why I'm taking so long. I have more friends at the office now." He smirked. "What?"

"Nothing love."

She turned and looked at him. "What did you do?"

"I didn't do anything. I can promise you that."

She shook her head. "I know you're up to something. Just spill it."

He kissed her neck and slid his hand into his pocket. "Don't you dare," she teased.

"Not doing anything beautiful," he replied as she felt the buzz start.

She grabbed his leg. "Ridge."

"Happy birthday," he teased.

They got to the restaurant and headed inside. As they walked them to the back room, Faith looked at him. "Promise me you didn't do anything insane."

"Like what? Invite people you haven't seen in over 10 years to our little two-person birthday party?"

She looked at him. "I mean it." He kissed her and walked

her in to see a bunch of her friends all there to celebrate, and ones that he'd even flown in. "You little sneak," Faith said as he kissed her.

"I love you beautiful."

"Just drinks right?"

He nodded and kissed her again. The plan was to have a visit for a little while with her friends then duck out and head to the restaurant he'd booked for dinner. Quick and easy. She visited, laughed and he talked to the boyfriends and husbands. Every once in a while, he'd slide his hand in his pocket and bump the remote just a little to see the look on her face.

Once everyone started heading out, they walked out the back and went to the restaurant he'd actually booked for dinner. It was a little quieter and a lot more fancy. Just what he needed to heat her birthday up to scorching. "You do realize that you taunting me is only making things worse right?"

He smirked and nodded as they sat down at their table. "Had to right," Faith asked.

"Your birthday. I wanted something special especially after the promotion and everything."

"And all of that party stuff was what, just warming me up?"

He nodded and kissed her as the waiter brought the drinks over and they ordered.

Once they were alone again, he smirked. "What," she asked as he slid his arm around her.

"I wanted to give you some life back. You've been here and working from home since we started this. You deserve to have time with your friends baby."

"Literally, every one of them is either divorced or separated. I'm still stunned," Faith replied as she took a sip of her drink.

"I had one guy ask me how we managed to stay together so long. That's why I told everyone about the engagement."

"Like I said, I barely see let alone talk to any of them anymore."

"Faith."

"What?"

"I love our little love bubble at home and all, but not seeing anyone else isn't healthy. You know that right?"

"I have my best friend. I don't really need anyone else." He smirked and kissed her, knowing that he needed to back off. He kissed her.

"I love it, but you still need to go outside at some point. We can't stay in bed for the rest of our lives."

When she smirked, he shook his head. "Really? So, you actually wanted me to turn it up?"

She smirked and kissed him. "That too."

He nudged the intensity up in more than one spot and she almost jumped in her seat. "You were saying?"

"Ridge."

"You really think that you can last all day and night?"

She looked at him. "No idea, but I do know that you need to turn it down."

He smirked and kissed her. "Nope."

Dinner came and Faith looked at him. "You started it Faith."

They had dinner and relaxed for a little bit, had a quick drink then the waitress smirked. She came in with chocolate silk pie with strawberry cream on top with two candles. Just two.

"Happy birthday sexy."

She smirked. "Had to didn't you?"

He nodded. "My fave, and yours from what I always remembered."

She smirked and kissed him. "Thank you."

He cut them each a piece, giving her the first, as per their tradition, and she saw the strawberries on the inside.

"My favorite." He nodded. They had dessert, packed the

rest up to take back with them and headed back to the house.

"We going back to the beach?"

He nodded and slid his hand in his pocket. "Don't you dare," Faith teased as he did it anyway. The remote was becoming fun.

"I swear." He turned it back down and Faith slid into his lap.

"Ridge, give it back."

He shook his head. "Nope."

She shook her head and he smirked. "This is a tickle Faith. You wanted the whole thing and you get it for your birthday," he whispered.

"Promises, promises," she replied as his hand slid to her leg and inched it's way up.

"We'll be back in 10," Kellen said as he made his way there. When he felt the lace of the panties, he started taunting her all on his own.

"Ridge." He kissed her and they finally got to the house. He picked her up and carried her inside and straight up to the main bedroom.

"Ridge," Faith said as he locked the bedroom door and pinned her onto the bed.

"Yes love."

"Off."

He shook his head. "Baby, that literally is kindergarten compared..."

She kissed him, grabbed the remote and turned it off.

"Faith."

"What?"

He shook his head, unzipping her dress. He kissed her and slid it off, walking into the closet and hanging up the dress. When he walked back in, the heels were gone and she was on the bed in the lingerie and nothing else. The ring, the lace, and the smile ear to ear. He kissed her and Faith went for the button of his pants.

"Nope."

"Ridge." He went into the drawer and grabbed the handcuffs.

"You touch, they go on."

Faith looked at him. "No."

"Then no touching." He kissed her, went into his closet, and slid into his jeans, coming back into the bedroom.

"Ridge."

"Yes love," he teased. "I want you over here." He smirked and poured out two glasses of Jack, putting them on the bedside table.

"Now, what were you saying," he asked as he leaned into her arms.

"Better," she teased as she kissed him.

"Wife to be, it's up to you what you want tonight."

"And if I said I get to tease you first."

"I'd say no. If I have to pull them out, I mean it Faith."

"And if I said I wanted us to just be together without all the other stuff so I can say thank you properly?"

He smirked and kissed her. "So, you aren't mad about the party?"

She shook her head. "I love that you did it, and that you loved me enough to do it. Honestly, I thought we were having dinner there."

"Babe, that's the birthday version of an engagement party. We barely told anyone, but I wanted you to have your friends to celebrate with you."

"With us."

"Babe." He kissed her and snuggled her into his arms.

"I saw a couple guys there that you knew at school."

"And they were either married or divorced from the ladies that you knew."

"Babe, those were your people."

She kissed him. "I love you," Faith said.

"Love you back beautiful."

"What about your friends?"

"Kinda all busy doing security for my really sexy fiancée."

She smirked. "That's all?"

Ridge nodded. "The guys I trust. They're the only ones."

She kissed him. "We can't give them a night off can we?"

"Depends on whether you wanted people to break in or not," he teased as Faith kissed him.

"Ridge."

"Wife to be."

"Is it ever gonna be over?"

"That stuff? Probably. Hopefully before the wedding. If not, they stay. We all have done a pretty good job keeping you safe. That's all I wanted. That's all your Dad wanted and that's all you wanted from them. You wanted a hell of a lot more from me though," Ridge teased as Faith's arms slid around him and he kissed her.

"You think so do you," Faith teased as he smirked.

"What," Faith asked.

"You wanted me because I was sexy. That all?"

"No."

"You sure that's not all?"

He leaned her onto the bed, sliding her arms above her head, and sliding the lacy lingerie off piece by irresistible piece.

"I wanted you here because you make me feel good."

"Good? Really? Not sexy? Not wanted? Not hot?"

"Burning."

He kissed down her torso and her toes curled. "Faith."

"What?"

"Because I make you hot?"

She nodded and he kissed her inner thigh. "How hot," he asked.

"Ridge."

He kissed, licked then nibbled at the apex of her thighs. "How hot Faith?" He could see her body's reaction. He could see how hot, but he was determined to hear it. "How hot?"

"You already know."

His fingers started to tease her. "Say it or this is getting even hotter wife to be."

"Ridge." When he intensified that feeling, she was almost

moaning his name. "How hot?"

"Ridge, please."

He kept going. One nibble. One strategic nibble was all that it took. One until her body was reaching orgasm. One until her entire body was humming. "And I haven't even warmed up yet," he teased. Faith reached for him and he shook his head, grabbing one of the toys that she'd loved. When the buzzing started, she knew. Either she answered, or he made it even hotter. "White hot," she said.

"And if I did this," Ridge asked as the toy made her toes twist into pretzels.

"Ridge."

"Wife to be," he replied as he kissed her hip.

"Come here."

He smirked and kissed her stomach. "What would you like sexy," he teased as the toy magically sped up.

"Please."

"More?"

"You." He kept going and kissed up to her breasts, nibbling and taunting even more. "Ridge," she said as her body throbbed.

"Yes love," he said as her leg slid around his. "Nope." He smirked and his hand kept taunting and it just got more intense.

"Ridge, please."

"Please what," he asked as he kissed her. "I want you."

"I know you do. You still haven't made it through appetizer. Wasn't there something about the full deal," he teased.

Faith shook her head. "Changed my mind."

She kissed him and he could tell that she was past the second round. "Faith."

"I want you. No more stupid toys," she said.

He smirked and turned the first toy off. "Really?" She nodded as she felt a slight bit of relief. "Faith."

"Yes," she said.

"Not even close," he whispered as she got goosebumps.

"Ridge, please."

He kissed her again, devouring her lips until her legs were curling around him. "Wife to be."

"What?"

He kissed her and she felt buzzing again. "Ridge, no."

He kissed her and started all over again. "Please."

He smirked. "I love you."

"Ridge, we don't..."

He kissed back down her torso and her legs were shaking. "You sure," he asked as the taunting tripled.

"Ridge, now. I'm not waiting anymore," she said as she reached for him.

He flipped her to her stomach. "Ridge, please."

He smirked, grabbed a condom, and slid it on. The one thing that he wanted to do was finally happening. He kissed down her back as she leaned back against him. "Ridge, please." He kissed her shoulder and then her neck. "No more waiting," she said. He kissed her. "Ridge."

He gave her what she wanted. Even when she turned to face him, they kept going, making out like teenagers, and having earth shaking sex. Even when she reached orgasm again, he kept going, deeper, harder, and only because she asked. When her nails were digging into his back and he was almost there, she kissed him and she felt his legs almost shake.

"I love you," Faith said as both of them collapsed onto the bed.

"Faith," he said as he slid to his back and she curled up and leaned her head onto his chest. "Yes husband to be."

He kissed her forehead. "Happy Birthday."

She shook her head and he kissed her. "I love you."

"Love you back sexy." He got up a few minutes later, cleaned up and handed Faith her drink, sliding into bed in boxers. "You are seriously such a party pooper," she teased.

"And if I said that I did it intentionally?"

"Oh, I know why handsome."

She kissed him and he pulled the blankets up over them. "Ridge."

"Yes baby."

"I love you."

"Love you to the moon and back a million times," he replied.

She fell asleep a little while later and, for once, there were no texts in the middle of the night, no stress, and a quiet, peaceful night of sleep. The first in a while.

***

The closer the wedding got, the more Faith wanted to just run away with Ridge and disappear somewhere so they could be alone. When it got to the rehearsal, he was past ready to just take her home. They were surrounded by friends and family and happy to just have everyone there. He was determined to get it all overwith. To take her home and take full advantage of his new wife. Badly.

"I'm not coming back to the beach house. I'm going to the house."

"Faith."

"We have to follow a tradition Ridge. This one. You know that my Mom and yours will lose it if we're in the same house."

"We'd sleep in different rooms."

She shook her head and kissed him. "Nope."

"Faith."

"What?"

"I left you something in your bedside table. Don't ask. Just follow the directions."

"To where?"

He smirked. "Ridge."

He kissed her, devouring her lips.

"Come with me."

"Ridge." He snuck out the back with her and slid his arms around her, pulling her tight to him. "What," Faith asked.

He kissed her again. "I'll meet you at the house."

"What?"

"Kellen is staying at the house to make sure that you're safe. I'll be there at 1."

"Ridge."

He kissed her and she felt something. "Ridge."

"Yes love. "Tell me you didn't."

He smirked, kissed her, and walked her to the SUV. "You ready," her Mom asked.

Faith nodded, kissed Ridge again and hopped in as he slid the remote in his pocket. When he nudged it on, he smirked and headed to the truck.

"You ready for guy night," Conner asked.

"No guy night. Just hanging out. We have backup security for both houses yes," Ridge asked.

Conner nodded. "Leo has 5 with him and Kellen, we have 6 plus Calvin and I."

"Good. And her folks place?"

"8 at the main house, 8 at the beach house just to make sure that it stays safe."

"Good. I might actually be able to sleep."

"And," Conner asked.

"If I take off in the middle of the night, not a word."

Conner smirked and nodded. They all headed off and went their ways, and Ridge headed to the beach house. He slid out of his suit as soon as he got back and sat down outside with a Jack in hand.

When his Dad came out to check on him, he smirked. "What's up Dad," Ridge asked.

"You happy," his Dad asked.

"I'll be happier tomorrow. We haven't been apart a single day since we got together. Honestly, I don't know if I'm even gonna be able to sleep."

"You love her don't you?"

"More than I ever thought was even possible. She's the best thing that ever happened to me. I didn't think I could have even been with her. You knew how much I loved her when we were kids."

"Son, I knew the moment you told me you two were together that this day was gonna come. You deserve the world. Always have. So long as you're happy, and you make her happy, you have everything you could ever want. Not just because of who she is, but because you two always loved each other just that much. You love her like I loved your Mom the minute we met again."

"And now, two married men. What are we gonna do with my little sister," Ridge teased.

"You know, she did mention that she had a thing for Calvin." Ridge shook his head and laughed. They sat out on the steps and talked until his Dad headed home. One look at his watch and he smirked. It was time.

He texted Faith and it took seconds for a reply:

> *Hello wife to be. This is your husband to be. Did you open the drawer?*

Hey handsome. Just about to. What on earth did you do? By the way, not fair with the remote. Not even close.

Follow the directions.

He knew just how long he had until she did it. Until she was alone:

And?

Done?

Yes.

He went into an app on his phone and pressed a preset he'd saved – Rehearsal.

He had exactly 20 minutes to get to the house. 20 until the preset had played through on the buzzy little friend he'd left in her drawer.

When he got to the house, he snuck up the back and bypassed her Mom's room that she was sleeping in, then snuck into her bedroom, closing, and locking the door behind him. When he walked into his closet, there she was.

"You are so…"

He kissed her, tossing the toy into the bag in his closet. He picked her up, sat her on his counter and devoured her lips.

"If you hadn't…"

He kissed her again. "What?"

"Ridge, no more taunting."

"Done." He kicked his jeans off, kicked his boxers off and slid the satiny nightgown over her knees. When she kissed him, she barely managed to let him up for air until they were having sex on that counter, then the bench, then the floor. When they managed to actually sit up, neither of them could stop laughing. "Nice present," he teased.

Faith shook her head. "How's that gonna work if we're always together?"

"Never know. Could just be warm-up," he joked. She kissed him and devoured his lips again.

"You do know that my Mom knew you'd show right?"

He nodded. "I needed to kiss you before I went to sleep. Can't sleep without it," he said.

She smirked. "And you'll never have to again. Not after tomorrow."

He kissed her, devouring her lips until they were curled up together on the floor. "Happy wedding day," Faith said. He kissed her again, got up and after another kiss goodnight, he snuck back out and went back to the beach.

Ridge got up the next morning, went for a run and sat down to have breakfast with the guys. "This showed up this morning for you by the way. Leo dropped it off. Happy wedding day," Conner said.

"Thank you my friend. Anything insane happen last night?"

Conner shook his head. "Short of that disappearing act, no," Conner joked.

Ridge opened the package that came, seeing a handwritten note from Faith on top in a card:

> *To my fiancée, the man I was destined to marry at 2 days old.*
>
> *I can remember you being in every memory of my childhood. Every happy Moment, every hard one, and still, you are standing right there again today, but this time as my husband. You are my soul mate and have been since we were babies. We both knew that. When you showed at my house that day, I got a feeling. Yes, you were sexier than you had been years before, but you gave me butterflies. The first time I've had that feeling since my first date. You had me daydreaming about us together. Even when you were determined to do things respectfully, you had me wanting you. Now, I have you and you have me for the rest of our lives and in a billion more lifetimes. See you soon my love. – your wife.*

Ridge couldn't help but well up. The woman he'd loved since they were babies just said the words he'd dreamt of. Through his insane military time, his 20s acting a fool, and the horrible things he'd lived through, she was still his. She always would be.

"You alright," Callon asked.

Ridge nodded with a smirk. "I'm marrying my best friend today."

He opened up the package in the box and saw a Rolex box. He shook his head, knowing that she wouldn't have done it. He hoped she hadn't. When he saw cufflinks and a key, he shook his head. It was worse than a Rolex watch.

"Do you know what this is," Ridge asked.

"She said it's in the garage at the house. You should probably get ready. We have a lot to get done," Callon said. Ridge nodded and cleaned up the breakfast dishes, got showered and dressed and his Dad and Faith's showed to drive with him.

Faith woke up that morning, still laughing at what had happened the night prior. She loved him. She always had. Now, it was all becoming a reality. All she had to do was slide on the dress. When she got a text, she smirked:

> *Hello wife. I can't wait to say it for real. Thank you for the note. You have a little surprise too. Kellen has it. No, it doesn't buzz (this time). I love you forever. See you soon. I'll be the one in tears at the end of the aisle.*

Faith smirked and Kellen knocked. "Miss Faith."

She walked over to the door. "What's up," she asked. He handed the package to her.

"He asked me to give it to you when you woke up. Eggs Benedict is waiting on you downstairs," Kellen said.

"Thank you." He nodded and headed back down and Faith sat down in the chair and opened the box. On top was a card that had a double eternity sign on it:

> *To my almost wife. My best friend, my love, and my life.*
>
> *I haven't always had the happy life. I went through my own hell years ago. I thought I had completely lost my chance with you then. When I saw you again, my heart raced. I never thought we'd be together let alone getting married. You're the woman I've loved my entire life. The best parts of my life have always had you in them, and today will be no different. I can't wait to wake up with my wife in my arms. I can't wait to see our babies, and their babies. Forever is what you always wanted. Starts today. Forever and a billion more.*
> *– Your soon to be forever husband.*

Faith got choked up and brushed tears away. She opened the box and saw diamond stud earrings and a sixpence. Under it was a tiny note:

> *The same one that Mom had in her shoe when she married my Dad.*

Faith shook her head. She messaged Ridge as she headed downstairs:

I love you back. Forever. PS buzzing would have got me laughing.

She slid her phone in her robe pocket and had breakfast with everyone then hair and makeup arrived to get her, her Mom and Ridge's Mom ready. They finished within a few hours and gave the Mom's their gifts.

"You don't have to do this. You know that right," his Mom said.

"Kinda do. You both told me that you were like sisters your entire lives. Now you are family. Real family. You're both part of our family now. Mine and Ridge's."

They both opened the presents and saw a photo of them all together. One from when Ridge and Faith were kids, and one from when they first got engaged.

"This is beautiful," her Mom said.

"Well, we sorta wanted to give you guys a happy memory. All of this is kinda crazy since we really don't have a best man or maid of honor. We wanted to include you both," Faith said.

"Meaning what," her Mom asked.

"Mom, if you can be my matron of honor. Ridge wants you to be his best Mom," Faith said as she looked at Ridge's Mom.

"What?"

"The Dad's do the warming of the rings stuff. That way everyone important to us is included," Faith said.

They all hugged and helped Faith into her dress. "What do you think," Faith asked as she looked up with her veil, the cape and the train all in their perfect place.

"Wow," her Mom said.

"You like?" When she nodded and started welling up, Faith hugged her.

"I wanted simple."

"Far from simple, but he's gonna be crying like a baby," his Mom said.

"Well, are we ready," Faith asked.

"Old, new, borrowed and blue," his Mom said. "

I got the sixpence from Ridge. Borrowed and Old," Faith said.

"Dress is new, all we need is the blue part," her Mom said as she handed Faith the blue sapphire bracelet.

"It's beautiful," Faith said as his Mom slid it on.

When her Dad showed, Faith and her Mom were coming down the steps. "Oh, my goodness," her Dad said.

"And?"

"Baby, you look like an angel," her Dad said.

"That was the look I was going for," Faith joked as her Dad hugged her. The photographer took photos, and they headed off, with Kellen, Leo, and Conner driving.

They made their way to the church and Faith saw Ridge in his tux. When she saw the roses and the lavender, she smirked. The guys looked great. They all headed inside and Faith came in the side of the church and they went into the bridal room. When she came in, wisteria was on the table with her bouquet. It was exactly as she'd dreamed when she was a kid. "Wow," her Mom said.

"I know that he wanted something special, but this is gonna be like walking into a dream," Faith said.

The music started and Ridge walked down the aisle with his Mom. His Dad had a grin ear to ear. When the music changed, everyone stood up to see Faith.

He was in awe. She had curls, sparkle, and everything was absolutely perfect. She sparkled as she walked down the aisle. He felt like he was in a daydream. She was like an angel walking towards him and his Mom handed him tissues as he started crying.

"Your life," his Mom whispered.

Ridge nodded and when they were face to face, she brushed his tears away. "Wow," Ridge said.

"Worth the wait?" He smirked and nodded, gulping back the tears. "What," Faith asked silently.

"Angel," he replied.

They got through the ceremony with everyone and when it came time to do the vows, Faith got a smirk ear to ear. She'd worked with all of those authors that long for a reason. She showed that she was 100% her Mom's daughter:

"Ridge, if I had known at two-days old that I'd met my soul mate, we never would've been apart for a single Moment. I fell in love with you long ago. When you walked back into my life, I was mesmerized and head over heels. We've already lived our worst, our best and everything in between. That promise will always be there. Good or bad, happy, or crying, healthy or sick, I'll never leave your side. I promise to love you with every ounce of my soul for the rest of time. You are my person. The man who's arms comfort me and hold me even when you're ready to kick my butt to the moon. I love you Ridge. I'm never letting go of you or this hand. Glue them together now my love. Forever starts now."

Ridge brushed tears away. "No more tears," Faith said.

He nodded. "Ridge," the bishop said as Ridge handed Faith a handkerchief:

"I remember the first time I knew I loved you. Sitting there watching you go on that first date. I wanted more than anything to tell you then, but I waited. Now, seeing the amazing woman before me, the woman that you became and the woman who fell in love with me too. I want all of you Faith. I want our beginning, our present and our forever with you and only you. I promise to tell you how much I love you every day and night. I promise to romance you until you beg for the music to stop. I promise our lives will never be filled with anything but love. I promise to be there through whatever life throws at us, and I promise to be an amazing Dad and remind you how amazing of a Mom you are when that time comes. Forever isn't even long enough. I will love you for the rest of time and then double infinity. You have me and always will."

Their Dad's came and handed them the wedding bands and they slid them on each other's fingers. Ridge kissed her hand and he smirked. All they heard beyond that was man and wife. Seconds later, he kissed her and dipped her just like an old black and white movie. The photographer snapped a few photos then they made their way back down the aisle with their Mom's behind them then went into the alcove to sign the papers with the bishop.

"There was a gift here for the two of you. Your Dad's wanted me to give it to you both after the ceremony," the bishop said as he handed them the box while they signed the papers.

"Mom," Ridge said.

"You two open it together," his Mom said.

They finished signing and sat down together to open it. When they opened the card, keys fell out.

"What in the.."

"Just read it," her Mom said:

> *To the second generation – If the two of you are*

here in this hallowed place doing what we all knew would come, then you received this note. This is a set of keys to my home. The one that your Dad grew up in Faith. The one that had every happy memory attached. You can sell it, live in it or give it to someone. It's yours. The deed is now in both of your names. The larger key is for a crate in the basement with your wedding gift. I knew when you two were babies this day would come. I knew when Faith's parents married, and when Ridge's parents did. I knew that you two were destined when you couldn't sleep if you were apart. I wish your home and your lives will be filled with love and a memory of forever. I'll see you both in heaven. – Gran

Faith looked at Ridge. "How," Faith asked.

"She told me when we were doing her estate paperwork. It's been there since she passed when you two were just kids. It's been maintained and is one of the biggest estates in Charleston. It's up to the two of you. We had requests to turn it into a hotel and a million other offers. It's now up to the two of you," her Dad said.

Ridge looked at him. "Seriously," Ridge asked.

Her Dad nodded. He handed Ridge the envelope with the papers as Ridge slid it into his pocket.

"Thank you," Ridge said.

"Congratulations," her Mom said.

They all hugged and made their way outside to see their friends throwing rose petals. They went and got into the SUV with Kellen driving.

"Congratulations," Kellen said.

"Thank you," Faith said as Ridge kissed her and snuggled her into his arms.

"Wife."

"Husband."

"Home?"

She smirked. "You have a reception to show off handsome."

"Are we allowed a detour?"

Faith kissed him and Kellen smirked. "You have an extra half hour, but that's it."

"I'll take it," Ridge teased.

They got back to the house, headed inside and Ridge carried Faith up the steps. "You keeping this thing on," he teased.

"Veil, no. Cape, until the first dance is over."

He kissed her, devouring her lips. "Dress off."

Faith shook her head. "I need to leave…"

He kissed her again. "Promise that you never ever let go."

He nodded. "Not even when we're both old and grey sexy wife."

"Even when I'm fat?"

"Meaning what?"

"In like 8 months."

Ridge looked at her. "What?"

"I took a test this morning before I had my shower." He looked at her.

"Faith." She nodded and he kissed her, devouring her lips again, then picked her up and swung her around.

"Baby."

"So long as it sticks, we're having a baby."

He kissed her again, wrapping his arms around her. "Baby, I love you."

"I love you too handsome husband."

"Amazing Mom," he said.

She kissed him. "I have to fix my lipstick then we can head out." Ridge nodded, kissed her again and hugged her.

"I love you wife." She kissed him again and went into the bathroom and touched up her makeup.

He shook his head, sitting on the edge of the bed where she'd talked him into being with her that first time. The first time he said he loved her was in that same spot. Everything had happened in that house. Her house. Their home. He brushed tears away. Every dream he'd had, had come true. Every wish he'd made on every falling star had landed in his lap. The woman she'd become was his person. She always had been if he'd managed to see past his craziness. She came out of the bathroom and looked at him.

"What," Faith asked.

He wrapped his arms around her. "My dream wife is now my wife," he said.

"And my sexy enough to hire man is my husband. Now what?"

"We go see the reception so I can drag you off to a beach where you only need a bikini."

She kissed him. "Then we should go so they can get the photos done so I can dance with my husband," Faith said. He kissed her forehead and they headed off with Kellen.

When they got to the house, they went out and did the photos then headed in to where the reception was. Nobody knew it was a tent from the inside. It was as if they'd walked into a midsummer's night's dream. The subtle lights. The wisteria and white roses among the lights. The white and silver tables. All of it was exactly how it was in her dreams as a kid. It's like she'd walked into a dream.

"Ridge."

"Wife."

"You did all of this?"

"Organized someone to help, but yeah. All for you. I love seeing that smile," Ridge teased.

"This is just beautiful," Faith said. Everyone was welcomed in and the dancefloor filled with mist. When the song came on from their prom that they danced their first dance to, Faith smirked.

"I love you husband," she said.

"Love you to little mama," he whispered.

*****

When they were three months, Faith invited the guys and their parents to the beach house. "What is all of this about," her Mom asked.

"I remember a long time ago when you told me about where you and Dad met again after all those years. I told Ridge about it. We decided to bring y'all over to give you the news," Faith said.

"What news," her Dad asked as he zipped up his sweater.

"Well, in August, we had a little bit of a blip. We didn't get a chance to meet them, but now, we do."

"What," his Mom asked.

"We're having a baby," Ridge said.

"Faith," her Mom said.

"We wanted to do it somewhere that meant something. This is where you always told me that you told Dad you were pregnant. Sort of works that we're doing things in the same place," Faith said as they all hugged.

"Do we know if you're having a boy or a girl," his Mom asked.

"Yes," Faith replied as she smirked at Ridge.

"What," her Mom asked.

"Well, here's the thing. We're having one of each," Faith said as she snuggled Ridge.

"What," her Dad asked.

"One little girl as amazing and creative, talented and beautiful as her Mom," Ridge said.

"And one amazing, handsome, protective and loving guy just like Ridge," Faith replied.

The rest of the night was a celebration filled with love, hugs, and happiness for the entire family. There were no more worries, no more stress and no more threats. Even the guys that were Ridge's friends joined in. They were all safe, happy and without a worry.

6 months later, Faith had her dream babies. Rose Addison Sams and Liam Emerson Sams. When their folks came in,

her Mom smirked and hugged his Mom. "What," Ridge asked after hugs and kisses of congrats to both of them.

"He looks just like Ridge did as a baby," his Mom said.

"And she looks just like you did," her Mom said.

"And now we're a family, just like you always wanted," Faith replied as her mom smiled.

Faith and Ridge headed home the next day, showing their babies their new home. They curled up together on the sofa that Ridge and Faith had curled up on their first night alone.

"So, now that you have the babies and the husband, what's next," Ridge asked.

Faith looked over at him with a grin ear to ear, just like the one she'd had that first night. "Now, we get to start forever." Ridge leaned over and kissed her as their babies nodded off. That beach started it all, and now it was part of a whole new generation.

The End – at least for Ridge and Faith